PENGUIN MODERN CLASSICS

The West Pier

Patrick Hamilton, universally known as the author of *Rope*, *Gaslight* and *Hangover Square*, was one of the most gifted and admired writers of his generation. Born in Sussex during the first decade of this century, he and his parents moved shortly afterwards to Hove, where he passed his formative years. He published his first novel in 1925 and within a few years had established a wide readership for himself. It seemed as though his reputation was assured, but personal setbacks and an increasing problem with drink overshadowed this certainty. Yet in spite of these pressures he was able to produce some of his best work, the seeds of his own despair almost feeding his vision, where an underlying sense of loss and isolation is felt beneath his tragi-comic creations. He died in 1962.

PATRICK HAMILTON

1904 Mar. 17-1962

THE WEST PIER

PENGUIN BOOKS

Penguin Books Ltd, Harmondsworth, Middlesex, England
Viking Penguin Inc., 40 West 23rd Street, New York, New York 10010, U.S.A.
Penguin Books Australia Ltd, Ringwood, Victoria, Australia
Penguin Books Canada Limited, 2801 John Street, Markham, Ontario, Canada L3R 1B4
Penguin Books (N.Z.) Ltd, 182–190 Wairau Road, Auckland 10, New Zealand

First published by Constable 1951
Published by Viking 1985
Published in Penguin Books 1986

Copyright 1951 by Patrick Hamilton
All rights reserved

Made and printed in Great Britain by
Richard Clay (The Chaucer Press) Ltd, Bungay, Suffolk
Typeset in Ehrhardt

AUTHOR'S NOTE

Although a complete story in itself, *The West Pier* is the first of a series of novels dealing with the character of Ernest Ralph Gorse.

There may be some readers who, on learning this, will feel that *The West Pier* is *not* actually a complete story in itself. The author is anxious to assure any such reader that it really is.

The final novel of this series will disclose the ultimate fate of Ernest Ralph Gorse.

CONTENTS

PART ONE

THE BOY GORSE

I

There is a sort of man – usually a lance corporal or corporal and coming from the submerged classes – who, returning to England from military service in distant parts of the earth, does not announce his arrival to his relations. Instead of this he will tramp, or hitch-hike, his way to his home, and in the early hours of the morning will be heard gently throwing pebbles up at his wife's bedroom window.

It is impossible to say whether he does this because he hopes to surprise his wife in some sinful attachment, or whether it has never occurred to him to use the telephone, the telegraph service, or the post. If the latter were the case one might suppose him to be merely unimaginative: but this type of person is actually far from being unimaginative.

What concerns us here is that such a person certainly belongs to a type, rare but identifiable. There may exist only one in a hundred thousand, or more, people: but, by a shrewd observer, they can be discerned and classified without mistake.

The main feature which characterizes these people is, of course, their silence – their almost complete dumbness and numbness amidst a busy and loquacious humanity. They are not, in fact, inarticulate: at certain times they will talk at great length. They are able, also, to laugh, though this is usually at a joke of a common-place, cruel, or dirty nature. But although they are able to talk and laugh, they seem to do this only spasmodically and on the surface: beneath this surface they are dreaming, dully brooding, seeming incessantly and as it were somnambulistically to contemplate them-selves and the prospects of their own advantage.

They are almost exclusively a male species. Seventy-five per cent of them belong to the submerged classes: the remaining (and perhaps most interesting) twenty-five per cent are scattered amongst all kinds of higher strata. They all tend to drift into the

Army. During wars, or in periods of social upheaval, they appear, as if vengefully, to come into their own, to gain ephemeral power and standing.

As boys at school they are generally bullies, but quiet ones – twisters of wrists in distant corners. As adults, naturally, they can no longer behave in such a way, and some of them wear on their faces what may be a slow, pensive resentment at being thwarted in this matter.

They use few gestures, and, like most great inner thinkers, they are great walkers, plodders of the streets in raincoats.

They are conspicuously silent and odd in their behaviour with their wives or their women. In public-houses, or in tea-shops, they are to be seen sitting with women without uttering a word to them, sometimes for as much as an hour on end.

It is extremely difficult to guess what goes on beneath the surface of their minds. It is only from their surface behaviour, and surface utterances, that the depths can be dimly understood or estimated.

It would be wrong to suppose that they are all of the same character, that there are not innumerable variations within this species. They are not all bullies at school, and they are by no means all bad and harmful. Indeed, it is likely that many of them serve a purpose as calm, honest, useful, though extremely dull citizens. On the other hand it is beyond dispute that it is from this type that the most atrocious criminals emerge.

We feel that the poisoner Neil Creame, the bath-murderer George Smith, and many others of a similar way of thinking belonged to this type.

Of this type Ernest Ralph Gorse, who was born in 1903, was clearly one or the other sort of member. He showed as much as a boy.

2   During a Thursday afternoon of the winter before the First World War, at Rodney House Road, Hove, there occurred, in a changing-room, an episode which was originated by Ernest Ralph Gorse.

Rodney House was a preparatory school for about forty boys, accepting pupils from many different classes of parents in the town. What may be roughly called an aristocracy of five or six boys came from the squares and avenues – Brunswick Square, Grand Avenue, First Avenue, and the like: what may be roughly called a *bourgeoisie* (the sons of merchants, dentists, estate agents, doctors, clergymen,

retired officers, and well-to-do local tradesmen) came from the
roads – Wilbury Road, Holland Road, Tisbury Road, Norton Road:
while the rest came from the villas – Hove Villas, Ventnor Villas,
Denmark Villas – or from obscure crescents and streets at the back
of Hove or of Brighton, or from humble western regions verging
upon Portslade. A few of this third class approximated to the *sansculottes*: at any rate, their clothes were laughed at, and they were
known to be 'common'.

Of these three classes the quietest, for the most part, were the
aristocrats and the *sansculottes* – the former, perhaps, because of
their smooth home atmosphere; the latter because of their rudely
published inferiority and consequent timidity. It was the middle
class which made all the noise, the middle class, which in the pursuit
of its many varied and violent pleasures, caused the establishment,
out of working hours, to resound to the skies.

These pleasures, like all pleasures, were subject to fashion, and
fashion of an even more fickle kind than that which operates in the
adult world. For a short period, for instance, the eager, clamorous
delight of almost all the pupils would centre around the persecution
of a single boy, who would be accused of being a thief, or a cheat,
or a 'sneak', or unclean in his personal habits, or all these things
together. Such a boy, however, would all at once be rescued from
the utmost spiritual and physical torment, would be permitted to
sink into a blissful state of nonentity, by the chance appearance at
the school of a mere water pistol of a new design. Not the human
boy, but water pistols of this design would now be the rage, though
not for long. Water pistols would be soon submerged in a suddenly
recurring wave of, say, model battleships, and so it went on throughout the year, a single one of which would embrace vogues moving
from boy-persecution to water pistols, from water pistols to model
battleships, and from model battleships to electric torches; to
catapults; to regimental buttons; to pocket knives; to miniature
trains; to fretsaws; to pistols exploding pink caps; to miniature
soldiers, guns, and forts; to whistles; to balloons; to instruments into
which one could hum tunes with a greatly enlarged volume of
sound; to small mirrors which sent mischievous reflections of the
sun into the eye of a distant enemy or friend; to highly coloured tin
beetles which raced along the floor; to tops; to cameras; to 'trans-
fers'; to white mice; to chewing gum; to miniature aeroplanes; to
solid imitations of spilt ink, and so on and so forth. All these
popular passions, ephemeral but returning in cycles, were accom-

panied by the perennial and perpetual creation and throwing of
paper darts and gliders, and the collection and exchange of cigarette
cards.

On that remote Thursday afternoon of that remote winter, an
interest in small electric torches was approaching its peak; and
Ernest Ralph Gorse originated the episode in question by removing
one of these from the pocket of one boy and putting it into the pocket
of another. He was able to do this unseen, because he was the first
to return to the changing-room after military operations on the
County Ground, which was within six minutes' walk of Rodney
House.

Thursday was the day on which Rodney House School, forsaking
games, applied itself diligently to military exercises. In the morning
there appeared a 'sergeant', who, establishing himself in a shed in
the back garden, taught a number of privileged boys (those whose
parents desired to pay for it) to shoot at a target pinned on a wooden
box. Such boys, in an expectant and excited condition, were called
in twos by rota from their classrooms. They left the room with a
silent, valiant, and dramatic air (which gave the impression rather
that they were going to be shot than going to shoot) and returned
about ten minutes later with their targets, riddled and showing their
scores, in their hands. These targets, despite the vigilance of the
masters, usually succeeded in being passed from desk to desk
around the room and coming back to their owners.

All this, in the morning, was pleasant and intelligible to the boys:
the afternoon was unpleasant and almost completely unintelligible.
In the afternoon they were dressed in the boots, puttees, tunics, and
caps of private soldiers, and, carrying wooden imitations of rifles,
were marched down to the County Ground and drilled – made, with
their coarse puttees tickling their immature legs, to shoulder arms,
present arms, port arms, form fours, right dress, stand at ease, etc.,
never, never satisfactorily, and again and again and again until they
were stupefied.

It was, oddly enough, not difficult to stupefy the boys of Rodney
House. They were, in fact, during the greater part of their day at
school, either making a noise which rang to heaven, or in a state of
stupefaction at their tasks. In the latter condition they wore a
bewildered, staring, idiotic, Bedlam, Bridewell look – many of them,
during class, biting their nails, blinking their eyes, or showing other
nervous twitching gestures.

This habit of staring, brought on by bewilderment and boredom, was almost certainly the original cause of the myopia which would make so many of them in later life wear spectacles.

Ernest Ralph Gorse was, however, not in any way bored by Thursday afternoons: the unintelligible was to him in some way intelligible. His boots were always clean; his puttees were rolled neatly and expertly; his buttons were the brightest of all; his execution of the requisite movements was so good that he was often called from the ranks to make a model demonstration and shame his fellows. Thursday afternoons stimulated rather than stupefied Ernest Ralph Gorse.

Even his expression and demeanour changed. A slim boy, with ginger silken hair which came in a large bang over his forehead, and an aquiline nose which seemed to be smelling something nasty – a boy with thin lips, a slouching gait, a nasal voice, and a certain amount of freckles, Ernest Ralph Gorse's normal expression was the dull, thoughtful one of a person proposing to remember an evil done to him. But on Thursday afternoons there was something different: his look was less obtuse and hoarding: he became, even, in his own way, lively.

It was, perhaps, an excess of this lively spirit which put into his mind, and inspired him to perpetrate, the mischief with the torch.

3   The changing-room was a dark, bare-boarded room in the basement – in the day overrun by boys, in the night by beetles. It was lined with lockers which did not lock, with hooks, and with benches. About twelve boys changed in here – those who occupied, roughly, an upper middle station in the school. A select band of seniors and a mob of juniors changed in their respective rooms elsewhere.

After Ernest Ralph Gorse (who, having removed the torch from the one pocket to the other, was by this time unrolling his puttees) there entered two boys.

One of these was named Ryan and the other Bell. Ryan was a carefree, impulsive, good-looking boy who did not pretend to be clever and did not specialize at anything; while Bell was a spectacled, old-looking boy who was extremely clever at his lessons and who specialized in the use of long words. He was using long words as he entered with Ryan.

'The relation of your proboscis appertaining to your external physiognomy', he was saying to Ryan as he entered, 'occurs to me to be somewhat superfluous.'

This remark of Bell's came completely out of the blue: nearly all such remarks of his did. Bell would go into a sort of trance, would remain absolutely quiet for a minute or so while preparing such sentences, which, though painfully obscure, were nearly always to be recognized as being of a bald, rude, gratuitous, and challenging nature.

Ryan now had to do some quick thinking. He had not understood what had been said: but he was certain that whatever had been said was unfavourable to himself. 'Proboscis', he at any rate knew, was long-languagese for nose: so presumably something nasty had been said about his nose. But what? Had it been called red, long, dirty, ugly? He floundered about in doubt (as Bell had intended he should) for a matter of ten seconds, and then, unable to make a retort in kind, rather shamefacedly took the easiest way out.

'So's yours,' he said, and a moment later added, 'Only worse . . .'

'That *happens* to be a *tu quoque*,' said Bell without hesitation, and Ryan, having been recently taught in class what a *tu quoque* was, this time did not hesitate.

'You're a *tu* silly ass,' he said. 'And I should say you've got a bit *tu* above yourself.'

This was definitely witty and clever, and it was Bell's turn to be momentarily dumbfounded. He paused for as long as he had previously made Ryan pause, and at last was only able to manage:

'Really . . . Your *brain* . . .'

'Really,' said Ryan, '*yours* . . .'

Honours might now well have been considered even, and so the argument might well have been allowed to drop. But the Ryans and Bells of life never on any account allow such arguments to drop. Only when a school bell rings, a master enters, or their attention is fortuitously distracted elsewhere, do such arguments end. There was now a pause during which the adversaries, while rapidly changing their clothes, and while other boys entered to change, were clearly mobilizing their forces behind the lines. Then Ryan went into the attack.

'Bell . . .' he said in an innocent voice, as if he intended to ask the other a detached or even amiable question.

'Yes?' said Bell.

'*Nothing*,' said Ryan, with the firm and gleeful air of having most cunningly enticed and then snapped a trap upon Bell.

This device, commonplace and, in fact, beneath contempt, yet had the power to hurt: for to the Ryans and Bells of life, in argument, there is hardly any ruse considered too conventional or too low.

'Very clever,' said Bell. 'Very clever indeed. You ought to have your bumps examined – by a phrenologist – just to see how clever you are.'

'I've got quite enough bumps, thank you,' said Ryan, 'playing football. And barges, too.'

Now Bell saw an opportunity of employing a counter-device. This device was, perhaps, not quite so base as the one just used by his opponent – but was, all the same, cheap and facile beyond measure. It consisted of repeating, word for word, and merely for the sake of annoyance, what the other person had last uttered.

'"*I've got quite enough bumps, thank you*,"' Bell quoted, '"*playing football. And barges, too.*"'

Ryan thought for a moment.

'Are you trying to imitate me?' he then said.

'"*Are you trying to imitate me*?"' said Bell.

'Don't be a fool,' said Ryan. 'Anybody can do that.'

'"*Don't be a fool*,"' said Bell. '"*Anybody can do that.*"'

'It's not funny, you know,' said Ryan.

'"*It's not funny, you know*,"' said Bell.

There was a pause.

'Well – I just won't say anything, that's all,' said Ryan.

'"*Well – I just won't say anything, that's all*,"' said Bell.

There was now a silence of nearly a minute's duration, in which it seemed that Ryan intended to adhere to his resolution. This silence was embarrassing and hateful to both, for to the Ryans and Bells of life there is nothing more unnatural and detestable than not talking. Much as he desired it, it was impossible for Bell to break the spell, for, had he done so, Ryan, he knew, would have at once started repeating his own words, and the whole position would have been fatally reversed. It was Ryan who at last relieved the situation. This he did by adopting a new tactic – or rather a familiar variation in this barren and frustrating form of conflict.

'Bell', he said, 'is the silliest fool at Rodney House.'

Now what? Without proclaiming himself the silliest fool at Rodney House, Bell was unable to maintain the ascendancy by continuing in the same course as before. Should he, then, remain silent? No – for that would be an admission of defeat. Also, being a Bell of life, Bell, as has been said, was temperamentally incapable of remaining silent. He saw that he had to compromise, and did so.

'Bell', he said, 'is *not* the silliest fool at Rodney House.'

'There you are. Got you!' said Ryan. 'You couldn't repeat me.'

'"*There you are. Got you!*"' said Bell. '"*You couldn't repeat me.*"'

'You didn't repeat me, and it's no use pretending you did,"' said Ryan.

'"*You didn't repeat me, and it's no use pretending you did,*"' said Bell.

Now it seemed to Ryan that, owing to his own folly, he was back exactly where he was before. Ryan, however, was an indomitable boy, and he used indomitability.

'Bell', he said again, firmly, 'is the silliest fool at Rodney House.'

'Bell', Bell replied with equal firmness, 'is *not* the silliest fool at Rodney House.'

'Bell', said Ryan, 'is the silliest fool at Rodney House and is not able to repeat Ryan's words.'

'Bell', said Bell, 'is *not* the silliest fool at Rodney House and *is* able to repeat Ryan's words.'

'Bell', said Ryan, 'is so Abso–Blooming–Lutely silly that Ryan doesn't intend to speak to him any more.'

'Bell', said Bell, 'is *not* so Abso–Blooming–Lutely silly that Ryan doesn't intend to speak to him any more.'

Who, now, was the winner? Who could ever be the winner? Ryan, undoubtedly, was morally and logically in the right, but appearances, which are all-important to the Ryans and Bells of life, were against him. He could not, by any means, establish his moral and logical superiority, and he could never get the last word.

How long this would have gone on, and what the outcome would have been, cannot be said. In a sense fortunately, the insoluble was at this moment solved by misfortune.

Misfortune, striking Ryan like a thunderbolt, caused him to go white in the face, and to dismiss from his mind all other things.

'Hullo,' he said frantically and whitely, going through the pockets of his coat. '*Where's my torch?*'

4   At first Bell, who was fundamentally of a humane nature, did not at all take in the seriousness of what had been said.

'"*Hullo,*"' he repeated automatically. '"*Where's my torch?*"'

'No, shut up, man,' said Ryan. 'I've lost it.'

And still Bell did not understand, and repeated Ryan's words again.

'No. Do shut up, really,' said Ryan. 'It's gone from my *pocket!*'

At this a hoarseness, even a hint of tears, in Ryan's voice caused

Bell to look at Ryan and see that his face was pale and his manner agitated beyond measure. Seeing this, Bell abandoned frivolity, though reluctantly.

'What do you mean – it's gone from your pocket?' he said. 'Don't be an *ass*.'

'It's gone,' said Ryan, still searching feebly, 'that's all.'

And now something of the real and peculiar horror of the situation was communicated to Bell. The horror was of a peculiar nature because of the character and reputation of Ryan's torch. Ryan's torch, in fact, dwelt in a heavenly realm above and beyond all other torches – was famous, one might say fabulous, in the school just at this time. To be permitted to look at it was a privilege, to hold it was an honour; to use it, even with its owner's sanction, was almost a blasphemy, frightening. This was to a certain extent because it was so wonderfully thin and small and covered with imitation crocodile leather; but principally because it had, at the top, a sliding apparatus which enabled its user to change the white light to red, and then to white again, and then again to green! What specific purpose, if any, this was intended to serve, nobody had as yet asked: everyone simply and instinctively knew that no one could ask for more. During the whole week it had been the making of Ryan: Ryan's being was the torch and the torch was Ryan's being. Ryan was a torch. If, then, the torch was lost, was not Ryan utterly lost, suddenly a nothing? Bell, looking at him, was genuinely appalled, and attempted kindness.

'Go on, man,' he said. 'Have another look. It must be there somewhere.'

'But it *isn't*.'

'But it *must* be.'

Bell was not entirely disinterested, and his voice also betrayed terror. For when he was not quarrelling with Ryan he had more than once been allowed to use the torch and had looked forward to much pleasure of this kind in the future.

Here Ernest Ralph Gorse, who, while methodically changing, had been listening to every word which had passed between these two, spoke.

'Are you sure it was in your pocket?' he asked Ryan.

'Yes. I know it was.'

'Absolutely sure?' asked Ernest Ralph Gorse.

'Yes,' said Bell. 'You might have left it somewhere else.'

'No, I didn't,' said Ryan. 'It was in my *pocket*.'

'Then someone must have pinched it,' said Ernest Ralph Gorse.

Ryan considered this for a moment. 'But *who* could have pinched it?' he said, and then, returning to life, he burst forth angrily and addressed the entire room. 'Look here,' he said. 'Is someone trying to be funny? Has someone pinched my torch?'

'Look here,' said a boy named Kerr. 'Are you accusing me?'

'No. I'm not accusing anyone. I'm just asking who's jolly well pinched my torch.'

'You'd better not accuse me, you know,' said Kerr, now anxious to be accused, and endeavouring to create the illusion that this had already happened. 'Because I'll jolly well punch your nose.'

'And you'd better not accuse me either,' said another boy named Roberts, perceiving and rushing with all his belongings towards the glorious Yukon of quarrelling which Kerr had discovered. 'Or I'll jolly well punch your nose, too.'

'I'll jolly well punch anyone's nose who's pinched my torch,' said Ryan. 'Come on. Who is it? Come on!'

Ryan himself was now, it can be seen, affected by the wild spirit of the gold rush, and assumed without further question that his torch had been stolen.

'Why not institute a search?' said Ernest Ralph Gorse.

This brought in Bell's support because he liked the long word 'institute' (of which he took a mental note).

'Yes,' he said. 'Let's institute a summary investigation.' (He was glad to have beaten 'search' with 'investigation' and was very pleased indeed with 'summary'.)

'Nobody's jolly well going to summary investigate *me*,' said Kerr. 'I'll jolly well summer and investigate their noses, if they do. And winter, too, if it comes to that.'

At this delightful play upon words, many of the boys could not resist openly giggling, while others reluctantly half smiled, and it looked for a moment as though a painful and strenuous situation might break up in humour and lightheartedness. But now another boy named Wills, changing in a far corner, poisonously reintroduced seriousness.

'I'll bet it's Rosen ...' he said.

Rosen was a dark, Jewish, short, quiet, passionate, long-haired boy, destined in later life to become a successful municipal and B.B.C. musical conductor. His quietness and aloofness, his gift for the violin (which enabled him most enviably to escape, during the week, quite a few hours in the ordinary classroom), together with his hopeless inability to keep a shred of his temper when falsely accused of the foulest crimes, all served to make him unpopular, a victim. He, above all, was one of those characters whom only vogues for water pistols, torches, model battleships, etc., could save from persecution. Now it seemed that the prevailing torch-mania, instead of mercifully hiding him, was by a wicked paradox fated to bring him into the limelight yet again.

'Yes, *I'll* bet it is, too,' said another poisonous boy.

For a few moments nothing was said, and in the silence it was generally felt that it was Ryan's business to make a formal accusation against Rosen. This Ryan did not at once do. Being, like his friend Bell, a humane boy, and not believing for a second that Rosen had stolen his torch, he was loth to begin. The continued silence, however, at last began to fill him with a sense of having to shoulder a public obligation, and, in a gingerly manner, he plunged in, or rather began to paddle.

'Have *you* taken it, Rosen?' he said, with an imitation of some hostility, but actually almost apologetically.

Rosen, who was already getting dangerously angry, made the pretence of considering it beneath his dignity to reply, and went on changing his clothes rapidly.

'Well. Go on,' said Kerr. 'Answer – can't you?'

But still Rosen, in his anger changing his clothes even more rapidly, affected mute and sublime dignity.

'Oh – so you can't answer,' said Kerr. 'Well – that's a proof of guilt, anyway. That's jolly well a proof of guilt.'

'Yes – that's a proof of guilt,' said Roberts, who was Kerr's shadow. 'Come on, hand it over, you dirty little thief.'

This caused the pent-up Rosen to explode. He stood as if at bay, his body quivered, and his eyes dilated.

'How *dare* you say that!' he said. 'How *dare* you! You *pig*!'

Alas, Rosen had succumbed yet again to his inveterate weakness – his inability to keep a shred of his temper when falsely accused. His mother had constantly spoken to him about this – so had his father: he himself completely accepted and eagerly agreed with what both his mother and father said; but it was all of no avail. He was totally unable to control himself when unjustly treated at school. A success in later life, certainly, he was going to be, with a fame to which his present tormentors (themselves having drifted into money-seeking, undistinguished, or even sordid obscurity) would allude with pride and pleasure, basely preening themselves with a morsel of his glamour: but here and now he created nothing but ignominy and suffering for himself. This was aggravated by the fact that when he lost his temper he always did so with the utmost *gaucherie*, bringing forth, in his lonely, alien, Jewish way, absurd, alien, outmoded expressions. At Rodney House, or at any preparatory school of its kind at that time, you simply did not say 'How *dare* you!' Nor, though in certain contexts you might abusively use the word 'pig', did you ever permit yourself the ridiculous, declamatory 'You *pig*!'

'Did you call me a pig?' said Roberts, fixing Rosen with a steady, detached, questioning look. 'Did I hear anyone calling me a pig?'

Rosen's answer was simple enough.

'You're a *pig*, a *cad*, a *swine*, a *hog*, and a *liar*!' he said.

'Oh – so I'm –' began Roberts, when Ryan cut in.

'Never mind about that,' said Ryan. 'All I want is my torch, and all I want to know is if you've got it, Rosen.'

'How *dare* you say I've got it!' said Rosen. 'How dare you *suggest* I've got it! Do you want to search me? Go on. Search my clothes! Search my locker! Search my desk upstairs! Search everything!'

'All right. We will,' said Roberts, and moved over towards Rosen's locker.

'If you *dare* to so much as *touch* my clothes I'll kill you!' said Rosen, contradicting himself.

'Oh – so you're afraid, are you?' said Roberts.

'No. I'm not afraid. Ryan may search. It's his torch. Go on, Ryan. Search!'

'No, *I* don't want to . . .' said Ryan, but Rosen would have none of this.

'Go on. Search!' he said. 'I *insist* that you search! I *demand* a search!'

Ryan still hesitated, but the other boys egged him on, only one of them recommending him to refrain from searching, and this not for Rosen's sake, but because of the inconvenience which Ryan might have to endure from 'the smell'.

Ryan began to search, and the others crowded round to watch him.

All at once a gasp of incredulity and ineffable exultation arose from the boys. Ryan had found the torch in Rosen's pocket.

'My *Aunt* – my Sainted *Aunt*!' said one boy, and 'Phe-e-e-e-w!' said another, and others said, 'My Giddy *Forefathers*!' and 'By George' and 'Great Scott' and 'Great Jehoshaphat' and 'My *Hat* –

my Giddy *Hat*!' And Bell said solemnly, 'By *Nebuchadnezzar's Toe-Nails* . . .' (Nebuchadnezzar's name was very frequently upon Bell's lips, because Nebuchadnezzar's name was so long.)

Then they turned upon Rosen. 'Well – what about it now, my young friend?' said Kerr. 'What about it now?'

'It's a trick! It's a trick! It was never there! It's a *conjuring* trick!' said Rosen in his old-fashioned way. 'Someone must have put it there! Someone put it there by *sleight of hand*!'

'Oh,' said Kerr. 'So you're accusing other people now. You're not content with stealing – you start accusing people of playing tricks.'

'Legerdemain . . .' said Bell.

'I tell you it's a trick!' said Rosen. 'And you all know it! If I'd taken it I wouldn't let you *search*. I *demanded* the search. Didn't I?'

'Yes,' said Bell fairly. 'He certainly requested an examination of his external apparel.' And the other boys were struck by the curiousness of this. They might, indeed, have remained in some sort of benevolent doubt had not Ernest Ralph Gorse, still standing apart and quietly changing, now cut in again.

'That was just a try-on,' he said. 'He knew he was caught, so he tried it on. He thought we wouldn't look. It was his last fling.'

'Yes,' said Kerr, highly grateful to Gorse for having so astutely readjusted the case against Rosen. 'It was your last fling, you filthy little thief, and now you're trying to use it as an excuse.'

'Filthy low thief yourself!' shouted Rosen, and 'What did you say!' shouted Kerr, advancing upon Rosen to make a physical attack, when there was an interruption from outside. Mr Oakes, a junior master, put his head round the door.

'There's a lot of noise going on in here,' he said, and then suavely suggested: 'Shall we have complete silence until you're all changed and upstairs?'

5   Mr Oakes' suggestion was not really a suggestion at all: it was a command: and Mr Oakes was capable, even with this violent, hardened, and for the most part brutish mob, of inspiring the greatest fear.

This was strange, because Mr Oakes was not in fact formidable, either in himself or to himself. Only twenty-two years of age, with a chubby face, curly fair hair, and spectacles, Mr Oakes was in his private life lonely, miserable, and afraid. He had a tendency to spots on his face; he suffered a good deal from earache; he caught colds easily; and he was treated, it seemed to him, contemptuously and basely by the headmaster. He had a mother who lived in Clapham, and to his mother he wrote letters which were on the surface hopeful and courageous, but in reality filled with great pathos. Over and above his unhappiness at the school he was 'in love', and the one he loved, also living in Clapham, he could not 'understand'. Also, it was clear that she did not 'understand' him. She had originally 'understood' him, had, he believed, 'loved' him, and that was what made it all so much worse. In addition there was a nagging mystery as to whether or not there was somebody *else*. He wrote to her almost daily (receiving much less frequent replies) and harped upon this mystery. She stated that there was nobody else: but this she did in an indifferent, and therefore cruel, way, and even if he had believed it he would only have been unhappier still: because in that case there would be no explanation for her erratic and extraordinary attitudes. Then, again, she might simply have *changed*. He only wanted, he told himself, to *know*. And so on and so on and so on, and so forth and so forth and so forth.

Yet the youthful Mr Oakes, weak and tottering as a private individual, had witch-doctor, like power in the school and was able to cause dread amongst savages. He had a mystical alliance and direct means of communication with the study-god, the headmaster Mr Codrington, whose hideous vengeance, with a 'report', he could at any moment summon into action. The boys were quite silent for fully a minute.

Then, one of the boys having crept to the door and ascertained that Mr Oakes was not within hearing distance, they began to whisper, and then, softly, to talk.

'Well – what are we going to do with him, Ryan?' said Kerr. 'It's up to you.'

'He jolly well ought to have his nose punched,' said Ryan.

'He jolly well ought to be stewed in boiling *oil*,' said Roberts.

'Except for the smell,' said the boy who had already pointed out the danger of any sort of physical approach to Rosen, and who did not desire this contribution of his own to the matter in hand to be overlooked.

'Yes. There is *that*,' another boy agreed, and then said 'Pooh!' as though he could already smell something.

'Stewed in boiling oil, turned upside down, have his guts taken out, and sent to Coventry for a week,' suggested Wills, Rosen's original accuser.

'*Cave!*' said the boy nearest the door, thinking he had heard Mr Oakes returning.

There was now a long, cautious silence, which gave Bell the time and peace necessary for creative thought.

'The advisability of dismissing the delinquent to the City of Cycles', said the gifted Bell, 'is not to be dismissed. But to submerge his physiology in the oleaginous substance does not appertain to civilized behaviour.' There was a pause. 'I therefore suggest', Bell went on, 'that the venerable and much-respected Order of the Boot be applied by means of pedal extremities to his nether proportions, and that the culprit be summarily dismissed.'

Bell had surpassed himself.

'*Cave!*' said the boy nearest the door, and this time it was not a false alarm. Mr Oakes again put his head round the door.

'Did I hear someone talking?' he asked, and most of the boys cried '*No*, sir!' indignantly; and Bell, who had, in addition to a command of length in language, nerve, said sweetly, 'By no manner of means, sir' – and there was thenceforth actually no word uttered in the changing-room until the school bell rang.

6   Rosen was sensible enough to prolong his changing until the exact moment at which the school bell was rung, and was the last to enter the third-form classroom.

This was a dreary and uncomfortable room, now rendered, owing to the time of year and day, even more dispiriting by the electric light which shone down upon it from two bright bulbs, with white porcelain shades, suspended from the ceiling.

Three rows of three age-worn desks (each of which seated, and harboured the school belongings of, two boys) confronted the smaller and higher master's desk, which contained, for the most part, objects which had been confiscated owing to their illicit circulation in class.

The boys, when brooding, looked either at this desk and the master seated behind it, or at a blackboard on a stand to the left, or at an enormous coloured map of England, showing each county in a particular colour, which hung in the middle of the wall facing them. They usually stared at the map, gloomily realizing, for the thousandth time, that Rutland (in pink) was indeed, as they had been told, the smallest county in England, and very small.

This afternoon, under the supervision of Mr Oakes, history was being examined, and history had recently arrived at the French Revolution. But this brought about no response, caused nothing but electric-lit, map-staring torpor in the spirits of the pupils. Nor was Mr Oakes responsive, his complications at Clapham and a threat of recurring earache almost wholly occupying his mind. While the boys read given pages, he himself pretended to read.

The boys' reading, too, was little more than a pretence. They relied on their wits somehow to see them through when Mr Oakes questioned them, and engaged themselves in many fervent underground communications.

Ryan, seeking in his mind for any sort of means of relieving his tedium, suddenly realized that Rosen had, certainly, to all appearances, behaved atrociously towards him in stealing his torch, and used this as an excuse for sending a note to a plump, spectacled boy named Appleby, who shared a desk with Rosen.

This note, which merely said, '*Kick Rosen for me and tell him just wait*,' was made remarkable by the elaborate manner in which it was addressed:

Appleby,
      Desk nearest door,
            Front Room,
                  Rodney House,
                        Hove.

– and was passed along to Appleby, who in three minutes' time had sent back a reply.

'*Can't kick him properly because he's too near, but told him to wait*,' wrote Appleby, using the address:

Ryan,
      Desk nearest window,
            Front Room,
                  Rodney House,
                        Hove,
                              Sussex,
                                    England.

Ryan, who had in the meanwhile been reading a little, and had come across in his book the curious name St Just, now inadvertently let Rosen escape from his mind, and sent another note asking, 'Do you think *St Just* was *Just*?' with the address:

Appleby,
   Desk nearest door,
      Front Room,
         Rodney House,
            Hove,
               Sussex,
                  England,
                     Europe,
                        The World.

To which Appleby replied, 'No, because he *Robed* himself with *Spears*,' which was a subtle allusion to St Just's colleague, Maximilien Robespierre, and was addressed to Ryan as follows:

Ryan,
   Desk nearest window,
      Front Room,
         Rodney House,
            Hove,
               Sussex,
                  England,
                     Europe,
                        The World,
                           The Universe.

This set Ryan a by no means easy problem, which he at last solved, he believed satisfactorily, by writing, 'Tell Rosen I'll *guillotine* him,' and using the address:

Appleby,
   Desk nearest door,
      Front Room,
         Rodney House,
            Hove,
               Sussex,
                  England,
                     The World,
                      The Universe,
                   Not Mars.

This, in its turn, was tasking Appleby to the utmost. How, now, could the point occupied by Ryan in eternal space conceivably be presented with more agonized clarity or accuracy?

However, after much thought, Appleby, like Ryan, solved the practically insoluble. He wrote:

Ryan,
    RIGHT HAND SIDE of desk nearest window,
        Front Room,
            Rodney House,
                Hove,
                    Sussex,
                        England,
                            Europe,
                                The World,
                                    The Universe,
                                      Not Mars.

and was just about to add, as a *coup de grâce*, 'AND NOT VENUS EITHER' (which, in fact, opened illimitable possibilities) when Mr Oakes, who had had his eye on both of these boys for some time, asked Appleby what he was doing.

'*Nothing*, sir,' replied Appleby in an injured tone. Yet, though injured, he blushed.

Mr Oakes then replied that Appleby certainly ought to be doing something – he ought to be reading – and Appleby began to stare hard at his book.

And so the afternoon, and the Rosen episode (originated by Ernest Ralph Gorse), bleakly wore on.

7   Between the ringing of the bell which broke up the class and the ringing of the bell which summoned the pupils to tea, there was no time to resume the assault upon Rosen in a systematic way. At the long tea-table itself Rosen occupied a seat next to another junior master, and immediately after tea came 'prep'. Most of the boys did this under supervision in the front room, but others were allowed to go home, where it was presumed that they did their homework, though they certainly did not unless there was something on paper to be shown next morning. Amongst the latter were Rosen, Ryan, Wills, Appleby, and Ernest Ralph Gorse.

Because these boys had recently slipped into the habit of making a great noise in the changing-room before departure, it had become the business of a junior master to see them quickly off the premises. Rosen was thus again temporarily protected.

Nevertheless, during tea, a plot had been hatched, between

Appleby and Ryan, who sat next to each other, to attack Rosen as soon as he was outside the school and in the dark. Appleby, in fact, had been inspired by a plan which served the double purpose of vengeance upon Rosen and use of the torch which he was supposed to have stolen.

This plan was curiously complicated and carefully rehearsed in theory beforehand. Ryan and Appleby, it was agreed, would get into their outdoor clothes with the utmost speed and leave the school by the back door, from which Rosen would presently emerge. When they were outside they would prepare to 'ambush' Rosen, but not together. While Ryan was to take his station at the door, Appleby was to stand at twenty yards' distance in the darkness. Then, as the other boys came out, Ryan was to 'signal' to Appleby with his torch. If the boy who came out was not Rosen, but another, a green light would be flashed to Appleby, whose nervous vigilance and strain would thus be momentarily relieved. If Ryan believed that Rosen was 'just coming' the white light would be flashed on three times (and this three times in succession) and Appleby would brace himself for the coming ordeal. When Rosen himself did come out, the red light, of course, would be used. Action, however, was not to follow instantly. It was now Appleby's business to 'track' Rosen, while Ryan followed Appleby – Appleby himself having an ordinary torch with a plain white light with which, behind his back, he would himself 'signal' to Ryan – and this in 'Morse', which he professed to have mastered. What was to happen after this had not been discussed, and the main point, really, was that light had been most cleverly thrown upon an obscure matter – sense and a positive utility had at last been found in what might have been thought a totally senseless and useless sliding apparatus at the top of Ryan's torch.

But all these plans came to nothing because the passionate but clever Rosen, on coming out of the back door, at once sensed that something was afoot, ran in an unexpected direction, and made his escape. It was impossible even to make an attempt at a chase. Ryan shouted and 'signalled' to Appleby, and they joined each other at the back door.

'It's no good. He's gone,' said Ryan, and at this moment Ernest Ralph Gorse, coming out into the night, heard what had been said.

'Who's gone?' he asked.

'Rosen,' said Ryan. 'He did a bunk and got away.'

'Well, that doesn't matter,' said Ernest Ralph Gorse. 'You can get him tomorrow.'

'Yes,' said Ryan. 'I suppose we can . . .'

Ryan spoke without enthusiasm, for he did not in his heart believe in Rosen's guilt, and, unlike most of his fellows, was not the sort of boy who was even more anxious to persecute the guiltless rather than the guilty. He was only anxious to make use of his torch. This he now did, turning on the white, the green, the red, the white, the green.

The other two boys stood observing these flashes, and a rather funny silence fell upon all three. This silence may have been due to their absorption in the unspeakably beautiful, the absolutely divine colours piercing the blackness: but it may, in addition, have been due to something else. It may, to a certain degree, have been caused by the fact that Ryan and Appleby, without knowing it, did not wholly like Ernest Ralph Gorse, and felt his presence to be an interruption of their pleasure.

'You'll wear out the battery,' said Appleby at last.

'Got three more in reserve,' said Ryan, and there was another silence . . .

'What are you going to do to him', said Ernest Ralph Gorse in his level, nasal voice, 'when you catch him tomorrow?'

Such a return to the question of Rosen, in the midst of the divine flashes, was instinctively felt by Ryan and Appleby to be a little coarse, boring, unnecessary, and odd.

'I don't know,' said Ryan halfheartedly. 'What would you?'

'I'd tie him up,' said Ernest Ralph Gorse, 'if I were you.'

And this extraordinary remark succeeded in surprising Ryan and Appleby on a conscious level.

'What do you mean?' said Ryan with a casual air which concealed his bewilderment.

'Yes. That's what I'd do, if I were you,' said Ernest Ralph Gorse. 'I'd tie him up.'

But he had not thrown any further light upon his meaning, and Ryan, flashing his torch off and on, made a brief mental endeavour fully to comprehend what had been said. Tie Rosen up? Why? And what when he was tied up? Or was 'tying up' some sort of new invention by Gorse, something to be regarded as a punishment in itself?

Ryan was unable to find a satisfactory answer, and was not the sort of boy to seek one for long. Asking a patient Appleby whether he now wanted to 'have a go' with the torch, he dismissed the matter from his mind, and here the Rosen episode in fact came to an end, for no one brought the matter up again next day.

Something more than a quarter of a century later, however, those words of Gorse, uttered while the torch flashed in the darkness of that night, were to return to Ryan, and were to have meaning.

II

Those flashes of the little torch in the night – the red, the white, the green! Were these, to Ernest Ralph Gorse, in any sort of way what they were to Appleby and Ryan?

Did he, as they did, standing there in excitement and rapture, see little holes being pierced into the blackness, holes through which one might gaze into paradise – now a cool green paradise, now a blazing red paradise, now a blinding white paradise in which the visible and glorious filaments of the bulb might have been the crystalline flower of paradise itself?

Seemingly he did not. He did not even wait to ask Ryan to allow him to use the torch. Without saying good night, he left the other two in the darkness and entered the lamplight of Rodney Road.

If not inspired by paradise, in what, then, could this boy be interested? Was he interested in anything at all? Yes – for he took pleasure, as has been seen, in military exercises, and he was, apparently, sufficiently interested in human nature to desire to see the results of surreptitiously slipping a torch belonging to one boy into the pocket of another.

Again, were these pure, artistic interests? Did he enjoy military exercises and the observation of human nature for their own sakes? Or was there something more to it than this? Did he, perhaps, dimly perceive and relish the huge potentialities for the infliction of universal pain behind the seemingly innocent and childish military drill? And was his little experiment with human nature in fact conducted mostly for the sake of watching the misery of the victim?

No certain answer can be given. The type to which Ernest Ralph Gorse belonged cannot ever be fully understood at depth: only shrewd or inspired guesses can be made.

Now that the boy was out under the lamps on his half-mile walk back to the house in which he lived in Denmark Villas, he had further business of an uncommon sort to do.

This consisted of sticking a large pin, which he carried for the purpose in the lapel of his overcoat, into the tyres of as many bicycles as he might find, on his way home, propped up against the kerb in dark places.

Although, in those faraway nights, there were many such bicycles, Gorse's task was by no means too easy. To avoid detection, a good deal of preliminary observation and lurking was necessary, and the deed itself required histrionic ability – the simulation of an air of nonchalance as he approached the bicycle, of a detached interest in its make or style. Often, in the pursuit of this hobby of his, Gorse would arrive home twenty minutes or more later than he would have in the ordinary way.

Tonight he met with nothing satisfactory to work upon until he was within fifty yards of his own home: but here his watchfulness was rewarded with a machine in a situation of the most delightful vulnerability. Here he had, also, the pleasure both of knowing that it belonged to a neighbour and of knowing who the neighbour was. He stuck his pin twice into the front tyre and twice into the back one, and half a minute later he was indoors.

Ernest Ralph Gorse never knew – because he felt that it was too dangerous to wait and see – whether these pricks with his pin brought about an almost immediate deflation of the tyre. He confidently believed, though, that a slow puncture was begun in nearly every case, and he was certain that eventual damage of some sort had at any rate been achieved.

2   Ernest Ralph Gorse's mother and father were dead: he lived with his stepmother: and he had a home background which caused him intuitively not to ask his friends back to tea.

He had taken, indeed, even at this early age, a dislike to his social beginnings, and this in spite of having been often told that he had much to be proud of in his father, George Gorse, who had been, in his day, a successful, and in certain circles even well-known, commercial artist – the creator of a famous cartoon advertising a tooth paste. But the precocious Ernest Ralph was not interested in art of any sort, and he did not fancy a connection with advertising and tooth paste.

Also, his father's second wife had at one time served behind a West End bar, and although Ernest Ralph was not aware of this, all his instincts informed him that there was something out of order in this second marriage.

He could remember nothing of his mother, and little of his father.

A solicitor uncle, Sydney Gorse, was his guardian, and frequently paid visits to the house in Denmark Villas.

His stepmother was one of those remarkable, fat, excessively genial women who are, for some reason, despite their somewhat advanced age and fleshiness, never without quite serious admirers. Known as good 'sorts', or great or grand 'sports', they seem to have the power of enslaving men physically purely by the warmth of their spiritual nature. (Service behind a bar undoubtedly has some occult connection with the creation of this type of woman.) Mrs Gorse was now fifty-seven, but little as her stepson could conceive such a thing, it was not totally impossible that she had notions of marrying again, and that she was actually in a position to put such notions into practice.

The relationship between Mrs Gorse, who made little active endeavour to conceal the fact that she had sprung from the people, and Ernest Ralph Gorse, who already knew that it was inadvisable to ask his friends round to tea, was of the weirdest kind, and marked by suspicion and caution on both sides.

The fault, needless to say, did not lie with the genial second Mrs Gorse. She had made every attempt to make the boy happy and reasonable, and, conscious without being ashamed of her social origins, had been scrupulously careful not to 'stand in his way', as she put it.

Although she believed that she might be capable of 'passing', she never attended, as most parents did, any of the cricket matches, sports, fireworks, parties, prize-givings, and plays given by the school: she never, in fact, made any appearance at the school, or had any interview or direct communication with the headmaster: all that was necessary in this way was left to the uncle.

All the same, she did not like the boy, and was unable to force herself to do so. And, although an extremely fine judge of character, as such a type of ex-barmaid always is, she was unable quite to name to herself what it was which she found so distasteful, if·not almost detestable, in her stepson. She contented herself with telling herself (and her intimate friends) that he was a 'funny' one, an 'odd' one, a 'rum' one, and she predicted that his future would be curious. She said that she never knew 'what he was thinking'.

To dislike and distrust anyone – let alone a child, and a child so closely connected to her – ran so much against the grain of Mrs Gorse's character that it caused her whole personality and manner, when in contact or conversation with him, to change. Normally a carefree, laughing, nearly boisterously uninhibited woman – one who was the life and soul of parties in the private rooms of the public-houses which she still discreetly visited – with Ernest Ralph Gorse she was actually timid, shy. When she spoke to him she spoke quietly, and looked at him. Often, when not speaking to him, she would look at him. And this for as much as a minute on end, as if she still sought to discover his secret.

Mrs Gorse's manner to himself seemed to be, and almost certainly was, a matter of indifference to Ernest Ralph Gorse. With such a character any kind of behaviour – kindness, cheerfulness, sourness, spitefulness, or even physical brutality – would have produced the same outward response. These would have been, in any event, the same slouching, inimical demeanour: the same slightly nasty smell under the nose.

3   Tonight, when her stepson returned, Mrs Gorse was not at home.

She had, in fact, been out most of the day, and was at this moment drinking stout with familiars in a remote private residence at Preston Park. But Ernest Ralph knew nothing of her whereabouts.

Nearly every week she was twice or three times away from home when he returned from school, but he was not neglected. A maid-of-all-work, Mabel, who was nineteen years of age and who slept in, was there to look after his needs.

The sentiments of Mabel in regard to Ernest Ralph Gorse were, unlike those of Mrs Gorse, uncomplicated: they were those of sheer hatred. This was not because she was, like Mrs Gorse, a fine judge of character. An inexperienced, lumpy girl, she was anything but this. She simply hated boys of this age on pure, academic principles. She had had to live with young brothers and her mind was warped in this direction, perhaps for life. She was, therefore, being unfair to the young Gorse, particularly because in point of fact he gave her very much less trouble (or 'sauce') than nearly any other boy of his age might have given her. He was not the sort of boy to give trouble of the conventional kind to which she was habituated.

Ernest Ralph Gorse did not make a noise, and was orderly in his habits. Also, curiously enough, he had hobbies which kept him quiet. It was curious that a boy who was not interested in paradise could be interested in hobbies. This contradiction was, however, possibly explicable on the grounds that his interest in hobbies was not essentially disinterested. He pursued hobbies for the sake of vainglory and prestige at his school. He had the largest and finest collection of cigarette cards at the school, and the largest and most intricately made fleet of model battleships. But he was a hoarder rather than a genuine collector. He would slowly assemble his fleet of battleships in secret, and then one day appear at school with a huge cardboard box containing them under his arm. Having caused general curiosity, he would open this box at an appropriate and if possible dramatic moment, and become the centre of attraction. All rivals would be snubbed, and he would glow with quiet, ginger-haired, level-eyed power.

He was clever with his hands, and was at present engaged upon an elaborate piece of fretwork. Fretwork was in the air at the school just at this time, was due to succeed torches, and by the employment of foresight he proposed to outshine his fellows with a masterpiece.

He had a hobby room on the first floor at the back, and to this he retired at once on returning. Here he remained until his supper at seven-thirty.

Mabel would cook Ernest Ralph's supper and lay it on the dining-room table, with an air of being meticulously just. However much she might abominate him, his supper was his due, and she was not going to let him gain any moral advantage by not getting his supper properly and punctually.

'Your supper, Master Gorse!' she would cry up from below, but the words, which in print would seem cordial enough, were shouted in a way which filled them with vindictiveness and the resentful intimation that she was keeping *her* side of the bargain.

'All right!' he would shout down, and these, on most evenings when they were alone together, would be all the words which passed between them.

Then Master Ralph would wash his hands (he was clean in his personal habits) and go into the dining room to eat.

After eating, this evening, he returned to his fretwork for another hour, and then, taking his cage of white mice with him, went into the bathroom and had a bath.

Then he took his five white mice from the cage and made them swim in the bath. This he did almost every night, whether he himself was bathing or not, and the ceremony seldom took less than half an hour.

His furry pets, their heads held painfully high, would scramble and scamper through the water from one end of the bath to the other and back again. It would be impossible to say for certain whether they enjoyed this on the whole or not: but probably they did not. Master Gorse would endeavour to engineer 'races' between different mice, but this was always a failure, as it was impossible to arrive at a decision with creatures who did not know what they were being set to do and every now and again gave signs of extreme panic.

Neither Mrs Gorse nor Mabel knew anything about this nightly immersion of his white mice. Had they done so, they would have put an end to it.

Having roughly dried off his white mice in the dark and merciful recesses of a bath towel, Ernest Ralph put them back into their cage, took the cage into his bedroom, undressed, put out the light, and went to bed. Before sleeping he lay on his back, and thought.

4   It may be assumed that the material for thought for boys of his age in those days was very different from what it is in these; but such was not, really, the case. There was remarkably little difference. The games were the same – cricket in summer and football in winter – there was the motorcar, the aeroplane, the battleship (from 'dreadnought' to submarine), the steam train, the bomb, the revolver, the air gun, the electric torch, and electrical equipment of all kinds, even including 'wireless' in its early state – almost precisely all those things, in fact, over which the juvenile mind today might brood blissfully before sleeping.

What went on in the social adult world of that day, on the other hand – a world not as yet emancipated from its watch chains, and still subservient to the walking stick – a world in which the horse-cab continued to plough its way through streets filled with a squat, bowler-hatted, vindictively moustached middle class and proletariat: a world whose 'politics' manifested itself in the wearing of Conservative or Liberal favours: a world menaced by the militant suffragette yet enlivened by the 'hobble-skirt', the 'tango', the 'knut', and 'ragtime' – what went on in this world certainly differed considerably from what goes on at the present day, but entered only in a blurred, practically meaningless way into the consciousness of the juvenile – was, in fact, as remote and freakish to him as it would be to a man of the present era attempting mentally to reconstruct that past. He would give it no thought in bed.

As Ernest Ralph Gorse lay awake tonight he could hear, even from this distance in Denmark Villas, the English Channel crashing against the beach in the dark – crashing in the dark against the watch chains, the walking sticks, the horse-cabs, the hobble-skirt, the knut, the tango.

The voice of any sort of water beating against any sort of shore at night may be construed in a multitude of ways – as soothing, as menacing, as cynical, as reminiscent, or as prophetic. If the English Channel had been prophesying that night there was certainly no one listening in the town who could have effectually interpreted its obscure though pounded and reiterated utterances – least of all any allusions it might be making to those expeditionary forces of soldiers which in the very near as well as more distant future were destined to float upon its own bosom.

III

To all those boys at Rodney House that summer was the longest and most golden of their lives, and this was not because it was (as it was in fact) an exceptionally long, fine summer; it was because it was the one immediately preceding the world war of that era. It was to stand out in their minds in rich, warm contrast with the four black winters to follow. Wars, on the whole, are remembered by their winters. Also, when the war was over, the boys were older, and so the summers were naturally shorter.

Under the arrangement that the boys of Rodney House should play and drill on the County Ground, it was in addition permissible for them to enter the ground free of charge when county matches were in progress. In term-time, under the supervision of a master, they were taken down to watch such matches in the late afternoons, and in the holidays very many of them would separately or in couples take advantage of this privilege. It thus came about that the commencement of the war was to many of these boys ever afterwards to be sunnily and rather weirdly connected with the County Ground and cricket.

One sunny evening, shortly after the gentle tea interval of a county match, something almost resembling a scene, or even a disturbance or riot, took place inside the County Ground. About a dozen men, wearing uniforms and blowing through brass instruments, began to march around the outer path encircling the seats and the stands. The noise they made could not possibly be ignored, and they were almost at once followed by a crowd of small boys as well as many inquisitive adults. Others, watching the cricket and desiring to continue to do so, did not quite know what to do, or what exactly this noise was intended to convey.

Before long, however, the intention became more and more clear. This blowing through military brass was being directed against the flannelled fool still at the wicket while his country was in peril; and soon enough the attention of the entire crowd was divided equally and rather uglily between the game and the band.

This entirely unnecessary, gratuitous, and largely bestial assault upon the players (curiously akin in atmosphere to the smashing up of a small store by the henchmen of a gangster) beyond doubt ended in the victory of the aggressor – though at the time of its happening very few people present were able vividly or exactly to understand what was taking place.

Ernest Ralph Gorse was amongst the crowd of small boys following the band – so also were Ryan and Bell. Ryan and Bell were delighted simply by the music. Gorse was not the sort of boy to whom music in itself appealed; nevertheless, he was much more pleased than they were.

He could not have said why. He inhaled unconsciously the distant aroma of universal evil and was made happy, that was all.

Astute and precocious as he was, he was unable to tell himself in so many words that his day had come.

2   Ryan and Bell were innocently delighted by the music; and, paradoxically, they were at first almost equally delighted by its sequel; for there was a good deal of paradise for the Ryans and Bells of life in the early days of the First World War.

There was colour: an air of a festival: flags. To the charms of the Union Jack they were almost dulled by familiarity: but the French Flag, the Belgian Flag! And even the Union Jack was tricked out in new ways, with likenesses of the King and Queen set in its middle, or displayed in conjunction with the French and Belgian flags. Then there was the royalty – the King and Queen, of course, but, better still, the Tsar, and, again, even better still, the King of the Belgians! Then the leaders – the plumed General Joffre, the medalled Sir John French, the more simply attired but by no means less inspiring Sir John Jellicoe! – their bright images littering every kind of place – even, indeed particularly, the lesser sweet-shops, where it was possible to buy, instead of sweets, small, glazed, coloured discs of any of these national figures – these discs being attached to pins which one might stick into the lapel of one's coat. The war was, to the Ryans and Bells, very much a small-sweet-shop war.

The 'Red Cross' itself, contributing its own flag, added further vivid colour: not least when assisting the return of wounded 'Tommies', who were depicted with bandages set heroically aslant one eye of their weary faces, and as carrying captured German helmets in their limp hands.

And against the 'Tommy' the 'Uhlan', and against the 'Uhlan', at a distance, the 'Cossack!' – and Kaiser and Kitchener, and new figures and flags and events each day to stir irresistibly the happy imaginations of Ryan and Bell.

Slowly, however, the hues of heaven began to fade from all this: the photograph of the scene, as the winter set in, was no longer tinted; it became, like any ordinary photograph, the colour of mud, possibly even muddier. By Christmas Ryan and Bell were looking forward to the end of the war, and were conscious of doing so. They said as much.

With Ernest Ralph Gorse, naturally, there was throughout an entirely different reaction to contemporary events. These never at any time bore the hues of heaven: nevertheless, he was stimulated and satisfied beyond measure in his own way. As on the drill-ground in peacetime he was brighter and more alert, a different boy. After all, was not what was happening the realization, on a vast and unforeseen scale, of all the latent suggestions and aspirations existing in the drill? Gorse did not talk much about the war (he never talked much about anything), but he studied the maps and the illustrated papers with a thoroughness phenomenal in one of his years, and with a peculiar look of complacency on his face – a look which never varied. Victories or defeats in arms for the Allies or for their enemies seemed to make exactly the same impression upon him. It was as if all were equally satisfying.

Many of his school companions at this period spoke of their anxiety to be in the forces, and of their regret that their age did not permit this. Such talk was, needless to say, pure nonsense and boyish pretence on their parts. Gorse, on the other hand, never made any such protestation, but it was likely that he in fact genuinely desired to be in the middle of the conflict. At any rate, he envied the wearing of an adult uniform – an officer's uniform, of course – with so profound a feeling that he was blinded to any perils that it might entail. He had now, as later, a sort of mania for uniforms – a fixation.

As the Christmas Term of 1914 at Rodney House wore on, and was followed by the Easter Term of 1915, life grew blacker and bleaker for the Ryans and Bells. Games were still played in sweaters and shorts, but moral precedence, as well as an enormous amount of free time previously allotted to games, was now given over to drill in uniforms with puttees which made the legs itch incessantly. The boys were made to march during what would normally have been happy breaks and half-holidays: they were even made to march to and from their games – the whole day throbbing hideously to the tune of Left-left,-left-right-left. As a crowning horror, on the night of November 5, 1915, there were no organized fireworks as before; instead there was a torchlight parade in the back garden of Rodney House. Parents were invited and the boys drilled and sang patriotic songs in front of them.

Three days before the Christmas Term began, that is to say three days before the end of the holidays of that long, uncanny summer before the First World War, a long and slightly uncanny interview took place between Mr Codrington, the headmaster of Rodney House, and a policeman dressed in plain clothes.

3   Throughout this interview, which took place on yet another sunny evening, Mr Codrington, a thin, spectacled man, was evasive, and at first he did not fully understand, or at any rate he pretended that he did not fully understand, what the precise point of the interview was.

The policeman, also, was politely evasive, though he fully knew what he was about. He had on his person a long statement, which he did not actually show to Mr Codrington, but which told a story which he roughly outlined to the headmaster.

The story seemed to be a peculiarly odd and unpleasant one to Mr Codrington; though to the experienced officer it was nothing very much out of the way.

A few evenings previously, it seemed, a young girl of eleven had been found in a shed underneath the grandstand of the County Ground. She had been found tied to a roller, and screaming in panic for help.

A junior groundsman, working late, had heard cries from a distance, and had finally located her and released her. He had then taken her home crying to her parents – humble people who kept a small tobacco-and-newspaper shop in George Street, Hove. The father had then taken the child, now mollified and perhaps not altogether displeased by the limelight which the adventure as a whole had cast upon her, to the police station, where she had been talkative and made a detailed statement.

This statement, though doubtless entirely truthful, had all the weirdness and unreality of nearly every statement made to the police under such circumstances. When read in court and afterwards published in the newspapers, they almost always puzzle, baffle, and even irritate the reader, who feels that there is something indirect, forced, and false about them. This, almost certainly, is owing to the fact that although they have all the appearance of being a series of direct utterances poured forth spontaneously, they are in reality the result of wearisome and plodding questions put to the witness during a long period of time.

Fragments of the statement made by Ethel Joyce, the little girl from George Street, will serve to illustrate this point as well as to give some impression of what took place on that summer's evening at the County Ground, Hove.

Having given her name and address and age, and after other preliminaries having thoroughly established her identity, the little girl went on thus:

'I was on my way home to George Street. I stopped at the sweet-shop in Alwyn Road, which is near the back entrance of the County Ground. The name of the sweet-shop is Gregson's. I am familiar [*sic*] with it. I go in there often. I went in to buy lemonade powder.

'When inside I spoke to a little man. He seemed to be a little man. He may have been a boy. I think he was a boy. He wore no hat, but carried a green cap in his pocket. I think it was a school cap. I am not certain but think so – it was definitely [*sic*] green. He had very fair hair. I would know him if I saw him again. He spoke to me and offered me a drink of lemonade ...'

Ethel Joyce then described how she drank two glasses of lemonade with the boy and then continued in the same irritating, because slightly mysterious and not fully comprehensible, way:

'After we left the shop he suggested that we enter the County Ground by the back entrance. I agreed. He said this was for fun. The back entrance was locked, but he said we could climb over. He assisted me to do so. There were spikes on the gate, but he showed me a way of avoiding them. We climbed up and jumped down from a pillar at one side.

'Having entered the ground, he took me to a shed underneath the big wooden stand. Here he found a rope. He did not have this rope when I met him, but I think he knew it was in the shed. I had a skipping-rope with me, but this was not a skipping-rope.

'He then suggested that I should tie him up for fun. I did as he said, and when I had untied him he suggested that he should tie me up as well. I agreed to this, and he tied me to the roller so that I could not free myself.

'He then left me, and as he did not return I became frightened and called out. He then returned and put his hand over my mouth and told me to be quiet.

'He had been gone about two minutes. Perhaps it was not as long as that – I cannot be certain. It was long enough for me to be frightened.

'I then asked him to untie me, but he was rude and said he had no intention of doing so. He seemed excited.

'He then said, "What have you got on you – eh?" and he took my purse from my pocket. The purse contained sevenpence-halfpenny – a sixpence and two coppers. He then put his hand over my mouth again and told me I had better keep quiet after he had gone. He said, "It will be the worse for you if you don't." He hurt me and bruised my face in putting his hand over my mouth.

'He then ran away and I was quiet as he had told me. He took my purse with him. After five minutes alone in the shed again I became frightened and began to cry out ...'

The child then went on to describe how she was found by the groundsman, released, and taken home to her parents. Towards the end of her statement she repeated her description of her assailant – the 'little man' who on reflection she believed was a boy.

'I am sure', she said, 'that the cap he had in his pocket was green. His hair was very fair. I was struck by his fair hair. I would know him again by it.'

Mr Codrington, listening gravely, not to this statement but to a précis of the story generally given by the policeman, only just succeeded in disguising a slight change of countenance – a sudden sharpening of interest in his eyes – when the green cap was mentioned. Here, he realized, was the matter with which he might conceivably be concerned. For the Rodney House school cap was of a startling green colour; and it was by virtue of wearing this cap that the boys were permitted by the turnstile attendants to enter the County Ground free of charge when county matches were in progress. The green caps were, in fact, a minor but familiar feature of the ground.

Mr Codrington also found himself disguising a thoughtful look behind his spectacles when mention was made of the unusual fairness of the boy's hair. He endeavoured rapidly in his mind to summon up any of his pupils who might be described as having fair, or outstandingly fair, hair, and for some reason which he could not understand he found his mind almost instantly fixed and concentrating upon Ernest Ralph Gorse.

He was the less able to understand his own lightning mental processes because Gorse's hair was not what one would, strictly speaking, call 'fair'. It was 'red' – or 'ginger'. With so many boys with genuinely fair hair in the school, why should his mind have been attracted with that astonishing magnetic speed to a boy whose hair was ginger?

As the policeman talked he attempted inwardly to find an answer to this problem and met with a certain amount of success. His mind had rushed headlong to Gorse, he believed, simply because his hair was of a remarkable colour, and the child who had been tied up and robbed in the shed had made it clear that she thought the hair of her assailant remarkable. Many boys at Rodney House had fair hair, but by no means in any remarkable way.

The small girl, Mr Codrington noticed, had made no mention of ginger or red hair, and if Ernest Ralph Gorse had been the delinquent, this was odd. But then the small girl was a small girl, and as such likely to be bewildered and unreliable: she had shown complete confusion of mind by first of all making that queer allusion to a 'little man' to whom she had spoken, and then afterwards saying that he was a boy.

Then something else occurred to Mr Codrington. He knew the shed underneath the stand to which the policeman was referring, and he knew also that this was used as a base for hide-and-seek, as a 'den', and for other childish, mischievous purposes by certain of his pupils: he had more than once had to clear the shed of these boys. And he knew, over and above this, that Gorse had always been present when such clearances had been made. He had always felt, in fact, that Gorse had been the ringleader of any boys playing in this shed. It had been, as it were, Gorse's shed.

Having reflected on these lines – and such reflections occupied less than a minute in time – Mr Codrington had a fairly good idea why his mind had in the first place flashed at once to Ernest Ralph Gorse.

His having succeeded in understanding his own mental processes

did not, however, make Mr Codrington in any way disbelieve in his
intuition about Gorse. On the contrary, it supported it. As a consequence his eyes, behind his spectacles, grew more and more
watchful, and his manner became subtly more guarded. For Mr
Codrington was not anxious for it to become known in public that
one of his pupils had tied up a small girl in a shed, seriously
frightened her, and robbed her of her purse.

Towards the end of the interview the policeman came candidly
to the point. He explained that the green school cap, taken in
conjunction firstly with the fact that the assault and robbery had
taken place in the County Ground, and secondly with the fact that
the juvenile assailant and robber was evidently acquainted with the
County Ground (so far acquainted as to know of the existence of
a rope in one of its back sheds), made it seem likely that a boy from
Rodney House was concerned in the matter. Could Mr Codrington
be of any assistance? Was there at Rodney House any boy with
exceptionally fair hair whom Mr Codrington might feel justified in
suspecting – any boy who had, perhaps, to Mr Codrington's knowledge, at an earlier date, misbehaved himself in some such manner?

At this Mr Codrington made an elaborate pretence of thinking
disinterestedly yet earnestly, and then answered in a negative
manner which simulated entire bewilderment. He said that there
were certainly several boys with fair hair in the school, but that did
not take one anywhere. There were boys with fair hair in every
school. There was certainly no boy at Rodney House who had ever,
to his knowledge, committed anything resembling any such offence.

Then, although the interview was conducted throughout on the
most friendly terms and in the spirit of co-operation, Mr Codrington went, as it were, over to the attack. He suggested that what had
been assumed to be a boy might, after all, have been a 'little man',
or at any rate an older and more mature boy than any at his own
preparatory school. He said that there were many other schools in
Brighton and Hove whose pupils wore caps incorporating the colour
green, and he mentioned one or two of these schools. He admitted
the singular and undivided greenness of the Rodney House cap, but
he did not think that this amounted to anything. How much of the
cap did the plainly rather unreliable little girl see sticking out of the
boy's pocket? Finally he made what he thought was a strong point.
Why, he asked, should any boy from his school find it necessary to
effect a difficult entrance into the County Ground by a spiked back
entrance when, by virtue of being a pupil at Rodney House, he was

entirely at liberty to enter in the proper way at the front? Were not the front gates open at the time of the incident, and was it not in fact a matter of the utmost ease to enter at these gates at such a time and such a season of the year, unseen by anyone? Was there not, therefore, every indication that the boy had no connection with the school and probably belonged to a rough, hooligan type?

The policeman, throughout the interview as shy and guarded in his manner as Mr Codrington, seemed to agree with most of this, and made it clear that he had visited Mr Codrington merely on the off-chance of gaining information or assistance. Soon afterwards he left, shaking hands with Mr Codrington, and talking about the weather and the war.

When he had gone Mr Codrington was only dimly aware that he had failed to tell the truth, the whole truth, and nothing but the truth. He had all the same failed to do this. He had not seen fit to tell the policeman that he was for certain reasons well acquainted with the shed underneath the stand, and it had therefore been impossible for him to say that this shed was associated in his mind with Ernest Ralph Gorse. He had also been disingenuous in his remarks about the spiked back gate to the County Ground, for if he had searched his mind thoroughly at the time he would have remembered that he in fact knew that there were boys from his school who liked to climb over this gate when it was locked. These boys had a passion for defeating the spikes for the sake of adventure, and only two summers ago he had, in the course of an admonitory lecture about various matters to the school as a whole, threatened to punish such dangerous folly. Finally, he had failed to tell the policeman that as the story had been unfolded the figure of Ernest Ralph Gorse, the boy with the remarkable hair, had flashed at once into his mind.

Though normally an honest man, Mr Codrington had on this occasion been dishonest, both to himself and to the policeman. For this reason, after the policeman had gone, he was faintly disquieted in his conscience.

As he had a lot of letters to write and work to do that evening in preparation for the coming term, this feeling of disquietude soon left him, and when he thought about the matter next morning he was confident that his attitude had been entirely correct. Any suspicions he might have had about Ernest Ralph Gorse, were, of course, fantastic. The whole thing, as connected with any boy at Rodney House, was fantastic.

The small girl had undoubtedly imagined or invented a good deal in what could have been nothing worse than some sort of prank, and, moreover, had come to no harm beyond the loss of sevenpence-halfpenny and a purse.

The policeman did not call again; nothing further ever came to light; and Mr Codrington almost entirely banished the story from his mind.

Nevertheless, when Ernest Ralph Gorse appeared at the school on the first day of the new term Mr Codrington found himself looking at him. And, as the term progressed, he for some reason still found himself looking at him. He would look at him in class for as long as thirty seconds, very much in the same way as Mrs Gorse would look at her stepson. It became a sort of habit. He would look particularly at his hair, and try to get an impression of its exact colour.

This habit became less easy to break because in the Easter Term which followed Gorse was promoted to the senior form, which was the one which Mr Codrington most frequently took. In fact, at last Mr Codrington reached a stage at which he had definitely to resolve to himself not to look at Gorse. But he was unable to achieve this.

Towards the end of the Easter Term the boy's guardian, Sydney Gorse, called upon Mr Codrington. He explained that the step-mother was moving to London – to Chiswick – and that the boy was to be sent to school not far away – to Colet Court in Hammer-smith. Later he would go on to St Paul's.

At the end of the term Mr Codrington invited Gorse to his study in order to give him the conventional headmaster's valedictory discourse. During this discourse he looked at him, behind his spectacles, more closely than ever. What was going on in Mr Codrington's head, during these last few moments of his acquaintanceship with Gorse, it would not be easy to say. Probably Mr Codrington had no idea himself.

It may be guessed, though, that Mr Codrington, in addition to being the first individual to protect Ernest Ralph Gorse from the results of a serious misdemeanour, was also (apart from Mrs Gorse) the first faintly to suspect that the boy had a remarkable future.

PART TWO

GETTING OFF

I

Towards dusk on a summer's evening three years after the First World War, two girls of about eighteen years of age walked arm in arm along the Brighton front.

One of these girls was exceptionally pretty; the other seemed to be exceptionally plain. The latter, who wore spectacles, was certainly not as plain as she seemed to be; her plainness was much exaggerated by the observer because she was seen beside her friend, who was indeed spectacularly pretty.

The fact of their walking arm in arm, as well as the way in which they did this, revealed the sort of class to which these two girls belonged. Though remarkably well dressed, they quite evidently came from a poor quarter of the town and were of working-class origin and occupation. The way in which they walked made manifest, too, the real object of their walking: so also did the time and place at which they walked – the hour of dusk on a sea-front. They were looking forward, or at any rate laying themselves open to, encounters with men, or with boys of their own age.

It may be thought curious that, their object being what it was, one of them should have been so pretty while the other was so plain. It might be supposed that normally a pretty girl would pair with a pretty girl, and a plain one with a plain one. But such is not the case. Owing to some mystifying law of psychology or expediency, couples of this sort are more often than not composed of such opposites, and this law has always been as dismaying as it is mystifying to those young men who are also walking in pairs and desiring to talk to girls. Who is to take, to put up with, to be palmed off with, the 'other one'?

The causes of this law must be numerous and complicated. Perhaps the pretty girl adopts the ugly one quite selfishly in order to enhance her own beauty by means of contrast. On the contrary, she may be moved by pity, an anxiety to help her friend. She might, indeed, have both these ideas in her mind at the same time. Then again she may choose to walk abroad with an ugly girl so that there is no question of a rival. Or she may do so for the sake of base vanity, of showing off her powers of attraction in front of one who, incapable of attracting men herself, will be duly impressed and will offer up incense. On the other hand, the relationship may often practically be forced upon the pretty girl by the ugly one. The latter, in order to bathe in something of the glamour of the former, may make herself so useful to her in a variety of ways, may show herself so wonderfully willing to listen to confidences, to advise and sympathize, or even to play the part of a go-between, that she makes herself at last almost indispensable to the other. Plain girls may have solid useful qualities which pretty girls may not be so foolish as to disregard. Whatever the answer to the riddle is, in any given case, there is probably some hidden bargain behind such partnerships.

These two girls were walking from the direction of the Palace Pier towards the West Pier, which they had nearly reached.

At about a hundred yards' distance from the West Pier some sort of suggestive nudging took place between their interlocked arms, and they turned away to the left to the railings overlooking the sea. They leaned over these railings and gave an imitation of observing the beauties of what remained of the sunset.

'Go on,' said the pretty girl to her companion. 'Have a look *now*.'

'No,' said the ugly girl. '*You look*.'

'No – *you* look,' said the pretty girl, and she was in due course obeyed. The pretty girl is usually ultimately obeyed on such occasions, for, in addition to her ascendancy for other reasons, she is the initiator, the senior officer, the skilled and experienced campaigner in operations of this nature.

'Yes,' said the ugly girl. 'Here they come.'

She was alluding to three young men whom they had believed to have been following them.

'All right. Just pretend to be looking out at the sea,' said the mature strategist, in a quiet, steady tone which in fact betrayed some nervousness by virtue of its quietness and steadiness.

'It's a lovely evening,' she added. 'Ain't it?'

2   The pretty girl bore a pretty name – Esther Downes – and the ugly girl bore an ugly one – Gertrude Perks. Fortune, in the case of these two girls, had made up its mind to use no half measures of any kind.

After they had been gazing out over the sea in silence for a minute or so – and after they had intimated to each other, by further imperceptible (indeed practically immaterial) nudgings, that each knew that the three young men who had been following them had caught them up and passed them from behind – Gertrude Perks spoke.

'I think', said Gertrude, 'they're going on the Pier.'

'Oh – are they?' said Esther, and there was in her voice something which suggested that she felt that she was about to receive a challenge of some sort.

'Yes – they're going on now,' said the vigilant Gertrude.

'Oh well,' said Esther, 'maybe *we'll* be going on too.'

Now Esther's voice showed quite clearly that she thought a challenge had been thrown at her – if not a positive affront. During the last few evenings these three young men had been passing and re-passing her and her friend in a manner which vividly conveyed only one thing – that they desired, and intended soon, to come up and speak to them, to 'get off'. Indeed Esther had been almost certain that they would do so tonight. And here they were coolly going on the Pier by themselves!

The Pier was intimately and intricately connected with the entire ritual of 'getting off'. Indeed, without the Pier, 'getting off' would have been to some minds inconceivable, or at any rate a totally different thing. The Pier was at once the object and arena of 'getting off', and usually the first subtle excuse made by the male for having been so bold as to 'get off' was his saying that he thought it might be 'nice' to go on the Pier. An invitation to go on the Pier was like an invitation to dance; it almost conferred upon 'getting off' an air of respectability. And so now these three young men, by going on the Pier by themselves, had, as it were, established their independence doubly – firstly by the act itself, and secondly by proving that they were in no way anxious to avail themselves of any excuse.

'All right. Let's go on, then,' said the eager and inexperienced Gertrude Perks.

But the wiser Esther replied that there was 'no hurry', and she continued to gaze out at the sea.

3   Esther had much to consider and weigh in her mind. Had she been affronted, and, if so, was the offence too gross for her to stomach? Was she making a mountain out of a molehill, or was she in danger of losing face by making a molehill out of a mountain? If

she went on the Pier now, might it not be a clear case of the unthinkable – of 'following' them? And, apart from any injury to her own pride, would not such a thing amount to an appalling mistake from a purely tactical point of view? On the other hand, was it not absolutely the truth that she had, when she had come out this evening, intended to go on the Pier in any case? Why, therefore, should these three impudent young men (if indeed they were intending to be impudent) be allowed to interfere with her original plan? Then there were her purely aesthetic desires to be considered. She genuinely liked walking on the Pier for its own sake: she liked its lights, its band, its slot machines, its smell of tar, its rusty foundations, its noise of people's footsteps clacking incessantly on wood just above the satin-surfaced sea, its curious iron-grille quadrangle at the end, and its vast views of twinkling Brighton and Hove. Why should she be deprived of these pleasures for the sake of childish pride or laboured devices? Who did these young men think they were? Did she not disdain to think of such things as devices in connection with them?

Convincing herself that she did, she at last made up her mind.

'All right,' she said. 'Let's go on.'

But that she still had devices, or pride, or the three young men somewhere at the back of her mind, she proved by her next utterance, which she made as they were walking on again, arm in arm, towards the turnstile of the Pier.

'After all,' she said, 'it's free for anyone to go on, ain't it?'

4   As the girls passed through the turnstile the three young men were outside the West Pier Theatre playing with a slot machine behind whose glass were miniature images of German soldiers on a field of battle. These Germans were waiting, in various positions and postures, to be shot down by a sort of pistol operated from outside the glass. It was necessary to aim between their eyes, and if a reasonable percentage of them were shot down the marksman was rewarded not only with the glamour of achievement but with the pecuniary profit of not losing his penny.

The young man peering through the sights of the pistol at the moment had a great deal of dark hair, a fine profile, and a generally graceful air in spite of his immaturity. This was Ryan, whose torch, several years ago, had mysteriously disappeared in the changing-room of Rodney House School. His two companions also had been educated at Rodney House. One was Bell (who had at that period specialized in the use of long words) and the other was Ernest Ralph Gorse.

All of these three wore grey flannel trousers – what they would have called 'bags'.

With these trousers Ryan wore a well-cut coat originally belonging to a dark blue lounge suit; Gorse wore a pepper-and-salt tweed jacket; and Bell wore a jacket of brown tweed.

None of them wore hats. Ryan probably had the smartest appearance, but he was followed closely by Gorse. The spectacled Bell was far behind: his jacket was shoddy and rumpled, his trousers were not creased, and his collar and tie were out of place. Love of long words had in the course of years led to a love of Learning, and the learned disdain too great an attention to their clothes. He bit, learnedly, a curved pipe.

Ryan and Bell were clean-shaven, but Gorse wore what he could manage in the way of a toothbrush moustache. Ryan and Bell had been to Brighton College. Gorse had been to St Paul's School in London.

Ryan was simple, eager, and shy in his demeanour and thoughts. Bell, in spite of affectations, such as curved-pipe-biting, was really very much the same as Ryan. Gorse was very different from both, in his demeanour and in his thoughts.

Gorse was reasonably tall and had a good figure. His reddish moustache improved him. It largely succeeded in removing what had been so noticeable in his face as a boy – that expression of smelling something nasty immediately underneath his nose. The expression was still there, but could only be seen every now and again, and then fleetingly, by someone who knew him well. A casual acquaintance might never observe it.

He was clean, and neatly dressed, and many might have thought him good-looking. He had even acquired a sort of dashing charm – a charm which, when he took the trouble to exercise it, not only made him seem more good-looking than when he was behaving otherwise, but drew attention away from that other defect he had had as a boy, and still had, a most unpleasantly nasal voice.

5   Gorse was not making any attempt to be particularly charming with his two companions at the present moment, and when, following Ryan in putting his penny into the slot machine and peering through the sights at the German soldiers, he spoke, his looks and voice were on the whole displeasing.

'Well,' he said. 'Do you think the "Birds" are on yet?'

Young women – and particularly young women of working-class origin walking along sea-fronts with a view to encounters – were in these days usually alluded to as 'Birds' by this class of young man. Gorse was asking his companions whether they thought Esther Downes and Gertrude Perks were already on the Pier; and they understood him without difficulty.

'What makes you think they're *coming* on?' said Ryan. He spoke a little nervously.

'Oh,' said Gorse, shooting down a German with a lazy, level accuracy all his own, 'they'll be on all right.'

'How do you know?' said Ryan. 'You seem to be jolly certain about everything.'

And now there was something closely resembling a gulp in Ryan's voice, a gulp of disappointment or grief. It was as if he believed that some fearful mistake had been made.

The truth of the matter was that Ryan loved the sight of Esther Downes – and this passionately. He had done so ever since he had been passing and re-passing her during these soft summer evenings: and passionately to love the sight of anyone, for a male of Ryan's temperament and Ryan's age (which was eighteen), is the equivalent of passionately (though almost sexlessly) loving them themselves – without any reserve. Alluding contemptuously to Esther Downes as a 'Bird' was pure defence and pretence on Ryan's part. If it could be done Ryan would have married Esther Downes tomorrow – married her and have sat in the dusk on the Pier with her (perhaps 'kissing' her) and have taken her to the pictures and caressed her hand, and have taken her into the country on the back of his motorcycle, and so on and so forth for ever and ever with the blessing of the law. No wonder, then, that there was a gulp in Ryan's voice, and that he resented the calmness of Gorse, who, he believed, had lost an opportunity which might never return.

It was all Gorse's fault. For Gorse was to Ryan and Bell, in matters of this sort, as Esther Downes was to Gertrude Perks – the initiator, the experienced campaigner, the acknowledged leader.

That this was so was, really, surprising, and for two reasons. Firstly, Ryan was actually and quite transparently a very much more attractive creature than Gorse. He was indeed one for whom 'all the girls', in the expression of that day as well as this, 'fell', and he might, therefore, be expected to be playing the dominant part in this trio of cavaliers. Secondly, he was by no means fond of Gorse, whom he inwardly and instinctively disliked and distrusted – as much now as when they were both children at Rodney House – and shy as he might be in his thought and demeanour, he had not the sort of character which would accept much domination of any kind.

The explanation was, almost certainly, that Ryan, despite his opportunities, had an attitude towards 'girls' singularly lacking in vulgarity and totally different from that of Gorse, and that he was, in the ordinary way, too easy-going generally not to submit to the mood and manners of anyone with whom he happened to be. So, with Bell as a nonentity hard at work at his pipe, Gorse was allowed to take the lead.

There was remarkably little in common between these three boys, who were now walking together in Brighton through the instrumentality of a letter-writing Gorse. Gorse was an assiduous writer of extremely lengthy letters. It was a sort of passion with him, and in order to appease this passion, he kept in touch with innumerable school companions, even those from his earliest days at school. His letters were largely facetious, and he fancied his own style immeasurably. This was of a fearful Wardour Street, Jeffery Farnol kind – packed with 'Thou'st', 'I would fain', 'Stap me', 'Beshrew me', 'A vast deal', 'Methinks', 'Albeit', 'Where-anent', 'Varlet', 'Knave', etc. – a style commonly used, for reasons hard to ascertain, by people either with very naïve or very unwholesome minds. But the mind of Ernest Ralph Gorse was by no means naïve.

Through all his days at Colet Court, and later at St Paul's, he had written regularly to Ryan and Bell, and now, as all three happened to be in Brighton at the same time, they had at Gorse's instigation met, and had taken to walking with each other.

All three had left school for good and were on holiday before embarking upon adult life. Ryan was to enter a firm owned by his uncle, an estate agent, in London; Bell was hoping before long to Matriculate and afterwards gain a footing in the scholastic world; Gorse had nothing particular to go to, but had expressed (to his stepmother and uncle guardian) a desire to be connected with the motorcar business. With the makes, intricacies, and secondhand prices of the motorcar, Gorse was, for his age, phenomenally well acquainted.

Although she still disliked him, perhaps because she did so, Gorse's ex-barmaid stepmother was singularly indulgent with him, and had urged him, barmaid-fashion, to 'have a good time' while he was 'young enough to enjoy it'. It was also possible that she was a little more indulgent with him than she might otherwise have been because her conscience was a trifle uneasy. Still, notwithstanding her decidedly mature age and figure, she was loved, and permitted herself to be loved by, elderly men – was 'having a good time' herself, in fact. Discreet as she was in these affairs she felt that, from the point of view of conventional respectability, she was here not playing quite fair with her stepson, who, she suspected – quite rightly – was not unaware of what went on. Gorse's uncle, now getting old and becoming increasingly less interested in Gorse, took a good view of the motorcar business, which he believed belonged to the future. At the age of twenty-one Gorse was due to inherit enough money at least to keep him from destitution.

All these three boys were, of course, in what is deceptively called the 'morning' of life – deceptively because the vigorous word 'morning' does not at all suggest the clouded, oppressive, mysterious, disquieted, inhibited condition through which the vast majority have to pass at this age. Ryan and Bell – in spite of their social cheerfulness – in spite of the one's motorcycle and the other's pipe – certainly belonged to this majority, but perhaps Gorse did not. No ordinary human rules applied to the baffling Ernest Ralph Gorse. He was certainly neither clouded in his ideas nor inhibited in his behaviour. To such a character this period may indeed have been a strange sort of 'morning'.

6   Gorse, having shot down his Germans and retrieved his penny, put in the same penny and shot the Germans down again, and then again put in the penny and retrieved it – all this with the air of an adroit executioner rather than a juvenile pier-gambler.

The others watched and waited in silence as he did this. Gorse never showed any dislike either of waiting or of keeping people waiting.

'Well – let's go and see,' he said at last. He was alluding, as his companions knew, to the 'Birds', concerning whose presence on the Pier he was so certain.

'Where?' asked Ryan.

'Follow thou in my footsteps, rogues, rapscallions, and rascally roisterers,' said Gorse, who enjoyed the art of alliteration along with the style of Jeffery Farnol. 'Thou shalt not be led astray.'

He now, in a large manner befitting his style of speech, put his hands patronizingly on the shoulders of the other two, and steered them down the Pier again in the direction of the shore, choosing the right-hand side of the seated and sheltered partition which ran from the Theatre towards the Concert Hall – the east side of the Pier, that is to say. He had a reason, as the anxious Ryan quickly and gladly perceived, in choosing this side. What there was of a breeze that night was westerly, and apart from a few eccentrics, all who were walking or sitting on the Pier had naturally chosen the east side because it was protected from the breeze by the partition.

Also, quite unaccountably, this side of the West Pier has, from far-distant times until the present day, been strongly favoured by the whim of the public.

They had walked scarcely thirty yards before Esther Downes and Gertrude Perks were observed.

The two girls had found a place, as near to the Concert Hall as possible and therefore amongst many other people, on the free seating accommodation which edged the Pier. With their backs to the sea they were looking at the passers-by and enjoying the music wafted from the Concert Hall.

No sooner had they been seen than Gorse began to hum in a gentle, meaning way; and, when he had finished humming, a deadly silence fell upon all three young men.

Absorbed, perhaps, by the music, and the passing people, and the faint, soothing sound of the sea beneath them, Esther and Gertrude were caught unawares.

It was, indeed, not until the three young men were within ten yards of them that Esther and Gertrude saw them, and Esther, for once, lost her head.

Catching Ryan's eye, she turned with absurd haste and looked down at the sea, while the spectacled Gertrude, thus abandoned and in a hideous state of fear and embarrassment, could only glance glassily at the three young men, at the other people passing, and at nothingness – at all at the same time, as it were, and with the self-conscious stiffness of a chained, alert macaw being too closely stared at on a perch at the Zoo. This, needless to say, made the ill-starred Gertrude look even uglier than usual – one might fairly say repulsive.

When this gruesome little episode was over, Gorse was the first to speak.

'The saucy wench showeth disdain,' he said. 'Doth she not?'

'Yes, she certainly does,' said Ryan, and from his voice it would have been difficult to tell whether he was disappointed or pleased by what had just happened.

On the one hand he was inclined to interpret Esther's gesture at its face value and as a firm rebuff: on the other hand it had been his own eye that she had caught, and he was not so completely lacking in self-assurance and sophistication not to suspect that extreme coyness had been her motive, and that such coyness was a good omen.

'And what about the other one?' said Gorse. 'I hadn't realized it was as bad as all that.'

'No,' said Ryan. 'She's certainly no beauty.'

And here both Gorse and Ryan gave a little look at Bell, who was silently biting and nagging at his pipe.

Why did Ryan and Gorse thus look at Bell?

Almost certainly this was due to the all too familiar but none the less horrid problem of the 'other one'.

It is not always realized that there are male as well as female 'other ones'. And poor Bell, because of his spectacles, his learnedness, and his general contempt for glamour or even ordinary tidiness in his clothes, had, it seems, either in the conscious or subconscious minds of his two companions, come to be regarded as 'the other one' in this situation.

Now the 'other one' has worse to suffer than the mere humiliation of being what he is. He has duties to perform. It is, in fact, his business to take, to put up with, be palmed off with the 'other one' on the other side. 'Other ones' are supposed not to mind this; indeed in the thoughtless baseness of human nature, they are supposed rather to like it. They are even assumed to have (most conveniently) a *penchant*, if not some sort of inexplicable longing, for their counterparts: like is said, after all, to attract like. But nothing could be further from the case. 'Other ones' worship at the shrine of pure beauty as much as – perhaps, because of their disadvantages, more than – the fortunate ones.

So Gorse and Ryan glanced at Bell – Ryan, possibly, not without a distant twinge of conscience. What Bell was thinking was well concealed by his pipe-biting. The matter, though, was of grave importance. Was Bell willing to undertake his responsibilities? Indeed, in view of the recent disaster – the finally established absolutely awful hideousness of Gertrude Perks – would anybody in their right senses be willing to undertake such responsibilities?

Nor was this the only difficult matter. Even if Bell could be taken to be out of his mind and prepared to withdraw Gertrude Perks from the arena, who, then, was to be the 'other one' in regard to the lovely Esther Downes? Ryan or Gorse?

In addition to having very little in common, these three boys knew very little about what each other was thinking. Bell, as we have seen, was an enigma to Gorse and Ryan, both of whom he found enigmatic, and Gorse was an enigma to Ryan. It was only the shrewd Gorse who knew at least one thing, and that was that Ryan, without having met her, was infatuated by Esther Downes, was unable even properly to keep an outward composure about her.

Ryan, then, would have been indisputably anxious to defeat Gorse, though, his nature being as amiable and easy-going as it was, he probably did not think of things in this way.

But what were Gorse's feelings about all this?

Again, because no ordinary human rules could be applied to this boy, the question is not an easy one to answer. Of one thing we may be sure – Esther Downes by no means infatuated him. His was a character incapable of infatuation – it was so for women at any rate. (Military uniforms and slow schemes for secret power are another matter.) He probably admired Esther Downes considerably, however, and had already fitted her in to some roughly formulated plan for the future. In the meanwhile he was clearly enjoying his tacitly acknowledged leadership in the chase as well as the exercise and exhibition of his ingenuity as a leader.

7   'Well, what do we do now?' asked Ryan, and Gorse, having said, Drake-like, that there was 'plenty of time', walked on and on, almost off the Pier. He did at last turn, however, and then persuaded his companions to lean over the railings near the shore, and to look down, not at the sea, for that did not rise as high as this, but at the beach, which was now almost in the darkness of the night.

Talking of detached matters, he kept them at these railings for about six minutes – which seemed to a frantic Ryan to be little less than sixty – but he at last relented and permitted a return journey in the direction of the spot at which it was presumed that Esther Downes and Gertrude Perks would still be sitting.

Wrongly presumed, though, as the unimportant Bell, oddly enough, was the first to perceive.

'Ah-ha,' said Bell, 'I see our "Birds" are flown.'

This was a pun, and as such might have been thought beneath such an austere thinker as Bell, it was, though, a Learned pun, and therefore perhaps permissible. Bell was imitating the famous remark of Charles the First on his entry into the House of Commons to arrest the five members who had departed, and whose names, as a knowledge-thrusting Bell would have been only too glad to remind Ryan and Gorse, were Pym, Hampden, Hazelrigg, Holles, and Strode.

But he was given no chance to do this, and his companions, in fact, did not know that he had made a pun at all and simply took his remark at its face value.

Ryan and Gorse had little Learning, and were, if anything, eager to expunge from their minds rather than retain what they had been forced to digest during the last twelve years or so.

'Yes, they've gone,' said Ryan, and added, in the phrase popular at that period, 'They've Done the Giddy Bunk, all right.'

Gorse was masterfully silent.

'And now they're *all* coming off,' said Ryan in despair.

The band had evidently played 'God Save the King', and the greater part of the populace had risen and was making its way to the turnstiles.

'Never mind,' said Gorse. 'When dirty work's afoot, the fewer the better.'

He now led the other two as far as the Theatre again, and then, inclining to the left, took them along the side of the Theatre to the extreme edge of the Pier proper.

Only the grilled quadrangle now lay between themselves and the French coast, but on the farthest edge of the quadrangle, gazing towards the French coast, were Esther Downes and Gertrude Perks. Dark as it now was, their figures were easily recognizable.

'Ah – here we are,' said Gorse, and leaned over the railings, staring through the heavy twilight at the two girls. Ryan and Bell submissively did the same as their triumphant leader.

'I fancy', said Gorse, 'that our Birds are trapped, should we be desirous of courting their favours.'

This was true. There were only two ways, on the east or the west side, of their leaving the quadrangle, and, when they did so, the young men could easily see which side they were choosing and without any haste be in time to intercept and accost them.

'But *are* we desirous? That's the point,' said Bell.

'Ah – that's a different matter,' said Gorse, still gazing at the sea-gazing figures. 'What think'st thou, Ryan?'

'Oh – I don't know,' said Ryan, 'I'll leave it to you.'

He spoke thus indecisively, not because he did not really know his own mind, but because now that a real opportunity had arisen, and a decision had to be made, he was desperately afraid. Also, he wanted to re-establish in front of Gorse an attitude of indifference which he knew he had failed to maintain during the last twenty minutes.

'Very well, then, leave it to me,' said Gorse.

Ryan had to make the best he could of this. Did Gorse, with his 'Very well, then, leave it to me', mean that he definitely proposed to undertake and lead the way in an almost immediate operation? Or had he not as yet made up his mind, and did he merely mean that the decision as to whether or not they were to accost the girls at all was to be left to him?

Ryan, dreading either answer, glanced at Gorse, seeking to discover his intentions.

But Gorse wore that composed and utterly noncommittal expression such as Satan, one imagines, unintermittently wears.

Soon the girls moved to the eastern side of the quadrangle, and then again stopped to look at the view – at the pretty lights of the Palace Pier, it seemed. They had an air, though, of being in conference and of trying to come to a decision themselves.

Then, after a minute or two, they walked in a determined way shorewards (as if anxious to go home), and up the stairs near to which Gorse, Ryan, and Bell were leaning. They could, of course, have chosen the stairs on the other side, and the fact that they did not do so possibly assisted Gorse in making up his mind.

As soon as Esther and Gertrude had reached the top of the stairs Gorse turned and spoke in a loud, cheerful voice.

'Hullo, girls,' he said. '*Quo Vadis* – eh?'

Now had come the agonizing moment – agonizing for Ryan in particular, but almost equally for all the others – except Gorse. Gorse was as immune from this sort of agony as he was from infatuation.

Was Gorse to be answered or totally ignored – given, as they would have said, 'the bird'?

(In the language of Getting Off, 'bird' was in those days used in two senses.)

There was a pause.

Then '*Quo Whattis*?' said Esther, and she and Gertrude stopped.

The sharpest agony had passed, and the climax had been at last reached.

The West Pier, resembling in the sea a sort of amiable, crouching,

weird battleship – a sex-battleship – had, at its prow, yet again
revealed its peculiar, traditional uses.

The Getters-off were Off.

PART THREE

OFF

I

Second sight and telepathy, along with other immaterial means of communication, are probably used by those engaged in these unearthly preliminaries to Getting Off.

Something he could not name had led Gorse to lead the other two to the prow of the Pier, and as soon as they had arrived there Esther Downes, though still gazing towards the French coast, had suspected that she was being watched from behind and who was doing the watching.

In taking Gertrude to the east side of the quadrangle to look at the Palace Pier lights she confirmed her suspicions beyond all doubt. She glanced upwards and sideways and unmistakably saw the young men – saw them, although in the darkness they were not in fact properly visible.

In looking at the lights of the Palace Pier, she had not actually been in conference with Gertrude but making up her own mind as to whether, on returning to the Pier, she should or not choose the steps nearest to the young men.

She had chosen, as we have seen, those nearest, knowing what must be the almost certain result of doing so.

That she had been followed to the limits of the Pier in this way had completely assuaged her pride: and she was, now, weary of immaterial skirmishing, and eager for battle.

She had never intended, if honestly accosted, to avoid battle completely. This was because (just as Ryan loved the sight of Esther) Esther loved the sight of Ryan. But this did not mean that she felt anything at all of what Ryan felt. She belonged to a different and, at the age of eighteen, a much more mature, cold, and enlightened sex.

She would not have married Ryan tomorrow; indeed, unless he behaved as she required she would not even meet him again tomorrow evening. She was extremely suspicious of Ryan, though she loved the sight of his unusually good looks.

She was extremely suspicious of all three, with the exception, possibly, of Bell, whom she had at an early stage of the proceedings identified as a typical 'other one', and who did not, therefore, really 'count'.

She was, in fact, abnormally suspicious, and, for one of her experience, abnormally inclined to caution.

This was largely because there were three of them – three against two (or rather two against one, since neither Bell nor Gertrude 'counted') – and largely because she was aware that they did not come from her own class. They had, it seemed to her, clearly been educated at what she would have called 'College', and for this reason were what she would have called 'gentlemen'.

Now the much-got-off-with Miss Downes was by no means absolutely unacquainted with 'gentlemen', but she was certainly not so much at ease with them as she was with young men of her own class. Though she had not as yet come to any sort of harm from 'gentlemen' she could still not quite rid herself of a picture of them as cads and traducers.

Also, they had either a flippancy which differed altogether from the crude flippancy of young men in her own sphere of life, or, however shy they might be, an ease which robbed her of her own ease and, therefore, of something of that complete ascendancy which she was accustomed to her beauty bringing her.

Nevertheless, she had made up her mind to take any risks of this sort, and, with her 'Quo *Whattis*?' had shown as much, and could not retreat.

II

It has been said that the sharpest agony had passed: but there was still much agony, of a different kind, to be endured. This was the agony of that laboured punning and fatuity in conversation which those who have just Got Off are absolutely forced to employ in order to conceal their embarrassment.

'*Quo Vadis*,' repeated Gorse. 'Meaning "Whither Goest Thou?" Latin. Ancient. In common parlance, where are you toddling off to, girls?'

'We're toddling off home,' said Esther, 'if that's all you want to know.'

'But it isn't all. By no means,' said Gorse, and added: 'Oh, excuse me, girls, I don't think you know my friends. Mr Ryan, Mr Bell.'

Gorse had now adopted his dashing and most amiable manner, and was completely in charge of things. The others smiled and murmured 'How-do-you-do' in a shamed way.

Ryan and Bell (and Ryan in particular) were ashamed of Gorse's vulgarity. To hear Gorse calling the girls 'girls' like that caused Ryan the acutest torture, and he trusted that Esther was not going to think of him as another Gorse. At the same time he was grateful to Gorse for what he had achieved and was achieving – which, really, could not be brought off without a certain amount of vulgarity.

'And may we escort you homewards?' Gorse went on. 'For that is whither we wendeth our own ways.'

'Certainly,' said Esther awkwardly, and as they all began to walk together shorewards there was a long, long, long pause – one which even the resourceful Gorse seemed unable to break.

Ryan now thought that he must, for the sake of his manhood, say something, and he did so, trying at the same time to dispel the atmosphere of vulgarity created by Gorse.

'Do you come a lot on the Pier?' he asked Esther, who was on his right. (She was on Gorse's left.)

'Yes,' said Esther, 'quite a lot. It's nice to hear the band and have a look at the people.'

'To *Peer* at people on the *Pier* – what?' said Gorse.

'That's right,' said Esther, smiling politely at this, his first shot in the inevitable play upon words.

'And did you see us three *Peering* at you?' asked Gorse.

'Oh yes. We saw that all right,' said Esther, looking ahead of her with a demure complacency which fascinated Ryan beyond measure.

'And a very nice *Pair* we thought you,' said Gorse.

'Did you?' said Esther, and there was a pause.

'Yes,' said Ryan, himself plunging into fatuity in his determination not to be left out of things. 'Without *Peer*, in fact.'

'Yes. Beyond com*Pare*, certainly,' said the quick-minded Gorse, and he looked at his hands. 'By the way, I'd've *Pared* my nails properly tonight if I'd known we were going to meet – just to be Pre*Pared*.'

This absurd irrelevant, untrue, and unfunny remark caused laughter.

'Well,' said Gertrude Perks, now feeling that she must somehow establish herself as a fellow wit, and speaking for the first time, 'we can't give you a *Pear*, as a reward, because they're out of season. Ain't they?'

But nobody laughed at this. 'Other ones' seldom cause laughter. They are not, really, supposed to speak at all. Instead of laughter there was some dim sniggering.

'Are they?' said the polite Ryan, and there was silence.

Now Bell, emboldened by hearing his opposite 'other one' speaking, broke into the conversation for the first time.

'"A drunk delight of battle with my *peers*,"' said Bell.

Learned again, needless to say. Bell was quoting from the poem *Ulysses* by Alfred, Lord Tennyson. Bell's quotation was even less relevant than the previous remarks of Gorse and Gertrude Perks, and, in his eagerness to disseminate the seeds of learning, he had neglected to notice that the word 'peer' had already been used by Ryan.

'Drunk *what*?' said Esther.

'"Far",' continued Bell imperturbably, sonorously, and not without grandeur, '"on the ringing of plains of windy Troy."'

'I don't follow,' said Esther, and appealed to Ryan. 'Is your friend always like this?'

'Oh yes. Don't mind him,' said Ryan. 'He's probably quoting poetry. Aren't you, Bell?'

'Tennyson,' said Bell. 'To be precise.'

'Well,' said Miss Perks, 'the only kind of Tennyson *I* know is Tennis on the Lawn. Do you chaps play? You look as if you do.'

'Chaps,' Ryan felt, was even worse than Gorse's 'girls'.

'No,' said Esther, who was anxious to educate herself, and had therefore a certain respect, an exaggerated one possibly, for learning. 'Was that Tennyson? I used to be taught him. I used to know *The Brook* right off by heart.'

'Oh – you did – did you?' said Bell eagerly. '"I chatter over stony ways . . ."'

'"In little sharps and trebles,"' said Esther with equal enthusiasm.

'"I bubble into eddying bays,"' said Bell.

'"I babble on the pebbles!"' said Esther triumphantly.

What was this? Was this 'other one', the uncouth and dishevelled Bell, to be the one to capture the beauty after all?

'"Till last by Philip's farm I flow,"' Bell went on, but this sort of thing had to be put a stop to, and Gorse firmly did so.

'Well,' he said, 'as we're all so poetical tonight, what about sitting down and drinking in the poetry of the scenery? What say you?'

They had now reached the long sheltered partition dividing the middle of the Pier, and Gorse indicated, with a sweep of his hand, where they might sit.

'All right,' said Esther. 'Though we haven't got long – have we, Gertie?'

'No – it's getting a bit late,' said Gertrude.

And so now they all sat down – Gorse by methods which were mysterious but did not permit of disobedience, arranging who should sit where. Esther sat between Ryan and Gorse, and on Gorse's right was Gertrude, and next to her was Bell. Bell was thus thrust into outer darkness, having the hideous Gertrude on his left and nobody at all on his right. This was probably a punishment given him by Gorse for getting above himself and gaining favour with Esther by quoting poetry.

Why he had made them all sit down no one exactly knew – not even Gorse. There was no question, for instance, of any of those things which precede, or go with, Kissing. The lights were quite bright here, and there were too many people still about, and they themselves were too ill-assorted, and unacquainted, and large in number.

Nevertheless, sitting down was the thing to do. Perhaps it paved the way, established a precedent for conceivable future sittings-down – these in darker places and when some sort of assortment and separation had been worked out and agreed upon by the individuals concerned.

'That's better,' said Gorse. 'Now – what were we talking about?'

'Poetry, wasn't it?' said Ryan.

Ryan, whose arm was touching Esther's, and who was gazing out to sea at the fairy lights of the Palace Pier, was in what may be called a 'poetical' mood. He had also been much impressed by Esther's interest in poetry, which he took as a sign of remarkable culture, sweetness, and intelligence in one of her class.

It may be said, however, that even if Esther had in the immediate past been totally foul-mouthed and low, Ryan would have found an excuse for her, and, more, somehow twisted things so as to see her in a favourable light for being so.

'Ah, yes. Poetry,' said Gorse, speaking to Esther. 'And Tennyson's your favourite poet, is he – Miss – I'm so sorry I didn't quite catch your name.'

'I don't remember giving it,' said Esther, with an air rather closer to that of flirtation than to that of snubbing.

'Ah, no. So you didn't. But you can now. Come along, then. What is it?'

'Why do you want to know?'

Esther felt a curious reluctance in disclosing her name. Girls do, on occasions like this. They are like new boys at school, afraid of having their names laughed at, or despised.

'Oh – we must be sociable, you know. Come along now.'

'Downes . . .' said Esther after a pause, shyly. 'Spelt with an *e*. . .' She was aware that the *e* gave it all its prettiness, and that without it one thought of things like the Sussex Downs to the north of Brighton.

'And very nice, too. And what's your name, Gertie?' said Gorse.

'How did you know it was Gertie?' asked Miss Perks.

'Because I heard Miss Downes calling you it just a moment ago. Come along now.'

'Perks,' said Gertrude, 'if you want to know.'

'Ah, very suitable for both of you. So when your friend's in one of her *Downes*, you *Perk* her up? What?'

'Yes. That's right,' said Gertrude. 'That's my job.'

It is intensely difficult to believe that sane young people ever talked like this. They did, however. Furthermore, they undoubtedly still do. Let the unbeliever sit on piers in the evening, and eavesdrop.

'Well – now that's all over, let's go back to Poetry,' said Esther, talking to Gorse. 'Who's *your* favourite poet then, Mr – you haven't told us *your* name, by the way.'

'Mine? Gorse. Ernest Ralph Gorse. Known as Ralph – pronounced Ralph or Rafe, whichever you prefer. Which are you going to use?'

'I don't know that I'm going to use either . . . Well – go on – who's your favourite poet, anyway?'

'Mine? I don't think I know. Or at least I know, but I don't know his name. He wrote a wonderful poem. Now – how did it begin? "There was a young lady of –" No, perhaps I'd better not go on with that.'

'No – I don't think you'd better,' said Esther.

There was a pause.

'And who's *your* favourite poet, as you know all about Poetry?' said Gertrude, speaking challengingly to Bell. She knew that Esther expected her to handle and to pair with Bell eventually, and she thought that the time had come to make a start.

'Mine?' said Bell. 'Well, there's a pretty extensive field – isn't there?' said Bell. 'I should say that my taste was eclectic, and that –'

'*Electric*?' said Gertrude sharply, and with all the bitterness which some people have against a word which is curious and unfamiliar to them.

'No, Eclectic,' said Bell, rather cowed.

'Well, I'm glad to hear *that*,' said Gertrude, but there was still acerbity in her tone.

'I flit from flower to flower, you see,' Bell went on, 'and still can't settle anywhere. One day it's Chaucer, then Milton, then Shelley, then Keats, then Byron (the noble lord), then Coleridge (the opium-eater). Then I'll suddenly tire of the Romantics and return to the clipped austerities of Pope.' (Bell, though cured of the grosser manifestations of his schoolboy malady, had not completely lost his love of long words.) 'I should say, though, that for lasting satisfaction, and real greatness and depth, the real master is Wordsworth, and if I had to vote for anyone I'd vote for him.'

'Oh no,' said Ryan. '*Not* Wordsworth, surely.'

'Why not Wordsworth?'

'What – *We Are Seven*, and *The Idiot Boy*, and *Goody Blake and Harry Gill*, and all that?' said Ryan, revealing a knowledge which neither Bell nor Gorse had suspected he possessed.

'Well,' said Bell, 'I'll admit that our Lakeland friend was capable of carrying simplicity to an exaggerated degree – even at times to the point of ridiculousness.'

'He certainly was,' said Ryan.

'Yes,' said Bell, 'but we've got to take him all in all. I mean to say, for instance, a man who can write such things as "Earth has not anything to show more fair, Dull would he be of soul who could pass by, A sight so touching in its majesty: The City now doth like a garment wear, The beauty of the morning, silent, bare, Ships, towers, domes, theatres, and temples lie . . ."'

Bell was reeling off his favourite poet's sonnet at a good speed, with no expression, and apparently without any intention of stopping until the end had been reached.

'Yes – I know,' tried Ryan, but Bell went inexorably on.

'"Open unto the fields and to the sky; All bright and glittering in the smokeless air . . ."'

This was not quite so terrifying to Ryan as it was to the others, for Ryan knew that there were only fourteen lines altogether, and that eight of them had been used. The others had no such advantage. For all they knew, Bell might be intending to go on until midnight, or dawn, or beyond.

'"Never",' continued Bell, '"did sun more beautifully steep, In his first splendour valley, rock, or hill; Ne'er saw I, never felt, a calm so deep! The river glideth at his own sweet will . . ."'

At this point Ryan became fascinated beyond measure in conjecturing as to how Bell proposed to finish the construction of the prodigious sentence upon which he had embarked. It had begun with 'I mean to say, for instance, a man who can write such things as "Earth has not anything," etc., etc., etc.,' and it was still going. How would Bell wind it up? Grammatically, with 'is worthy of consideration' or something like that? Or would Bell draw breath and start again, with something like – 'Well – I mean to say, a man who can write like *that* is worthy of consideration'?

The precise Bell now solved the problem in a way which Ryan had rather fancied it would have been solved.

'"Dear God,"' said Bell, '"the very houses seem asleep; And all that mighty heart is lying still" – is not to be lightly dismissed. Don't you agree?'

'Oh yes,' said Ryan. 'He's fine when he's in form.'

'Nor', said Bell, 'would I like to say –'

'But he's not always –' said Ryan.

'*NOR*,' went on Bell, now completely inebriated by the exuberance of borrowed words, and practically shouting Ryan down. 'Nor can we allow such inspiring passages from the Lucy poems as "She dwelt among the untrodden ways, Beside the springs of Dove, A maid whom there were none to praise, And very few to love. A violet by a mossy stone, Half hidden from the eye! Fair as a star, when only one Is shining in the sky. She lived unknown and few could know When Lucy ceased to be; But she is in her grave, and, oh –"'

Here Ryan, who knew that the last line was just coming, again waited in a sort of anguish for the accurate completion of the sentence. 'Nor can we allow such inspiring passages from the Lucy poems as' had been the beginning, and then the poem had followed. Would Bell repeat his idiotic adherence to the strictest rules of grammar – which was really an idiotic pretence that he was not really declaiming poetry, as if invited to do so on a platform?

Bell did.

'"The difference to me," be regarded,' said Bell, 'as anything other than in the front rank of English verse.'

'My word,' said Gertrude. 'You can't half spout.'

'And then even the familiar "Daffodils",' said Bell. '"I wandered lonely –"'

But here Ryan was completely at home and able to take the ground from under Bell's feet.

'"As a cloud,"' said Ryan, raising his voice,

> '"That floats on high o'er vales and hills,
> When all at once I saw a crowd,
> A host, of golden daffodils . . .
> Ten thousand saw I at a glance,
> Tossing their heads in sprightly dance"'

Ryan was doubtful if this was enough, and so, as a *coup de grâce*, gave a little more.

> '"Continuous as the stars that shine
> And twinkle on the milky way
> They stretched in never-ending line
> Along the margin –"'

but we can't go on pouring out poetry like this all night – can we?'

'Well, I sincerely *hope* not,' said Gertrude, but Esther was very much impressed.

'So *you* know all about Poetry too?' she said to Ryan, looking gravely at him.

'No,' said Ryan. 'Only a bit. Nothing like Bell.'

Gorse, who did not care for Poetry and so knew nothing about it, had been perforce silent all this time. Gorse did not like being silent or left out of things. When such a thing happened his expression was thoughtful and displeasing; that faint smell under his nose came back.

Now Ryan had silenced Bell, Gorse saw a chance of entering the conversation.

'And what about the Immortal Bard?' he said. 'What about the Swan of Avon?'

'Oh, he goes without saying,' said Bell.

There was a pause.

'I have, as a matter of fact,' said Bell, 'a copy of Wordsworth on me.' He produced a selection from the poet's work – a cheap paper edition – from his pocket.

'Handy for the pocket,' he said, 'and, as you can see, extremely well Thumbed.'

It was indeed well Thumbed. It was a good deal more. Bell being in the habit of reading at meals – particularly breakfast and tea – the book, in addition to being well Thumbed, was well Fingered, well Porridged, well Marmaladed, well Jammed, well Baconed, well Coffeed, well Tea-ed, well Cocoa-ed, well Crumbed, well Biscuited, and well Buttered. Nor would a keen examiner with a microscope have found the book totally unsausaged, unspinached, unpotatoed, uncauliflowered, unstewed-plummed, unapple-charlotted, unriced or uncurried.

'Yes,' said Gertrude. 'It certainly looks well read. And so that's all Electric, is it? Or Effectic, or whatever you call it.'

'Eclectic,' said Bell.

'And may I ask what that means?' asked Gertrude. 'It sounds funny to me.'

'Oh – gathered from all sources – taken from all schools.'

'You've been to a lot of schools, I should say – by the look of you,' said Gertrude, gazing at him. 'Haven't you? One or two too many, I should say.'

'No – no more than my friends here.'

'We were all at school together,' said Ryan, breaking into the conversation because he felt that the too determinedly philistine Gertrude was being over-harsh with the too determinedly cultured Bell.

'Well, anyway,' said Gertrude, looking at the book, 'if that's Wordsworth, you seem to've got your Words *Worth* out of it all right.'

'Yes,' said Bell, finding nothing else to say.

Gertrude had now as it were come into the lead in the fatuity race, which we are not compelled to follow any further. It may, however, be mentioned that these five, having exhausted the subject of their Favourite Poet, went on to discuss the matters as to Who was their Favourite Musician, Who was their Favourite Painter, Who was their Favourite Sculptor (this originated by Bell), Who was their Favourite Actor, Who was their Favourite Architect (Bell again), and, finally, Who was their Favourite Character in History.

Then Ryan, who was getting very tired of all this, put in a remark about the pretty lights of the Palace Pier. Other lights on the front were then discussed – including those of the Hotel Metropole.

Then the Hotel Metropole itself was discussed – this with results very much more momentous than any one of these young people would have been able to conceive.

'Would you like me to take you there one evening?' said Gorse to Esther.

All heard this, but no one knew exactly what to say. Esther at last replied.

'I'd like to see you doing it,' she said, showing clearly that in her mind the supreme heights of fatuity had been reached.

'Very well, then, you shall,' said Ernest Ralph Gorse.

Esther now used these absurd heights as an excuse for saying what she had wanted to say for a long time.

'Well,' she said, 'we've got to be buzzing off home. I don't know about you.'

She half rose, the others half rose, and then all rose completely and walked towards the shore.

2   By the same semi-mystic yet adamant measures which Gorse had employed while seating the company, he now arranged how it should go off the Pier. Gertrude Perks, Ryan, and Bell went ahead. Gorse and Esther walked behind – so far behind, finally, that they were out of earshot of the other three.

But the anxious Ryan saw to it that all of them met at the turnstiles. They went through these, and it was clearly time to say, 'Well ...'

'Well, when do we all meet again?' said Ryan, and Gorse said 'Yes, when?' and there was a general atmosphere of 'Well ...'

Then Gorse suggested that they should all meet at the entrance to the Palace Pier (to make a change) tomorrow evening at seven-thirty.

All agreed to this, and all looked at each other with great shyness and suspicion.

But there was more than the usual shyness and suspicion which takes place on occasions like these. There was a funny, shifting glitter in everybody's eye.

This was probably because Gorse, while walking alone with Esther, had made a private arrangement with her, and the others, quite subconsciously, suspected it.

PART FOUR

GORSE AND ESTHER

I

Getters–off do not usually disclose their home addresses at the first encounter: indeed, more often than not these are never disclosed at all.

Even Gorse, in spite of his private arrangement with Esther, had made no inquiry as to any such thing, and the thought of actually doing so would never have even entered Ryan's mind.

This does not mean that Ryan had not longed to do so – in order to dispel that peculiar dread necessarily attendant upon the hours intervening between a first meeting of this sort and the second – the dread that the other party may vacillate, change its mind (or perhaps it never even *had* any mind to keep its promise), 'think better of it', and so not 'turn up' and, having left absolutely no clue as to where it might be sought, disappear for ever.

Ryan that night, on his bed in the darkness of his bed–sitting room in Tisbury Road, Hove, lay awake a long while wondering where and how Esther lived.

2   The where, actually, would have furnished a fairly vivid picture of the how. The lovely Esther lived in conditions of grave squalor in Over Street, near Brighton Station, and no one who lived in this street at that time lived otherwise.

Esther shared a bed with a small brother and sister. Her father was a porter at Brighton Station, her mother an ex-seamstress who still made a little money by sewing and mending.

Another family, of three, lived in the same house, whose passages were densely perambulatored.

Over Street, then, was a slum, and Mr and Mrs Downes were not happy people. That they were less acutely wretched than they might have been was because a sort of apathy, even towards wretchedness, had overtaken them. Overwhelmed and overworked boxers are sometimes called 'punch-drunk': Mr and Mrs Downes might have been called 'slum-drunk'.

Of the two, Mr Downes, the porter, perhaps suffered the most.

Some people in this world totally fail even to know, while others fail fully to appreciate, the fact that being a porter involves what nearly all people on this earth detest more violently than nearly anything else on earth – namely, *Carrying*. Indeed, they detest this so much that they will part with money in order to get other people to carry the lightest articles over the smallest distances. Being a porter also entails what many people detest even more than Carrying – that is, *Waiting About* – waiting about, sometimes, in the coldest, wettest, or vilest weather – waiting about, worst of all, hopefully, and, as often as not, with hopes dashed to the earth and so without any monetary gain.

Again, a porter is compelled to endure what many people dislike even more than carrying or waiting about – that is, being snubbed, or even insulted, continuously. People who have just alighted from, or who are about to get upon, trains are usually of an anxious, foreboding temper; and this usually manifests itself either in an air of disdain, in irritability, in furious excitability, or, lastly, in sheer savagery. The porter is made the butt of all these types of behaviour.

In those distant days, of course, it was permissible (for the rich at any rate) to indulge in disdain, irritability, excitability, and savagery to a degree in which the youthful gentle reader will not be able to believe. And the amount of money Mr Downes earned, and the amount of hours of the day and night which Mr Downes spent in carrying, waiting about, and being virtually spat upon, would, if revealed and believed, make such a reader's hair stand on end.

Over and above all this, Mr Downes was asked questions by people all day and night. This may be thought of as some sort of compensation, for people, on the whole, like answering questions. But the novelty soon wears off, and Mr Downes was questioned by passers-by in an incredibly rude way. Indeed, more often than not he was hardly what could be called questioned: he was brutally cross-examined.

It may be added that sometimes – something more than a dozen times a year – Mr Downes, on account of some imaginary piece of inefficiency or insolence, would receive no payment at all for an arduous service. And for this Mr Downes had no redress.

There would, however, be a rare saint, lunatic, or drunkard, returning from a successful day at the races, who would give Mr Downes as much as five shillings. (Or even half a sovereign!) Such characters Mr Downes and his fellow sufferers would, in those days, call 'toffs'.

It may be fairly said that without these occasional 'toffs', and the hope of serving one, Mr Downes' miserable existence could hardly have continued.

From all this it may be assumed that Mr Downes looked upon himself as a being who had indeed sunk low in the world. But not at all. Mr Downes was confident that he had risen in the world, and believed that he was a success. This was because Mr Downes had vivid memories of his father, with whom he often compared himself.

3   Mr Downes' father had also been connected with Brighton Station – but not in any official capacity. Mr Downes' father had worn no uniform – he had worn rags, and he had not worn shoes. He was not allowed on to the platforms: instead of this he hung about the horse-cabs outside the Station.

When a train of any importance came into the Station, Mr Downes' father would eagerly watch these cabs as they were loaded with luggage by the uniformed porters, and, with a discrimination learned from long experience, would choose a cab, which he would follow, running, to its destination. He did this because he hoped that when it reached its destination, wherever that might be, he might be permitted to help with the unloading of the luggage, and be given a copper for doing so.

Mr Downes senior – who was, by the way, a consumptive – was not obliged to move at a great speed while his cab was moving along thoroughfares in which the traffic was thick, but when the emptier streets or roads were reached he had to run like mad. And, if he was unlucky, he had to run like this for a matter of three or four miles.

Was the hopeful Mr Downes senior, at the end of the pursuit, rewarded with the copper he had sought?

The answer is that nine times out of ten he was not. On the contrary, he was ordinarily threatened and shooed away with the greatest violence. Policemen were mentioned menacingly, and, if one happened to be present, used.

In extenuation of this cruelty on the part of the users of the cabs it should be mentioned that the consumptive Mr Downes senior, small as he was, at the end of his run presented an appalling sight – a frightening sight. The users of the cabs were frightened, and did what they did largely in panic. It must also be remembered that the man was looked upon as a beggar, and a beggar in those days was roughly identical wth a criminal of the worst sort.

But the same extenuation cannot be extended to the servants of the households at which Mr Downes pantingly arrived. These were by no means afraid of the runner, and, in their treatment of him, were much more cruel than their employers. It is a mysterious and hideous truism that the oppressed are often much more harsh with the oppressed than are the oppressors.

Again the youthful gentle reader will be finding it practically impossible to believe that people of the type of Mr Downes senior existed in the Edwardian era. But they did, and many men alive today, men no older than forty-five, will testify that they did. Moreover, such men have been, and for the rest of their lives will be haunted painfully by the memory of what they saw as children – by the picture of one of these agonized, humble creatures as they asked gently to help carry in the luggage (which they were hardly capable of doing), and then, after vindictive expulsion, the way in which they hesitated for a moment, like dogs, and at last turned, and slunk wearily back to the Station from which they had come.

It is astonishing that characters like Mr Downes senior are capable of reproducing their kind, but, weirdly enough, in this direction such persons seem to be as, or more, prolific than the healthy and well-to-do. Mr Downes senior succeeded in having two children, a daughter who died at the age of three, and our Mr Downes – though neither was born in wedlock.

No wonder, then, that Mr Downes, with memories of his father and his mode of living, looked upon himself as one who had risen in the world. He wore a uniform; he lived in part of a house; he had married (above himself); he had three children who were decently fed, clothed, and shod. Despite his general misery and slavery to the Station, he knew he had much for which to be thankful.

4   Mr Downes saw remarkably little of his daughter Esther: working as he did, he hardly had any time in which to do so. But sometimes, on a Sunday, he would see her for an hour or so, and even eat at the same table with her.

He was aware that she dressed extremely well, and that she was beautiful. This made him proud. But it also frightened him, for, not altogether unreasonably, he associated beauty, in one of her origin and class, with the danger of sin.

Esther, on the other hand, was not proud of her father. She was ashamed of him, or at any rate of his profession and manners – this without disliking him. Nor did Esther take the view that the Downes family had risen in the world. She imagined that it had sunk low, because her mother had married beneath her.

Esther's mother was in fact of higher social origin, and had been more kindly educated than Esther's father. She had at one time been a housemaid, and afterwards a nurse, with a well-to-do middle-class family in First Avenue, Hove. She was still acquainted with this family – the mother of which still gave her a good deal of sewing, as well as recommending her, for the same task, to other women of the First Avenue type. In this way Mrs Downes – an ailing, tired, but fanatically industrious woman – made quite a good deal of money, and she was rich in comparison with the average Over Street wife. This money was hoarded, or spent upon her children – upon Esther in particular.

Thus Esther was, in a variety of ways, singularly blessed in her mother. For such a mother, having lived in households and nursed children of a much higher class than her own, had taught Esther graces of habit, speech, and manner which would otherwise have been denied her. Also, Mrs Downes, being an expert sewing-woman, not only made for Esther remarkably good and remarkably cheap dresses, but taught her the art of dressing well. She gave money to Esther, too. Most of this Esther herself had to hoard – but she was permitted to spend some of it frivolously upon herself.

Over and above this, Esther made a little money for herself. She worked and served at the counter in a sweet-shop – a rather large and rather low pink-and-white sweet-shop – particularly pink-and-white because it specialized in Brighton Rock – and popular in the season because it was situated in the Queen's Road. Swarming day-trippers, arriving at Brighton Station, and desiring to reach the sea as soon as possible, were then, as they are now, compelled to use the Queen's Road.

Esther, herself looking slightly pink-and-white in this thronged pink-and-white atmosphere (and fully conscious of each minor sensation caused throughout the day by her extreme prettiness), was a good deal happier than her fellow worker here, Gertrude Perks.

All the same, she would not concede that she was happy. Miss Downes was, probably, 'spoiled' and, if not already 'above herself', likely to become so. With all her advantages and good fortune for a girl in Over Street, she pictured herself as one in a miserable, penurious, and frustrated situation, from which she was anxious to escape as soon as she possibly could. She was acutely ambitious.

To return to Over Street, after an evening on the West Pier in the company of young men, and to sleep in the same bed with her small brother and sister, made her very seriously despondent. And as she lay awake long into the night – as she nearly always did, listening to the movement of trains and other station sounds – her depression and anxiety became deeper and deeper.

This slowly increased nocturnal melancholy was almost certainly partially attributable merely to her nearness to Brighton Station.

Large stations (termini especially) are at night evil things. To the listener in bed they seem to be making semi-hellish suggestions: they cast forth an aura of wickedness which extends as far as a quarter of a mile away from themselves, if not further.

It is difficult to discern in what this wickedness of large stations consists. Conceivably it is because they convey, to the sleepless mind, all the pain, futility, and folly of travel, of coming and going – the horrible inevitability, like that of birth and death, of arrival and departure.

They are boisterous and disquieting things during the day as well, and they can never be quite at ease in their souls who dwell near one.

Brighton Station was, as usual, the distressing audible background to Esther's thought: and she had much to think about.

She had to review in her mind the evening she had just spent on the West Pier. She had to appraise the characters and intentions of Ryan and Gorse. She did not have to worry about Bell. He was too spectacled and silly.

5   Ryan and Gorse (and even Bell) were what Esther thought of as 'gentlemen'. Esther flattered herself that she could 'tell' a gentleman 'the moment' she saw one.

Esther, the lovely walker on the front so often accosted, had some experience of gentlemen: and on the whole, as has been said, she distrusted their intentions and disliked their bearing. They were either too flippant ('la–di–dah'), or too sure of themselves, or too indifferent, or too much inclined to use obscure idiom far removed from her own.

At the same time Esther had a great hankering after gentlemen. She wanted to marry one of the right sort.

Ryan and Gorse, to her way of thinking, were good types of

gentlemen – Ryan in particular. Indeed she entertained strong suspicions that Ryan was a 'perfect' gentleman. She also thought him almost divinely good-looking and attractive. She would have liked to marry Ryan, but she would not have entered into such a bond with the same precipitancy as Ryan would have entered into it with her. Though junior in age to Ryan by several months, she was, by virtue of her sex, at least three years his senior mentally in some ways. Before marrying Ryan she would have wanted much time in which to discover and ascertain many things.

Gorse presented a totally different problem. He was probably not a 'perfect' gentleman. Esther even doubted whether he was fully a gentleman. This was because of his swaggering manner, and of his rather distasteful nasal voice and look, which made themselves apparent every now and again.

All the same, Gorse had an air – an effrontery which did not displease, which rather engaged, Esther. And, what far exceeded these advantages, he had made a most astonishing and exciting proposal to her. He had invited her to drink a cocktail with him at the Metropole Hotel.

This had happened during the brief period in which Esther and Gorse had somehow fallen behind while the five were leaving the West Pier.

'And what about you and I having a cocktail at the Hotel Metropole one evening?' Gorse had said. It will be remembered that this hotel had only just recently been discussed by all of them.

Esther had thought he had been joking, and had replied, 'Don't be so silly. I'd like to see you and I sitting in the Metropole.'

'No,' said Gorse. 'I mean it all right. What about tomorrow night? Do you think I don't mean it?'

At this Esther looked at him, and met his eyes, and had a sudden mad feeling, a sort of uncanny inspiration, that he did in fact mean what he said. She obeyed this inspiration.

'All right,' she said. '*I* don't mind, if you don't.'

'All right,' said Gorse. 'That's settled. But we've got to do it cleverly, if we want to be alone.'

'And how do we do that?'

'Listen,' said Gorse. 'When we all meet up again in a minute, and decide where to meet again, I'll see that it's outside one of the piers. Well, if they choose the Palace Pier, you and I meet outside the West – and *vice versa*. And at the same *time* that's chosen. Got the idea?'

'Yes.'

'And you'll do it? You'll fill the bill all right?'

'Yes,' said Esther. 'I'll fill the bill.'

And less than a minute afterwards they had perforce joined Ryan and Bell and Gertrude at the turnstiles.

6   At the time of agreeing to this proposition Esther, completely staggered, had hardly known what she was doing. Now, lying in bed listening to the trains, she was only a little less staggered, and knew practically nothing about what she actually intended to do.

A cocktail at the Metropole! With a 'gentleman' – secretly and deceptively! The decision she had now to make involved such vast and hideous intricacies as this old campaigner in Getting Off had never encountered, had never dreamed of encountering.

First of all, did he mean it? Would he 'turn up'? Was he not making (or trying to make) a fool of her?

Somehow she instinctively still believed that he was serious. But, even if he was, how could such a young man, a stripling certainly not much more than a year older than herself, take her into the *Metropole* and give her a *cocktail*? 'Gentleman' he possibly was, but how could he have the nerve?

She could have swallowed the idea of a cocktail, though this frightened and rather thrillingly scandalized her, but the *Metropole*! – that palace of mad, Oriental opulence, that haunt of the fantastically rich, the gorgeously successful theatrical, the aristocratic – that vast cathedral to Mammon outside which she had so often lingeringly passed, and through whose revolving doors she had caught glimpses of fur coats and cigars – the Metropole was too much for her. How could he *afford* it, in any case? (She had a subconscious idea that you had to pay something like five pounds even to pass through those doors, and even then have to produce credentials of some sort.) Even if he was a 'gentleman', she was certain he was not a rich one. He had worn grey flannel trousers and no hat – a thing which the rich Metropole-haunter would, she knew, not do. But did he perhaps have a hat, and a proper suit, which he would wear tomorrow?

And what about her own dress? Could she possibly dress up for the Metropole? She believed that, owing to her skill in dress inherited from her mother, by the skin of her teeth she might possibly 'pass'.

But he was so young, young, *young*! And she was younger still. Would they not (if not actually refused admission) be laughed at cruelly? Would they be served with a cocktail? Once more she suspected that it was a joke, and that he would not turn up.

But even if he did turn up, there were countless other difficulties with which she had to contend. She would, if she met him outside the West Pier, be guilty of a deception of the most crude and brutal sort. Her close friend Gertrude, and Ryan, and the other one (as ill-assorted a trio as you could find in the world) would meet in the open outside the Palace Pier and find themselves betrayed – betrayed while she sat inside the palace sipping a cocktail. What excuse could she make afterwards to Gertrude for not turning up? And what (and this could so easily happen) if she was found out?

Or could she let Gertrude into the secret beforehand? This seemed not impossible, indeed quite easy, for Gertrude was her admiring subordinate and might eagerly encourage her in such a scheme – but still this meant the betrayal of Ryan.

And this brought her to the question of Ryan. Was not Ryan far and away her favourite – the possibly 'perfect' gentleman, the one whose looks and manners she loved, the one who, she believed, strongly admired her, the one whom, after proper investigations, she would be willing to marry?

What if Ryan 'found out' – discovered her hideous treachery? Nothing could be more likely. Would he forgive her and continue to know her? Almost certainly not.

Was she, then, to forsake Ryan for Gorse, for whom she had no particular feeling? Was she to lose Ryan for the sake of one absurd, flashy, material vanity – a cocktail at the Metropole?

Or was there some way round? Need Ryan find out – and even if he did, could not some excuse – a lie, of course, and one made in collaboration with Gorse – be found, and might not Ryan accept this? Might she not without undue exertion eat her cake and have it too?

Esther rebuked herself for contemplating succumbing to treachery on behalf of a material pleasure. But here she wronged herself. What she had in mind was, really, a romantic pleasure. Cinderella's motives could hardly have been called material. What the Ball was to Cinderella, the Metropole was to Miss Downes of Over Street. The romance of Ryan conflicted with the romance of the great seaside hotel – that was all.

Finally – and, in view of her ignorance of Gorse's real character, pitifully – she decided in favour of the Metropole.

She came to this conclusion at about a quarter past one in the morning. She knew that this was the time because she had just heard her father come in – the porter returning after his day and night of waiting, carrying, and being insulted.

II

Ryan, Gorse, and Bell, after leaving Esther and Gertrude that night, had soon parted, and had made no arrangement to meet each other until all three met the 'birds' again outside the Palace Pier the next evening at seven-thirty.

Purely by accident, however, at about eleven on the morning of the next day, Ryan ran into Bell in a small tea-coffee-cake restaurant in Preston Street. Bell was seated at a table eating a large ice cream.

Ice cream, really, does not consort with Learning: ice cream lacks austerity; it is not food befitting a sage. Milton, letting his

> lamp at midnight hour,
> Be seen in some high lonely tower

would certainly not, even if such a thing had been obtainable, sustained himself with ice cream.

Bell, therefore, looked a trifle ashamed of himself – and perhaps the more so because Ryan, the comparative philistine, ordered a sophisticated coffee.

They talked about various matters, and then came to the proposed meeting with the two girls in the evening. Bell suggested that he himself should not appear at this. He was, he said, 'odd man out'. Ryan at first warmly persuaded him to come. Ryan was anxious to · be polite: and also he secretly felt that Bell was not actually odd man out: it was Bell's function to draw off the hideous Gertrude.

But Bell persisted. Bell also was privately conscious of his real function, and he had no desire whatever to fulful it.

Ryan at last gave in. It was really a matter of indifference to him. Only Esther was his object and only Gorse was his possible rival.

He was not, really, at all certain that Gorse was his rival. He was quite sure that Gorse had no feelings towards Esther to be remotely compared with his own. Ryan even doubted whether Gorse was capable of natural, commonplace reactions towards girls. Gorse was an unpredictable and curious as well as slightly distasteful character. Gorse, though, by mere virtue of his indifference and calmness, might be all the more powerful a rival.

Ryan left Bell and spent the greater part of the day on his

motorcycle. He had a late high tea in his bed-sitting room in Tisbury Road, and then dressed with great care.

In his anxiety to be early for the appointment he somehow managed (as people in the same situation so often do) to be late for it – late by two minutes. People get it into their heads that they have an enormous amount of time to spare, and consequently walk about the streets in the vicinity of the meeting place, almost disregarding time altogether.

Outside the Palace Pier, Gertrude was waiting. Neither Esther nor Gorse was present.

2   'Oh – hullo,' said Gertrude, and Ryan said the same, and apologized for being late, and they clumsily shook hands.

'Where've your friends got to, then?' asked Gertrude.

This was Gertrude's initial indirect lie. She had more to tell. She knew perfectly well at least where one of Ryan's friends was. He was, unless he had proved a deceiver, drinking, or about to drink, a cocktail at the Hotel Metropole.

'I don't know,' replied Ryan. 'At least I know about Bell. He's not coming along. But I don't know about Gorse.'

Now he came to the matter horribly nearest to his heart.

'Where's yours, by the way?' he asked with fairly well-assumed indifference.

Here Gertrude braced herself for the great and indirect lie. Esther, at the sweet-shop that morning, had confided almost all the truth to her, and had instructed her in regard to the falsehood she was to tell.

'Oh – I'm ever so sorry,' she said rather breathlessly. 'Esther sent a message she can't come. She's got a little brother who isn't at all well. He's got a temperature. And Esther's got to stay in and look after him. She told me to say she's ever so sorry, and she hopes she'll meet you again.'

Esther, having invented this lie for Gertrude to tell, had been visited by pangs not only of conscience, but of fear. She was a victim of that curious superstition, and consequent inhibition, under the spell of what human beings feel that if they say that one who is near and dear to them is ill, then Fate, or an angered God, will make that person ill in fact.

Because Gertrude was not a good liar, and spoke breathlessly, Ryan was at once suspicious.

'Oh,' he said. 'I'm sorry. What's the matter with him?'

'He's got a bad sore throat and a cough,' said Gertrude. 'And with a temperature, too, you don't want to neglect that sort of thing – do you?'

The bad sore throat and cough had also been Esther's invention, and she had thus secretly scared herself dreadfully. For, according to this strange superstition, God, provoked, gives the imaginary invalid precisely the illness he or she is imagined to have, and in a much more severe and dangerous degree than is originally pictured. Esther, therefore, had a vision of her little brother dying, within a few days, of influenza, bronchitis, or pneumonia.

'No,' said Ryan, still suspicious. 'I know one mustn't neglect that sort of thing. Is he seeing a doctor?'

'Yes,' said Gertrude. 'I think he's coming tonight.'

This was Gertrude's own invention. Esther had not thought about the necessity for a doctor.

'Well – I'm very sorry,' said Ryan, and though still not quite credulous, realized that he could not press the matter further. Instead he said: 'Well, I wonder where our friend Gorse has got to.'

Ryan, of course, was very seriously disappointed about the absence of Esther, but not in despair: for Gertrude had at any rate turned up with a message from Esther, and through Gertrude he could send messages to her and arrange another meeting later – tomorrow, perhaps. He meant, also, to get Esther's address from Gertrude.

But what on earth was he going to do about Gertrude this evening? How was he to get rid of her? The prospect of spending a whole evening with this plain, spectacled, common girl was too awful to contemplate. And yet he could not see how, in common politeness, and if she desired it – and she clearly looked as if she did – he could do otherwise.

This being so, he longed for Gorse to appear. Gorse would at least help him out. Indeed, Gorse was such a deep and resourceful character that he might well invent some remarkable excuse for both of them to get away quickly.

'He's very late, ain't he?' said Gertrude. 'You were late yourself, but he's later.'

'Yes. He certainly is,' said Ryan. 'Well, we'll give him five minutes – shall we?'

It had occurred to Ryan that Gorse quite probably would not appear. Gorse, he knew, was an extremely punctual person; he was also an extremely unpredictable one. Gorse, Ryan felt, would either be at an appointment on time, or not turn up at all. That is why he gave Gorse only five minutes – anyone else he would have given ten minutes, or a quarter of an hour.

'Yes,' said Gertrude. 'Let's just give him five minutes.'

Something frightened Ryan in this utterance of Gertrude. Perhaps it was the word 'just'. That word betrayed an eagerness to give Gorse as little time as possible. And that, in its turn, indicated a wish to spend the evening alone with Ryan – conceivably a strong desire. And such a thought was decidedly intimidating.

Ryan and Gertrude stood talking about the weather and the passing people for five minutes, and then Gertrude said:

'Well, his five minutes is up. Let's go on by ourselves, shall we?'

By 'go on', she meant go on the Palace Pier. Ryan had been right about her attitude. Bold and extraordinary thoughts had entered the unfortunate Gertrude's head.

3   Gertrude had been given, by her friend Esther, many lessons and lectures on the subject of young men and the manner in which they were to be captured and, when captured, treated.

At the end of these lessons Gertrude had frequently pointed out to Esther that they were of little use. They did not, she would say, properly apply to herself. For, whereas Esther was beautiful and attractive, she, Gertrude, was plain and lacking in magnetism.

To which Esther would reply – half out of politeness but half because she believed it to be true – that it was not Beauty that mattered, it was *Personality*. *Personality* and *Boldness* – cheek, sauce, courage, wit, the art of repartee, a way with one.

Esther would also never concede (but here she was lying in order to be kind to the other) that Gertrude was plain. Now Esther was an extremely kind girl and a fine liar. As a consequence she had made Gertrude believe quite often that she was not anything like as plain as she thought she was, that she was, perhaps absurdly, underestimating herself.

Being in her best dress, and 'got up to the nines', she was tonight in one of these optimistic moods, and there had come into her mind the staggering notion that she should take advantage of the present favourable circumstances and employ Personality and Boldness upon Ryan, and conceivably capture him by such measures!

It must not be thought that Gertrude had any idea of behaving treacherously to Esther in thus trying to win Ryan's admiration or love. She had never suspected for a moment what was in fact true, that Esther was emphatically interested in the good-looking young man. This was because Esther had in another way been untruthful. In her pride she had always pretended, in front of Gertrude, that young men as a whole are contemptible, to be treated disdainfully, merely used. Gertrude certainly did not think in this way about young men, but she believed absolutely that Esther did. Therefore, it was quite clear to Gertrude that Ryan was not a person of the smallest consequence to Esther, and there was no question of her 'stealing' him.

And so she had said to Ryan, 'Well, his five minutes is up. Let's go on by ourselves, shall we?'

4   Ryan, staggered and terrified, tried to do some rapid thinking. But no amount of thought, quick or slow, could extract so kindhearted a being as Ryan was from the situation in which he found himself.

And so he said, 'All right, then. Let's.' And they moved towards the turnstile.

Here Ryan, who was by no means rich, realized that he had to pay for this torture, and he did so gracefully.

As soon as they had got through and were walking on the planks seawards, Gertrude was the one who was trying hardest to think quickly. *Boldness* and *Personality*, she kept repeating to herself. But Boldness of the kind she contemplated was, she realized, of no use until it was Dark. At the moment the sun had barely set in a cloudless sky.

How then, until night had fallen, could she at least exercise Personality?

Thinking of these things, she said nothing, and, Ryan having nothing to say, there was a long, very embarrassing silence as they walked along.

At last Ryan was compelled to descend to banality.

'It's a lovely evening, isn't it?' he said.

'Yes, it is,' said Gertrude. But she could not go on, and there was another silence.

'In fact, we've really had a lovely summer,' said Ryan. 'Taking things all round.'

'We have,' said Gertrude. 'Really.'

And again there was silence.

At last, as they approached some slot machines, Gertrude saw a chance of bringing Personality into play.

'Are you a kid, like I am?' she said. 'And like to play with slot machines?'

'Oh yes,' said Ryan. 'I love slot machines.'

'Ah – then you are a kid,' said Gertrude. 'I thought you were.'

'I suppose I am,' said Ryan.

'You look like one, anyway,' said Gertrude. (Personality, sauce, cheek, an air!)

'Do I?'

'Yes, you look as though you want taking in hand and looking after – to *me*.'

'Do I?' said Ryan.

'You certainly do,' said Gertrude. 'Come along. Let's be kids and play at one of these.'

Ryan assented, and they went up to a machine behind whose glass were small and crude images of moustached footballers. These footballers, on one side, wore green jerseys, and, on the other side, red. The stitches which had gone to make these jerseys were greatly out of proportion. They would, if they had been worn by real footballers, each have been as large as, or larger than, footballs.

To play at this game it was necessary to put in two pennies – the winner receiving one back. Gertrude offered to put in her own penny, but the chivalrous and generous Ryan would not permit this. '*More* money!' was Ryan's thought. But he meant, before he had parted from Gertrude that night, to get Esther's address from her. And that would be worth his entire fortune. Ryan put in the pennies, and they began to play.

The reader will possibly blush in his soul almost as much as Ryan did on learning that, as they played this game, Gertrude, while peering through the glass to decide what sort of shot to make with her side of footballers, put her head and hair so close to Ryan that they almost touched his own. She did this more than once, too. But at last Ryan managed to shoot a goal and was temporarily relieved.

They next went to a machine again requiring two pennies and behind whose glass were imitations of race horses.

At this game it was impossible for Gertrude to assault Ryan in the same way – it was too quick.

Ryan, therefore, made them play the game as much as five times. He won the first two races, and then suggested giving her a 'start'. Gertrude won the last game, and they moved on again.

Now some clouds had appeared in the sky and it was darker, but not dark enough for Gertrude's intentions.

She therefore took Ryan to the end of the Pier, and then made him walk four times around the Palace Pier Theatre. This she supplemented by making him stop at other slot machines.

At last it was dark enough. She led him towards a deserted covered bench which she had in mind and which faced the West Pier.

'Come on,' she said. 'Let's come and sit down here.'

And (she hoped fascinatingly) she took his arm in order to compel him to do so. He complied. For about ten minutes she talked, and he answered as well as he could.

Now it was really dark enough. She had not yet released his arm.

'Yes,' said Gertrude reflectively, 'it isn't half a lovely night – isn't it?'

'Yes, it certainly is,' said Ryan.

'Or a night for love,' said Gertrude. 'Which?'

'I don't know,' said Ryan.

'Don't you?'

'No ... I don't ...'

'Sure?'

'Yes.'

'Well – *I* think it's a night for love.'

And here Gertrude put ('nestled' is the word vulgarly used) her head on Ryan's shoulder.

He had anticipated abominable enough things, but nothing so eerily ghastly as this. He felt he must say something.

'Do you?' he said.

'Yes. Don't you?' said Gertrude.

'I don't know,' said Ryan.

There was a pause.

'You're Cold,' said Gertrude. 'Ain't you?'

Here Ryan made the perfectly honest mistake of believing that she was alluding to the temperature of the Pier.

'No,' he said, 'I'm quite all right, thank you.'

'No,' said Gertrude. 'I don't mean Cold in that way.'

'Oh,' said Ryan. 'Don't you?'

'No,' said Gertrude. 'Don't you know the way I mean it?'

'No. I don't,' said Ryan yet again.

'Oh yes, you do.'

'No. I don't. Really,' said Ryan.

Now, of course, he was not telling the truth.

'Well – shall I tell you?'

'Yes. Do.'

'Well. Not Warm. Warm in the Heart.'

'Oh. Aren't I?'

'No.'

'Oh. I'm sorry.'

'Not warm in the heart,' said Gertrude. 'Not warm in the heart towards poor little Gertrude.'

And, to cap this horror, she put out her hand and began, with her fingers, to play flirtatiously with the middle button of Ryan's coat.

'*Are* you?' said Gertrude.

'I don't know,' said Ryan (it now seemed to him for the eightieth time).

'Don't you?'

'No. I don't . . .'

'I'm warm in the heart about you, anyway. I was, ever since I set eyes on you, and I am still.'

'Are you?'

'Don't you think you could ever get warm in the heart about your little Gertie-Wertie?'

(*Gertie-Wertie!*)

'I don't know.'

'Well, I wish you'd make up your mind –' Here Gertrude paused. 'What's your Christian name, anyway? I've told you mine.'

'Peter,' said Ryan.

'Peter,' repeated Gertrude. 'That suits you. I like it. Don't *you*?'

'I don't know,' said Ryan.

5   It is not necessary further to embarrass, or tire, the reader with a narration of Gertrude's further Boldnesses during the next twenty minutes.

It need only be said that she continued to be Bold, thinking that she might wear him down (Esther, in addition to Boldness and Personality, had unfortunately recommended Persistence to her) and that Ryan went on saying 'I don't know' and 'Are you?' and 'Do you?' and 'Don't you?' until he was nearly out of his mind.

Then, quite suddenly, Gertrude gave in. She withdrew her head from his shoulder, and her hand from the middle button of his coat, and she looked at him, pityingly and pitifully.

'No – it ain't any good, is it?' she said.

'I don't really know. What do you mean?' said Ryan

'Oh yes, you do,' said Gertrude. 'And I know *why* it ain't any good.'

'Why?'

'It's because I'm not pretty – ain't it?' said this now very genuine girl. 'It's because I'm so darned ugly.'

'Don't be silly,' said Ryan. 'You're not ugly. You're very pretty.'

He had not meant to say this last. It had slipped out in his sorrow for her pathos.

'No. You don't mean that.'

'Yes, I do. Of course I do.' What else could he say? And how could he say it without pretending as cleverly as he could that he meant it? And yet how cruel he was being, and what unutterable confusion he was causing in the wretched Gertrude's mind!

For, so convincing was his manner, that Gertrude half believed he was speaking the truth. And if this was so, why did he not accept her advances?

Gertrude, hoping for the best, but feeling in the bottom of her unhappy heart that she was probably deceiving herself, alighted upon an explanation.

'It's *She* you're after,' she said. 'Isn't it?'

'Who?'

'Esther.'

There was a pause.

'Is that her name?' asked Ryan.

'Ah – so you're ever so keen to know her Christian name – ain't you? It *is* her you're after – ain't it?'

'I don't know . . .' said Ryan.

'But I do,' said Gertrude. 'And I can't say I blame you. She's very beautiful – ain't she?'

'Yes. She's certainly very pretty.'

'Not ugly. Like I am.'

'You're not ugly. Don't be silly.'

'Oh yes, I am. And you and she'd make a proper pair. She doesn't think much of boys as a rule, but I think she might like *you* – if you tried.'

'Do you think so?'

'Yes.'

'Really?'

'Yes. I think so. And you're ever so keen to know – ain't you? Come on. Own up. You're crazy about her – aren't you? There's plenty that are – I can tell you.'

'Well – I do think she's very lovely . . .'

Gertrude persisted.

'And you're crazy about her – ain't you?'

'Well – perhaps I am. A bit.'

'Yes. I thought so.' Gertrude was in a way pleased because his confession confirmed her hope that it was only because he loved Esther that he had rejected her advances. Being pleased, she was very generous.

'Well,' she said, 'can I help you in any way? I know her very well – and what I said might count.'

'Do you think you could?' said Ryan. 'It's very nice of you.'

'Yes. I think I could. What do you want me to do?'

'Well – I'd like to know her address, really. Just in case we didn't meet on the front again and I couldn't find her.'

'All right,' said Gertrude. 'It's Over Street. Two hundred and six Over Street. Can you remember it?'

'Yes. I can remember. Two hundred and six. Over Street. Thank you. It's very good of you.'

'And do you know where Over Street is? It ain't a very swell district.'

'No.'

'It's just by Brighton Station. I don't know I ought to be telling you all this.'

'Oh, it's all right. Really. I wouldn't take advantage. It's only just in *case*, you see. To write to her.'

'Yes, I see,' said Gertrude. 'And anything else, Mr Peter Ryan?'

'No – I don't think so. No – I'm sorry there *is* just one other thing.'

'And what's that?'

'I don't know if it's all right for you to tell me – but tell me if you can. It's just that I want to know whether it was true that her little brother was ill tonight. Or was it just a sham, because she didn't want to turn up?'

'What makes you think it wasn't true?'

Gertrude said this in order to gain time in which to think. She had temporarily forgotten the problem of Esther having lied, and of probably being with Gorse at the Metropole at the present moment.

What was she to do? She was maternally eager to help Ryan, but how could she do so without betraying Esther? She would like Ryan to know, too, that his alleged friend Gorse was betraying him. And

had not Esther betrayed him as well? Gertrude fully understood
Esther's motives, and had already forgiven her, had even warmly
supported her in what she had done. And Esther was to be further
forgiven, too, for she had had no knowledge of Ryan's feelings
towards her. Had she had, she would probably have acted differently.

As these thoughts rushed through Gertrude's head, Ryan
answered her.

'Oh – I just thought it might not be true,' he said. 'There was
something in the way you said it, I think. Not that I can complain.
There's no reason why she shouldn't make an excuse and not turn
up. I know I probably don't mean anything to her. Not at present,
at any rate.'

He spoke with such naïveté, charm, and simplicity that Gertrude
was tremendously tempted to be of assistance to him by telling him
the truth. But no – she must resist this. Esther came first. And
tomorrow morning she had to get instructions from Esther about
this new state of affairs.

'Oh no. It was quite true,' she said. 'Her little brother's ill all right
– and that's the only reason she couldn't come.'

'Oh well – I'm very glad to hear it,' said Ryan.

What on earth would happen, Gertrude wondered, if she and
Esther and Gorse were found out? Esther had, she realized, caused
a complication dangerous from innumerable aspects.

'I mean', Ryan went on, 'that as long as she wasn't making an
excuse, she might even be a bit interested in me, or come to be
later.'

'Yes,' said Gertrude. 'I'm sure she might. And there's plenty of
other opportunities – ain't there? I'll be seeing her tomorrow, and
so do you want me to give any message to her?'

'Oh,' said Ryan. 'Would you? It's terribly good of you, and you're
terribly nice.'

'No, I ain't. What do you want me to tell her?'

'Well. Would you ask her if she could meet me?'

'Where?'

'Well – what about the same time and place that you and I met
– outside the Palace Pier – seven-thirty?'

'And when? Tomorrow evening?'

'Well, yes. If her little brother's better and she can manage it.'

'Oh – I expect he'll be better, and that she'll manage it. Anyway
– that's the message I'll give her.'

'Well – thank you so much. You're terribly nice.'

'Don't be so silly ... And now I think it's time we was toddling off home – don't you? Me, at any rate.'

'Oh no. Do let's stay, if you'd like it,' said the kindhearted and grateful Ryan. He was so grateful that he would have stayed with Gertrude till midnight, or beyond, if she desired it. But this was not what he wanted to do. He wanted to go home at once and dream and scheme about Esther, and brood upon his probable meeting with her tomorrow evening.

'No. It's quite late, and I'll only get into trouble with Mother,' said Gertrude. 'Come on. Let's wend our way.'

And she rose.

Ryan rose too, and they began to walk towards the shore.

They began to speak about Brighton – its climate and amenities.

When they had passed through the turnstile and were on the front, they stopped and looked at each other shyly.

'Well,' said Gertrude, 'I suppose it's good-bye. I'll give Esther that message all right, and I'm sure she'll be here. You've got her address, anyway, now, haven't you?'

'Yes. I have. Thanks to you. I really can't thank you enough. Just tell her seven-thirty – just here – where we're standing – will you?'

'Yes. I'll tell her that.'

At this, chivalry and gratitude again attacked Ryan.

'And will you be coming along too?' he asked. 'I hope you will.'

'No. I don't think I'll be along.' Gertrude smiled at him. 'I don't think *that'd* be very wise, would it?'

'Oh yes, it would. Surely it would. Do come along.'

'No. I won't come. But thanks for asking me all the same.'

'Well – we'll be meeting again – won't we? Of course we'll be meeting again.'

'Yes. I daresay we'll be meeting. Especially if you get friendly with Esther.'

'Oh yes, we *must* meet,' said Ryan. 'All *three* of us must go out together.'

His earnestness, sweetness, and *gaucherie* completely overcame Gertrude.

'You ain't half a baby – ain't you?' she said. And she kissed him on the cheek, and ran away before he could reply.

Soon after they had parted, the minds of each began to work roughly on the same subject – that of Esther and Gorse. Ryan wondered what Esther was doing now, and he wondered why Gorse had not turned up.

Gertrude, who knew all, wondered what Gorse and Esther were doing now, and what they had been doing all the evening.

What, indeed?

III

Gorse had arrived at the West Pier three minutes before the time appointed. Esther, on principle, had seen to it that she was half a minute late.

Esther was dressed well as she knew how to dress – which meant that she was dressed very well; and Gorse, for one who remembered him in his jacket and 'bags' of the previous evening, was a transformed being. He was in a well-made dark blue lounge suit; he wore a fawn-coloured trilby hat, a stiff white collar, and a striped but modest tie.

Our dear old friends The Nines, in fact, had been paid due respect by both. But this discreetly – not too officiously or subserviently.

Esther was enormously reassured on seeing Gorse dressed so well. Now it did not seem so incredible that they would be allowed into the Metropole. Her main concern was as to whether she herself would 'pass': but on the whole she believed she would.

Having shaken hands, Gorse said, 'Well. Off to the good old Met. That's where we said we were going – wasn't it?'

'Yes,' said Esther. 'That's what you said.'

'*Bon*,' said Gorse, and nothing further was said as they crossed the road: nor was anything said as they walked along in the direction of the Metropole. At last Esther found the silence embarrassing, and she decided to break it.

'Do you go to the Metropole a lot?' she asked.

'Oh yes,' said Gorse. 'Quite a good bit.'

But this was a complete lie. Gorse had never been inside the Metropole in his life. Moreover, he was almost as frightened by the idea of doing so as Esther was herself. Indeed, in a manner, he was more so. For whereas Esther had him to lean upon, to believe in, he had no such prop. He had to lead the way, find a table, deal with the waiter. Even the cold, inscrutable Gorse on certain occasions knew the meaning of the word 'cowardice'.

This was why he said nothing as they walked along. This struck

Esther as being curious, for he had been so loquacious, too much so, yesterday evening.

Without having uttered another word they reached the entrance and walked up the steps to the revolving doors.

These were swung round for them by a porter from within. The porter did this rather too quickly, and there was something of a rush and panic as Gorse made the trembling Esther go through first.

Then they were inside, and Gorse was face to face with his difficulties.

He now regretted deeply having told Esther that he had been in here before, for he was, in fact, entirely bewildered, and felt that she would detect his falsehood.

'Well. There're a lot of places we can sit,' he said. 'Where would you like to go?'

'I don't know,' said Esther. 'I'd rather leave it to you.'

As they had as yet not been turned out she was regaining confidence.

'Well, let's try down there – shall we?' said Gorse, and he led her straight forwards. About twenty-five yards ahead he had spotted an adult couple seated at a table drinking. He had also seen a vacant table not far away from them.

Nothing was said as they walked towards this table.

Esther, in spite of her more confident feeling, was too overwhelmed by the grandeur of the place and the people and the carpets to speak; Gorse did not speak because he was too frightened, and too much on the watch in order to behave properly.

This state of mind in Gorse caused him, as such a thing does with many more ordinary people, to lift his chin high and to put on an air of the greatest *hauteur*.

Then suddenly he realized that he had not taken off his hat, and he believed this was highly incorrect. He therefore snatched it off clumsily, and so lost the impression of *hauteur*. Then, having lost it, he resumed it with even greater and more painful intensity.

At last the table was reached, and he motioned to Esther to sit down, and sat down himself. Now he did not know what to do with his hat. He thought of putting it on to the table, but he was visited by the hideous idea that he ought not to have a hat with him at all: that he should have put it in the cloakroom or something. And so, hoping that no one had seen him do it, he put it under his chair. But Esther had seen him do it, and had noticed his furtive look.

Now what was he to do? How was he to find a waiter? Esther still had not uttered a word, and he was conscious that she was looking at him. The couple opposite were taking no notice of them, and Gorse was at least grateful for this. (Esther was glad of this too. It helped to make her feel that she had 'passed'.)

By the grace of God a waiter came hurrying by. Gorse put up his hand and snapped his fingers. He had an impression that it was vulgar to snap one's fingers (particularly so loudly), but he could not risk losing the waiter.

The waiter turned and came up to them.

Now Esther was wondering whether Gorse looked old enough to be served with drinks, and Gorse himself had his doubts.

'Yes, sir,' said the waiter, and bent over them politely. This was better. Gorse suddenly regained confidence.

'Well,' he said, looking and smiling at Esther. 'What's your choice?'

'I don't know,' said Esther, who had suddenly and completely lost confidence again. 'Really . . .'

'Well, you must make up your mind, you know,' said Gorse, and now he smiled almost confidentially, or even winkingly, at the waiter.

'I don't really know,' said Esther.

'Now. Come along,' said Gorse. 'You've got to make up your mind, you know.'

'I don't know.'

Esther was in a panic.

'But you must know,' said Gorse. 'Surely it's easy enough to think of a cocktail – isn't it?'

Esther absolutely lost her head.

'Oh – very well, then,' she said, 'I think I'll have a Benedictine.'

The unfortunate girl had heard of Benedictine, and had always somehow imagined that it was a cocktail.

'A *What*?' said Gorse in a shocked way. He had no particular desire to humiliate Esther, but he wanted to keep up his dignity in front of the waiter.

'A *Benedictine*,' repeated Esther in a wretched attempt at defiance. But she knew she had made some shocking error, and she blushed.

'Well,' said Gorse, 'you can have a Benedictine if you like – but it's not a cocktail – is it? And I think you'd find it a little sickly if you have it before dinner.'

Young as he was, Gorse – along with his many other rapidly

developing snobberies – was an incipient wine-snob (perhaps the most unattractive form of snobbery on this earth), and he already knew something about these matters.

'Don't you agree, waiter?' he said, once more very nearly winking.

'Yes, sir. It might be.' The waiter smiled.

Humiliated almost unbearably, Esther at last saw a way out.

'Well – what are *you* going to have?' she asked.

(Why on earth, she wondered, hadn't she asked this before?)

'Well, I'm going to have a Gin and It,' said Gorse. 'Will you try one?'

'Yes. I think I'll have that,' said Esther. She put in the word 'think' in order to make it seem that she was making a choice. But in fact she did not know the name of any cocktail.

'Good,' said Gorse. 'Two Gin and Its, then, waiter.'

'Yes, sir. Thank you, sir,' said the waiter, and he went away.

There was a silence.

'Sorry if I made a fool of myself,' said Esther. 'But I'm not used to cocktails and places like this, you see.'

'You didn't make a fool of yourself at all,' said Gorse. 'And it's very easy to make mistakes about these things. I used to myself, anyway. Actually Benedictine's a liqueur – not a cocktail.'

'Is it? And what's a liqueur? I don't even know what *that* is.'

Gorse began to explain, and soon the waiter returned.

Gorse paid, tipped the waiter handsomely, and was thanked with the utmost deference. Gorse was now beginning to feel splendidly at home in the Hotel Metropole.

But he, as well as Esther, looked at the drinks (which had a cherry stuck into them at the end of the stick) with some diffidence.

Esther was certainly not going to tackle her drink until Gorse had tackled his and she had been given some intimation of the proper way to approach a cocktail with a cherry in it.

Gorse hesitated for a moment. Then he put the cherry into his mouth, and the stick on to an ash tray, and he raised the glass to his mouth and said, 'Well – cheerio,' to Esther.

Esther did exactly the same.

'Like it?' said Gorse.

'Yes,' said Esther. 'It's ever so nice.'

But although she had not much objected to the cherry, because of its sweetness, she had really hated her first sip at the cocktail.

After they had been talking and sipping for about five minutes, however, Esther found that she disliked the taste of the drink much less. Also, she experienced a warm feeling in her heart, a not unpleasant giddiness in her head, and a curious temptation to behave much more audaciously than she had so far. She succumbed to this temptation.

'That's a nice tie you're wearing,' she said. 'Where did you get that?'

'This? Oh – it's just an old-school-tie, as a matter of fact.'

'Really?' said Esther, secretly awed. 'What school?'

'Westminster,' said Gorse.

The tie Gorse was wearing was in fact an old Westminster tie. But Gorse had been to St Paul's, and he was therefore, masquerading in such a tie.

Gorse had not thought St Paul's quite good enough, and had chosen Westminster. He had contemplated adopting Eton or Harrow, but had then thought that this might be going a little bit too far. Westminster was his compromise. He only seldom wore this tie, for he was afraid of being exposed as an impostor.

But on special occasions – and bluffing his way into the Metropole tonight was certainly such – he would put it on with his best blue suit.

Westminster conveyed practically nothing to Esther. She thought only of Westminster Abbey. Only Eton and Harrow – or, because she had been brought up in Sussex, Brighton College or Lancing – would have impressed her very much.

The drink by this time had just affected Gorse's head.

'Yes,' he said in a languid way. 'All my people went there, from time immemorial, so I had to go there too.'

This again awed Esther, and she was once again bolder than she would have been if she had not taken drink.

'And what sort of people are yours?' She spoke in a saucy way, which failed to conceal her deep curiosity.

'Oh – Army People,' said Gorse. 'Nearly all of them. They're a dull lot, really.'

Gorse, when he said this, believed he was lying. But, if what he had said were to be taken literally, he was not. His ancestors, on the whole, *had* been 'Army People'. They had been, very many of them, low and lewd privates in slightly second-rate wars.

'Well,' said Esther, who was more impressed than ever. 'I wish I had some Army people in *my* family. *My* people are pretty humble, as I expect you've guessed.'

'What do you mean?' said Gorse. 'We're all the same – aren't we

– under the skin? The Colonel's Lady and Judy O'Grady are sisters under the skin – what?'

He was quoting Rudyard Kipling. Gorse, though he disliked poetry intensely in a general way, was not completely lacking in appreciation of the baser sort.

Esther did not know that he had quoted Kipling, but understood his general meaning.

'Yes,' she said. 'I suppose we are. All the same, I wish I'd been born to better things. I work in a sweet-shop all day, and it's pretty nearly a slum, where I live.'

'Well, if you work in a sweet-shop – that's bringing coals to Newcastle – isn't it?'

Esther did not understand this compliment – Gorse's first.

'What do you mean?' she said.

'Well – a perfect sweet amongst the sweets – what?'

She understood this.

'Don't be so silly,' she said, not displeased.

They continued to talk in this way, and then Gorse insisted that they should have another cocktail, and Esther, after a few protests, succumbed.

Halfway through the second cocktail Esther was hilariously happy (she did not know why, for she did not connect drinking with hilarity). Then she suddenly felt 'swimmy' and knew that she must stop drinking. She therefore made Gorse finish off the remaining half of her drink.

Gorse did this quickly, and was, by now, himself quite inebriated. Gorse, throughout his life, was never able to take drink very well.

He suggested that they should go and walk on the West Pier, and Esther gladly assented.

On the way to the West Pier, and while walking on it, Gorse did something which, throughout his life, he always did when he had taken too much to drink. This was his 'Silly Ass' act.

The 'Silly Ass' act had a patter which he had half invented himself and half borrowed from 'Silly Ass' actors on the stage or the music-halls. There was a great deal of 'I say!' 'Bai Jove!' 'Weally!' in it, and before he started his performance he took a monocle from his pocket and stuck it into his eye.

Needless to say, the cultured, watching this, did not, in their shame, know where to look; but the uncultured were often genuinely amused, or fascinated simply to see someone genuinely making a fool of himself.

Esther, though clever, was not very cultured, and tonight the drink had gone to her head. She was therefore highly pleased by Gorse's performance. She laughed at it, and encouraged him to go on with it.

At last, however, he put away his monocle and behaved normally and quietly again. By this time it was dark, and Gorse suggested that they should sit down. He chose the same spot as the five had used last night.

Looking at the lights of the Palace Pier (had she had a telescope and had it been light), Esther could have seen the bold Gertrude and the agonized Ryan sitting beside each other. Esther became pensive and serious. Gorse sensed her mood and imitated it.

After a while Esther said: 'My word – I haven't half got a conscience about those other three.'

'Which other three?' asked Gorse.

'Why – your two friends – and Gertrude.'

Of course she really had no conscience about Gertrude (who was in the secret) or about Bell (who didn't count). But she did feel conscience-stricken about her own deceitfulness, and about Ryan, who, she was certain, must have been disappointed not to see her.

'Oh,' said Gorse. 'I wouldn't bother about them. They'll be getting on all right.'

'Yes. But they must've been waiting for us to turn up.'

Another lie – for Gertrude had been there to tell that she, Esther, at any rate, was not coming because of the illness of her little brother. The Over Street girl was beginning to have some glimmering of what a tangled web we weave when first we practise to deceive.

'Oh, I don't expect they'll wait long,' said Gorse. 'If I know my Ryan, he's not the sort to wait long.'

'Is that his name?' asked Esther. 'I know you introduced us last night, but I didn't take it in. But I can remember yours. It's Gorse – isn't it? Like what you see on the Downs.'

'Thats right.'

'And what's your friend's Christian name? I mean the better-looking one – Ryan.'

'Well, of all the cheek,' said Gorse facetiously. 'Here am I taking you out, and you ask Ryan's Christian name, but not mine. And on top of it you call him good-looking.'

'Oh – I'm sorry. Well – what is it? I mean yours.'

'I told you last night.'

'Well – I didn't take it in. I wasn't taking a thing in, somehow, last night. Go on. What is it?'

'Ralph,' said Gorse. 'Pronounced Ralph or Rafe – whichever you prefer. Which do you?'

Esther thought about this.

'I think I prefer Ralph,' she said. 'Rafe's a bit too La-di-dah.'

'Very well, then. And will you call me Ralph, Esther? I remember your name all right, you see.'

And here Gorse moved closer to Esther, and put his arm around her waist.

'Oh – I don't know about that,' said Esther.

She was fighting for time. She had had many previous experiences of this kind, and believed she knew how to deal with them expertly. But Gorse, somehow – was a new type of problem. She now believed that he was a 'gentleman'. His blue suit, his hat, his manner and success at the Metropole, his old-school-tie – all these had practically convinced her. Also, she thought she 'liked' him. He had dash, and she had laughed a good deal at his 'Silly Ass' act. But still there was just something wrong which made her suspect and *not* altogether like him. This was to a certain extent instinctive in her, but there was also the concrete fact that he had shown duplicity in making a private arrangement with her to go to the Metropole. If he could deceive others, could he not deceive herself? (In thinking thus, Esther completely overlooked her own deception.)

'Come along, Esther, now,' said Gorse. 'Won't you call me Ralph?'

'All right, then. If you like,' said Esther after a pause.

'Well, go on. Say it. Say Ralph.'

'All right, then. Ralph.'

'Good. And will Esther gave Ralph a kiss?' said Gorse.

'Oh – that's *quite* a different proposition,' said Esther.

But she had hardly got the words out of her mouth before Gorse was kissing her on the mouth.

This, although she submitted, Esther greatly disliked. She always did with any young man.

Then Gorse kissed her again, and Esther discovered that there was something unusual in the way in which he was kissing her. There was about it an intensity, even a viciousness, to which she was not accustomed. No 'gentleman', or proletarian of her own class, had ever kissed her in this way. They had been too timid.

And this lack of shyness, restraint, and inhibition, Esther, averse as she was to kissing, did not exactly dislike.

'Now then,' she said at last. 'That's quite enough of that.'

Gorse obeyed her, but, leaning back in the seat, still kept his arm around her. He did not speak, and she thought she must break the silence.

'Well – what *is* his Christian name, anyway?' she said. 'You still haven't told me.'

'Who?'

'Your friend's.'

'Ryan, you mean?'

'Yes.'

'Peter, if you must know. But I still think it's damn sauce for you to ask me, you know.'

'Don't swear.'

'Do you call "damn" swearing?'

'Yes.'

'Well, in that case you're going to hear a lot of swearing before your life's finished.'

'I think it's Unnecessary,' said the demure beauty.

'And I think it's unnecessary for you to ask me someone else's Christian name while you're out with me. And by the way, if you're so interested in Christian names, why didn't you ask me Bell's?'

'Is that the name of your other friend?'

'Yes . . . Well, why didn't you want to know *his* Christian name?'

'I don't know,' said Esther.

'Don't you?' said Gorse. '*I* do.'

Thus Gorse had shrewdly discovered something of Esther's feelings towards Ryan.

'You know a lot, don't you?' said Esther.

'Yes. Quite a lot. I'm not such a fool as I look. And I hope I don't even *look* too much of a fool. Do you think I do?'

'No, you don't look a fool. Anything but. Except when you're playing the silly ass,' said Esther, alluding to his act.

'Ah – but that's put on.'

In this semi-flirtatious way they continued to talk for about half an hour. Then Gorse began kissing her again, and Esther was again slightly fascinated by his lack of restraint.

Having asked the time, Esther found it was unexpectedly late, and she said that she must 'fly' home. Gorse made no attempt to make her stay and they walked towards the turnstiles.

When they had passed through these Esther stopped, as if to say good-bye.

'Don't you want me to see you home?' asked Gorse.

'No, thanks. I'd rather rush off by myself, really. I wouldn't like you to see where *I* live, anyway.'

'Oh – what does it matter? Won't you let me?'

'No. Honest. I'd rather go by myself.'

'Very well. Have it your own way. But let me know when we're going to meet again, at any rate.'

'Well – that's up to you.'

'All right. Let's make it seven o'clock tomorrow evening – just here. Then we'll go and have another cocktail. That suit you?'

'Yes. That sounds all right to me.'

'All right. Seven o'clock tomorrow – at the hour of the setting sun. Just here. *Eau voir*, madame,' said Gorse, and offered his hand.

Esther shook hands with him, said 'Good-bye' shyly, and went away, almost running because of her shyness.

As soon as her walk had returned to a normal pace she realized that she had not offered him a word of thanks for the evening, and she reproached herself bitterly for such a breach of good taste – particularly with a 'gentleman'.

This failure was made all the worse by the fact that he had spent a lot of money on her and given her an entirely delightful evening. She could not remember ever having spent a more delightful one. He had taken her to the Metropole and she had 'passed'! And he had been responsible for all this.

She was grateful to him and liked him enormously. She was sure of that.

But was she sure? She did not quite know. Still there was something about him which intuitively made her suspicious.

In spite of his generosity, did she like him as much as Ryan? No – of course not. He was not so good-looking, anyway, and he was not so 'perfectly' a 'gentleman'.

She would like, if he was all he seemed, to marry Ryan. She did not somehow take to the idea of marrying Gorse.

Nice as he undoubtedly was.

PART FIVE

ESTHER AND RYAN

I

Though very busy, Esther and Gertrude had plenty of time for conversation, though some of it had to be furtive, at the sweet-shop at which they both worked.

Gertrude, therefore, next morning, had no difficulty in describing to Esther her evening with Ryan, and in letting Esther know that Ryan was 'crazy' about her.

She also told Esther that she had made an appointment for her to meet Ryan outside the Palace Pier at seven-thirty that evening.

All this disturbed Esther very much. She had had no idea that Ryan's feelings were so strong; she liked Ryan much the better of the two; and yet she had made an appointment to meet Gorse at seven o'clock outside the West Pier.

She could not, in honour, abandon Gorse. (And, because of his Metropole and his cocktails, she didn't really want to!) But she desired intensely to meet, not to lose, Ryan. Could there not be some compromise? Could she not somehow again contrive to eat her cake and have it too? Could not cleverness find a compromise?

Cleverness could. Cleverness combined with wickedness. She had arranged to meet Gorse outside the West Pier at seven o'clock. The appointment which Gertrude had made for her with Ryan was at seven-thirty outside the Palace Pier. Was it not possible to meet both? Might she not meet Gorse, lie to him, and then rush off to meet Ryan? Then, having met Ryan, spent a little time with him, at least kept him in tow, she might even return to Gorse.

She wondered what lie, if she did this, she would tell Gorse. What, but her little brother? She felt herself sinking deeper and deeper into crime. She would, she felt, in fact kill her little brother if this sort of thing went on.

Then it occurred to her that those two – Ryan and Gorse – might easily meet and compare notes. Thus she would be disclosed as an adventuress, and probably lose both.

But she felt that there was some way of forcing Ryan (her slave, after all) to hold his tongue. She could do this either by telling him some lie, or even, by telling him the truth.

Truth has always been the liar's most able and trustworthy lieutenant.

And what if she did fail in these schemes and was put to shame? Did it matter? Did she not despise young men? Had she not always avowed her scorn of them to Gertrude – and must she not stand by her words? Was not the whole matter of the smallest account to her? Were there not 'plenty of other fish in the sea'?

Esther thought of these things all day as she worked, and at last came to a decision.

She had decided again to take the risk of killing her little brother.

2   Because she had a conscience and wanted to get her lying over quickly, and because she wanted to be in good time to meet Ryan afterwards, Esther abandoned feminine principle and was actually outside the West Pier three minutes before the appointed time. Gorse arrived two minutes later.

They shook hands, and she dashed into it at once.

'Look,' she said, 'I'm ever so sorry, but I can't spend tonight with you – at least not all of it. I've got my little brother ill at home. He's got a temperature and I've got to go back and mind him while Mother's out. I'm ever so sorry.'

'Oh dear,' said Gorse. 'What's the matter with him?'

'I don't really know. But he's got a nasty cough, and a temperature, and he's in bed. I'm ever so sorry.'

'Oh – that's all right. But can't you stay a little while?'

'No. I think I ought to be off, really. But I'll tell you what. I could meet you later, if you liked. But I don't expect that'd suit you.'

'Well – what time, about, were you thinking about?'

'Oh. Nine – or something like that.'

'Well, do you think you could make it eight-thirty? Then it'd be worth while. Otherwise I might as well go to a cinema.'

Esther pretended to hesitate. Then 'Yes,' she said. 'I think I could make it eight-thirty – if that's all right by you. I might be a bit late.'

'Yes. That's all right. And where shall we meet?'

'Oh, here. That's the best place, isn't it? And now I'd really better be popping off.'

'All right. Eight-thirty. I'll be here.'

'What are you going to do in the meanwhile?' asked Esther. 'Going to have a cocktail in the Metropole by yourself?'

She asked him this in order to find out where he was going to be during her interview with Ryan, so that she could see to it that there was no possibility of their running into each other. She wanted Gorse absolutely safely at the Metropole. Esther wanted practically everything. Esther, the beauty in danger of becoming 'spoiled', had recently developed the bad habit of wanting practically everything.

'Yes. I think I probably will,' said Gorse.

'Good. Then you'll be nice and comfy,' said Esther in a voice which was warm because this had made her feel nice and comfy herself. 'Well. So long.'

'So long,' said Gorse.

'Oh, and I'm ever so sorry,' said Esther as an afterthought, 'but I never thanked you for last night. It was a lovely evening, and thanks ever so much.'

'*Pas du tout*, madame,' said Gorse. 'The pleasure was all mine.'

'Well. Ta-ta!'

'Cheerio,' said Gorse, and Esther, having waved, raced off.

Esther now had some time on hand, and she made for the small streets behind the front which she knew intimately and in which she could, as it were, hide, and waste time, until she met Ryan outside the Palace Pier at seven-thirty.

She had believed Gorse when he had said he was going to the Metropole. But it is hardly necessary to say that Gorse had no such intention.

Gorse was not so credulous as Ryan, and although Esther was a better liar than Gertrude, he was not to be taken in by ill little brothers.

And so he followed Esther.

To do this, undetected, amongst the small streets behind the front was no easy matter. Nevertheless, Gorse did so.

And at the end he observed, from a distance, Esther meeting Ryan outside the Palace Pier.

Esther's mother had incessantly told Esther never to Tell a Lie. To do so, she had explained, would only be to attract very evil consequences.

11

Esther, returning to her principle, made herself two minutes late for Ryan.

She saw him looking in a sort of despair in many directions, and was reassured in her belief that he was her slave.

'Hullo – how are you?' she said, softly stealing up from a direction in which he had not thought to look, and taking him by surprise.

'Oh, hullo!' he said, and they shook hands.

'Hullo. I hope I'm not late.'

'No. You're just on time, I think,' said Ryan nervously. 'I'm so glad to see you. I thought you mightn't be able to manage it.'

'No. I managed to make it, all right.'

'And how's your little brother? Is he any better?'

Her little brother was beginning to get slightly on Esther's nerves. She never knew what exactly had to be said about his state of health. It had to vary.

'Well – he's better. But he's not all right. And that's why I'm terribly sorry I can't stay very long with you tonight. I'm afraid I'll have to be home about eight-thirty.'

'Oh dear. What a pity. But when somebody's ill, it's got to come first – hasn't it?'

He led her automatically towards the turnstile of the Palace Pier; they went through, and walked seawards.

Ryan was so happy merely because Esther had appeared that he could not be downcast because she had to leave him so soon.

'Yes. It must come first,' said Esther. 'But I'm sure he'll be better very soon now.'

This was said to placate God, and so possibly secure her little brother's endangered life.

'And what did the doctor say?' asked Ryan.

This took Esther completely aback. She had no idea there was a doctor. Gertrude had failed to tell her that she had last night been compelled to invent one.

'Oh,' she said after a slight pause. 'He says he'll be all right. So long as he stays in bed. And he *is* better today, too. A *lot* better.'

(Esther was again speaking to God.)

'Oh well. That's good,' said Ryan.

2   As they walked along Esther looked at him. He had no hat; he still wore grey flannel trousers, and had made few concessions,

if any, to The Nines. All the same he seemed to her to be even more divinely attractive than when she had first met him. His shy manner, too, confirmed her in her suspicion that he was a 'perfect' gentleman – more 'perfect' than Gorse.

But Gorse had the Metropole behind him! He was drinking cocktails in there now. Ryan, hatless and in grey flannel trousers, would never, she imagined, be allowed into the Metropole.

They played at a few slot machines, and walked to the prow of the pier, and then played at a few more slot machines. Although it was getting dark Ryan made no suggestion that they should sit down, and this made the experienced Esther admire him the more. It was a sign either of his shyness, which she so much liked, or conceivably of indifference, which she did not exactly like, but which made him all the more desirable.

When they were somewhere near the middle of the pier Esther asked him the time, and was told it was five past eight. She said that she must be hurrying off, and they walked towards the turnstiles.

'Well,' said Ryan. 'May I meet you again soon? It's been very short this time, and it'd be nice if we could have a bit longer together.'

'Yes,' said Esther. 'Of course you can. Certainly. I'd like it very much.'

'Well, I'll tell you what,' said Ryan. 'I've got an idea. I've just got a new motor bike, and I thought that if you didn't mind sitting on the back – it's very comfortable – we might spend an afternoon in the country together. Would you mind? It's quite easy to sit on the back.'

'No,' said Esther, who had actually sat on the back of more than one motorcycle already. 'I wouldn't mind it at all. I'd like it. But I don't know about an afternoon. I'm a working girl, you know.'

'Yes. But don't you ever get an afternoon off? A Saturday, for instance? Or what about a Sunday?'

'Yes,' said Esther. 'I get each other Saturday.'

'And what about this one?'

'Yes. I'm off this one.'

'Well,' said Ryan. 'Could we meet – do you think? Then I could take you out to the country, and we could have some tea somewhere.'

The day was Thursday.

'Yes. I'd like to. Very much. That's the day after tomorrow, then.'

'Yes. That's right. I'm so glad you can manage it . . . Well, where shall we meet?'

'I don't know. I'd better leave that to you.'

'Well – what about outside the West Pier? About two-thirty. I'll be waiting for you there. And then, if it isn't fine, we might go to a cinema.'

'Yes. That suits me. Two-thirty – outside the West Pier – Saturday afternoon.'

'Yes. That's fine.'

Now Esther realized that the time had come to practise a further deception, one which she had worked out in her mind carefully beforehand.

'Tell me,' she said. 'Will you do me a little favour?'

'Why, yes. Of course I will. I'd do anything. You must know that. You've only got to tell me.'

This was Ryan's first open intimation of his adoration of her.

'Well,' said Esther. 'You know that friend of yours – the sort of ginger-haired one – I think his name's Gorse or something, isn't it?'

'Yes. That's right.'

'Yes. Well – do you meet him a lot? Do you go about a lot together?'

'Yes. We meet quite a lot. Why?'

'Well,' said Esther. 'I know you'll think it's funny – but will you *not tell* him that you've met me tonight and that I'm going out with you on Saturday?'

'Why, yes. Certainly. But why on earth?'

'Well, now, I know it seems ever so funny and silly, but just at present it's a little secret. I've a reason. There's nothing of any importance in it, but it's a little secret. I'll tell you later. But will you do what I say – just for the time being?'

'Yes. Of course. As long as you promise it's not important. And as long as you'll tell me afterwards. Will you?'

'Yes. It's not the tiniest bit important. And I'll tell you after-wards.'

'Promise?'

'Yes. I promise.'

A conscience-stricken Esther was on one hand sorry to have had this promise extracted from her. On the other hand, if Ryan turned out to be all he seemed to be, she certainly meant to tell him everything afterwards. For if Ryan was the Ryan she hoped and believed he was, all this might easily become a matter of Love. And in Love, Esther had always believed, there were no secrets.

'Well – that's all right, then. I promise, too,' said Ryan.

When they were on the front again Ryan asked her whether he might see her home.

'I know your address, you know,' he added.

'Oh – and how do you know that?' asked Esther flirtatiously, because, through Gertrude, she in fact knew how he knew it.

'Well, I asked your friend – Gertrude – last night. Well – may I see you home?'

'No. I'd really rather you didn't – though thanks ever so much. I wouldn't like you to see where *I* live. It's only a slum, you know. Or pretty near it.'

'Well – does that matter? It certainly doesn't to me.'

'Well. It does to me. No – thanks ever so – but I'd really rather go off alone. Well – thanks for the meeting – and I'll see you on Saturday – two-thirty outside the West Pier?'

'Yes. That's right.'

They looked at each other shyly. They did not shake hands. They were already on too exciting and intimate a footing.

'Ta-ta,' said Esther, and 'Good-bye,' said Ryan, and she hastened away.

In order to reach the West Pier again she used the same streets she had used in coming thence, and on the way she reflected deeply upon Ryan and his motorcycle. Quite apart from Ryan's other charms, Ryan's new machine almost cancelled out Gorse's hotel.

Because of her flurried state of mind she was three minutes early for Gorse, who was waiting for her.

They went at once on to the West Pier, and much the same happened as last night. Gorse did a little more 'Silly Ass', and, when they were seated, kissed her again in the same uninhibited way, and Esther found this even more pleasing, or rather less displeasing, than she had the night before.

After this Esther practised the same deception on Gorse as she had practised on Ryan an hour or so earlier. She asked Gorse not to tell Ryan that she and Gorse had met. She said that she had a 'reason' and that it was a 'secret' which she would finally tell him. But whereas with Ryan she did hope finally to confess, she had no such intention with Gorse. She did not at present totally like or trust him: she was merely irresistibly bewitched by his hotel.

Gorse at once promised secrecy. He said he would not have told Ryan in any case.

As they were parting outside the West Pier, Gorse asked her when they might meet again, and then suggested tomorrow evening, Friday. He said he would like to give her cocktails at the Metropole again.

This, of course, suited Esther down to the ground. Ryan had not asked to meet her until Saturday. She agreed; she thanked him for the evening; and, having arranged to meet once more at seven outside the West Pier, they left each other.

At this moment Ryan was already in bed at Tisbury Road, dreaming about Esther. Ryan, blinded by love, absolutely believed in her story about the 'funny' little 'secret' in regard to Gorse. He had given the matter little further thought.

But Gorse, now returning to his room in Norton Road, of course had not believed her story. He had seen Esther meeting Ryan, and he would not have believed it in any case. And, unlike Ryan, he gave the matter a great deal of thought. Gorse was a great thinker.

PART SIX

WELL-WISHER

I

On returning home from work to Over Street, the next evening, Esther's mother told her that there was a letter for her. Her mother said, with an air of discretion, that she had left it in Esther's bedroom.

Miss Downes of Over Street received letters very seldom. And this letter was addressed in a hand unfamiliar to her mother. That was why her mother had had an air of discretion.

Esther, on hearing about this letter in her bedroom, at once thought that it had come from Ryan. He had told her that he knew her address. The idea filled her both with pleasure and fear. She would be delighted to have a letter from him, but it might be one putting off the motorcycling appointment tomorrow afternoon.

What she found inside, when she opened the envelope, completely surprised her.

She found, pasted upon a plain postcard, some letters, mixed with whole words, which had obviously been cut out from a newspaper. These, all askew, went to form the following disgusting (because anonymous) message:

look out *for* **R** y an I KNOw him Do Not go out with him ON cycle d *an* **G** er OuS Take *WARN* in g

A WELL **W**ISHER

Esther did not for a moment suspect that this had come from Gorse.

But, naturally, it had.

Gorse had not, of course, actually known that Ryan would invite Esther to go on his motorcycle. But he had been almost certain that Ryan would do this.

2   Esther's reactions to this communication were those, first of surprise, then of bewilderment, then of fear, and then of panic – a panic which very nearly sent her rushing downstairs to her mother.

But she restrained herself. Her relationship with her mother, as regards the matter of young men, was, although loving and sincere, rather strange, shy, and furtive.

Esther's mother was fully aware of Esther's beauty, and she had on more than one occasion given Esther advice upon the serious dangers which attended this. Esther had always promised her mother that she completely understood these dangers. Her mother had then said that she completely trusted Esther in every way.

For this reason Mrs Downes, although she knew that a great deal took place on the Brighton Front, and the West Pier, made a point of questioning Esther as little as possible. As a consequence a kind of convention had at last arisen between them that nothing should be said at all about these things. And so Esther did not at once rush downstairs to her mother.

Instead she began to dress for her meeting with Gorse at seven-thirty. Doing this soothed her, and to a certain extent assuaged her feeling of fear. It also prevented her temporarily from giving the matter too much thought.

As soon as she had left the house, however, and was on her way to the West Pier she began to think violently.

Now her fear had left her, but this was replaced by that sort of nausea, that overhanging pall of filth and evil which an anonymous letter always creates – even if it is not (and this one was not) of a threatening nature.

The main question was, of course, who on *earth* could have *sent* it?

Who on earth knew about her meeting with Ryan yesterday? Who had *watched* them? Could it be, possibly, some boy of her own class to whom she had in the past rejected or been cruel? She had a few such boys on her conscience. Moreover, she felt certain that message was of low-class origin. It had a slum air about it.

She had looked at the envelope and had seen that it had been posted in Portslade. But she knew no one in Portslade. And, of course, the poster might have been careful to post it far away from where he lived.

Then, who on *earth* could know that Ryan had a motorcycle?

Who, but Gorse?

Or the other spectacled one? She could not bring herself to believe that the latter had done this. He was not the sort of boy who 'counted' enough to get up to such a thing.

But what about Gorse? He would know about the motorcycle, and she still faintly distrusted him.

Could he possibly be capable of such infamy?

She thought it just possible – only just.

But, on the other hand, what could his motive be? He knew nothing about her meeting last night with Ryan (Esther, of course, was wrong here) and so he could not in any way be jealous.

Or did Gorse in fact know that Ryan was 'dangerous'? And had he, for some obscure reason, chosen this way of warning her?

And *was* Ryan dangerous? She simply could not bring herself to believe this.

And yet had not her mother often told her, and had she not often read, that the greatest villains are usually infinitely more plausible and charming than others?

And dangerous in what way? If she went out into the country with him, would he attempt to assault her? Or kill her? Or both? Esther was a reader of *The News of the World*.

Or dangerous merely in the sense of being a seducer and trifler? She was quite sure she could deal with *that* sort of thing.

But she did not believe that the message intended to convey this lighter meaning. She was certain that dangerous in the fullest sense of the term was being conveyed to her.

It was all hideously disturbing, and she was so upset that she was outside the West Pier six minutes before the time, and Gorse was not there.

He arrived three minutes later, saying politely that he hoped he was not late, and she had to concede that he was not. This normally would have annoyed Esther, as she would not normally have liked to be found 'hanging about', three minutes too early, for any young man. Tonight, however, she was too upset even to think about it.

Gorse, after his success the night before last, had now completely lost his fear of the Metropole, and he was loquacious and cheerful as they walked along towards it. But Esther was distracted, and could only answer him briefly. Gorse noticed this in Esther, and, as the sender of the anonymous message, suspected its cause.

As they went through the revolving doors and entered the Oriental palace Esther was still so worried that she was not in the smallest way impressed by its splendour. She walked and behaved like one who went into the Metropole every evening of her life.

The table they had found the night before last was again vacant, and they sat down at it. The same waiter served them with the same drinks.

Esther had not taken many sips at her own before she began to experience that warm, confident feeling which had come upon her that other time. She was still very worried indeed, but inclined to look upon her trouble more lightly.

By the time the second drink had appeared Esther was not only feeling confident: she was feeling confiding.

Why not, she thought, confide in Gorse?

It was all but inconceivable that he could have sent so foul a message. And, even if he had (but he *couldn't* have!), there would be no harm in confiding in him.

She would, she was sure, be able to detect any deception on his part. Esther thought that she was very clever at this sort of thing.

And then, if he was innocent, which she was certain he was, he might be able to give her some advice – which she seriously needed. She decided to confide in him.

This involved some humiliation and confession.

'Listen,' she said. 'I'm afraid I've got something to confess to you.'

'Oh. What's that?'

'I hope it won't make you angry.'

'I'm sure it won't. Go on.'

'Well – you know when we made that secret appointment to go to the Metropole together . . . ?'

'Yes. Go on.'

'Well – the next day I told Gertrude to make an excuse to your friend Peter Ryan. I don't know why I did it. I suppose I just thought I was being rather mean – not turning up – and I don't know for the life of me why I didn't tell you – really.'

'Yes. Go on. Anything worse?'

'Yes. Quite a lot . . . Well, Gertrude met him and he asked her if he could meet me outside the Palace Pier the next evening. And

I don't know why – I suppose I felt sorry for him or something – but I thought I *would* meet him – just for a little while. And so I came and told a fib to you.'

'About your little brother?'

'Yes. Are you angry?'

'No. Not a bit. Anything more?'

'Yes ... There's still a lot. Well, I *did* meet him, and he asked me if I'd go out on his motor bike into the country on Saturday. That's tomorrow.'

'Yes? ...'

'Well – and then I came back to you at the West Pier. I don't know why I didn't tell you, and I'm sorry. I was afraid you'd be angry, I suppose. I was just being silly.'

'Yes. It was a little silly – I'll admit that. You see what trouble one gets into if one doesn't tell the truth? I didn't believe in that little brother story for a moment.'

'Didn't you? Why not?'

Esther was not altogether pleased to learn of her failure as a liar.

'Oh – I don't really know,' said Gorse. 'I just didn't. But go on. If there's any more.'

'Yes, there is. I'm just coming to the real point – now I've confessed.'

'Well? ...'

'Well – I made this appointment to meet your friend, you see – and then, this evening, I got a most horrible letter – if you can call it a letter.'

'Really? What was it about?'

'Well, I've got it on me, if you'd like to see it. Would you?'

'Yes. I would. Certainly.'

Esther produced it from her bag, and handed it to him.

Gorse took the card from her, and looked at it. Then, feigning bewilderment and short sight, he took out his 'Silly Ass' monocle from his waistcoat pocket and looked at it again. The glass of his monocle was quite plain. Later in life he was clever enough to have a lens made.

'Ah,' said Gorse after scrutinizing the document from several angles for more than a minute. 'Most interesting, very interesting indeed.'

There was a pause.

'Well – what do you think about it?' said Esther impatiently.

'I don't really know. Just at the moment,' said Gorse. 'But on first

thoughts I'd say that there are just two things you ought to do with
something of this sort.'

'What? Which two?'

'Well – one is to put it straight into the wastepaper basket and
forget about it. And the other is to take it straight to the police.
They're nasty things – anonymous communications – like this.'

With his mention of the police, and by his general attitude, Gorse
completely duped Esther. She had, now, not the slightest doubt that
Gorse was not the originator of the situation.

'Oh – I don't want to go to the Police,' said Esther, rapidly and
with determination. The very idea of the Police scared the humble
Miss Downes out of her wits. And, when she had been naughty as
a child, her mother and father had often frightened her with the
Police.

'Well, then, put it into the wastepaper basket.'

'Yes. But what if it's *true*? What if there *is* something dangerous
about him? Should I go out in the country on his bike?'

'Ah, yes,' said Gorse. 'I was coming to that aspect of the matter.
Now that, I must admit, is a differing thing.'

'What do *you* know about him? You were all three at school
together, weren't you? Do you *know* anything about him?'

'Well, we were only at school at Hove together. I've written to
him since then, but I haven't seen him all the time I was at –' (Here
Gorse inadvertently very nearly said St Paul's but saved himself in
time.) 'Westminster,' said Gorse.

Along with Gorse's astuteness there was, occasionally, a curious
folly and lack of caution. He had worn an old Westminster tie for
Esther's benefit. Now it was quite possible that he and Ryan and
Bell and Esther might meet again, and that Esther might mention
that he had been to Westminster. In which case Ryan and Bell, who
knew for a fact that he had been to St Paul's, might easily expose
him.

All impostors, of course, must take risks: but this particular risk
had never even entered Gorse's head.

'Yes,' said Esther. 'But you did know him at your first school,
and you know him now. Do you *know* anything about him?'

'Well, now, that's not quite a fair question, is it? If I did know
anything against him it wouldn't be right for me to tell tales about
a friend – would it?'

'Yes. I think it would. You're my friend, too, aren't you? And I'm
really very worried. I think it'd only be fair to *me*.'

'Ah – I don't know about that,' said Gorse, putting his fingers together, leaning back in his chair, and looking at her in a manner which hinted that he had a good deal to tell if he could.

Esther rose to this suggestion in his eye.

'I believe you *do* know something, you know. Come on. You must tell me. If you do. Do you?'

'Well, now,' said Gorse, still looking at her meaningly. 'That's rather difficult to say, you know.'

'No, it isn't. Not if it's going to help me it isn't – is it? Go on. Say it.'

'Well, I'll say this much, at any rate,' said Gorse. 'I don't personally really trust Ryan. And I don't really think he's the sort of person *you* should trust.'

'But *why*?'

'Oh – it's only just a feeling – probably. Perhaps I'm doing him an injustice.'

'No. There's something else. You know something more. Go on. Tell me.'

'Well . . .'

'Yes?'

'Well. There *were* some rather funny things which took place at school – I'll admit that.'

'What sort of funny things?'

'Oh. Just funny things.'

'But what? Did he steal or something?'

'No. He didn't *steal*.'

'Well, *what*, then?'

Gorse paused.

'You know, really it's not the sort of thing I'd like to discuss.'

'But you *must*!'

'No – it's not the sort of thing.'

Esther braced herself to speak more boldly.

'But you must. Tell me. Go on. Was it something to do with ¬' said Esther, here hesitating before she took the plunge. '*Sex*?'

'What made you think that?'

'I don't know. It just came into my mind. Was it?'

Gorse did not answer.

'Go on,' said Esther. 'Was it? Because if you don't answer you make me think it was. Go on.'

'Well . . .'

'Go on.'

'Well . . . Yes.'

There was a pause.

'What *sort* of thing to do with sex? Come on, now. Tell me. We're both grown up, after all.'

'No. Now you're going too far. That's not the sort of thing a gentleman discusses with a girl.'

'But what was it? How could it make him "dangerous", as that beastly card says? Could it?'

'Well . . . it *could*. But I really don't want to go on talking about this.'

'You mustn't go on mystifying me like this. Tell me. Something about sex?'

'Well,' said Gorse. 'I'll tell you this much. I think Ryan thinks a little too much about sex. We all do, of course. I do myself. But Ryan carries it a little bit too far, and he's not at all scrupulous in the methods he uses of getting what he wants. There, now, that's enough for you, surely.'

'No. It's not. I want to know if *you* think he's dangerous, and if I ought to go out with him tomorrow.'

Gorse was again silent.

'Well. *Do* you?' said Esther.

'Do you want me to tell the truth?'

'Yes.'

'Well. I don't think you should. It *might* be all right, but I wouldn't advise it. Not after you've received this card. It's signed Well-Wisher, and he may really know something. I have a feeling that things have got worse since Ryan's school days. Now – let's leave the subject, shall we?'

'But I can't leave it. I've got to make up my mind about to-morrow!'

'Well – you've been given my strong advice. You must just take it or leave it. And so now let's drop the subject, shall we? Will you?'

'Well, I suppose I must. If you say so. But it's very worrying. Who on earth could have *sent* the letter?'

'Well – that's the mystery. It couldn't be Ryan, of course . . .'

'No. Of course it couldn't.'

'But it might, of course,' said Gorse humorously, 'be Me.'

'Don't be so silly.'

'But it *might*, you know. Didn't that ever strike you?'

'Yes, it did. Just for a moment – if you want the truth. But of course I know it's absurd, now.'

'Well, it is actually, you know. If I'd wanted to warn you I could have done it by word of mouth – very easily – couldn't I? I wouldn't have sat up all night pasting bits of a newspaper on to a postcard. It must be hard work – finding the words and letters – apart from the pasting.'

'Yes. It must. That's what makes it so beastly. Do you think it could be that other friend of yours – the one in spectacles?'

'Bell? . . . No,' said Gorse benignly. 'I don't think poor Bell would do a thing like that.'

'Did *he* know about this – Sex thing?'

'I don't really know. Possibly.'

'Then he *might* have done it. He seems to have got a pretty funny mind – with all his jabber, jabber, jabber about Poetry and all that.'

'No. I think we can exclude Bell. I like and trust Bell, in spite of his eccentricities,' said Gorse. 'He's not the type – although one can never be absolutely sure with human nature – can one?'

'No. And it must be a pretty low type. It couldn't be a gentleman. The whole thing *looks* sort of uneducated – doesn't it?'

'It certainly does.'

'That's what makes me think it might be someone in *my* class. But how could they know about the *motor bike* and all that?'

'Yes. It's all very baffling, I must say. But I'm very sorry you began to suspect me.'

'Don't be so silly. But you see that's what a thing like this does to one. It makes you suspect *everyone*, and it sort of hits at you every way – if you see what I mean.'

'Yes. I certainly do.'

'And so your advice is for me not to go tomorrow?'

'Yes. That's my advice. My *very* strong advice.'

'Well. I'll have to think about it.'

'Yes. It's for you to make up your mind. But if you *should* decide to go, by the way, I hope you won't tell him what I've said about him. I still feel in a way I shouldn't have told you.'

'No. Of course I won't. I wouldn't dream of it.'

'And if I were you, I wouldn't dream of going. But that's your business. Now let's change the subject – shall we?'

'Yes. Let's.'

But Esther could not change the subject – at least not with any pleasure. She kept on coming back to it.

Tonight she was so distraught that she finished her own second cocktail, and, though she felt a little dizzy, the drink did not go to her head as it had last night.

Then Gorse suggested that they should go, and they rose and went out into the air.

'Where are we going?' said Esther, and it was clear to Gorse that in her present state of mind she had no desire to go on the West Pier and repeat the performance of the two previous evenings. He was wise enough not to invite her to do such a thing. He stopped.

'You know, I don't think you feel like the Pier tonight – do you?' he said. 'I think you'd rather go home – wouldn't you?'

'You know, I honestly think I would. I don't want to disappoint you, but I'd really rather. It's very nice of you to think of it. Would you mind if I did?'

'No. But may I see you home?'

'Well. Part of the way.' She smiled. 'You know I don't want you to see where I live. Come with me as far as the Clock Tower – will you? That's quite near where I am.'

'Very well. Always your humble obedient servant. To the Clock Tower.'

When they reached the Clock Tower Esther said, 'Well – here we are,' and Gorse asked her when he might meet her again.

'Well – I don't think tomorrow – do you? I still *might* decide to go out with him. What about the day after?'

'Very well. That'll be Sunday. What about seven-thirty again, outside the West Pier? And then we'll go to the Metropole.'

'Yes. That'd be lovely. You're ever so good to me. And thank you ever so for the evening, although it was a little bit spoilt. Good-bye, then, and thank you again.'

And feeling suddenly grateful for his kindness, his generosity with his cocktails at the Metropole, and the fact that she had him at least to turn to in her trouble, she impulsively kissed him on the cheek. Then she ran away.

This was the first time that Esther had ever been the first to kiss a young man. She had made a strange choice in the one she had singled out for such an honour.

Gorse returned to Norton Road very deeply satisfied with the evening, the success of his schemes, and his knowledge that he had entirely deluded Esther.

What, it may be wondered, were Gorse's motives in all this? They were, roughly, threefold.

He had no particular feeling for Esther. His vicious kisses were feigned. Lovely as she was, there was no question of his being in love with her. Gorse was never, in all his life, capable of sentimental emotion. But he knew that she was lovely, that she dressed beautifully, and that in a right setting, such as that of the Metropole, she definitely 'passed'. Hence he liked to be seen with her: everybody looked at her with admiration, and then, of course, looked at him and envied him. In this way she was an asset: and he had no intention of losing her. He was only just trying his wings in places like the Metropole, and she was of the greatest assistance to him. Such was his first motive.

Not being in love with her, he was not particularly jealous of Ryan. He saw, however, that Ryan was a danger, and he had taken steps to meet this danger. This was his second motive.

His third motive, however, was really much more powerful and irresistible than the other two. It was the sheer pleasure of scheming and deceiving, of knowing that he alone possessed a secret – and one with which he could wield secret power.

He had almost intoxicated himself with pleasure while pasting those letters on to the card. He had found it much more deliciously easy than he had expected. He had done it from only one evening paper. He had easily found the 'Ryan' (which he had thought might be considerably difficult) by using an 'R' and 'Y' (in headline letters) – followed by the first two letters of the word 'and'. And the rest had been child's play.

He was even more exhilarated by the restraint and brilliance of his performance with Esther at the Metropole this evening.

He did not think that Esther would meet Ryan tomorrow. His schemes had succeeded. He had, as he put it to himself in his own dirty way, 'done the trick all right'.

II

Gorse, for once, was wrong.

Esther, for some reason – possibly some obscure physical cause – woke up in a peculiarly calm frame of mind the next morning.

The anonymous card, she found as she dressed, was not anything like the horribly disturbing thing she had found it last night. She even thought that she had made a mountain out of a molehill.

This balanced mood continued as she worked at the sweet-shop. She was very busy because it was Saturday morning and the trippers were in full force. And hard, bustling work soothes the mind in much the same way as cocktails do.

A picture of Ryan was in her mind almost incessantly as she worked, and she simply could not bring herself to believe that he was what the author of the anonymous message had said he was. And, if he was not, what right had she to break the appointment? Would he not be infinitely pathetic – desolate – if she forsook him? And did he not know her address and be bound to continue his pursuit in any case?

And did she not, very nearly at any rate, Love him – like him a hundred times more than any other boy she had met?

And if he *was* 'dangerous' – could he be so in public? Clearly not. What was his present idea of what they should do this afternoon? He had suggested that they should go out on his motorcycle and 'have tea somewhere'. Well – he certainly couldn't do anything 'dangerous' while she was on the back of the motorcycle. Nor could he do anything in a tea-shop.

But what about Quiet Lanes? What about Shady Nooks? What about Woods? Suppose he invited her into one of these? Well, she could always refuse to accompany him. She could make some excuse to keep him in the open. And if he insisted she could become angry and leave him.

Finally, was she not in duty bound to defy an anonymous letter writer? Was not such a one so low a creature that he (or it might be a she) must be treated only with the supremest contempt?

Esther at last made up her mind to meet Ryan.

2   Ryan was outside the West Pier twelve minutes before the time. He filled in the time he had to wait for Esther with polishing and playing with his delightful new machine.

So absorbed was he in this that he did not notice the arrival of Esther, who was herself early.

Men are at their best when quietly absorbed in the workings of a machine. There is something charming, disinterested, and child-like about it. Her heart grew even warmer towards him than ever before as she approached him. Oh – if only that *filthy* thing had never been sent to her!

'Hullo,' she said, completely surprising him. 'Is that the bike?'

'Oh. Hullo!' he said. 'I didn't see you. Yes. This is it. What do you think of it?'

'It looks lovely to me. I'll bet you aren't half proud of it – aren't you?'

'Yes. I must say I am, a bit.'

They gazed at it.

'Yes. It's lovely,' said Esther.

'Well,' said Ryan at last. 'Where would you like me to take you with it?'

'Anywhere you like. I'll leave it to you.'

'Well, I'll tell you what. I have an idea. Do you know Hassocks? It's a little village about seven miles from here.'

'Yes. I've heard of it. I've never been there.'

'Well, I thought we might go there. And then go on to Hurst – do you know Hurst? – for tea. Do you know Hurst? It's about three miles away from Hassocks, and I know a tea-shop there.'

'Yes. That sounds fine.'

'You see, I was born at Hassocks, and I know all the walks round there. There're some lovely walks all about there.'

Esther did not this time reply that this sounded fine. She was far too frightened. Some Lovely Walks. Did not Lovely Walks possibly imply Quiet Lanes, Shady Nooks, Woods?

'Oh – are there?' she said.

'Yes. I thought we might go for one, if you liked.'

'Yes,' said Esther, and added awkwardly, 'Well – we'll see when we get there – shall we?'

This rather mysterious remark made Ryan glance at her. And, of course, the glance, innocent as it was, again frightened Esther. She read it as a glance with some meaning behind it – she did not know what exactly.

'Well – let's start, shall we? Now – I'll get on, and then you get on. I think you'll find it quite comfortable. Have you ever done this before?'

'Yes. I have. Once or twice.'

'Oh . . . Good.'

Soon they had adjusted themselves and started. Ryan made for the London Road.

'It's a glorious day – isn't it?' Ryan shouted back to her against the noise of the machine.

'Yes. It is!' she yelled.

After this they said practically nothing until they were past Preston Park and approaching the country. Then Esther spoke.

'Where's the walk you're thinking of taking me?' she asked. 'Have you got a special one in mind?'

'Yes. I have, as a matter of fact. It's where I used to walk as a child. It's along by the railway line. I love walking by railways – don't you?' Both were yelling, of course.

'Yes. I do.'

'It's what we used to call the Cinder Path when I lived there. It may be still, for all I know.'

'The Cinder Path?' said Esther, and added. 'You mean a sort of *public* Path.'

'Yes. That's right.'

Again Ryan thought there was something curious in what she said, but he was, of course, unable to glance at her. Esther was slightly reassured by his assurance that the Path was public. All the same she still wondered about Quiet Lanes, Shady Nooks, and Woods leading from this Path.

Now the Gorse-created evil of Ryan's situation resided in this. He was a young man in love – desperately and sentimentally so. And what, pray, is a young man in such a condition likely to think of most when taking the loved out into the country? What, but Quiet Lanes, Shady Nooks, and Woods?

He had, in fact, a Wood in mind. It adjoined the Cinder Path. Here he had picked primroses as a child, and here he proposed to take Esther. He meant, furthermore, to take her into the middle of this wood, and tell her that he loved her. Then, if she would permit such a thing, he would kiss her. And then, if his wildest hopeful dreams came true, she might consent to be his own. She might become *Engaged* to him! Or, failing that, Promise to Think about it.

He knew that a romantic setting was necessary for this, and so he had chosen his Wood carefully.

Because he loved Esther so much he was desperately afraid of the immediate future, but he was swearing to himself, as he drove along, that he would show courage and determination.

Ryan had never before taken a girl into a Wood, Nook, or Lane. But girls had more than once made him go, reluctantly, into such places; and because this had happened he did, at moments, have a feeling of confidence.

3   At the entrance to the Cinder Path Ryan stopped, and both dismounted.

He left his motorcycle at the side of the road.

The Cinder Path at Hassocks runs southwards, parallel to the Southern Railway, and very near it. It is little frequented on week-days, but on Saturday afternoons Hassocks villagers and others use it a good deal.

This was Saturday afternoon, and, to Esther's unspeakable relief, a dozen or more people had passed them before they had been walking a quarter of a mile along it.

Ryan's Wood, however, was about three quarters of a mile away, and, as they approached it, people became scarce.

They stopped, every now and again, to watch a passing train, and talked about trains. Ryan was an expert on trains (his father and himself shared a model railway), and he interested Esther with his talk and explanations.

But, at last (and alas!) the Wood was reached. It was on their left and could be entered without difficulty at any point. Ryan began to talk less and less. Esther talked less, too. She had noticed that Ryan was talking less, and she had noticed that, on their left, was a Wood which could be entered without difficulty at any point.

At last Ryan found his courage.

'Let's go in here, shall we?' he said. 'It's awfully pretty. This is where I used to pick primroses when I was a child.'

And he led the way into an easy path through the wood. Esther, trying so hard to think quickly that she was unable to think, followed him.

She had, though, seen a man walking at a distance along the Cinder Path in their direction. Otherwise she probably would not have followed Ryan.

When they had walked about fifteen yards into the wood, Esther suddenly stopped and looked around at the trees.

'Yes. It's ever so pretty,' said Esther, and she tried to make every motion of her eyes and body imply that it was very nice to have gone fifteen yards into a wood in which he had once picked primroses, but that it was now obviously time that they returned to the public path by the railway.

Ryan immediately sensed that she did not want to go any further. But they were fifteen yards inside, and not visible to a passer-by. Therefore, summoning up all the courage he had promised himself all the afternoon that he would, he said: 'Well, shall we sit down for a bit? I'm a bit tired, I don't know about you. It looks quite dry and cosy here. Shall we?'

He indicated a dry place on the ground, filled with last year's leaves.

Esther said 'Yes,' and, with Ryan's assistance, sat down.

Ryan sat beside her.

The man in the distance, Esther reflected, must be much nearer by now. And they were, after all, very near the path by the railway, and other people must soon be passing.

Ryan began to talk – again about trains. He had never thought that his knowledge of trains would be of such service to him.

But trains were not enough. Something else had to be said or done. He forced himself to do it. He put his hand upon hers as he talked.

Esther did not at once withdraw her hand. One of the reasons for this was that her attention was at the moment elsewhere. She was listening to the sound of footsteps. They were obviously those of the man whom she had seen in the distance.

She heard him (but there was no way of seeing him) as he came striding by.

Then his footsteps died away, and there was complete silence.

There was not even the sound of a distant train. Also, Ryan had stopped talking. He was looking at her.

She drew her hand away, and uttered meaninglessly the word 'Yes . . .'

Ryan pretended not to notice this, and went on talking. Then he took her hand again.

Once more, because she heard people approaching, she let him retain her hand. Then the people passed, and she took it away.

But he persisted, and a few minutes later once more tried to take her hand. But this time she drew it away at once.

'You mustn't do that,' she said.

'Why not?' asked Ryan.

'I don't know you well enough,' said Esther feebly.

Now the Gorse-created evil of Esther's situation was this. She was enormously attracted to Ryan. She wanted him to hold her hand. She even wanted him to kiss her – a thing she had never really desired from any young man in her life before. But what is a young girl, confronted with her Prince Charming, to do, when she suspects that the latter may be a dangerous lunatic, a sex-maniac, some kind of *News of the World* slaughterer? She remembered Gorse's warning, as well as the anonymous letter.

If she let him hold her hand, it would be definitely encouraging him. It would lead to further things, and the hypothetical maniac might be seized by his mania.

'I know you don't know me well,' said Ryan, making no further attempt to take her hand. 'But a lot can happen in a little time, can't it?'

There was a pause.

'*What* can happen?' asked Esther.

'Well – one can get attracted – can't one? May I call you by your Christian name?'

'Yes. If you like.'

'Well – Esther – well, you see, it's hard to explain. But there *is* such a thing as love at first sight, isn't there?'

'Is there?'

'Yes. You know there is. Do you know the words of the old song:

> 'I did but see her passing by
> And yet I love her till I *die*?

Well – that's what's happened to me, that's all.'

Esther did not like his use or stressing of the word 'die'. To begin with, it reminded her unpleasantly of death! And it was too passionate a thing to say at this stage of their acquaintanceship. It confirmed her fears.

'Well,' she said. 'I don't know what to say.'

'Don't you like me at all?'

'But I don't know you. I don't know anything *about* you.'

'But that's not the point. The point is do you like me?'

'I don't know.'

'Well – do you think you could *come* to like me? Do you think if we went on meeting you could *come* to like me?'

'I don't know. I'd have to know more *about* you.'

'Why do you keep on saying that? I mean about knowing *about* me. There's nothing particular to know about me. I'm just an ordinary person, and I'm terribly in love with you.'

'Well, then I want to know you better, let's say.'

'Well, I hope you will. Tell me. Is there anybody else? There must have been dozens of people in love with you – but is there anybody *you're* in love with?'

Esther hesitated before replying. Suppose, she thought, it was later somehow proved that Ryan was incapable of wickedness, that the anonymous sender of the letter was the foul slanderer which such a person must almost certainly be, and that Gorse was mistaken? Surely she must give Ryan some sort of chance. And if, now, she said there was somebody else, she would lose him. He was (if innocent) not the type to persevere after being told such a thing, Esther imagined.

'No,' she said. 'I don't know that there's anybody.'

'Oh – then there *is* some hope, then. Say there is.'

'I don't know . . .'

Here Ryan made a fatal error.

'Oh – *do* say there is,' he said, and seized her hand – this time more violently. Worse still, when she tried to release it, he did not immediately permit her to do so.

There was, indeed, something not far removed from a struggle, and Esther, when her hand was released, at once rose.

Ryan rose too.

'I'm sorry,' he said. 'I'm really sorry.'

'It's all right,' said Esther. 'But I think we'd better be getting on – don't you?'

'Yes. Perhaps we'd better. I'm sorry. Let's go back to the bike, and then we'll have tea.'

Thus Gorse, after all, had 'done the trick' – temporarily, at any rate. If it had not been for this young man's crafty intervention Esther would have allowed Ryan to hold her hand, and afterwards to have kissed her. And after that, almost certainly, it would not have been long before Ryan would have realized his ultimate ambition. They would have become 'engaged'.

But instead of this they walked back to the path by the railway, and then returned in the direction of his motorcycle.

Ryan changed the subject. He was not utterly crestfallen. He thought that Esther's attitude might easily derive from maidenly coyness, and that he still might have a chance. There was, though, in her attitude, something which he could not define and which slightly puzzled him.

He told her some things about his childhood, and she told him something about her own.

When they were not far away from the motorcycle, he pointed out that it was Sunday tomorrow. Because of this she would be free, and perhaps able to meet him. He asked her if he might take her to the Palladium Cinema in the evening. There was a film he particularly wanted to see, and would like her to see.

Esther remembered that she was meeting Gorse tomorrow evening. She would have liked nothing better than to go to the Palladium with Ryan. There could be no 'danger' in that. But she could not do so, and had, she supposed, to tell another lie.

She was seized suddenly with a violent revulsion against these incessant falsehoods. Why not, for once, tell the truth – and afterwards tell Gorse that she had done so? She saw nothing against it, and attempted it.

'Well, that's going to be difficult,' she said. 'You know that friend of yours. His name's Gorse, isn't it?'

'Yes.'

'Well, I ran into him last night – quite by accident.'

Esther saw that, in her magnificent attempt at truth-telling, she had told yet another lie. Oh – what *was* she to do!

'Yes?' said Ryan.

'And he took me to have a drink at the Metropole.'

'The Metropole!' said Ryan. 'I say – *he's* going it a bit – isn't he?'

'Yes. I suppose he is. And he asked me if I'd meet him tomorrow for another drink. And I don't see how I can let him down, really. You don't mind, do you?'

'No, not a bit,' said Ryan. 'But why didn't you tell me before?'

'It just didn't come into my head.'

Another lie, thought Esther.

'Where did you run into him?' asked Ryan, slightly suspicious and disturbed.

'Oh – on the front. Between the two piers.'

And another!

'And what did you have to drink?'

'Oh – Gin and It, I think it was.'

'How many did you have? Didn't it go to your head?'

'No. I was all right. We only had one.'

And another.

'And what did you do afterwards?'

'Oh – we just said good-bye outside the Metropole.'

And another still.

Truth, it seemed, was out of the question, beyond her powers. She had told him that she had had only one drink, because she did not want him to be shocked. And she had told him that Gorse had left her outside the Metropole, because she did not want to hurt him by letting him know that Gorse had escorted her most of the way home – a privilege she had not granted Ryan on Thursday. She did not want Ryan to think that she was in any way interested in Gorse.

Now they had reached the motorcycle. They mounted it and drove off towards Hurst.

This was a great relief to Esther.

The noise of the machine excused her from talking, and so, briefly, from telling further lies.

4   It was only after they were seated at the tea-shop in Hurst, and after the tea and bread-and-butter and cakes had been put before them, and Esther (being 'Mother') had poured out the tea, that something occurred to her which, for some extraordinary reason, had never occurred to her before.

Why should she not tell Ryan about the anonymous postcard and give him a chance to defend himself? And why had it never crossed her mind to do so?

This was precisely what these hideous communications did to one. In addition to all else, they threw you off your balance – robbed you of your normal reasoning powers.

What could be wrong with this proposition? She looked at Ryan. He was eating his bread-and-butter, and sipping at his tea, and looking out of the window at the pretty garden with a sort of dejection and quietness which touched her heart immeasurably. Why should she not put him out of his pain – and, perhaps, by candour – and fearlessness and truthfulness – escape from her own pain?

Something held her back. There were, after all, reasons why she should not do this. In the first place, if he was in fact guilty and 'dangerous', he would certainly not confess that he was. He would lie with all the charming plausibility which he so obviously possessed.

Then (supposing he *were* 'dangerous') Esther perceived that above all things she must be cautious. She must think about it carefully; and this she could not possibly do while sitting with him over a tea-table.

Then, supposing he was innocent, she was afraid of offending or disgusting him. Her real belief still was that the postcard came from someone in her own class – her own low class. Would not a gentleman, and particularly a 'perfect' gentleman, be so horrified by such a thing that he would decide to abandon her, utterly disconnect himself from such slum-filth?

This was all getting too much for Esther. To whom could she go for help?

At this point it occurred to her that she might tell her mother.

Then she decided that she would do this. She loved and trusted her mother, who had always told her never to tell lies, and who, as a wise woman, might extract her from those upon which she had embarked.

5   After tea, a subdued Ryan peacefully drove her back to Brighton.

There was a discussion as to where he should leave her. Ryan knew that Over Street was near Brighton Station, and suggested the Station itself. To this Esther agreed.

Ryan had a minor motive in naming Brighton Station. Here, he knew, he could get the latest edition of the evening paper. He was anxious to read the Cricket Results. At Ryan's age such things as Cricket Results can enter the head of even the most dejected or frenzied lover.

When they had got off the machine Ryan told her that he wanted to buy a paper and asked her if she would accompany him to the stall in the Station. She consented.

But she had no sooner done so than she regretted it. She had remembered that she might easily encounter her father inside the Station, and she did not want to be seen by him with a young man. Esther's father, unlike her mother, had no tacit mutual arrangement about her young men. Esther's father, really, was not supposed to know that young men happened at all. (And, in fact, he was too busy a man to know fully that they did.)

When he had bought his paper Ryan made the foolish and unnecessary mistake of trying to say good-bye inside the Station.

'Well,' he said. 'I suppose this is good-bye, isn't it? Just for the present. When can I see you again? Tomorrow evening seems to be out – *so what about the evening after that?*'

Because of a great noise of engines, and because of the flood of returning Saturday trippers, almost bumping into them, Ryan raised his voice.

Esther, already alarmed by the thought of her father seeing her, was further disconcerted by Ryan's raised voice, and the noise of the engines, and the danger of trippers bumping into them – so much so that she could hardly think. She had promised to go out alone with Gertrude one night early in the week, but she could not remember which night this was.

'I don't know,' she shouted back. 'I've got to go out with Gertrude one night. I just can't think at the moment.'

And now a sort of panic seized both of them. Standing where they were, in the midst of the noise and bustle, they both got the impression that one or the other of them had to catch a train. Moreover, they quite madly thought that the train was going out at once, and that they had only a few seconds in which to speak.

It was this insane unconscious impression which had originally panicked Ryan into saying good-bye here instead of peacefully outside.

Esther, too, imagined that she had seen her father at a distance – her father coming in their direction.

What if her father came up and spoke to them? Such a thing was extremely likely, and then she would be shamed doubly. There would be the shame of being discovered by her father with a young man, and the shame which would be caused by Ryan seeing that her father was a member of a low profession – that of a porter. In addition to this, Esther knew that her father, apart from his being a porter, had the appearance of a low person. He was bowed, and he wore a moustache which he frequently neglected to wipe.

And so her panic increased. All she wanted to do was get away. And when Ryan said, 'Well – couldn't you *think* of a day?' all she could reply was, 'No. I don't know. I can't think.'

Esther's panic had increased Ryan's.

'But you *must* think!' he shouted against a violently hissing engine. It was as if he were speaking harshly, and shouting – not against the engine – but at Esther. This further frightened, and slightly offended her.

'But I can't. Just at the moment. And I *must* go, you know,' said Esther, again thinking that her father might be upon them at any moment. 'I'm ever so late.'

'But when are we going to *meet*?' cried Ryan in despair.

It still did not occur to either of them that they might walk out of the Station to his motorcycle, and there say good-bye and make their arrangements peacefully.

'I don't know,' said Esther, looking at him miserably.

The atmosphere of trains and journey-taking gave Ryan an inspiration.

'Well, can I *write* to you?' he said. 'I know your address.'

'Yes. That's right. You can write to me. You know my address.'

'All right. I'll write. And you'll answer, won't you?'

'Yes. I'll answer all right.'

'Promise?'

'Yes. I promise.'

'All right, then. Well, I suppose it's good-bye for the present.'

'Yes. I suppose it is. Well – good-bye, then.'

She shook hands with him and fled from the Station.

As soon as she was back at Over Street and had calmed down, Esther perceived that she had yet again failed to thank a young man for taking her out. Esther, whose ambition it was to behave like a 'lady' in whatever circumstances, bitterly reproached herself for this omission.

Ryan, deeply disturbed, went into the Station Buffet and had yet another cup of tea.

Upset as Ryan was, however, he did not fail to open his paper and look at the Cricket Results.

PART SEVEN

SAVINGS

I

Gorse was in excellent form when Esther met him on the following Sunday evening, and he took her with great dash to the same table at the Metropole.

'Well, what news on the Rialto?' he said, when their drinks had come. 'Eh?'

And he stuck his monocle into his eye and looked at her ruminatively.

He was really seeking to confirm his conviction that his ruse had succeeded, and that Esther had not gone into the country with Ryan.

'I don't think there's any, really,' said Esther. 'At least none of any importance.'

Something evasive in the way Esther said this gave Gorse an idea that his ruse had failed after all. He came straight to the point.

'Did you go out with our friend Ryan?' he asked. 'Against your Uncle Ralph's advice?'

'Oh yes. I'd forgotten about all that.' (But Esther had not forgotten about all that.) 'I *did* go, as a matter of fact, after all. I thought I was making a mountain out of a molehill, and that I knew how to look after myself, and so I decided to go after all.'

'Oh – you did – did you?'

'Yes. And – oh – by the way, there's something I ought to tell you.'

'Oh – what's that?'

'It's not of any importance. It's just that I suddenly got tired of telling lies, and so I told him I'd met you, and had a drink in here, on the Friday evening. I told him I met you by accident, and you took me in here.'

'But that's still telling lies, isn't it?' said the quick-witted Gorse. 'Because you didn't meet me by accident – did you?'

'No. But you've got to *try* and tell the truth. You've got to get

as far it as you can – haven't you? And it didn't do any harm –
telling him – did it? *You* don't mind, do you?'

'No. Not in the least. And I'm all for telling the truth, whenever
it's possible, certainly.'

'Yes. I knew you would be. So that's why I told him. And I told
him I was meeting you tonight. That's all right, too, isn't it?'

'Perfectly,' said Gorse, still looking at her. 'And tell me. Did
anything happen?'

'Happen? When?'

'When he took you out.'

'What do you mean by "happen"?'

'Come along now. You know perfectly well what I mean.'

Esther hesitated.

'Well. No . . .' she said, and added, 'If you mean he tried to hold
my hand, he did. But that's all.'

'And did you let him?'

'No. I didn't . . .'

'Sure?'

'Yes.'

'And where did all this take place? I hope you won't think I'm
cross-examining you. But I'd just like to know.'

'Oh, just in a place by the railway. It was at Hassocks.'

'What sort of place?'

'It was a wood.'

'Ah. A wood. Really,' said Gorse, with much meaning.

'What's wrong with a wood? It was only just inside, and there
were quite a few people about.'

'And did anything happen after he'd held your hand?'

'What sort of thing?'

'You know what I mean.'

'Do you mean did he try to' – Esther dragged the word out – '*kiss*
me?'

'Yes.'

'No. Not a thing like that. I didn't even let him hold my hand
properly. And then he gave up, and we walked back to where his
bike was.'

'And did you make any arrangement to meet again?'

'No. No appointment. He said he'd write to me.'

'Oh – he did – did he?' said Gorse, again with much meaning.

'You know,' said Esther, 'I've thought it out and I'd swear there's
nothing really wrong in that quarter. I don't really believe that awful

letter, and even if he *did* do something wrong as a boy I'm sure he's all right now. I'd swear to it. I would – really.'

'Well,' said Gorse. 'You certainly seem to have got over your fright about the letter.'

'Yes. I am getting over it. I don't think I ought ever to have got in such a state about it. It ought to have been treated with contempt. He behaved so *well*, you see.'

'Yes. But that's just what they do – isn't it?'

'What do you mean?'

'Well – they behave well three or four times, and then, when they've got your confidence – something happens.'

'What?'

'Oh – something.'

'Tell me. Won't you still tell me what happened – what he did – at school?'

'No. I won't,' said Gorse. 'But don't look so frightened. And don't think I'm trying to damage Ryan in any way. He may be a perfectly decent chap. Uncle Ralph's just giving you his worldly advice, that's all.'

'I know. And it's very good of you. But all I can say is that he behaved like a perfect gentleman – that's all.'

'And what do you mean by a perfect gentleman? What do you mean by a plain gentleman, if it comes to that?'

'Oh. You know.'

'No, I don't. What?'

'Oh – don't be so silly.'

'No, I don't. You've said Ryan's a gentleman. Would you call me one?'

'Yes. Of course you are.'

'Why?'

'Why – it's written all over you.'

'What's written?'

'Oh – you know well enough. You've been to College, and all that. You were born better. You're not like me. I'm not a gentleman – I mean a lady. Although I try to be.'

'Why aren't you? *I* should say you are.'

'Oh, don't be so silly. It's a question of *birth*,' said the tormented Esther. 'Birth, and where you're brought *up*.'

'Is it? Well, how were you born? Who were *your* people, if you *must* go on about it? Who's your father, for instance?'

Esther paused.

'My father's a porter at Brighton Station, if you want to know. And I live in something pretty near a slum. I've told you about the slum before. But I haven't told you about the porter.'

'Well, what's wrong with being a porter?' said Gorse. 'I've no doubt he's a very worthy man.'

This last remark was typical of Gorse. He had spoken fairly gracefully to Esther so far, but now he had slipped up. Even the struggling, bewildered Esther somehow knew that it was very seriously caddish to allude to a person's father as one who is 'no doubt a very worthy man'.

Gorse was to do this sort of thing all his life, and it did not help him.

Esther, having much finer taste than his, took offence a little.

'He's a very nice man, anyway,' she said.

'I'm sure he is,' said Gorse. 'And what about your mother?'

'Oh – she's a bit different. She's in a much better sort of class, really. She worked as a nurse to some children in a very good family. They lived in First Avenue, in Hove. They were related to a General – General Sir Arthur Atherton-Broadleigh. I don't know if you've ever heard of him ... So you might call my mother a much better class.'

Esther, if the truth must be known, had brought in this General as a kind of counter-blast to Gorse's Army People.

There was, really, remarkably little social snobbery about Esther. But she did, as we have seen, desire to 'better herself'. And she thought it politic, on certain occasions, to 'hold one's own'. And so she had dragged in this obscure connection with an obscure General obscurely related to a family in First Avenue, Hove.

'And who were your grandparents?' asked Gorse. 'Do you know about them?'

'No. Not much. Mother's mother was a sewing woman, I know that. But I hardly know anything about my father's father.'

Esther's grandmother had, actually, been a hideously sweated seamstress of the type in which Beatrice Webb had interested herself. About Esther's grandfather, the consumptive runner, we know.

'So you found Ryan a perfect gentleman, did you?' said Gorse, returning to their previous conversation.

'Yes. I did. I must say I did.'

'More perfect than yours truly, for instance?'

'Don't be so silly. Of course not. You're both the same.'

Gorse had been profoundly chagrined to learn that Esther had after all been out with Ryan. This, still, was not because he was really jealous of Ryan. It was because his plotting had unexpectedly failed. (While discussing Esther's parentage he had been wondering what his next move was to be.)

The time came for their second cocktail, and Esther made a proposition.

'Won't you let *me* pay for a change?' she asked. 'I know it's not done, but I don't see why *you* should always go on forking out.'

'What!' said Gorse. '*You* be seen paying in a place like this! No – I don't think that'd quite do.'

The flash of the cad again – shaming her. She flushed faintly.

'No,' she said. 'I didn't mean that. I meant doing it all secretly. Or waiting till we got outside.'

'Well – that's very good of you,' said Gorse. 'But I really can't accept it.'

'Well, I wish you would – just once. It seems unfair on you all the time.'

'And are you as rich as all that?' said Gorse. 'I thought you said you were so poor.'

'Well, I *am* poor. But I've got a little put by. In fact, I've got quite a lot, for a girl like me. It'd surprise you. My mother always made me save, you see.'

Esther had, indeed, what she looked upon as a great fortune. And of this she was proud. She liked to tell her intimates about it.

'What do you mean by quite a lot?' asked Gorse.

'Oh – lots.'

'Pounds, shillings, or pence?'

'Oh – pounds. A lot of them.'

'Five?'

'No.'

'Less?'

'No.'

'More, then? Ten?'

'No.'

'More?'

'Yes.'

Esther was enjoying this game, and had no objection to disclosing the great amount of her savings. Not only was she proud, in a general way, of these. In this particular context, in the Metropole with Gorse, they might give her a further sense of satisfaction. If she

disclosed the great amount she might seem of much more consequence, both to Gorse and herself. The General, taken together
with her savings, were, she fancied, impressive, if only in a small
way.

'Fifteen?' asked Gorse.

'No. More,' said Esther. 'You see, my mother makes quite a lot
on the side by her sewing, and she's given me money to save ever
since I was a kid.'

'Twenty?'

'No.'

'Twenty-five?'

'No.'

'*Thirty?*'

'No.'

'More?'

'Yes.'

'*Forty*, then?'

'No.'

'Am I getting warm?'

'Warmer.'

'Fifty!' exclaimed Gorse.

'No,' said Esther primly. 'More.'

'All right. We'll try sixty.'

'Ah, now you *are* getting warm.'

'Then what about seventy?'

'No. You've gone just too far. It's sixty-eight pounds, fifteen
shillings, if you want to know.'

'Well – I'd call that a pretty tidy little sum – if you ask me,' said
Gorse. 'And where do you keep it all?'

'In the Post Office. Of course, I hardly ever draw on it. But it
gives you a sort of feeling of security.'

'Yes. It must,' said Gorse.

'And I do draw on it a little, every now and again. That's why
I wanted to pay for a drink tonight . . . And now I've got to tell you
I've gone and told you another lie . . .'

Esther could not resist having yet another of her wretched little
shots at the truth.

'What is it this time?' asked Gorse.

'Well – my money isn't really in the Post Office. My mother tells
me to say it is, that's all. It's at home.'

'At home!' said Gorse.

'Yes. My mother feels that way about money.'

'What way?'

'Well – she doesn't like *putting* her money into anything. She's had friends who've lost all they've got that way. She likes to keep it at home.'

Esther was again speaking the truth. Esther's mother was, in fact, a victim of this eccentricity – an eccentricity to be found more amongst the very poor than any other class. Mrs Downes, sane as she was, did not fully trust even the Post Offices or Banks. She had painfully forced herself to put a small proportion of her money into the Post Office, but most of it was at home. This was kept in her own bedroom, in an extremely inaccessible place. Esther's money was kept in an extremely old tin safe, which was hidden amongst old clothes in an old tin trunk in Esther's bedroom.

There is probably more ready cash available in little streets like Over Street than in the largest and most opulent Avenues, Crescents, or Squares of this world.

'Well – it doesn't sound very wise to me,' said Gorse. 'You're losing a tidy bit of interest to begin with … And how much have you got on you tonight, pray?'

'Three pounds. It's got to last a long while, though. And it's really money for a new bag that I've got to buy sometime this week. This one's worn out.'

'Is it? It looks all right to me.'

'Oh no, it isn't. You're only a man, so you wouldn't know. And the lining's all gone inside, anyway.'

'Can I have a look? Or is there anything private?'

'No. There's nothing private,' said Esther, handing it to him. 'And you just look at that lining.'

Gorse took the bag and looked inside it.

'Yes. It certainly is a bit torn,' he said, and handed it back to her.

'Thank you,' said Esther, herself examining the lining. 'And that beastly letter's still in here, I see. I suppose I ought to put it on the fire.'

'Oh, is it? I didn't see it.'

'Yes. Here it is all right.'

Gorse had, really, seen it, but he had to pretend not to have done so, because the card had now been put into its envelope, and he had not been shown this before.

Gorse, a few nights ago pasting the letters from the newspaper on to the card, had suddenly grown tired of his amusement. He had therefore decided to address the envelope in a disguised hand. He knew that there were certain risks attached to this: but he fancied himself as a forger.

He had not sent the postcard without an envelope, for he feared that a postman might report the matter either to Esther's father or mother, or even the police, and in this case it might never reach her.

'Perhaps,' said Esther, 'you didn't see it because of the envelope. I didn't show you that before.'

'Envelope? Oh – so there was an envelope, was there? No – you didn't show it to me before. But of course there must have been. The other side was blank. And I *did* see an envelope in there. Could I have a look? It's in somebody's hand, and it might throw some light on things.'

'Yes. Here you are.'

Gorse looked through his monocle carefully and at some length at the envelope.

'Portslade postmark, I see . . .' he said.

'Yes. But you don't know the handwriting – do you? It isn't any friend of yours, is it? Not your friend what's-his-name? Bell?'

'No. At least it's very cleverly forged if it is. And as you suspected me for a moment, I may as well tell you it's certainly not mine. I use a fountain pen with light blue ink. This looks like an ordinary pen, and the ink's pretty well black. If you still suspect me, would you like to see my fountain pen? I've got it on me. And would you like to see a specimen of my handwriting? You could take it to a handwriting expert, and he might prove it was me.'

'Oh – stop ragging me about that,' said Esther. 'I've said I'm sorry.'

When Esther was halfway through her second drink she began to feel dizzy, and she made Gorse finish it for her.

When he had done this they went out and on to the West Pier once more. Gorse repeated his 'Silly Ass' act, took Esther to the same seat as usual, and kissed her as before.

She again allowed him to escort her as far as the Clock Tower. But here, as they said good-bye, something unexpected happened.

'I say,' said Gorse. 'Something's just struck me. Do you think you could do me a favour?'

'Yes. I hope so. What is it?'

'Well, the truth is,' said Gorse, going through his pockets, 'I'm pretty well completely out of ready cash. That doesn't matter, because I don't want any tonight. But tomorrow morning I've got to be up with the lark to go and see an old uncle of mine over at Preston Park. He's a bit of a tyrant and a martinet, but as he's absolutely rolling in money, and I'm hoping a lot of it's coming to me, one's got to toe the line, if you see what I mean.'

'Yes? Well?'

'Well, although I've got enough of the ready to get home tonight, it's going to be the devil tomorrow morning waiting for the bank to open and then get to Preston in time. And I hate being without money on me. And so I was wondering if you could loan me something.'

'Yes. Of course I can. How much?'

'Well – could you manage a quid? Or even two – if you can manage it. I hate not having enough on me. And then I can go to the bank when I've left the old boy, and pay you back tomorrow evening. You can meet me tomorrow evening – can't you?'

'Well, I'm not quite sure,' said Esther.

She was, though she tried not to show it, decidedly taken aback by what Gorse had asked her.

Apart from the smallest sums to intimate girl friends, she had never lent money before. And the sum he had mentioned – two pounds – quite staggered her.

And over and above this, he was not an intimate friend. She had only met him three or four times. And he was a man, not a girl – a very different thing in money matters. And, further still, he was a man she still did not instinctively fully trust or like.

She knew exactly what her mother would say about this. She would say that it was very wrong of Gorse to have asked such a thing from a working girl: that it was a thing she didn't 'like the look of', and that it would be highly rash, asking for trouble, to let him have the money.

Then he had said that he would pay her back tomorrow evening at the Metropole. But tomorrow evening she had promised to go out with Gertrude alone.

She could, of course, put Gertrude off until another evening. But, if she decided to do this, she certainly would not mention her appointment with Gertrude to Gorse. Firstly, her putting it off would give him too great a sense of his own importance; secondly, it would look as if she were too anxious to get her money back quickly.

Gorse was speaking to her.

'Why? What's the matter?' he was saying. 'You've got the money on you – haven't you? But I don't want to press it, of course. I can manage easily enough.'

'No. It's not that,' said Esther. 'It's just that I've got to buy things with it. There's that bag, for instance.'

'Oh. Can't you put the bag off, just for a day? One never wants to rush at buying, you know. It's good policy to wait.'

Esther made her decision.

She desired to 'better' herself: it was for this reason that she liked mixing with 'gentlemen': and Gorse was one. But if one mixed with 'gentlemen' one had to behave in a gentlemanly way. And ladies and gentlemen, she had always imagined, did not fuss about small money matters. A matter of two pounds would be a small one to them.

Furthermore, a gentleman would certainly not like to find a lady not trusting him. Gorse might easily take offence, and that would be the end of the Metropole.

'Oh – I suppose you're right,' she said. 'And it was only the bag I was thinking about. How much do you want?'

'Well, I'd like two. But one would see me through.'

'No. You have two.' She gave them to him. 'There you are.'

'That's very nice of you,' said Gorse, pocketing the notes. 'And thank you very much indeed.'

'Not at all. And now I must be buzzing off.'

'You know I thought for a moment you didn't trust me,' said Gorse, smiling at her. 'Did you think I was going to run off with your hard-earned savings?'

'No, it was only the bag. I've told you. I promise you it was only the bag.'

'Well, I *might* be a crook, you know,' said Gorse. 'Anyway, now you'll *have* to turn up tomorrow – won't you? If only to get your money back.'

Esther suddenly thought of telling him frankly about her appointment with Gertrude. But she decided against it. If she did she would have to meet Gorse on another, later evening, and she did not want this. She wanted, she knew in her heart, to see the colour of her money as soon as possible!

And so that she could do this, poor Gertrude had to be sacrificed.

'Yes,' she said. 'I'll be there. Seven o'clock, West Pier?'

'That's right. And then we'll go to the good old Met. again.'

'Fine. Well – ta-ta!'

'Cheerio,' said Gorse, and they parted.

Gorse indulged in more deep thought on his walk back to Norton Road.

He now had two schemes on hand. One concerned Ryan. The other concerned Esther. Esther's sixty-eight pounds, fifteen shillings had interested the precocious and enterprising young man very much.

II

On Monday morning Esther received another letter. Before she had opened it she was sure it was from Ryan, and it was. It read:

Dear Esther,

Please forgive me for writing to you so soon, but I know how you must be booked up, and I thought it best to be in good time.

When we left each other yesterday evening we were in such a fluster (I don't quite know why) that it must have been difficult for you to have thought of a free day.

Would Thursday do? Say seven-thirty, outside the West Pier? Could you let me know? I know you are busy, but you need only just write a line, and I am enclosing a stamped addressed envelope. I never told you *my* address!

I am so much looking forward to seeing you again, and I do hope that you can manage Thursday. I thought we might go on to the Pier, if it is fine, but if it is wet we could go to the Palladium. I still very much want to see the film I told you about, and I would like you to see it too.

I hope you are keeping very well.

Yours,

Peter (Ryan)

Esther found this letter charming, and she spent a good deal of time in trying to find out whether he had signed himself 'Your', which was passionate, or 'Yours', which was less so. He had purposely put a little squiggle after the *r*. He had wanted to write 'Your', but thought it might be too bold, and 'put her off', and so he had hit upon this clever ambiguity with his pen.

Esther also admired his modesty in the way he had signed his name – the 'Ryan' in brackets. She would not have liked a plain Peter nearly as much. The perfect gentleman had hit (as he had tried to do) upon the perfect compromise.

2   From Ryan's point of view this letter (although he had
feared he had sent it too early) had arrived a little too late. For by
this time Esther, as she had promised herself she would, had
confided in her mother, and her mother's advice about Ryan de-
tracted from the charm of the letter.

Esther had confided in her mother on the Sunday night – shortly
after she had left Gorse.

The opportunity had arisen quite accidentally, and Esther had
taken advantage of it. She did not have to 'go' to her mother. Her
mother, on hearing her come in, had invited her into the sitting
room to join her in a cup of cocoa, which she was just about to make
for herself.

Mrs Downes had had no motive save that of having the com-
panionship of her daughter for a quarter of an hour or so.

Cocoa is not, like alcohol, a great stimulant: but, if taken in front
of a warm fire at the end of the day, it induces confidences.

Esther plucked up her courage and told her mother very nearly
the truth, the whole truth, and nothing but the truth.

3   She began with the first meeting of all five on the West
Pier. Then she told her mother about Gorse, and about her having
gone to the Metropole with him.

The nature of the hotel surprised and slightly alarmed Mrs
Downes. But some pleasure was mixed with her alarm – for she had
always felt certain that her lovely daughter was destined to enjoy
astonishing delights. And she believed, as have all mothers since
civilization began, that young people nowadays get up to extraordinary things for which allowances simply have to be made.

But then Esther came to the anonymous postcard, and her mother
was horrified. On Esther's showing it to her, she became more
horrified still. Indeed, after a lot of staring at it and thinking about
it, she said she would keep it and show it to Mr Stringer. Mr
Stringer was an elderly ex-policeman who lodged in a small room
three or four doors away in Over Street, and he was a personal friend
of Mrs Downes, whom he awed with what he believed was an
intimate and intricate knowledge of the law.

So, Esther reflected, it was going to the Police after all! She almost
regretted having confided in her mother. She only trusted that poor
Ryan was not, through her instrumentation, going to have the Police
set upon him!

Then Mrs Downes began to advise Esther. She said, first of all, that she must never see Ryan again. The message on the postcard might well be purely malicious, and untrue, but no risks could possibly be taken. In cases of this sort, she said, there was only one thing to do – and that was completely to remove oneself from the sphere of evil. When mud of this sort was being thrown near one, however pure Esther might be, some of it might strike and stick to her. And this was no ordinary mud: it was dangerous, and endangered Esther perhaps physically as well as socially.

Then Esther pleadingly told her mother how she had been out into the country with Ryan, and how he had behaved, throughout the entire afternoon, like a perfect gentleman.

But this made no impression at all on Mrs Downes. He might easily, she said, behave like a perfect gentleman at the beginning.

This, Esther noted secretly, was an almost exact repetition of Gorse's advice. Could both be wrong?

'But what if he *writes* to me?' asked Esther. 'He knows my address and said he would that evening.'

'Well,' said her mother, after reflection. 'You mustn't answer it, that's all.'

'But suppose there's nothing really wrong about him? Wouldn't it be rude and unkind to not answer?'

'No,' said Mrs Downes firmly. 'You mustn't answer. You've got to risk being rude and unkind. You've got to be kind to yourself, and keep out of trouble at all costs.' A thought struck Mrs Downes. 'You're not at all – keen – on this young man, are you, by the way?'

Esther could not quite bring herself to admit that she was.

'No,' she said. 'I like him very much, though – what I've seen of him. And I've told you he behaves like a perfect gentleman.'

'Well – I'm glad to hear you're not,' said Mrs Downes. 'You must keep out of this.'

'But what if I *meet* him again, on the front? I can't very well refuse to speak to him.'

'No. But there're ways and means – and I'm sure you know how to use them. I expect you've had to do things like that before. You can be cool and cut the meeting short – can't you? You'll know how to choke him off.'

'Yes. But if he's really all right I don't *want* to choke him off,' said Esther, and then asked about Gorse. Should she go on meeting Gorse?

Esther's mother gave this matter some reflection, and then said that this might be permissible. But Esther must take the utmost care. It would really be preferable, she said, if Esther never saw any of these boys again.

Then Esther asked whether she should not show the postcard to Ryan and give him a chance to exonerate himself. But Mrs Downes said that such a thing would be useless: he would certainly not admit any guilt, and have some extremely plausible lie ready to hand.

And, said Mrs Downes, repeating her exhortations, Esther must certainly not voluntarily see Ryan again. In addition to this, Mrs Downes said that she herself wanted to keep the letter and show it to Mr Stringer.

Finally Esther said that she would take her mother's advice, and her mother, adopting her usual method, said that she completely trusted her daughter, and she kissed her as she went to bed.

Hard as she had tried, Esther still had failed to tell her the whole truth, or even the truth, to her mother.

Her mother, for instance, had asked her what she had had to drink at the Metropole with Gorse, and Esther had said that she had had lemonade. This had been done in order not to shock her mother, but it was another plain lie.

She had failed to tell the whole truth in two ways. She had not told her mother about Gorse's hints concerning Ryan's strange crimes at school. She had been, somehow, too eager to defend Ryan to do this. And she had not told her mother that she had lent Gorse the sum of two pounds that very evening. She knew that this would scandalize her mother, who would probably make her promise not even to see Gorse again.

Esther was up early the next morning, and found Ryan's letter in the hall before her mother was down.

She knew that it was her duty to show this letter to her mother. But what harm could there be in reading it first? She did this in her bedroom.

When she had read it, and had been charmed by it, she thought that she would like to think about it before she showed it to her mother. What harm was there in this? Anyway, her mother was at the moment, she could hear, very busy, and she could show it to her in the evening. Her mother had made her swear no oath.

During her day at the sweet-shop, because her mother had not made her swear any oath, she decided that she would not show the letter to her mother at all, at present. And she decided that she would write to Ryan and agree to meeting him on Thursday evening.

Esther Downes was not a dishonest or untrue girl – rather the contrary. But she was not yet eighteen: she was weak, and found herself in unique circumstances. Any circumstances created by Ernest Ralph Gorse were almost always of a unique character.

4   On Monday night, Ryan, returning to his bed-sitting room yet again to think and dream, himself received a letter.

This at once puzzled him: for his name and address on the envelope, instead of being written in the conventional manner, had been cleverly formed by letters from a newspaper being pasted on to it. And, on opening the envelope, he found a postcard upon which other letters had been pasted.

These letters went to make the following message:

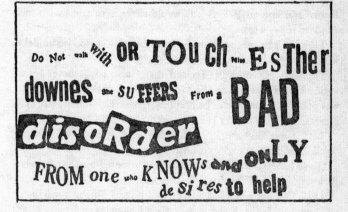

Do Not walk with OR TOUCh him EsTher downes she SUFFERS From a BAD disoRder FROM one who KNOWs and oNLY de si res to help

Ryan was not as frightened by this postcard as Esther had been by hers. But now it was his turn to think as laboriously as she had.

III

Gorse was again in splendid form when he met Esther outside the West Pier on the Monday evening.

Perhaps the writing of anonymous letters removes from the blood of the sender that amount of evil which it casts upon others. The evils of this life, after all, should be shared.

They found, at the Metropole, the same table and the same waiter; and Gorse ordered the same drinks. The moment these had been paid for and the waiter had gone away, Gorse, feeling in his hip pocket, said:

'Well – to begin with first things first – here's the money you lent me last night. Here we are. There you are.'

He put two pound notes down on to the table.

Esther did not quite know in what manner to take these. It was an entirely new situation for her. In her anxiety to be a 'lady' against his 'gentleman' (and in her flurry of happiness at seeing the colour of her money!) she even thought of trying to refuse the notes – to give them to him. But her common sense saved her from doing this.

'Oh well,' she said, picking up the notes and putting them into her bag. 'That's very kind of you.'

Before she had finished saying this Esther realized that it was absurd and not ladylike. A lady would never have said that it was 'kind' to repay a loan.

'How do you mean – "kind"?' said Gorse. 'It was just a debt which I've paid back – that's all.'

The cad once more. It seemed that Gorse could never resist letting Esther know when she had made a fool of herself. But there was possibly some motive behind this: it kept her in her place and increased his power over her.

'No. It was silly of me,' said Esther, and changed the subject. 'Well, how did you find your uncle?'

Gorse had almost forgotten about his invented uncle at Preston Park; but had no difficulty in extemporizing.

'Oh – he's not a bad old boy, really,' he said. 'Bit of a martinet, you know, as I said. You know – retired Colonel type.'

Gorse made him a Colonel as a means of utterly squashing Esther's faint, faint, faint, pathetic connection with a General.

'In fact,' he went on, 'you might say he had a heart of gold – beneath a rather frightening exterior. He's got a purse of gold, too – and a very large purse. And although I don't want to be mercenary – one does have to take that into account. Because I think he's taken a bit of a fancy to yours truly – I can't imagine why – and when he dies I have an idea most of his money's coming to me.'

'How old is he?'

'Oh – well into his seventies, and I have a feeling he's not going to last very long. Not that I want the old boy to go. I'm very fond of the old thing in an odd way.'

'What's his name?' asked Esther quite innocently – that is to say with no intention of trying to cross-examine Gorse to catch him out. She entirely believed in this Colonel uncle.

Gorse had neglected as yet to invent a name. He hesitated.

'Why do you ask?' he said, to gain time to think of a name.

'Oh, only curiosity,' said Esther. 'I don't really know why I asked.'

'He's a Gorse too,' said Gorse. 'My father's eldest brother. He's a Ralph Gorse, too, like me. Colonel Ralph Gorse. Perhaps that's why he's taken such a fancy to me.'

'Well,' said Esther, 'I wish *I* had expectations from a rich uncle.'

'Yes, I suppose I *am* pretty lucky, one way and another.'

'You certainly are.'

There was a pause.

'Oh – by the way,' said Gorse. 'I've got something for you.'

Esther had noticed, the moment she had met Gorse, that he was carrying a neat parcel, and she had somehow felt as though it contained something which he was going to give to her.

'Really?' she said. 'What's that?'

'Here you are,' said Gorse, handing her the parcel. 'You open it yourself and find out.'

Esther undid the string, and removed the paper, and found a flat cardboard box. On opening this she found tissue paper, and on removing this she found a woman's handbag.

'Good heavens!' she said, and took it out and gazed at it, shocked with delight. It was a handbag such as she would never have dreamed of possessing. She guessed that it must have cost two pounds at least. She was right. It had cost Gorse two guineas.

'There you are,' said Gorse. 'You said you wanted a bag, so I thought I'd save time for you and get you one.'

Accidentally Gorse had said this in such a way as to fill Esther with the dreadful suspicion that it was not a present – that he had merely bought this fearfully expensive article on her behalf. She had to be reassured at once.

'But I can't afford a thing like this,' she said disingenuously. 'It's good of you to have thought of buying it for me, but it's too expensive!'

'What do you mean – "afford"?' said Gorse. 'It's a present.'

'But you can't! You can't!' said Esther.

'I can, I will, and I do,' said Gorse. 'If you'll accept it.'

'But what can I say? I mean how am I ever going to thank you?'

'Don't thank me,' said Gorse. 'Thank God. He gave me the wherewithal to buy it – so I should thank God.'

'But it's lovely! It's lovely. I simply don't know how to thank you.'

'I've told you. You're not to try. I'm only too grateful that you like it.'

Esther, dizzy with pleasure at the gift, looked at the giver.

He was looking at his best, and behaving at his best. Was there, she thought, perhaps much more 'to' this young man than she had ever thought there might be before? The gift had truly captivated her. Was it possible that he himself might come truly to captivate her? At that moment she thought such a thing far from impossible.

'Well,' said Esther. 'I can only say thank you – from my heart. In fact, I'd like to kiss you for it, if I could, in a place like this.'

'Well – I can only say I wish we weren't in a place like this.'

'No. You're sweet. You are really. What shall I do? Put it back in the box?'

'No. Put the old one back in the box and wear the new one.'

'All right.'

She gleefully emptied the contents of the old bag, and put them into the new one, and then put the old bag into the box. Then she held up the new one to the light and gazed at it.

'Look at it!' she said. 'What on earth'll people think? They'll think I'm getting above my station.' An unpleasant thought struck her. 'Oh lord,' she said, changing her tone. 'What'll my mother think?'

'What's your mother got to do with it?'

'Well – I don't think she likes me taking presents. And I'm afraid an expensive one like this is going to shock her a bit. She's very old-fashioned, and she'll want to know all about you.'

'Well, you can tell her – can't you? There isn't anything to conceal, is there?'

'No. I suppose there isn't.'

'Or you could hide the bag.'

'Yes. I suppose I could.'

'That is, if you think your mother wouldn't approve of me. Do you think she wouldn't.'

'I can't see why on earth she wouldn't.'

'Well, I hope she would. Because I have an idea she's got to do a lot more approving before she's done.'

Esther did not at all get anything of his meaning.

'How do you mean?' she said.

'Well,' said Gorse, 'things might go further, mightn't they?'

'In what way?' said Esther, now roughly following his drift.

'Well – they might get a lot further – mightn't they? Then we *would* have to ask her approval. Your father's too.'

Though unable to believe her ears, Esther had an impression that Gorse was alluding to marriage – or an engagement to marry.

'How do you mean?' she said. 'How much further? And why should my father and mother come into it?'

'You know what I mean.'

'I don't really.'

'Well – must I explain?'

'I wish you would.'

'Well – just suppose – it's only a supposition – suppose I asked you to marry me. And suppose – and I expect that's even more unlikely still – that you – accepted me. We'd have to tell your father and mother then – wouldn't we?'

Here even the experienced Esther blushed, half with pleasure and half with embarrassment.

'Well,' she said. 'It's only supposing, isn't it?'

'No,' said Gorse. 'It *isn't*. I'm extremely serious.'

'Look here,' said Esther. 'What are you doing? Are you trying to pull my leg? Are you trying to say you're proposing marriage or something?'

'I don't quite know. I'm looking into the future. We don't know each other very well just at present, do we?'

'No. We don't . . .'

'But things do happen – don't they? In fact, things are happening. To me, at any rate. And if things go on happening, and we get to know each other better, I can see myself asking you to marry me – that's all . . . Tell me – if I did – do you think there'd be any chance of your saying yes?'

'Look here,' said Esther. 'Are you being serious?'

'Extremely serious,' said Gorse, looking seriously into her eyes as he leant back in his chair. 'I'm a very serious person. Though I may not seem to be on the surface. But tell me. Do you think there'd be any chance?'

'I don't know,' said Esther, looking away as he looked at her.

'Well,' said Gorse. 'I just thought I'd tell you that's the way my mind's working. I'm ready to wait – because you don't know me properly yet, and I know it's wise to wait. But I'm pretty sure that that's what's going to happen on my side.'

'But how *could* you marry me! It's all so absurd.'

'What's absurd?'

'You and me. We're not in the same *class*. It'd never work.'

'What's the difference in class?'

'Well – you're a gentleman and I'm just a shopgirl. It's absurd.'

'Well – even if you're right – *I* don't see that it matters. If there's one thing I'm not, it's a snob. I think you can see that.'

'No. You're certainly not a snob.'

'And I know that I'd be proud to have you for my wife. Anybody would. And, after all, that sort of thing happens every day nowadays. Peers marry chorus girls almost every other day. Not that I'm a peer, or that you're a chorus girl. So that side of it doesn't matter. You've only got to read the newspapers.'

'All the same, I still say it's absurd.'

'And I still say it isn't. Now will you tell me something else?'

'Yes.'

'Is there anybody else?'

'No.'

'Sure?'

'Yes.'

'You're not enamoured of our mutual friend Ryan, for instance?'

'No.'

'Sure?'

'Yes.'

'Not that I'm against him. Let the best man win's my motto. Have you heard from him, by the way?'

'Yes. He wrote to me.'

'What did he say?'

'He asked me to meet him on Thursday evening.'

'And are you going to?'

'I don't know. I suppose I might as well.'

'Where are you meeting him, and where are you going?'

'He asked me to meet him outside the West Pier. And he said we might either go on the Pier, or to a cinema. I can't see any harm in that – can you? It's a public place.'

'No. So long as it's in a public place it's all right. But see that it's in a public place – won't you?'

'Yes. I will.'

Gorse changed the subject.

'And now the time's come for me to finish your cocktail – hasn't it?' said Gorse about ten minutes later. 'That is, if you don't want it yourself.'

'No. I don't want it.'

When Gorse had finished drinking they went out of the hotel. On the way out Esther again spoke fervently about the beauty of the bag he had given her.

When they were in the street Gorse asked her what she would like to do.

'I don't know,' she said. 'I'll leave it to you.'

She presumed that he was going to ask her to go on the Pier, where he would again kiss her. But Gorse was too clever for this.

He knew that going on the Pier must entail kissing. And he knew that Esther would think, when he kissed her, that he was seeking a return, exacting a reward, for his generosity about the bag. She would be, as it were, under an obligation – and Gorse saw that this was inadvisable.

Gorse was not capable of sentimentality, or even sentiment, towards women. He had at times strong and unusual sexual desires, but he was otherwise cold.

In spite of this, or perhaps because of it, he had, throughout his life, a remarkable tact, skill, and understanding of the mentality of girls and women he met. He showed this quality tonight.

'Well, I'll tell you what,' he said. 'I've had rather a hard day, and I'm a bit tired, and I've got three letters I ought to write tonight – so shall we say good-bye early tonight? It's just as you like.'

Esther was inwardly delighted. Charmed as she was by Gorse, she certainly had no desire to go on the Pier and be kissed by him. Now she would get off scot-free with her bag! Gorse had read her mind correctly.

'No. I'm a bit tired too,' she said. 'I'd like an early night.'

'Well, then, may I just see you back as far as the Clock Tower again?'

'Oh no. Don't bother. I can easily go by myself. And you're tired, too, and it's right out of your way.'

'No. Please let me. I'd like to, really.'

He took her back to the Clock Tower, and on the way made an appointment for the following evening.

At the Clock Tower she thanked him for the evening, and again for the bag. Then, as on the previous night, she kissed him lightly on the cheek and quickly left him.

As each went homewards tonight it was Esther who was thinking the hardest. She had to grind over in her mind Gorse's amazing suggestion, his near proposal of marriage.

Could she marry Gorse? She believed almost that she could.

Since meeting him tonight she had completely lost her distrust of him. She did not quite know why this was. Perhaps it was the way he had instantaneously returned the money she had lent him. Perhaps it was the bag. Perhaps it was his talk of marriage, and what she thought was his complete lack of social snobbery. Perhaps it was his manner tonight – his generosity, chivalry, and reticence. She now believed that he was, along with Ryan, a 'perfect' gentleman.

Would he ask her to marry him as he had prophesied that he would? She believed so. And was the idea of marrying him as absurd socially as she had proclaimed it to be at the Metropole?

Did not peers, indeed, marry chorus girls? And was she not remarkably beautiful, and had she not always felt in her heart that she was destined for remarkable things? Even her mother had hinted as much.

She told herself that she must not make the fatal mistake of underestimating herself.

PART EIGHT

ADVICE

I

Ryan, as has been said, had not been as frightened as Esther on receiving his anonymous postcard.

His first impulse had been to tear it up and forget about it.

But he did not do this because he wanted to study it, to discover the sender, to have it, perhaps, as evidence.

This is another evil of the anonymous letter: their recipients hoard them. They simply cannot part with them.

And then, slowly, though he was still not really frightened, the muddy filth and nagging puzzlement attendant upon these things crept over Ryan, and at last completely gripped him.

'*Do not walk with or touch Miss Esther Downes she suffers from a bad disorder from one who knows and only desires to help.*'

Ryan began to reflect. 'A bad disorder.' What did this lewd expression mean?

Did Esther suffer from some plague – so serious that it was dangerous even to 'walk' with her?

Or did she have some dreadful rash or something, which was concealed by her clothes and infectious to one who 'touched' her?

Or was venereal disease being suggested? Ryan knew little about the latter, but his lack of knowledge made him dread it the more.

Ryan thought that, on the whole, this was being hinted, but surely you could 'walk' with such a victim. Surely you could 'touch' such a one.

'Touch.' Could this conceivably be the reason why Esther, at Hassocks that day, had been so reluctant to allow him to 'touch' her, to hold her hand?

Ryan, for whom 'all the girls fell', had not before encountered such reluctance. He had thought it strange at the time, and had put it down to her extreme beauty, which enabled her to behave in a high-handed way with young men.

But there had been other strange little things about her

behaviour. Could Esther have been trying to protect him from some malady from which she suffered? Such a thing seemed not at all unlikely.

Then Esther had confessed to living in a slum. There were many slum diseases, he imagined.

Did Esther have lice on her body? Or in her hair? Such a thing might account for the words 'walk' and 'touch'.

Or was she consumptive?

Then, of course, there was the problem of who on *earth* could have sent the message. Ryan, as had Esther with her pasted post-card, felt that it must come from the slums – from some incredibly low quarter.

But how would such a person know his address?

Who, in Brighton (the letter had been posted in Brighton) knew both his address and the fact that he had met Esther? Only, so far as he knew, Gertrude Perks, and Bell, and Gorse.

He could not possibly believe such a thing of the ugly but amiable Gertrude. She had tried to help him – had made an appointment with Esther for him.

True, as an intimate girl friend of Esther's, she would be in a position to know more about any malady than any man. And, of course, Gertrude might be a villainess – angry because he had rejected her advances, and jealous of Esther. This might be her way of taking her revenge. All the same, he could not believe it of her.

Bell? No – that was utterly out of the question.

Gorse? That, too, was surely out of the question. Ryan somehow disliked and distrusted Gorse, but it would be absurd to think him capable of baseness of such an order.

Ryan went over and over the thing, and backwards and forwards, late into the Monday night.

He hoped, on the Tuesday morning, to have a reply from Esther to his letter, and that she would have consented to meet him on the Thursday as he had suggested. Now, more than ever, he could hardly wait to see her.

He decided that, on the Tuesday morning, he would ask advice from a friend. He had only two of these in the town – Gorse and Bell.

Now Gorse was far and away the most sophisticated of the two, and likely to give the best advice. Nevertheless, Ryan decided to go to Bell.

There was still just enough of that little suspicion of Gorse to make him choose the naïve Bell.

2   The naïve Bell was lodging with an aunt in a little house in Bigwood Avenue, which was not far away from their old school, Rodney House.

In the morning no letter had come from Esther, and Ryan, in a state of impatience, took out his motorcycle very early and arrived at the house in Bigwood Avenue before Bell had quite finished his breakfast.

The naïve Bell was at his naïvest. He was smoking his curved pipe with the remains of his coffee, and was studying a chess problem on a small folding chess set which lay open upon the tablecloth.

Bell was by no means displeased to be accidentally discovered in this learned posture.

Indeed, instead of going to the door and letting Ryan in (he had seen him arrive on his motorcycle), he had let the maid do this, and had carefully held the chess picture of himself until Ryan had entered – and for some time after Ryan had entered.

'One moment,' he said, staring at the board. 'I'm delighted to see you, but I suspect I have just found the key move, and I don't want it to elude me. Sit down. I'll be with you in a moment.'

Ryan did what he was told, and waited patiently while Bell went on making an idiot of himself. This Bell did, in silence, for something like a minute.

Then 'No', said Bell, still gazing at the board. 'No. It won't do. It has eluded me again. A question of discovered check which I had missed. We'll have to abandon it for the time being. It's only a two-mover, but the ingenious problemist has defeated me for more than three quarters of an hour.'

Bell rose.

'Well, my dear Ryan,' he said, very nearly saying 'Watson', for at the moment he had a strong impression that he was Sherlock Holmes being called upon at an early hour by an anxious client. 'I'm delighted to see you. You come at an early hour – and the earlier the better.'

He had nearly added, 'And what can I do for you, sir, pray?' but realized just in time that he was not really Sherlock Holmes.

But he puffed mightily at his pipe, and took a rapid, nervous sip at his coffee – thus giving a clever impression both of smoking 'poisonous shag' and of being a drug addict.

'Yes. I know I'm early,' said Ryan, who saw through all these affectations and now rather regretted having called. 'But I thought it'd be nice to see you again. I'm sorry if I'm too early.'

Ryan did not want to confide in Bell until the latter had stopped making a damned fool of himself – had calmed down.

In about ten minutes' time Bell had done this. He was once more natural, and showing that somewhat sweet and pathetic nature which was really his.

At last, 'As a matter of fact, there's something I want to talk to you about,' said Ryan. 'I want to ask your advice.'

'Oh. Do you? Go ahead. I'm only too pleased to help in any way.'

'Well – it's rather a long story,' said Ryan.

'Go ahead. The longer the better.'

Ryan then reminded Bell of the first meeting of the five on the West Pier, and he told Bell that he had taken Esther into the country, and he confessed that he was 'rather keen' on her.

'Ah yes,' said Bell. 'I rather fancied that Cupid's dart had struck home in that quarter.

> 'Cupid and my Campaspe played
> At cards for kisses – Cupid –'

Bell perceived, in fairly good time, that he was reciting poetry which was utterly irrelevant to Ryan's problem, and stopped himself and went on to say, 'However. Proceed.'

'Well, I've had the most funny letter,' said Ryan. 'And I want to know what you think about it.'

'Really? Have you got it on you?'

'Yes. Here it is,' said Ryan, producing it. 'I think it's absolutely filthy, and I ought to tear it up and forget about it. But I'd like you to look at it and give me your advice.'

Bell read the pasted postcard carefully.

'Yes,' he said at last. 'I agree with you. I'd put it on the fire.'

'But who *sent* it?' said Ryan passionately. 'And could there be any *truth* in it?'

Now, at Bell's age (unless one has received one oneself, and one is personally concerned), anonymous letters are regarded as low, but not as being of tremendous importance. Therefore, Bell did not understand Ryan's passion and was of little assistance to him.

'Who cares who sent it?' he said. 'One simply doesn't consider such things. The only thing is the fire or the wastepaper basket. May I put it in this one – here and now?'

'No. I'd rather keep it, I think,' said Ryan. 'I don't know why, but I rather would.'

'Well, I think you're wrong – but here you are,' said Bell, handing it back to Ryan. 'My advice to you is to throw it away and forget all about it.'

But, as Ryan subconsciously perceived, Bell had not *received* the letter and was not *concerned*!

'Yes, that's all very well,' said Ryan. 'But supposing what it says is *true*. What about that?'

'Oh – I don't know about that,' said Bell lightly.

'Do *you* think it might be true? Go on. Tell me.'

'No. I shouldn't think so. It probably comes from some filthy rascal in a low district, and he may be jealous or something.'

'But do you think it *might* be true?'

'Well. Yes. It *might*, of course,' said Bell unconcernedly.

For Bell, having not received the letter, was not concerned.

'But then who *could* have sent it? How did they know my *address*?'

'What does it matter? I've given you my advice. Just forget all about it.'

'But it *does* matter, you know. Tell me. Do you think it might be that friend of hers – the ugly one – Gertrude Whateveritis?'

'It might be.'

'But do you *think* it is?'

'*I* don't know. And I don't care. Neither should you.'

But Bell did not care because he had not received the letter and was not concerned.

'It might be her,' said Ryan. 'I think she's got a bit of a crush on me, and she might be jealous.'

'Yes ... She might ...'

'You think it's possible?'

'Yes. It's possible.'

'But then I don't think she knows my address. And that brings me to something else I want to ask you. There is a person who knows my address – and you'll probably think me mad for even thinking of such a thing – but do you think it *could* somehow – be Gorse?'

'Well, I know your address, too – don't I?' said Bell.

'Don't be silly,' said Ryan. 'I'm just asking you if you thought it might be dimly on the cards that it was Gorse. Tell me. Do you think so?'

Bell puffed at his pipe for about ten seconds.

'No,' he said. 'I think that's entirely out of the question. I think you're letting your imagination run away with you. I've told you. Forget it all. It's certainly not Gorse.'

'Well, then. We have to fall back on Gertrude Whateverher-nameis. But I still don't really believe it's her. So who could it be?'

'I don't know. What does it matter?'

But it did not matter to Bell because he had not received the letter and he was not *concerned*!

Ryan was becoming slowly infuriated by Bell's complacent and inconsequent attitude – so much so that he had a strong feeling that he would like to get up and knock Bell's pipe out of his mouth. At the same time he knew that Bell was giving him the correct advice. It was exactly the advice he himself would have given to another.

Anyway, there was no sense in nagging at Bell, who clearly was not going to be of any assistance to him. He gave in.

'Well,' he said. 'It's no use going on about it, I suppose. Would you like to come out and have a ride on the bike?'

'Why, yes,' said Bell. 'That's very kind of you – I would. And it certainly might be as well to rid ourselves of the nauseous fumes of tobacco, and inhale the pure oxygen of the open air.'

In three minutes' time they were outside the house and driving away on Ryan's machine.

Ryan took Bell as far as Worthing, where they had a cup of coffee, and then they returned to Brighton. Doing this soothed Ryan considerably. Next to Esther he loved his motorcycle. And, after his motorcycle, Cricket Results.

I I

On Wednesday morning Ryan was further soothed by a letter from Esther. She wrote:

Dear 'Mr Ryan',

I was very pleased to recieve your letter, and will much look forward to meeting you outside the West Pier on Thursday – 7:30. Hoping you are keeping well.

Yours

Esther Downes.

Ryan was very glad that she had put 'Mr Ryan' in inverted commas. He had never for a moment hoped for a plain 'Peter'. He noticed that she had spelt 'receive' incorrectly. Apparently she had not been taught the '*i* before *e* except after *c*' rule. He was touched by her mistake, and loved her the more for it.

That night he put the letter under his pillow, and, defying a fear that he might be contracting some obscure contagious disease, kissed it several times.

2   On Thursday evening, Esther, not being particularly flustered, maintained her usual principle and arrived a minute and a half late for Ryan.

Esther had shown her mother the bag which Gorse had given her, and her mother had not disapproved very greatly. Esther had also told her mother that Gorse had a rich uncle who was a retired Colonel. Perhaps this had made Mrs Downes disapprove of the present of the bag less than she would ordinarily. The truth was that Gorse had succeeded in deceiving Mrs Downes almost as much as he had deceived her daughter.

Indeed, Mrs Downes at moments had even gone so far as to entertain high hopes about this mysterious young man.

But Esther had not told her mother that she had written to Ryan and agreed to meet him.

The squalid spiritual tumult caused by the two anonymous letters had, by Thursday evening, both with Esther and Ryan, somewhat subsided. They were both worried, but there was no panic.

They said 'Hullo', and shook hands shyly, and talked about the weather, and went through the turnstile, momentarily forgetting the cloud which overhung them both. But, having no conversation as they walked seawards along the west (the least populated) side of the West Pier, the cloud returned.

In sending an anonymous letter to Ryan as well as Esther, Gorse had, really, made yet another of those curious and gross blunders which he was to make throughout all his life.

Ryan had only to show his own letter to Esther, and all would have been well between them. Esther would have at once shown hers to him, and they would have both realized that there was a conspiracy against them. And they would, because of this, almost have been thrown into each other's arms.

But Gorse was, on this occasion, lucky. Or perhaps Gorse, in the extreme depths of his extremely deep mind, had been wise. Perhaps, in these depths, he knew that these two would not disclose such a secret to each other. He had, possibly, a sort of genius in regard to anonymous letters – knowing the curious effect, the passion for secrecy, which they have upon the minds of their recipients.

Just as Esther had never (until she had been at tea with Ryan at Hurst) for a moment thought of showing her own letter to Ryan, so it had not, as yet, occurred to Ryan that he might show his to her.

Esther and Ryan went to the extreme end of the Pier and looked, in a romantic atmosphere, towards the French coast. As it grew darker they returned, and played the slot machines outside the West Pier Theatre.

It was while they were doing this that there came to Ryan the same inspiration which had come to Esther at Hurst. Why not show her the letter, and free his mind from the beastly thing for good and all? Would it not, also, only be fair to her? What was against it?

Well, on second thoughts, there were reasons why it might be better to keep the thing secret.

In the first place, because the letter and the suggestions contained in it were so low, he would find telling her about it a hideously embarrassing thing to do. And it would not only be embarrassing to him: it would be even more so for Esther. It would shock her dreadfully if the letter had no truth in it; and if there were any truth in it the situation would be more awful still.

Then, quite apart from truth and falsehood, merely to show her such a filthy missive would be to disgust and frighten her. It was not a thing a proper person – a man with sensitive and decent feelings – could really do. It was, really, his duty, as Bell had advised, absolutely to ignore the thing. And if he did otherwise she might easily be 'put off' him – quite rightly put off.

But Ryan's father had always taught him to charge at difficulties – and to do so, really, belonged to his own temperament. Therefore, he did not quite put from his mind the notion of showing her the card.

It was now dark, and Ryan, leaving the matter in abeyance, manoeuvred Esther towards the part of the covered bench, facing the lights of the Palace Pier, upon which all five had sat upon that first meeting and to which Gorse had always taken Esther when he meant to kiss her. Such is the force of habit.

Esther was not much afraid of sitting with Ryan here. The place was dark, but a few people passed, and she was certainly within screaming distance of help.

After about ten minutes of talking Ryan tried to take Esther's hand, but she withdrew it.

'I told you you mustn't do that,' she said.

'But why?' said Ryan. 'What's the matter with it?'

'There's a lot the matter with it,' she said, being unable to think of anything else to say.

But there was, accidentally, something in the words she used and the way in which she used them which struck Ryan forcibly. Was Esther, conceivably, trying to intimate to him that there was something the matter with herself – that she suffered from some malady which made it dangerous to 'touch' her, as the missive had put it?

In which case had not his opportunity come? Should he not show her the letter, or somehow lead her on to talk about herself, or tactfully ask her about herself?

The impulsive Ryan believed that his opportunity had come and that he would be a fool to let it go by.

'But what *is* the matter?' he asked, looking at her earnestly.

'Well . . .' was all Esther could manage, and this encouraged Ryan further.

'Go on. Tell me,' he said. 'There *is* something the matter, isn't there?'

At this Esther was tempted to tell him about her own anonymous letter, but remembered her mother's advice not to do so.

She was merely silent, and Ryan was encouraged further still.

'Go on, tell me. What *is* the matter?' Ryan took the plunge. 'Tell me, is there anything the matter with you?'

'With me? How do you mean?'

'Well. The matter. With you. Personally. Tell me.'

'Personally? How do you mean?'

'Well. Personally. Is there anything wrong with you?'

'How?'

'Well – do you *suffer* from anything?'

'From any what?'

'From any illness. It's hard to put, but you must tell me. I have a reason. Now. Go on. Tell me. Do you, or do you not, suffer from any personal illness?'

Ryan was so eager and emphatic, and his question was so mysterious, that it struck Esther that he might be out of his mind. In that case, the warning put on to the postcard was a genuine one.

'What on earth do you mean?' she said. 'Do I suffer from a personal illness?'

'Just what I say.'

'Of course I don't,' said Esther. 'What on earth should make you think I do? I've never had any illness in my life so far – apart from the measles and whooping cough as a child, and an occasional cold.'

Because she was speaking the truth Esther's statement was utterly convincing, and Ryan was utterly convinced.

He bathed in delicious relief. At the same time he reproached himself for ever having even entertained such a suspicion. He should have taken Bell's advice and completely expunged the thing from his mind. He had behaved in a low way.

Esther, on the other hand, was now more than ever inclining to the opinion that Ryan might be mad. She therefore pursued a subject which Ryan was now only too anxious to drop.

'What on earth made you ask me such a question?' she asked.

'Oh – I don't know . . .'

Ryan, as well as feeling, was looking ashamed of himself.

'But there must have been a Reason. Go on. What is it?'

'No. There wasn't.'

'But there must. Go on. Tell me.'

'No. There wasn't.'

'There was. I can see there was. Come on. Tell me.'

Ryan hesitated.

'Well,' he said. 'There was a little reason – but it was an absolutely absurd one, and I don't want to talk about it.'

'But please do.'

'No,' said Ryan. 'It's a little secret. I'll tell you one day, perhaps, when I know you better.' Ryan had an inspiration. 'By the way – talking of little secrets, what about *your* little secret? The one about Gorse. You said you'd tell me later.'

'No,' said Esther. 'That's still a little secret. Like yours.'

Esther now had a shot at some more truth.

'By the way, I've been out with him twice since I last saw you,' she said.

'Oh. Have you? I knew you were meeting him on Sunday evening, of course. Did he take you to the Metropole again?'

'Yes. He did.'

Gorse, if he had been listening to the dialogue which had just passed, would have been disquieted. Esther and Ryan had very nearly disclosed to each other their separate secrets. But now the danger had passed, and Gorse would have been relieved.

'And did he give you another cocktail?'

'Yes.'

A cocktail and a *half*, thought Esther, would have been the real truth.

'Well, he certainly *does* seem to be going it,' said Ryan. 'What did you do afterwards?'

'Oh – he just saw me home – part of the way.'

'How far?'

'Oh – just as far as the Clock Tower.'

'Oh – he did – did he?' said Ryan, and added, after a pause, 'Do you think he's keen on you? Like me?'

'Oh no, there's nothing of that sort.'

Remembering the kisses which had taken place on the very spot upon which they were now sitting, together with Gorse's near proposal of marriage, Esther knew that she had told another flagrant lie. On the other hand, it might be thought of as a legitimate lie. It was not Ryan's business, and his question had been, really, impudent – 'sauce'.

Ryan, as we know, was not really afraid of Gorse as a rival.

'No,' he said, 'I didn't really think there would be. I somehow don't believe Gorse really likes girls. At least not in the way other people do.'

That's what *you* think, was what Esther wanted to say. She was, of course – remembering the kisses and marriage offer – quite certain that Ryan was wrong.

But, actually, it was Esther who was wrong.

'What makes you think he doesn't?' asked Esther.

'Oh. I don't know . . . It's just an instinct.'

'What sort of instinct?'

'I can't really say. He's rather a funny one, our friend Gorse . . .'

'Funny? In what way? I don't see how he's funny.'

'Don't you? Well – I can't put my finger on it – but there it is. It's only an instinct. No doubt he's really very nice.'

'Well. I don't see anything funny about him. I think he's very nice.'

Esther, who now completely trusted (and, almost with her mother's approval, was contemplating marrying Gorse), was annoyed by Ryan's attitude. Also, she felt that it might derive from spite and jealousy. Also, she knew that 'funny' people were the first to call other people 'funny'. And all this not only lowered her opinion of Ryan as a completely sane person, but refreshed her grave suspicion that he was mad.

Ryan sensed her annoyance at once.

'Yes,' he said. 'I just *said* I thought he's probably very nice. Don't be angry.'

'I'm not angry.'

The subject was changed, but Esther continued to be slightly annoyed, and said that it was time for her to go home a good deal earlier than she might have otherwise.

As they walked towards the shore Ryan asked her if he might meet her tomorrow evening. She told him that she had arranged to meet Gorse – which was the truth.

'Oh,' said Ryan with a rather irritating lack of concern. 'Then what about Saturday?'

'No, I'm afraid that's no good. I've got to work this Saturday.'

'Oh yes. I'd forgotten. But couldn't we meet after your work – in the evening?'

'Well, no. I'm afraid that's no good. I get very tired, and I always spend the evenings with Mother on the Saturdays I work.'

Esther (the nearly 'spoiled') had now worked herself into a temper.

They had passed through the turnstile.

'Well,' said Ryan. 'Now may I see you home? Just as far as the Clock Tower?'

'No. I'd really rather go alone,' said the bad-tempered girl. 'I'd really rather – if you don't mind.'

'No. Of course I don't mind,' said Ryan, his calm infuriating Esther more than ever. 'But when am I going to see you again?'

'I don't know.'

'Well – what about Sunday? Perhaps we might go out on the bike again.'

Esther, in her anger, and the perturbation caused by her anger, thought that she must certainly not at present risk going into the country with Ryan again.

'No,' she said. 'I'm afraid I can't manage Sunday afternoon. My father's home on Sunday afternoons, and I don't see much of him, and so I have to stay in. I'm sorry.'

'Well, then – what about Sunday *evening*?'

Ryan was now getting a little angry himself.

'Yes,' said Esther. 'That seems all right.'

'Good. Then shall we meet just here? Seven-thirty. Sunday evening? All right?'

'Yes. Right you are. Seven-thirty – Sunday evening.'

She thought of thanking him for the evening. But she was in a temper, and he had only taken her on to the Pier (not to the Metropole), so she did not.

'Very well, then,' said Ryan. 'Good-bye.'

And he offered his hand in rather a cool way. She shook his hand with equal coolness, and left him quickly.

Ryan, as he walked home, was fully aware that something very nearly approaching a quarrel had just taken place. But this did not bother him. It might, even, be taken as a good sign. Other girls had quarrelled in this way with Ryan, and such quarrels had certainly not shown disinterest on their part.

A little later, on his walk home, it struck Ryan that Esther was, perhaps, just a silly little ass, or a coquette whom he ought to leave stone cold – who should be allowed to stew in her own ridiculous juice.

Many things she had said and done pointed to this conclusion: and Ryan was for a few minutes exhilarated by the notion of quickly and dramatically abandoning Esther.

But this mood and theory did not last long. Our poor, infatuated Ryan, after a few minutes, was unable to sustain and fortify himself with this new idea.

PART NINE

THE CAR

I

When Esther met Gorse outside the West Pier on the Friday evening she found him in a state of subdued excitement.

This was feigned by Gorse, but Esther was completely taken in by it.

'Well – where are we going?' he said. 'The good old Met. again?'

'That suits me, if it does you.'

'Yes. That's what I'd like.' He took her arm as they crossed the road. 'And let's get there quickly, as I've got some news.'

'Yes. I thought you had. Good or bad?'

'Oh – good. Decidedly good, if only everything goes all right.'

'What is it? Tell me.'

'No. Let's wait till we're sitting down over our drinks. It needs a lot of talking over quietly.'

'Why – do you want my advice about something? Or does it concern me?'

'Yes, as a matter of fact, it *does* concern you. I hope, of course, that everything that concerns me concerns you – but this, as a matter of fact, concerns you in any case.'

'It all sounds very mysterious. Won't you tell me?'

'No – not until we're sitting down and drinking.'

'Very well.'

As soon as their drinks had come, at their usual table inside the Metropole, Esther said: 'Now then. The time's come. Go ahead.'

Gorse took a sip at his drink, sat back in his chair, and put his fingers together.

'Well,' he said. 'What would you think of yours truly as the owner of a car?'

'A car!'

'Yes, and not only a car – but one of the sweetest little semi-racing things you've ever seen in your life.'

'It sounds lovely to me. But where do I come in?'

'I'm coming to that in a moment. As I said, it's the loveliest little thing I've ever seen in my life. It's secondhand, actually – but as good as new, and going for a song. I know a lot about cars – I've been brought up with them as a child.'

'Yes. I'm sure it's wonderful, but I still don't see where I come in.'

'Well – would you like to be part owner of a car?'

'How'd I do that?'

'Oh – just put in a little money for it, and then you'd be part owner. And then, when I've sold it again, you'd get your percentage – double your money back, probably. If I can only get it, it'll be one of the finest investments in the world.'

'But why is it going so cheap?'

'The man's hard up for ready cash. I know that for a fact. He's having to make a rush sale. I've known him since I was a kid.'

'Who is he? What's his name?'

'Gosling,' said Gorse, who had prepared himself for this question. 'He's got a garage out on the London Road ... Well – are you coming in on it? It's the chance of a lifetime, I can assure you.'

'But how much would I have to put in?' asked Esther. 'About?'

'It's not a question of "about". I know the exact sum. It's fifteen pounds.'

'Fifteen pounds!' exclaimed Esther. 'But I couldn't manage all that!'

'Don't be silly. Of course you could, if you've got all that money saved. And you're going to make double – or only a little under.'

Esther did not like this at all. The two pounds she had handed over to Gorse (and had back) was one matter. Fifteen pounds was another.

'And what's the full price of the car?'

'Ah – that I'm not quite sure. It's going to be pretty stiff, and I'm going to haggle.'

'Then how do you know it's so cheap?'

With this Esther nearly tripped Gorse up.

'Oh – I know roughly,' he said. 'He's mentioned eighty, and it'll only be a matter of five or ten pounds either way. Well – are you in?'

Esther was deeply reluctant. Fifteen pounds! She thought of what her mother would say about all this.

She decided to make a stand.

'You know, I'd really rather not,' she said. 'I don't like "speculation", or whatever you call it, and I know my mother wouldn't approve.'

'But you needn't tell your mother.'

'No. But I don't like it myself. Honestly I don't. I'd really rather you left me out. It'll be your car – so why don't you buy it on your own? I'd really rather not. Do you mind?'

There was a pause. Gorse took a sip at his drink, and leaned back again, and looked at her.

'Well,' he said. 'To tell you the truth, I'm afraid it's a bit too late, and you've *got* to come in.'

'*Got* to? How?'

'Well – you've got to unless I'm going to lose it – and it's the chance of a lifetime.'

'How? I don't see.'

'Well – it's all rather a long story.'

'Tell me.'

'Oh dear – I'm afraid you'll think I'm trying to borrow money from you again, but I'll tell you all the same. You see, it's a question of a deposit.'

'Deposit?'

'Yes. You see, there are a lot of other people after it, and if I'm going to get it I've got to give this man Gosling a deposit – and he's asked for fifteen pounds. He's so hard up that he wants even that. And I said I'd give it to him.'

'Then why don't you? If you've got the money to buy the car!'

'Because I haven't got fifteen pounds.'

'Not fifteen pounds if you're going to buy the car for eighty?'

'No. Now I'm coming to the story. I haven't got all that money just at the moment, and if I don't give him the fifteen pounds tomorrow, Saturday, it'll go to somebody else. I *know* it.'

'But when will you get the money – I mean the fifteen pounds?'

'On Monday – absolutely for certain. That's when my stepmother pays my allowance in to my account. She does it monthly. So I can pay it back to you on Monday. And then, on Wednesday, unless there's any hitch, there's a hundred and fifty pounds coming to me, and all's well.'

'A hundred and fifty! Where's that coming from?'

'It's coming from my aunt. She died two or three months ago, and left it to me.'

Esther reflected that Gorse went in for rather a lot of aunts and uncles. There had been, so far, only one uncle and one aunt, but still this somehow seemed to her too many.

'And why haven't you got the money – if she died three months ago?'

'Oh – you know all these maddening legal delays. Or perhaps you don't. I do – I've had to suffer from them enough. It's a question of probate, and all that. I don't expect you know what probate means. However – it's all over now. I had a letter from my lawyer only this morning and he said I should get the cheque by Wednesday – or Thursday at the latest. I think I've got the letter on me.'

Gorse began to fish in his breast pocket. 'Would you like to see it, or do you still not trust me?'

'No,' said Esther. 'Of course I trust you.'

Gorse had expected her to say this, but was relieved that she had. Otherwise he would have had to pretend that he had left the letter at home.

'Well,' he said. 'I'm very glad you do. If you don't trust me, that means you don't really like me, and that's the end of all my hopes, isn't it?'

'What hopes?'

'You know exactly what I mean. But as I can't make love to you in the lounge of an hotel, perhaps we'd better drop the subject and return to where we are. Tell me now – will you help me in the chance of a lifetime? I've put all my cards on the table. Don't if you don't want to – of course.'

'No. It's not that. It's just that I hate speculation, as I said. And I know my mother wouldn't approve. And it was she who *gave* me all that money – wasn't it?'

'Yes. I know,' said Gorse. 'But do be a sport. I always thought you were one, and I believe you are still. Won't you?'

'I can't make up my mind,' said Esther, clearly weakening.

'I know your mother must be very nice,' said Gorse. 'But all mothers are old-fashioned – aren't they? And one's got to be modern and a sport – hasn't one? One's got to take risks – that's doing things the right way. And if one doesn't do things the right way, one never gets anywhere. One just gets stuck where one is.'

Thus Gorse, with that peculiar insight into women's minds which characterized him, was playing cleverly upon Esther's strongest inner passion – the passion to 'better' herself, and, in order to do this, to behave exactly as those 'better' than herself did. His use of the words 'the right way' won the day for Gorse.

'Well,' said Esther. 'Perhaps you're right.'

2   Gorse saw that he had won the day.

'Of course I'm right,' said Gorse. 'And just think of it. You and I, going wherever we like, and driving up to the Metropole in one of the smartest little cars on the road. Of course, it's not a Rolls, or anything like that, but I'll bet you there'll be plenty of Rolls owners who'll envy us. You just wait till you see it.'

Esther, already a little intoxicated by her cocktail, was additionally intoxicated by this picture.

Esther, although she had been on the back of motorcycles, had never actually stepped inside a car in her life. And the idea of doing so, and driving up to the Metropole, completely went to her head. All her fears left her.

'All right,' she said. 'Then it's a go.'

'Good,' said Gorse. 'I knew it would be. I knew you were a sport.'

A thought struck Esther.

'But how am I going to get the money to you? It's got to be by tomorrow, you say, and I have to work all Saturday.'

'Yes. It's got to be tomorrow – and tomorrow afternoon, too – or I'll lose it. Can't you take it to your work – and then meet me somehow?'

'Yes,' said Esther. 'I suppose I can.'

'I'll look in at your shop and buy some sweets early in the afternoon, shall I?' said Gorse. 'And then you can slip it to me. The money's got to be with Gosling by four o'clock.'

'All right. If you don't mind seeing me at my worst.'

'How worst?'

'Well – serving behind a counter.'

'I don't think you'll be at your worst. There's no worst with you,' said Gorse. 'At least not to me, at any rate. Everything's always the best.'

After this compliment there was a pause.

Then another thought struck Esther.

'Are you old enough to drive a car?' she asked.

'Ah,' said Gorse. 'There are ways and means.'

And for Gorse there certainly were. The precocious Gorse was more precocious in the matter of cars than in any other department of life. When it came to car-buying, car-selling, or car-trickery, Gorse probably knew more than any other young man of his age in England, Europe, or the world.

'Then, when I meet you after that,' said Gorse, 'I'll take you for your first spin in it. I know he'll let me take a run or two in it before I've actually got it. If he will – what about going out in it on Sunday afternoon?'

'Oh – I'm sorry. Sunday afternoon's bad for me. It's about the only time I ever see my father, and Mother likes me to stay in.'

'Well, then – Sunday evening?'

'Oh lord – that's no good either. I've gone and promised to meet your friend Ryan.'

'Oh – I'd forgotten about Ryan,' said Gorse truthfully, for, in the somewhat strenuous extraction of the fifteen pounds from Esther, he actually had. 'How did you get on with him?'

'Oh – all right . . .'

'Where did you go?'

'On the Pier.'

'And what did you do there, pray?'

'Oh – we walked, and played with a few slot machines, and sat down for a bit, and then came home.'

'Is that all?'

'Yes.'

'Did he hold your hand again?'

'He tried to.'

'But you didn't let him?'

'No.'

'Why not? There's not much harm in holding hands, if there're people about.'

'Oh – I don't know. I suppose I'm a bit afraid of him.'

'Naturally. And what did he do when you refused him?'

'Oh – he behaved all right. But you know, I *do* think there's something funny about that boy.'

'Ah-ha. So you're beginning to see that your Uncle Ralph knows a thing or two, after all. But what did he do funny?'

'It wasn't what he did. It was more what he said.'

'What did he say?'

'I don't know. It was just *funny*, somehow.'

'But he must have said something. Go on. What was it?'

'I can't quite remember now. But he asked me if there was anything the matter with me – whether I suffered from any illness.'

At this moment, for the first time, Gorse saw that he had made a serious blunder – that the two might compare notes. He looked thoughtful, and there was a pause.

'How very strange,' said Gorse. 'And what did you reply?'

'I said of course there wasn't, and I asked him if he'd gone mad.'

'And what did he reply?'

'I've forgotten how it went now.'

'Did you ask him why he asked?' asked Gorse.

'Oh yes. So I did.'

'And what did he say?' Gorse, although Esther did not perceive this, was looking gravely yet anxiously at her.

'He said it was a secret – a little secret. He wouldn't tell me. And that's funny in itself.'

'It certainly is,' said Gorse, breathing again.

'I mean *why* should he ask such a question?' said Esther. 'Can *you* think why?'

Gorse thought before replying, and was inspired.

'Well. I *could* make a guess,' he said.

'What?'

'No. I'd rather not say.'

'Now. Come on. You're my friend – aren't you? And you're advising me. You can't keep me in the dark if you're doing that. It's not fair. Go on.'

'Well – it's very difficult to put.'

'Go on. Out with it.'

'Well, if he wanted, later on, to go further than – just holding your hand. And if he wanted to go further even than kissing you – well –'

'Go on. What do you mean by further than kissing me?'

'Really. This is a bit indelicate, you know.'

'Go on.'

'Well, if he wanted to – to –' said Gorse, hesitating. 'Well – to *go the whole hog* – if I've *got* to say it. You know what I mean ...'

'Yes. I know. Go on.'

'Well, if he wanted that, he might want to make certain beforehand that you were quite well, in a certain way. I don't know if you know it, but there *are* certain diseases, you know.'

'Yes. I know. But what a filthy idea.'

'Yes, very filthy. But people with twisted minds develop filthy ideas – don't they? Of course I may be wrong – I may be completely maligning him on this particular point.'

'I hope you are,' said Esther. 'But it was a funny thing to ask me. And then the funny thing about it all is that he called *you* funny.'

As soon as she had made this indiscretion – one forgivable

because characteristic of girls of her age – Esther regretted it. She had, she realized, started 'making mischief'.

'Oh, he did – did he?' said Gorse. 'Did he say in what way I was funny?'

'No. He just said he thought you were – a bit.'

'And did you ask him why he thought me funny?'

'Yes.'

'And he said?'

'He said he didn't know.'

'A very curious character,' said Gorse. 'Do *you* think me funny?'

'Me? No. Anything but. *You've* got your head screwed on all right. Anybody can see that.'

'Well, I believe I have, fairly well,' said Gorse, and added, 'Of course it's typical of funny people to go about calling other people funny.'

This, it will be remembered, was exactly the thought which had visited Esther at the time.

'Yes,' she said. 'I know it is.'

'But you're still going about with him?'

'Well, I don't see really how I can get out of it. He's very polite and he hasn't done anything wrong so far. And I'll see that it's always in public places.'

'Very well,' said Gorse indulgently. 'Go your own way. But if you get into trouble don't say your Uncle Ralph didn't warn you. And now let's change the subject – shall we?'

The subject was changed, the second drinks were finished, and they went outside and on to the West Pier.

When it was dark enough Gorse took her to the familiar spot, and kissed her in the familiar way. While doing this he said: 'You know, I'm going to ask you a very important question very soon now.'

'Are you?' said Esther.

'Yes,' said Gorse. 'Have you any idea what sort of answer you're going to give?'

'I don't know,' said Esther.

'Very well,' said Gorse. 'Uncle Ralph'll have to wait. He's a patient fellow – is Uncle Ralph.'

'Is he?'

'Yes. But he knows what he wants, and quite often he gets what he wants,' said Gorse.

Esther allowed him to escort her as far as the Clock Tower. He arranged to call at the sweet-shop at two-thirty tomorrow (Saturday) afternoon in order to collect the fifteen pounds. Then they were to meet at seven-thirty outside the West Pier on Monday. He would then, he said, have the money to pay her back.

Esther was lighthearted as she left Gorse, but Gorse had a lot of thinking to do.

3   Ryan had had the effrontery to call him 'funny' to Esther.

Also, Esther and Ryan, despite all Gorse's efforts, were still meeting each other. And, this being so, they might easily still disclose to each other their anonymous letters from himself.

Previously Gorse had had little jealousy or hatred of Ryan. The anonymous letters had been sent mostly for the pure pleasure of the thing. But now Gorse, in working against Ryan, had two definite motives.

Ryan, if he went on meeting Esther, might at last show his letter, and, by doing so, perhaps win her. In this case Gorse's plot in regard to the car might fall through: for Ryan (who also knew a lot about cars) might advise and sway Esther.

Gorse's other motive was that of revenge. He did not propose to be called 'funny' without returning the blow – and this with double force.

Gorse, on his way home, decided that what he called to himself 'stronger measures' would have to be taken with the person he called to himself 'Master Ryan'.

II

On Saturday morning Ryan again arrived early, and on his motor-cycle, at the house belonging to Bell's aunt in Bigwood Avenue.

Because Bell's lighthearted advice about the anonymous letter had shown itself to be so entirely and beautifully correct, Ryan's heart was warm towards Bell, and, as a reward, he proposed to take Bell for a long trip into the country. The Sage, Ryan knew, enjoyed riding on the back of a motorcycle as much as he enjoyed ice cream.

Bell saw and heard Ryan arriving, but, as chance would have it, he had neither folding chess set, nor book, nor even pipe, to hand: and so there were no means of making an ass of himself. He went unaffectedly to the door, and invited Ryan to come into his front room.

They talked for a little while, and then Ryan said:

'Oh, by the way – about that anonymous letter – you were quite right. It was simply drivel. I've found out for a fact. I ought to have taken your advice in the first place, and thrown it into the waste-paper basket. I'm sorry I didn't, and I want to thank you for it.'

'Not at all,' said Bell. 'Only too glad if I've been of any help.'

'And as that cloud's passed,' said Ryan, 'and it's another cloudless day, what about you and I having a nice long trip on the bike into the country?'

Bell readily agreed to this, and in five minutes' time they were both on the motorcycle.

They travelled that day over a great deal of Sussex, having lunch at Haywards Heath, and tea at Hurst. At about six they returned to Bigwood Avenue, and washed, and then strolled down to the Brighton Front.

Between the two Piers they saw Gertrude Perks, who was walking alone.

They did their utmost to cut her, but she came up to them, saying, 'Hello – how are you two boys getting on?'

2   Ryan and Bell were walking in the direction of the Palace Pier.

After Ryan and Bell had greeted her politely, Gertrude walked with them in the same direction.

Ryan and Bell now tried very hard to do two things – to remain polite, and to think of an excuse for getting away from Gertrude. They were fairly successful with the former, but not adroit with the latter.

As all three drew near the Palace Pier, the situation was extremely, almost unutterably, painful.

Because of its painfulness, the naïve and *gauche* Bell could not resist giving Ryan a Nudge with his elbow.

Because Bell was so naïve and *gauche* this Nudge was an enormous one – ridiculously so. So much so that Gertrude herself observed it.

Ryan, agonized both by the Nudge and by his almost certain knowledge that Gertrude had observed it, was thrust into two minds – several minds.

Did the Nudge mean merely 'Isn't this awful?' Or did it mean 'What are we going to do? For heaven's sake get us out of this. You're more experienced than I am and you ought to find a way'?

Or did it mean, perhaps, that Bell wanted to be alone with Gertrude?

Ryan inclined very strongly to this last point of view. Wishes are, unfortunately, and as we all know, the parents of points of view, even with such sincere and delicate-minded people as Ryan. All Ryan wanted to do was to escape at the earliest possible moment – to run for his life, in fact – and here was his chance.

His reason, in due course, childlike, began to obey his wishes. Was not Bell an 'other one'? Was not Gertrude an 'other one'? Did not 'other ones' naturally desire to pair with each other? Would it not be simple tact on the part of Ryan, would it not, perhaps, be his *duty*, to leave these two alone?

When they were within about fifteen yards' distance from the entrance to the Palace Pier, Ryan made his decision.

'Well – this is where I have to buzz off,' he said, stopping and looking at his watch as if he had suddenly realized he was in a dreadful hurry. 'I've got to put the bike away, and the garage closes at eight. So will you two forgive me?'

'Yes,' said Gertrude with alacrity. 'Of course. If you're in a hurry. Nice to have met you. I only hope we'll meet again soon.'

'Yes. I hope we will. Well – I *must* go. So long – both.'

'So long!' said Gertrude cheerfully.

'So long,' said Bell.

Thus Ryan had done his duty by Bell, and should have been pleased with himself. But, unluckily, as he had left the couple together, he had looked at Bell's face, and had caught an unspeakably forlorn and deserted expression upon it.

And so, as he walked home, Ryan had an uneasy feeling that he had not, really, done his strict duty.

3   Gertrude had, as Ryan feared, observed Bell's enormous and ridiculous Nudge.

Now the real meaning of Bell's Nudge had been merely 'Isn't this awful?' –nothing more at all. But Gertrude had interpreted it quite differently.

Gertrude had, in fact, put exactly the same construction upon it that Ryan had. With Gertrude, as with Ryan before her, a wish had given birth to a thought. Not that Gertrude was in any way attracted by Bell. She thought him plain, affected, eccentric, and what she would call 'soppy'. But Gertrude was susceptible to flattery, and if the Nudge meant what she thought it did – 'I want to be alone with this girl' – it was a compliment of a serious kind.

And this made her see Bell in a new light. His 'soppiness' and other defects practically all vanished and she believed she could even discern in him some charm.

The unfortunate thing was that Ryan had absolutely confirmed her interpretation of the Nudge by his hasty departure with an obviously false excuse.

4   'Well,' said Bell weakly. 'What are we going to do now?'

'Well – as we're outside the Palace Pier – what about going on it?'

Bell tried to think of an excuse, but the feat was beyond him. Also, in common politeness, he could not make an excuse so immediately after Ryan had made his. The wretched girl would know that she was being left stone cold – stranded.

'Very well,' he said, and they went through the turnstile, Gertrude offering to pay, but Bell not permitting this.

As they walked seawards remarkable thoughts entered Gertrude's head – thoughts very similar to those she had entertained some nights previously when she was with Ryan.

What if 'other ones' (she thought) were, after all, destined to pair with 'other ones'? What if they had no other choice? What if they must simply make do with them?

And here was Bell, who had nudged his friend in order to be alone with her. Would she not be foolish to reject him? Was it not her business to encourage him?

Though he was now much more attractive in her eyes than before, Gertrude still could not say that she had any feeling for Bell. But, apart from anything else, after her rebuff, kindly as it was from Ryan, she was in desperate need of reassuring herself – of proving that she could at least magnetize someone. And here was her chance.

Bell was very untalkative as they walked along, and Gertrude put this down to sudden shyness or fear.

Was it not, therefore, her business to dispel this shyness and fear? Must she not, in fact (as with Ryan before), employ Personality and Boldness? She decided to do this.

'Do you like playing with slot machines?' she asked.

'I don't really know,' said Bell. 'Do you?'

'You seem doubtful,' said Gertrude. 'Do you think it too childish?'

'Well – quite apart from the expense involved – I'd certainly say I should regard it as a somewhat puerile – indeed, I might say sterile – form of activity. Don't you?'

'I don't know. You see, I don't know what "puerile" or "sterile" means. What do they? What's "puerile"?'

'Oh – just boyish – as of a boy. Derivation from the Latin.'

'And "sterile"?'

'Well – arid – leading to nothing. Unproductive.'

'And what does "arid" mean?'

'Dry,' said Bell. 'Dried up.'

'You know, you're a bit dry yourself, you know,' said Gertrude, 'with all your long words. Have you *got* to use them?'

'No. I haven't got to. I just like the right expression, that's all. I like to hit upon the *mot juste*.'

'The Mow *What*?' said Gertrude rather violently.

'The *mot juste*,' repeated Bell. 'That's French and means exactly the correct word.'

'*Joost* the right word, in fact?' said Gertrude jocularly.

'Yes,' said Bell. 'If you like to put it that way.'

'You with your French and Latin,' said Gertrude. 'You know, a lot of people might think you're a bit conceited.'

'Might they?'

'But I don't,' said Gertrude. 'I can see through you all right.'

And it had just occurred to Gertrude that she could, indeed, see beyond Bell's affectations. Furthermore, it now seemed to her that these were so childish that they might come to be slightly enchanting rather than a flaw in his character.

'Well, I certainly hope I'm not conceited,' said Bell.

'No. I don't believe you are. You're just a baby, really, in spite of all your long words,' said Gertrude, and she took his arm and led him towards the footballing slot machine with which she had played with Ryan. 'Now come and forget all about your French and Latin and have a bit of fun with me.'

Reluctantly Bell obeyed her. He tried to put in both pennies, but she would not allow this, and put one in for herself.

There is little skill required in this game, but there is just enough to make a person with enthusiasm and his wits about him beat a person who is devoid of either. Needless to say, Bell lost. Gertrude made him play again, and he again lost. Then, at the third game, she instructed Bell and absolutely forced him to win.

As with Ryan previously, while playing, Gertrude managed to get her head extremely near to Bell's. This did not terrify him as much as it had Ryan. In his inexperience he thought it must be an accident, or even as something necessarily belonging to such a game.

He was rather pleased at winning the third game, and when Gertrude (taking his arm again, which he did not like) led him on to the next machine (the race-horse one) he was more willing to play.

Of course he lost again. But Gertrude cleverly deluded him into the thought that he had won the third race by his own merits, and she could see that he was again not displeased.

'Third time lucky seems to be your motto,' said Gertrude. 'You can beat me easy when you learn. Only you're such a slow starter, that's all.'

In this last remark there was a double meaning which Bell completely missed.

She took his arm again, and they walked on.

They did not have to walk long before it was dark enough for Gertrude's purposes. She took him to the same seat to which she had taken Ryan. The force of habit again.

After a while Gertrude repeated, exactly, her tactics with Ryan.

'It's a lovely night – ain't it?' she said. 'Ain't it?'

'Yes. It certainly is.'

'Or a night for love?' said Gertrude. 'Which?'

The foolish Bell still had no inkling of her meaning or intentions.

'Yes,' he said. 'Gazing at the stars in their firmament is certainly an ennobling experience – small as it makes one feel.'

'Yes,' said Gertrude. 'It makes one feel lonely. Doesn't it you?'

'Yes. It certainly does,' said Bell gravely.

Bell had said this in all innocence, but Gertrude, remembering that he had nudged Ryan in order to be alone with her, was certain that he meant it as an invitation. And, remembering his shyness, she decided to take the initiative. She put her arm round Bell and endeavoured impulsively to 'nestle' her head against his shoulder.

But she was too impulsive and something went wrong. Instead of arriving on Bell's shoulder, her head somehow bumped into Bell's face, and her spectacles hit his own, with a clattering noise and very nearly knocking them off.

Only spectacle-wearers who have been embraced awkwardly by other spectacle-wearers will be able to comprehend fully the ineffable gruesomeness of the noise made by the clatter of lens against lens, and rims against rims.

Bell nearly jumped up, but managed to remain seated, and a

moment later Gertrude had properly 'nestled' her head upon his shoulder.

'Aren't *you* lonely?' said Gertrude. 'Aren't *you* lonely – like poor little me?'

'Yes ...' said Bell. 'Indeed ... Yes. I am ...' Then he managed to throw in 'I suppose ...'

'I thought you were,' said Gertrude. 'You're like me. You're all solitary. There you are. There's one of your long words for you – "solitary".'

Bell, fantastically unsophisticated as he was, now knew roughly the sort of thing Gertrude was after, and tried to think of some means of defence.

All Bell had learned in life had been Learning – and so his mind at once flew to this. He had never thought that Learning would be of assistance to him in a predicament such as this.

He loved, in his own way, Learning for its own sake, and he also hoped to advance in life by using it. But now it was to be used on a Pier in the darkness against an importunate girl!

'Ah, yes,' said Bell. 'Solitude. A serious problem indeed. In the words of Keats, "Oh solitude if I must with thee dwell, Let it not be among the jumbled heap. Of murky buildings; climb with me the steep – Nature's observatory – whence the dell Its flowery slopes, its rivers' crystal swell, May seem a span: let me thy vigils keep, 'Mongst boughs pavilioned, where the deer's swift leap. Startles the wild bee from the fox-glove bell. But though I'll gladly trace these scenes with thee, Yet the sweet converse of an innocent mind, Whose words are images of thoughts refined, Is my soul's pleasure: and it sure must be, Almost the highest bliss of human-kind, When to thy haunts two kindred spirits flee." Very finely put – don't you think?'

'Yes,' said Gertrude, who had not understood a word of the sonnet, and who, of course, did not want this sort of thing at all. However, she decided to go on trying.

'I like to hear you reciting Poetry,' she said. 'Go on. Recite some more.'

'Some more about what?'

'About solitude. It's romantic. Go on.'

Bell was silent.

'I can't think of one about solitude,' he said – weakly, because exhausted by thought.

'Well – about anything romantic. Go on.'.

Bell went on thinking.

'Well,' he said. 'As it's dark – what about darkness? Complete darkness. What about Milton on his own darkness? You know your Milton? You know that he was blind?'

'Yes,' said Gertrude, who did know this.

'Very well,' said Bell. 'Let's try this – "When I consider how my light is spent, Ere half my days in this dark world and wide, And that one talent which is death to hide, Lodged with me useless ..."'And Bell completed a second sonnet.

Gertrude, who was still hardly able to understand a word, was, however, quite clever enough to see that Bell had been clever enough to dodge Romance.

'Yes. That's nice, too,' she said. 'Now go on. Let's have some more.'

'But what?'

'Oh – anything. Just about the night and the stars, *I* don't mind.'

Keats' *Bright star, would I were as steadfast as thou art* came into Bell's head, but he was quick enough to see that the end of this would be most appallingly and pertinently romantic.

'Are you interested in the stars?' he said, with a new clever idea in his mind. 'In Astronomy?'

'Yes,' said Gertrude. 'I like hearing about Astrology.'

'No. I said Astronomy – not Astrology,' said Bell.

'What's the difference?'

'Well – one is the art of divining the future by the stars – that's Astrology. The other's the science of the stars – of the constellations.'

Bell felt that he was getting nearer the shore, and that, if only he went on swimming hard, he might reach it.

'All right, then,' said Gertrude. 'Tell me about your old Astronomy.'

'Very well,' said Bell. 'You see that star, there? The large one just above the extreme tip of the West Pier?'

'Yes.'

Luckily, amongst the branches of Learning which Bell had climbed, a little knowledge of Astronomy was included. He now proceeded, for a matter of ten minutes, to explain constellations to Gertrude.

He had reached the shore. Gertrude gave in. She was deeply hurt. So she could not even touch the heart of another 'other one'!

But she was not a resentful girl.

'All right,' she said at last, forgivingly interrupting Bell's flow of talk, and removing her head from his shoulder. 'We can't go on talking about the stars all night – can we? They're cold – and I'm cold, too. Shall we go off home? It's getting late.'

'Yes. It is a bit late, and I'm rather cold, too,' said Bell, and they rose and walked towards the turnstiles.

Bell offered to see her home, but she would not allow him to do so.

Deflated and wearied by her experience, Gertrude walked home. Exhilarated and stimulated by his escape, Bell did the same. These two made a very tragic couple.

For, when Bell was in bed, he remembered the warmth of Gertrude's body against his own, and half regretted what he had done. He even hoped he might meet her again. Gertrude, in bed, also remembered the warmth of Bell's body, and that night she cried before going to sleep.

They were not fated to meet again.

Bell was a bachelor all his life. Gertrude, on the other hand, by a mixture of divine luck and intense labour, married the son of a fishmonger in George Street, Hove. The fishmonger died, and his son inherited his father's business. Gertrude had three children by this son. These were hideous, noisy, and ugly, but consoled her. Bell consoled himself with the thought that Learning was to him both wife and mistress.

But Gertrude and Bell were not effectually consoled.

III

Esther and Ryan met outside the West Pier on Sunday at the time appointed and spent an evening which was not particularly eventful.

Esther was amiable and in an unusually carefree mood.

She had completely thrown off that fear she had momentarily had that she was 'speculating' and might not recover her fifteen pounds.

Gorse had called at the sweet-shop on the Saturday afternoon, and, serving him with sweets for which he had jokingly asked, she had secretly passed the notes over to him. He arranged to meet her on the Monday evening, and he said that, if Gosling would allow it (and he was almost certain he would), he might have the car with him when he met her.

She had liked the joke with the sweets (he had asked for pear drops and had been very amusingly particular about their size and colour), and when he had gone she knew she was beginning to like and trust Gorse more and more.

Also, she was excited about the car itself, in which Gorse had said she might still have a share, if she liked. She almost contemplated doing this.

Esther, as we know, had never stepped inside a car in her life, and the thought of doing so exhilarated her to a degree which cannot easily be understood by those who have entered or driven cars. Esther, in fact, was looking forward tremendously to tomorrow evening – could hardly wait for it.

2   Ryan, of course, benefited by her good spirits, which he at once sensed, and which made him happier and more hopeful. If he had known to whom and what he was indebted for this renewed hope and happiness, his spirits would have fallen low.

When it was dark, and they had played gaily at several slot machines, Ryan tried to take Esther to the usual spot on the covered bench. But this, for once, was occupied. They therefore went to the other side of the Pier, and sat down on a bench facing Worthing.

The very distant lights of Worthing Pier were just discernible, and Ryan told her that when it was so clear that Worthing Pier was visible from Brighton it was usually a sign of bad weather to come. Esther told him that she knew this. It is, in fact, an old Brighton legend.

They began to talk about Brighton. Ryan knew it well, but Esther knew it better and chattered to him cheerfully.

Then Ryan took her hand, and Esther did not withdraw it.

Ryan had by now, of course, almost completely forgotten about his own anonymous letter. And with Esther the passage of time, together with her excitement about the car, had very nearly removed the cloud. As these two sat facing Worthing at this moment neither of the two letters was in the minds of either of them.

Having held her hand in a variety of increasingly affectionate ways, Ryan was emboldened to kiss Esther. She allowed this, and he put his arm round her, and kissed her again from time to time.

Esther in some ways enjoyed Ryan's kisses more than Gorse's, but in some ways she did not. After Gorse, Ryan seemed a little timid, tame, even lukewarm.

Then, all at once, Esther recalled the hypothesis that Ryan was a dangerous lunatic, and she said, 'We mustn't go on doing this, you know.'

Ryan at once assented. His highest hopes had been exceeded; he was a good deal more than content; and he knew that this was the moment to leave well alone.

It was he himself who, after looking at his watch, suggested that it was time to go home.

When they were on the front again he asked if he might see her home, and she said, 'Oh no – don't bother.'

Determined not to press anything, Ryan at once agreed to leave her, but asked her when he might see her again.

'Now, let's think,' she said. 'Tomorrow's no good. Nor the day after. What about Wednesday?'

She had thus easily dodged telling him what she was doing tomorrow evening. She did not quite know why she implied that she was engaged on the day after. Perhaps it was because, if Gorse had the car on Monday, he might also have it on Tuesday, and then she would get two drives in it on successive evenings. The car had gone to Esther's head.

'Very well,' said Ryan. 'It's a long while to wait, but I'll put up with it somehow. Seven-thirty – here – Wednesday?'

'Right you are.'

They shook hands, and Ryan thought he would throw in a final compliment.

'You know I'd wait for you – don't you? For however long,' he said. 'You know I'd do anything for you. I'd die for you.'

'Would you?'

'Yes – die or do *murder* for you,' said Ryan solemnly, and he looked at her with burning eyes. 'Good-bye.'

Coming from one who was possibly a raving maniac, this remark was not a happy one.

Nor were the burning eyes exactly of any help to Ryan.

IV

On the Monday evening Gorse was waiting for Esther at the usual place, and as they walked towards the Metropole Esther noticed that Gorse was talking in a rather strained, self-conscious way.

Outside the Metropole, Esther observed, among a few other cars, a slim, exquisite, beautiful, open car, painted bright red – a dream-car.

She looked at this, and then at Gorse, who, it seemed to her, was purposely, and with an effort, not looking at it.

2   Her heart leapt with joy and hope. Could it be possible?

Once, when Esther was a child, she had been taken to a Christmas party for children. At this party there had been a Christmas tree, and, on this Christmas tree, presents for the children had been hung. Amongst these was a small doll's house, with miniature furniture, and on this doll's house, the moment she had seen it, Esther had set her heart passionately. She wanted absolutely nothing else on earth. Could it conceivably be for her? She had been compelled to wait in anguish until the Christmas presents were given to the children, and then, to her indescribable joy, she was given the doll's house.

Her emotions now were almost exactly the same as then. Could this dream-car be the one Gorse had acquired – or rather was in the process of acquiring? She wanted absolutely nothing else on earth.

3   They found their usual table at the Metropole, and as soon as their drinks had come, and they had sipped at them, Gorse said, 'Well – a little business transaction first, I think,' and began to fish in his back trouser pocket.

'Oh – must we be so businesslike?' said Esther, very pleased that he was being so, for all that.

'Yes, we must,' said Gorse. 'At any rate, in the present stage of our relations. Perhaps a time'll come when all my money's yours and all yours is mine. My money arrived all right.'

Another near-proposal of marriage, Esther observed.

'Well, here you are,' Gorse went on, counting the notes and putting them on to the table. 'Unless you want a share in the car, and you want me to keep it for you. But I don't think you want that – do you?'

The curious thing, now that she had seen the money, was that Esther was not absolutely certain that she did not want precisely this. Indeed, if the car was the red dream-car outside, she really believed that she would like to have a share in it. She did not pick up the notes from the table, and she played for time.

'Oh – I don't know,' she said. 'I've been wondering about that. Tell me. Did he let you have the car this evening?'

'Yes. He did. And if you're agreeable we'll go out for our first little spin in it together this evening.'

'Where is it? Where have you left it?'

'Ah – never you mind. It's not a long walk, though.'

'Tell me. What *sort* of car is it? What does it look like?'

'You're very curious, aren't you? Well – curiosity killed the cat. You must hold yourself in patience for a little. You'll be seeing it soon enough.'

Esther was now quite sure that the red dream-car was the one.

'Well,' she said. 'It's difficult to make up one's mind – I mean about taking a share.'

'Ah – so you're seriously contemplating it?'

'Well, I am *thinking* about it. It *would* be an investment, wouldn't it?'

'Oh yes – it'd be that all right. As I've told you, I'm going to sell that thing, after I've had some fun with it for a bit, for pretty nearly double the price – if not quite. I know about cars, as I've told you too, and I know when I'm on to a good thing. And it's not the first time I've done it, by any means – though my previous deals have only been more or less with little tin Lizzies.'

'Well – if it *is* an investment, I don't see why I shouldn't.'

'In which case I retain the fifteen pounds?'

'Yes.'

'And give you a receipt for it?'

'Yes. I suppose so.'

Gorse looked at Esther. He had not anticipated that Esther would trust him to this extent. He had to make up his mind quickly as to what he was to do in this new situation – to see if he could exploit it in any way.

After a pause in the conversation, he hit upon what he thought would be the best thing.

'No,' he said. 'I'm not going to let you.'

'Why not?'

'Well – you said you were afraid of speculation – didn't you? And I don't want to be the one to introduce you to bad ways – if you call them bad.'

'I don't. And I'm not really afraid any more. Honestly.'

'No. I know you think you're not. But I believe you still are at the bottom of your heart. And I'm sure your mother is.'

'Oh. That's a different matter. I needn't tell her.'

'No. I think it'd be wrong not to tell her. She gave you all your money, after all. And if you tell her, she'd be shocked. I know these old-fashioned mothers. And I want to keep the right side of your mother, above all things.'

'Why?'

'You know why.'

She did, but had to pretend that she did not, and said, 'No, I don't. Why?'

'Well, if you should look favourably upon a certain proposition which I've told you I may make very soon, your mother'd be a very important person, then, wouldn't she? And so would your father.'

'Oh – I don't think he'd count very much. Although he's very nice.'

'No,' said Gorse firmly. 'I'm not going to let you. I've got an instinct it's wiser not to. Although there *is* another idea.'

'What's that?'

'You keep the fifteen pounds, and let me *give* you a share in the car – fifteen pounds' worth.'

'No,' said Esther. 'That's certainly out of the question.'

'Why?'

'It'd be the same as giving me a present of fifteen pounds.'

'It'd be giving you thirty pounds, actually, when the car's sold. But I still don't see what's wrong.'

'Well, I do,' said Esther. 'It's out of the question, and that's *that*.'

'Very well, have it your own way,' said Gorse, and he picked up the notes and handed them to her. 'There you are. Put them away safely and don't lose them.'

'All right, then, and thank you very much,' said Esther, taking the notes.

Here, although he had no notion that he had done so, Gorse had made yet another of those strange, sudden, appalling blunders which he was always to make in spite of his astuteness generally.

He had returned to Esther the identical notes which she had given him, and if she had taken note of the numbers she might have noticed it, and this would have proved that no deposit had been paid to the man Gosling.

The man Gosling did not actually exist. But a man named Randall did. He dealt in cars, and Gorse had gained his confidence. He had let Gorse, a prospective buyer, use the car tonight. He had previously let Gorse use other cheaper cars. He had asked for no deposit.

In returning to Esther the fifteen pounds, which he had in the interval kept in his pocket, Gorse was using a very old-fashioned, one might say hackneyed, method of gaining confidence.

Fortunately for Gorse, Esther, reader of *The News of the World* as she was, knew nothing about this stale trick. Even more fortunately for Gorse, Esther had not looked at the numbers of the notes, and so did not realize that she was being given back just those which she had given Gorse.

Had she done so, Gorse's game might well have been up. Expert and resourceful liar that he was, he would have had great difficulty, on the spur of the moment, in explaining the matter away. Certainly he would have lost a little of her trust. And, if he was to achieve his ultimate object, he wanted all of Esther's trust, all the time and until the very end.

'And all in my new bag, too,' said Esther. 'You aren't half generous to me. Oh lord – I shouldn't say "aren't half".'

'Why not?'

'It's common. I know that. I ought to've said you're *very* generous to me.'

'I don't see that it matters. I like the way you say and do everything. And it's easy to be generous when you feel like that.'

'All the same, you *are* generous. I've never known anyone so generous. And if I say "aren't half" again – will you tell me off?'

'If you like.'

'And if I make any other mistakes, will you tell me? I try hard enough, but I don't always know, and I'm always tripping up.'

'All right, I will. All the same, I like you as you are.'

'Yes, but I don't like myself, and I'd like your help. I'd like you to teach me.'

This, perhaps, was the greatest verbal concession Esther had so far made to Gorse.

'That's very flattering,' said Gorse. 'And it makes me feel very hopeful.'

'Does it?' said Esther, and blushed.

Gorse changed the subject.

'And did you meet our friend Ryan last night?' he asked.

'Yes.'

'And how did he behave?'

'Oh – he was very harmless.'

'Did he hold your hand?'

'Yes.'

'Did he try to kiss you?'

'Oh,' said Esther, eluding the question. 'You know how boys go on. I know how to deal with them all right.'

'Are you sure?'

'Yes. Of course I do.'

'Yes. I believe you do – with the normal boy. But I'm afraid I don't think Ryan *is* a normal boy. Aren't you ever going to take Uncle Ralph's advice? When are you meeting him again?'

'Wednesday evening, I said.'

There was a silence, for Gorse was again thinking. He was wondering how this would fit into the plan he had in mind.

'Wednesday – the day after tomorrow – eh?' he said. 'Very well, do as you like. And now I think we'd better finish these drinks and go for a little spin. I'd suggest having another, but I don't want to be had up for driving under the influence.'

They went outside, and he led her to the red dream-car.

'There you are,' he said. 'What do you think of it?'

Esther was enraptured. It was, indeed, a sensational car – of the type at which connoisseurs, passing by, stop to look. There was a man looking at it as they approached it, and another man stopped to look. There was, Esther realized, practically a crowd ! – and one of which she, in a way, was the centre of attraction. At that moment Esther was a deeply, deeply, happy girl.

'It's *glorious*!' she said.

'Very well,' said Gorse. 'Step in.'

He opened the door for her, seated himself at the wheel, and drove away.

4   Gorse was an even more expert driver than he was a liar. He made no blunders.

He took Esther to the back of Hove, and then into the country, towards Devil's Dyke.

As they sped along the country road, Esther, exhilarated by the air as well as all else besides, said:

'You know, I wish you *would* let me have a share in this.'

'No,' said Gorse. 'This is where your Uncle Ralph puts his foot down sternly. You can have a share if you like, but I won't take the money.'

'Well,' said Esther. 'I think it's mean of you.'

'No. It's not mean,' said Gorse. 'Just wise. And, anyway, you might come to have a share in it in quite a different way. But I admire your attitude.'

'What attitude?'

'Oh – taking a risk. Not that it *is* a risk in this case. But that's the only way to do things in life. Do things in the proper style. That's what makes the difference between, well – *proper* people, and those who aren't.'

'You really mean common people and gentle-people – don't you?' said Esther.

'Yes,' said Gorse, after deliberating. 'If you like to put it that way. And you've proved to me to which type you belong.'

These words were to have a great effect upon Esther's future conduct with Gorse. They had been intended to do so.

Gorse was clever enough not to stop the car on a lonely road and kiss her. He drove as far as the Devil's Dyke, and then said that they must get home quickly or Gosling's garage would be shut.

He drove home with all his skill at a thrilling speed. He left her at the Clock Tower, arranging to meet her again tomorrow evening – Tuesday.

As Esther walked back to Over Street that night she did more than tell herself that she would like to marry Ernest Ralph Gorse: she hoped that he would quickly and firmly make the proposal.

PART TEN

WARNING

I

Returning from her work on Tuesday evening, and entering the house in Over Street with the object of dressing before meeting Gorse, the smashing blow fell upon Esther.

Her mother was out; so were both the children, who were with their mother.

The house was quiet, and seemed to be empty. On the floor of the perambulatored passage on the ground floor lay a letter.

It was addressed in letters from a newspaper pasted on to the envelope.

Because the house was quiet, and seemingly quite empty, Esther went whiter in the face than she might have done otherwise.

2　　Esther took the letter up to her bedroom. Now her face was red. She opened the letter.

She found, inside, a card upon which letters from a newspaper had been pasted. This read:

Esther read this three or four times in order to discern its full meaning behind its lack of punctuation.

Her impulse, then, was to rush down to her mother. But her mother was out, and the house, she believed (and actually it was), was entirely empty. She looked at the letter in the dusk (it was a cloudy night) and listened to the emptiness of the house.

She began to dress herself for Gorse.

When she was almost completely dressed, and ready for Gorse, she heard her mother come in with the two children. All three went into the sitting room on the ground floor.

She thought of calling her mother up to the bedroom. But she had not told her mother that she had met Ryan again, and so would have to reveal that she had betrayed her mother's trust in her.

Also, if she were going to meet him at the appointed time, she would be late for Gorse. She would have to talk to her mother for at least a quarter of an hour.

She decided that she would tell her mother later – or not tell her at all – and she slipped out of the house quietly without even greeting her mother or the children.

3   Gorse was again in very good spirits when he met Esther outside the West Pier, and he was loquacious as he took her to the Metropole. Esther noticed that the red dream-car was not tonight outside the hotel. But she was not now really interested in the red car.

'I'm sorry,' said Gorse. 'But we haven't got the car tonight. Old Gosling's a bit sticky about it.'

'Is he?' was all Esther could say.

'Yes. Very sticky, as a matter of fact,' said Gorse. 'Tell me, though – you seem a bit worried. Is there anything on your mind?'

'Yes. There is.'

'What?'

'I'll tell you when we're inside,' said Esther.

'Serious?'

'Yes. Very,' said Esther. 'I want your advice.'

'You shall have it,' said Gorse.

Their usual table was occupied, but they found one opposite it. When the drinks were ordered Gorse said. 'Well. Go ahead.'

'No. I'd rather wait till I've had a drink.'

The drinks came, and Gorse said, 'Well – go ahead,' again.

Esther sipped at her drink, and said, 'Well, I've had another – that's all.'

'Another what?'

'Another of those letters,' said Esther.

'Yes. I rather thought so,' said Gorse. 'If you've got it on you, will you let me see it?'

'Yes,' said Esther, producing it from her new bag. 'Here it is.'

Because of the seriousness of the occasion, or because Gorse desired to make the situation seem as serious as he possibly could, he did not put on his monocle to read the card.

He scrutinized it carefully for something like two minutes. Then he spoke, still looking at the card.

'Now this is serious – you know. Really serious,' he said. 'In fact, it's very dangerous.'

'Yes. It's pretty awful – isn't it?'

'Yes,' said Gorse. 'In fact, I should say that this is now definitely a matter for the police.'

'On no. Not the police. Surely.'

'But it is. In fact, if you'll let me have this card I'll take it to them myself,' said Gorse. 'Will you?'

'Oh lord. I don't want the police dragged in.'

'But I don't think you understand how serious all this is. The other letter was just a warning. This is a threat. And a very nasty threat. Did you read that bit about the body?'

'Yes. Of course I did. It's terrible, though I don't quite know what it means.'

'Well – it might mean anything – you know. You don't want to be set upon in a dark place – you don't want to be disfigured for life – do you?'

Esther went whiter than she was already.

'What do you mean?' she said.

'I mean what I say. This obviously comes from a very low quarter, and the type of person that doesn't stop at anything – *anything* – do you understand? I don't think you know the shadier side of life. How should you? I happen to have come across them – on racecourses, and other places. And the bad part of Brighton's as bad as any place on earth. This is a matter for the police.'

'Oh dear. I still don't want to go to them.'

'Well – even if you don't, your other course of action is absolutely clear now.'

'What other course?'

'I mean about Ryan. It's quite clear that you can never meet him again.'

'Oh lord . . . But I've *promised* to meet him, tomorrow night.'

'Well – you just don't turn up – that's all.'

'But supposing he's *innocent*? Supposing there's nothing behind these filthy letters?'

'You just can't afford to take the risk, and that's that. Anyone can see this man – the man who wrote the letter – means business. He must be a low type himself. He *may* be warning you for your own good, but he's probably got a grudge against Ryan. Ryan mixes with some very low people. I can tell you that, because I've seen him with them – unknown to himself.'

'Have you?'

'Yes,' said Gorse, moving away from the subject. 'And then has another thing struck you? You've been watched – incessantly watched. You've probably been watched coming here, and you'll be watched going home. And that brings us to another interesting thing. You and I must have been watched as well. But he's got no grudge against me, and you've been out with me more than Ryan. So it looks like a grudge against Ryan – I should personally say a justified one, but that's not the point. The point is that you're not going to meet Ryan again. That's absolutely certain, if ever anything was.'

'Oh dear,' said Esther. 'It does seem –'

'You see,' said Gorse, interrupting her, 'these sorts of people stop at nothing, and they usually strike through the girl. They've got twisted minds, and it's one of their pleasant little habits. It's the girl they go for. The girl's weaker.'

'But what could he do to me?' said Esther. 'I mean – "disfigure" me.'

'Oh, please don't let's go into that. I'd really rather not. The point is that it happens. It's happening incessantly. You've only got to read the newspapers. Isn't it?'

'I suppose it is.'

'Now. Will you promise me you'll do what I say?'

'I suppose I'll have to.'

'But *do* you? Solemnly?'

'I'd like to think about it. You see, if he's innocent, it does seem awful not to turn up – just leave him waiting there . . . He's never done me any harm. He's always behaved like a gentleman.'

'Believe me, gentlemen – or so-called gentlemen – can be more dangerous than any others in the world. You must know that.'

'Yes – but if he *is* all right. It does seem mean.'

'By the way,' said Gorse, 'you're not in love with him by any chance, are you?'

'Good heavens, no,' said Esther. And, in her present state of perturbation, she certainly was not. 'It only just seems mean – with him waiting there.'

'Well – there's a way round that.'

'What?'

'You can write to him and tell him you're not coming.'

'But it wouldn't reach him in time. Not even if I wrote it and posted it tonight.'

'No. But you could write it tonight and post it in the morning. Then it'd probably reach him before he left in the evening.'

'Yes. I suppose it would.'

'Then write it tonight and post it in the morning.'

'But what am I to *say*? What excuse am I going to make?'

'Oh, you can make any excuse. That's easy enough. But what you ought to do is to tell him that you don't want to meet him again at all. And an excuse for that might be just a little more difficult.'

'It certainly would.'

'But not impossible. In fact, on second thoughts, it's perfectly easy. Can't you just tell him there's somebody else?'

'I suppose so. But it's difficult.'

'Say there's been somebody else all the time – someone you're in love with. And then you can say that this someone's put his foot down at last, and said that you mustn't go out with anyone else. You can say you're very sorry, and all that.'

'But I told him – that day in the country – that there wasn't anyone particular.'

'Well – tell him that you weren't telling the truth. That's easy enough, isn't it?'

'Yes. I suppose so. But, if he's really all right, I still think it's mean. Especially if he doesn't get the letter in time. I *still* don't quite believe there's anything wrong with him, and I hate to think of him standing – waiting there.'

Esther, it will be seen, was putting up a brave, indeed a noble, fight for her romance – for her ideal of Beauty. For she thought Ryan beautiful, and he was the one she really loved. But Gorse was too much for this ignorant, frightened girl.

'I don't care if he stands and waits for hours. You've got to get

out of this. When there's evil going around you've just got to run
away from it. You've got to get out of its orbit.'

Esther did not know what the word 'orbit' meant, but she realized
that Gorse was giving her almost exactly the same advice which her
mother had given her.

'Yes,' she said. 'I know all that.'

'Have you told your mother about all this?' asked Gorse, by pure
luck hitting upon Esther's thought.

'Yes,' she said. 'Some of it. Not all. And she said just what you said.'

'Of course she did. And you ought to have told her all. And now
I can tell you this. If you don't do what I say, *I'll* do something.
You've had enough threats already, and heaven knows I don't want
to start threatening you. But I'll tell you this. If you don't do as
I advise, I could go to your mother myself – couldn't I? In fact, I
could go to your mother and father. And you know what'd happen
then – don't you? *They'd* soon put a stop to it – wouldn't they?'

'Yes. They would . . . But I don't want you to go.'

'Neither do I. But it might be my duty – just my plain, simple
duty. Now – will you promise to write that letter tonight?'

Esther paused.

Then she said:

'All right, then. I'll write the letter.'

(I've promised, but if I change my mind I needn't post it, was
her thought.)

'Very well. That's a good girl. I know I can trust you, and you've
taken a weight off my mind.'

'Oh – lord,' said Esther. 'I don't half feel bad – I mean I feel bad.
Not not half. I'd like another drink. Can I?'

'Of course you can. And you shall drink all of it tonight.'

'It looks as though I'm going to the bad, doesn't it? – taking to
drink.'

Esther spoke jokingly, but she had come very near to the truth.
In later life Esther was to drink a great deal too much, and this
brought upon her many evils. It is disasters (of the proportions of
the one from which Esther was suffering now) which, taken in
conjunction with early youth and the use of alcohol, bring about the
habit of heavy drinking.

'Don't be so silly,' said Gorse, and ordered more drinks.

They talked about other matters, but Esther could not properly
bring her mind to them. When she was halfway through her second
drink (which went to her head) Esther suddenly burst out with:

'You know I *still* don't believe there's anything wrong with that boy.'

'Now then,' said Gorse. 'Don't let's go back to that. You've made your promise, and that's that. You won't weaken at the last moment, will you?'

'I hope not.'

'Well, I'll jolly well see that you don't. Listen. What time are you supposed to be meeting Ryan tomorrow evening?'

'Seven-thirty.'

'Good. Now I'll tell you what. You meet me in here at seven o'clock. I'll be sitting here waiting for you. Then I can hold your hand – well, in a metaphorical sense, anyway. Will you do that?'

'Yes. All right.'

'Promise?'

'Yes.'

'Good.'

They again went on to discuss other matters, but Esther was still unable to concentrate.

At last, 'It's no good, is it?' said Gorse. 'You can't think of anything else.'

'No – I'm afraid I can't.'

'Very well, then, drink up that and we'll go off home. And I'm going to see you the whole way home tonight.'

'Oh no. Only as far as the Clock Tower. Please. It's so awful where I live.'

'Well, then, as far as the street. I want to see you going safely into your house tonight.'

'Why? Safely? I haven't done anything wrong tonight – have I? I mean wrong by this awful person, whoever he is?'

'No. You haven't. But I like to take every precaution. And I have a little idea. I want you and I to leave each other outside the Metropole. Then, at a distance, I'm going to follow you. You're probably being watched tonight, and I might find something out about the gentleman – what he looks like. I'll probably fail – but it's on the cards. So I'll just see you to the end of your street, and see you go into your house. Agree?'

Gorse, of course, was only trying to terrify Esther further with all this nonsense. He succeeded.

'Oh lord,' said Esther. 'It's pretty awful – this feeling you're being watched.'

'Yes. But remember you're being watched *over*, too. You've got me there to look after you – haven't you?'

'You're very good to me,' said Esther.

'It's very easy to be good to you,' said Gorse. 'And now let's get going – shall we? We'll just say good-bye in a normal way outside.'

'Very well,' said Esther, and they rose.

As they walked towards the revolving doors Gorse said:

'And you'll promise you'll write that letter tonight?'

'Yes. I promise.'

When they were outside Gorse said good-bye to her in a rather exaggeratedly normal and loud-voiced way.

Esther walked home.

Although it was not strictly necessary for his purposes, Gorse did in fact follow Esther to the end of her street and watch her go indoors.

He had a feeling that Esther would look back occasionally on her walk home, and that it would be politic to be seen following.

He was right. She did look back, once or twice. And, when she reached the door of the house in which she lived, she saw Gorse standing at the end of the street.

II

That night Esther wrote a letter to Ryan, using much labour in its composition. Its final version read as follows:

Dear Mr Ryan,

I am very sorry I cannot meet you tomorrow night.

I have also to say that it is impossible for me to meet you at all in the future.

I am afraid I have not played quite fairly with you. You asked me in the country whether there was anyone else and I said there was not. But there is someone else, who I love, and he says that I must not go on meeting you.

Please do not make any attempt to get into touch with me, either at the above address or by letter. It will be of no use.

I feel sure you will understand. I apologize for my bad behaviour, but I feel sure you will understand. I will always have very pleasant memeries of our friendship.

Yours gratefully and sorrowfully,

Esther Downes.

Esther put this extremely pathetic letter into an envelope and addressed it. But she left the envelope open, and she did not stamp it because she had no stamp.

She left the envelope open because she wanted to read the letter again in the morning.

She slept well, and in the morning was a good deal less frightened.

On her way to her work she bought a stamp and stuck it on to the envelope. But she still did not post the letter, or close the envelope.

All day she brooded upon her trouble, and still, still she had a feeling that Ryan was guiltless, and that she should defy the author of the low, menacing letter. For this reason she still refrained from posting the letter to Ryan, and had it in her bag when she met Gorse at the Metropole at seven that evening.

2   Gorse rose directly he saw her, and shook hands. She noticed that there were two drinks ready on the table.

'Never been so glad to see you,' he said. 'Now sit down and have a drink.'

Esther did so.

'I saw you following me last night,' she said, after she had had her first sip.

'Yes,' said Gorse. 'And I saw you looking back. You shouldn't have done that, really. A watcher doesn't like to know that the one who's being watched is trying to watch him. But it doesn't matter.'

'Well – *was* there a watcher? Did you find anything out?'

'Not a thing. He was probably behind – watching me. Or he may not have been there at all. He's as clever as paint, whoever he is. Well – did you write the letter?'

'Yes . . .'

'And post it?'

'No . . . I didn't.'

'Why not?'

'I don't quite know. I've got it here in my bag. I suppose among other things I wanted you to see it first.'

'Well – that's foolish in a way, you know. Now Ryan'll have to wait outside the Pier. However, may I see the letter?'

'Yes. Here it is.'

Gorse put his monocle into his eye and studied the letter.

'Yes,' he said. 'That seems all right. Very good, in fact. And now we'd better post this – hadn't we?'

'Oh lord. *Must* we?'

'Yes. And at once.' Gorse licked the envelope and closed it. 'I can do it here. In the hotel.'

Gorse rose.

'I won't be half a sec,' he said.

'But *must* we? Can't we wait a bit? I've got an idea.'

'Yes. I'm afraid we must,' said Gorse, and walked away and put the letter into the hotel box, and returned to Esther.

'Well,' he said, sitting down again, 'what's the idea? Or rather what *was* it?'

'You shouldn't have posted it, you know,' said Esther, ignoring his question. 'I started with "I'm sorry I can't meet you tomorrow night", and it ought to be *last* night, now.'

'Well, that doesn't matter – does it? That's your fault for not posting it. Now he's got to stand waiting, that's all. But what was your idea?'

'Well – *has* he got to stand waiting? Why shouldn't I be brave and meet him, after all? Why not show him those two filthy letters and give him a chance to defend himself?'

'Out of the question,' said Gorse. 'Don't be silly.'

'But I don't see why it's silly. The letters might just have come from a harmless lunatic. I've thought about it.'

'*Might* is the word you used,' said Gorse.

'And couldn't we *both* go along to meet him? Then we could all talk it over. I'd have a man with me.'

'Now listen,' said Gorse. 'You're talking complete nonsense and you know you are. He'd never admit anything. He'd just lie – I happen to know he's one of the best liars existing – and you don't get anywhere. And you'll have disobeyed the instruction in the letter. And that means danger. I don't want to talk about Disfigurement again –'

'Oh – don't do that, for heaven's sake.'

'No. I don't want to. But I'm telling you this. If you go out and meet Ryan tonight, I know exactly where I'm going tonight. I'm going straight to your father and mother in Over Street, and tell them everything. And you know what'll happen then. I'm sorry to be so stern, but there we are. And you know in your heart I'm right. Don't you?'

'Yes,' said Esther, after staring miserably at nothing for a few moments. 'I suppose I do.'

'Very well, then – the subject's closed, and the letter's posted anyway. You know, you ought to think yourself very lucky to have someone like myself to advise you.'

'Yes. I know,' said Esther. 'I'm very grateful, really.'

'Well, let's say no more about it – shall we? Let's talk about other things.'

'All right,' said Esther. 'Let's.'

And it was with these words that Esther, after her very fine struggle, finally lost Ryan – though she was destined to meet him once more in Brighton.

3   Gorse entertained Esther with his conversation and succeeded fairly well in holding her attention until twenty minutes to eight. Then she broke away.

'Oh, it is *awful* to think of him waiting there!' she exclaimed.

'Now then,' said Gorse. 'Don't be foolish. He's probably gone by now. He's not the type that waits.'

'I should have thought that's just what he is.'

'No. You don't know him as well as I do – believe me. However, I'll tell you what I'll do. I'd like to do it any case. I'll just hop out now and see if he *is* waiting. I might see someone else too. He must be watching, and I might still find something out. Do you mind if I leave you?'

'What? All alone here? I can't sit in a place like this all by myself. I'd look silly – and it's wrong – isn't it? – for a girl to sit in a place like this all by herself.'

'It depends on the girl,' said Gorse. 'And if you're embarrassed, I'll go and get you a newspaper to hide behind. They've got some papers at the porter's desk. Excuse me, I'll go and get one at once. I want to hurry.'

He went to the porter's desk, bought a newspaper, and returned to Esther.

'There you are,' he said. 'You read the news and tell me all about it when I come back. I'll only be about ten minutes. Cheerio.'

He left Esther, who saw him pass hurriedly through the revolving doors.

All this nonsense was, again, only perpetrated by Gorse in order to frighten Esther, and he was again extremely successful.

She sat, longing for his return, in anguish – anguish about the waiting Ryan, anguish about the whole situation, and anguish about sitting alone in the great hotel.

Esther, temporarily, had lost her taste for Oriental splendour.

Gorse, who (largely because it was still light outside) had never had any intention of going anywhere near the West Pier to look at Ryan, walked about in the small streets behind the front. He did this for nearly twenty minutes. He knew exactly what sort of anguish Esther was suffering from, and he thought it desirable to prolong it, and thus increase it.

Then he returned, apologizing for being so late. Curiosity, he said, had got the better of him.

'And was Ryan there?' said Esther. 'And did you see anybody else?'

'Yes,' said Gorse. 'Ryan was there. And, to do him justice, I must say he stayed longer than I thought. In fact, he only left a little before I did. And I drew a complete blank about anybody else. There was no one loitering or looking suspicious at all.'

'Didn't Ryan see you loitering? It's still quite light outside, isn't it?'

'No. I'm sure he didn't. I'm pretty good at that sort of thing. Now let's have another drink.'

They did so, and the subject was changed. Esther again finished the whole of her drink.

When it was time to go Gorse said:

'I don't imagine you want to go on the Pier tonight. I expect you'd rather go straight home.'

'Yes, I would rather.'

'Very well,' said Gorse. 'And tonight, if I may, I shall escort you as far as the Clock Tower. There's no sense in following you, like last night. You've done what you were told, and the danger's over now.'

'You think it is?'

'Yes. Of course it is. Well, let's go, shall we?'

On their way home Esther asked Gorse, quite accidentally, an amazingly shrewd question.

'Tell me,' she said. 'Suppose whoever wrote those letters had told me I wasn't to meet *you* – not Ryan. What would *you* have done?'

Gorse was very nearly knocked out by this: he was certainly on the floor while the referee started counting. But somehow he managed to survive.

'Ah,' he said. 'That's a very difficult question.' He was silent, and then went on. 'That's a very difficult question indeed ... Very difficult ... But I think I know the answer.'

'What?'

'Well – it sounds an awful thing to say, but I think there'd only be one thing I *could* do. I'd have to stop meeting you.'

'What – completely leave me?'

'Yes. It sounds awful, I know – but I don't see any other way. There'd be two reasons. One would concern me, and the other yourself.'

'What are they?'

'Well, in the first place, I personally don't like to get mixed up with that sort of thing. As I told you, you've just got to run – get out of its orbit. And I think anyone with any pretensions to being a gentleman would do the same. But that's only me. What's more important is you. I couldn't possibly expose you to such a risk. And so for your sake I'd have to leave you. There'd be nothing else to do. I need hardly tell you it'd break my heart. *And* ruin all my hopes of the future into the bargain. And I hope it would hurt you a little. Would it?'

'Yes,' said Esther, simply and candidly. 'It would.'

'But the question's an absurd one, really,' Gorse continued. 'Ryan's Ryan and I'm myself. Ryan has obviously done something very wrong somewhere, and he obviously mixes with very low people. Well – I *don't* mix with low people, and I've never done anything very wrong – so far as I know, at any rate. And so of course I'm not the sort of person to *get* a letter like that – or even to be mentioned in one. Do you follow me?'

'Yes,' said Esther meekly. 'I do.'

The referee had counted six and Gorse was up.

As they said good-bye at the Clock Tower, Gorse asked her if he could meet her tomorrow. She said, truthfully, that it was really time that she gave Gertrude an evening.

Gorse allowed her to do this, and arranged to meet her, not outside the West Pier, but inside the Metropole, at seven-thirty, on the day after tomorrow.

He was secretly glad to have missed a day. Doing so fitted in with the schemes he had in mind.

III

Ryan's first emotions, on receiving Esther's letter next morning, were those of one suffering from great grief and irretrievable disaster.

But, as the day wore on, his mood changed.

Having read the letter about twenty-five times, he decided that there was something 'funny' about it.

To begin with, it had been posted (as he saw from the postmark) in the evening, but she had begun her letter with 'I am very sorry I cannot meet you *tomorrow* [Ryan's italics] night.'

Did this not point to the fact that she had hesitated a long while, perhaps a whole day, before posting it, and had only at last done so reluctantly? And was not this a hopeful sign?

But there were other 'funny' things. He could not quite make himself believe in this 'someone else'. He did not appear to be a nice character, anyway – forbidding her to meet anyone else – threatening her, it seemed.

There was something strange, too, in her 'Please do not make any attempt to get into touch with me, either at the above address or by letter.' Why should he not at least write to her – even if it was only a letter of farewell? This seemed to confirm the idea that she was being threatened.

Then she had signed the letter, 'Yours gratefully and sorrowfully.' The 'sorrowfully' struck him as being written in all sincerity. And this was further reason for hope.

Then Ryan was touched by the immaturity of her handwriting and her misspelling of the word 'memories' as 'memeries'. He felt that she was in trouble, ignorant, and needing help.

But what was he to do? Clearly he must not visit her or write to her. But might he not contrive somehow to meet her, apparently by accident?

And, even if there was a genuine 'someone else', had he not been brought up to believe that faint heart never won fair lady, and that all was fair in love and war?

He was anxious to consult someone, and thought of Bell. But he remembered Bell's abilities and enthusiasm as a consultant on a previous occasion.

Gorse came into Ryan's head, and he saw that there were advantages here. Gorse was in the habit of meeting Esther: he took her to the Metropole.

Might he not get Gorse to plead for him – plead for another meeting, at any rate?

Gorse, also, was much more sophisticated than Bell – indeed more sophisticated than himself. He might have good advice to give.

The idea of going to Gorse was distasteful; for Ryan, as we know, disliked and somehow distrusted Gorse. The advantages, however, seemed to outweigh these sentiments, which after all were only faint and instinctive.

By the end of the day Ryan had decided to seek advice from Gorse.

2   Ryan, the early riser and motorcyclist, called at an early hour upon Gorse on the next day, Friday.

Gorse was still in bed with his breakfast.

When Gorse's landlady announced Ryan, Gorse was for a moment a little alarmed. He feared that objects in his room might disclose some of his occupations – such objects as paste, scissors, postcards, and clipped newspapers. But a glance satisfied him that all of these were effectually concealed.

'Ah-ha,' said Gorse from his bed. 'Our worthy Ryan. Thou callest at an early hour – dost thou not?'

'Yes. I'm sorry,' said Ryan. 'Do you mind?'

'No. I'm delighted,' said Gorse. 'But what bring'st thou here? Any matter of urgent moment? Thou wearest an anxious look. Come and sit on the bed.'

Gorse had also been struck for a moment by the fear that all had been discovered, and that Ryan had come round to fight with him.

'No, nothing frightfully urgent,' said Ryan, sitting on the bed. 'I've really only come round to ask your advice about something.'

'Go ahead. Only too glad to help in any way.'

'Well,' said Ryan. 'You know that girl – Esther Downes?'

'Yes. I do indeed. I've taken her out.'

'Yes. I know. She told me. Well – it's difficult to put – but I've got pretty keen on her.'

'Yes. I rather thought so. You showed it that first night.'

'Did I?'

'Yes. It seemed obvious to me. But go ahead.'

'Well – before I do that,' said Ryan, 'will you tell me something?'

'Certainly. If I can.'

'*You're* not keen on her by any chance – are you? Tell me if you are.'

'Not in the slightest,' said Gorse, more than ever convincing because he was telling the truth. 'I can give you a straight answer there, I promise you.'

'Then why do you take her out? Don't think I don't believe you, but why do you go out with her?'

'Well – it's rather hard to explain. I suppose it's vanity, really.

I like to be seen with a pretty girl. She's not my type, but she's tremendously pretty and she dresses beautifully. I've even taken her to the Metropole. Though I don't share in your feelings – I completely understand them. Well – go on.'

'Well,' said Ryan, producing Esther's letter from his pocket. 'I thought I was getting ahead pretty well with her, but yesterday I got this letter. There seems to be something funny about it, and I want your advice.'

'Funny?' said Gorse. 'Let me look.'

Gorse read the letter carefully.

'Well,' said Ryan. 'What do you think?'

'Well – I don't want to hurt your feelings – but at the moment I don't see anything funny about it at all.'

'You mean it means what it says – that there *is* someone else?'

'I'm sorry to have to say it, but I do, frankly – yes.'

'Tell me,' said Ryan. 'Has she ever spoken to *you* about anybody else?'

Gorse deliberated.

'Now, that's interesting,' he said. 'As a matter of fact, she has. She's given very strong hints that there is. And the funny thing is that it crossed my mind that it might be you.'

'Then your advice is to take the letter at its face value?'

'You know, I'm very sorry to have to say that it is. I wouldn't worry too much. There're plenty of other fish in the sea, you know.'

'Now there's something else,' said Ryan. 'Thank you for your advice. I'm not sure it's right, but thank you for it. But I was wondering if you could help me. Are you meeting her again?'

'I am indeed,' said Gorse. 'In fact, I'm meeting her again this very evening. At the Hotel Metropole.'

'Now, *that's* funny, too,' said Ryan. 'If this "somebody else" objects to her meeting me – why shouldn't he object to her meeting *you*?'

'Oh – that's very easy to explain,' said Gorse. 'She's probably told him that you're "keen", as you put it, on her. And she's probably told him that I'm not – that I'm quite harmless. Do you see?'

'Yes. I suppose I do,' said Ryan.

'But how can I help?'

'Well – if you're meeting her again – tonight – I was wondering if you could put a word in for me. I still think there's something mysterious about it all, and why I'm not allowed even to write to her *or* see her, I can't see.'

'Yes?'

'So would it be possible for you to ask her why? To ask her if we couldn't have just *one* more meeting, at any rate? You're detached, and so she'd respect your advice. And you might find out about this "somebody else". Could you help me?'

'Yes. Of course I could,' said Gorse. 'And I will. I'll speak to her tonight. Honestly, I don't think there's much hope, because I believe there *is* somebody else. But I'll try and pump her, and do everything I can for you.'

'You know, this is awfully good of you,' said Ryan, genuinely grateful to Gorse, whom he decided to flatter. 'And I know you're awfully good at that sort of thing.'

'I don't know that I am. But I'll certainly do my best.'

'And I nearly thought of going to Bell for advice!' said Ryan.

'No,' said Gorse. 'I don't think that'd have been wise, exactly. Bell's an admirable character, but not of much use in cases like this, I fancy.'

'By the way,' said Ryan, who at the moment liked and completely trusted Gorse. 'I suppose I couldn't come *along* to the Metropole tonight and join you, could I?'

'No. I think that'd be fatal. You can, if you like, of course, but I don't advise it. She's said you're not to meet her, and young ladies – particularly pretty ones – don't like to be disobeyed. It'd be butting in and might ruin everything. You take my advice, and leave it all to your Uncle Gorse. I can't promise anything. In fact, I don't hope for much, as I told you. But I'll do my best. You know in your heart I'm right – don't you?'

'Yes,' said Ryan miserably. 'I suppose I do. And thank you very much.'

'*Pas du tout,*' said Gorse. 'And now I suppose it's time for the Emperor – Gorse the First –to arise from his bed.'

'No – Gorse the Good,' said Ryan, and then asked Gorse, because he wanted to reward him, whether he would like to ride on the back of his motorcycle.

But Gorse, the motorist, was above motorcycles – very much above riding on the back of them.

He politely rejected the offer, and Ryan, who was anxious to soothe himself with riding, asked him when they were to meet again so that he could hear the news.

'Now, that's difficult,' said Gorse. 'I've got to spend all tomorrow with an ancient and venerable uncle of mine at Preston. Suppose you call on me, at the same time, on Sunday morning. I don't mind how early you are.'

Ryan again thanked his benefactor, who was left to his thoughts.

PART ELEVEN

RELIEF

I

On returning home from work on that Friday evening, Esther, going upstairs to dress before meeting Gorse, was called down by her mother, who asked her to come into the sitting room.

There was an air of mystery about her mother, who was alone in the sitting room, and who asked Esther to shut the door.

Esther, already frightened, was made more frightened by what her mother said.

'Another of those letters has come,' said her mother, 'But it's all right.'

'Oh lord,' said Esther. 'Where is it?'

'It came in the afternoon,' said Mrs Downes. 'It was addressed to you, but I couldn't keep from opening it. You don't mind – do you?'

'No. Of course not. But where is it? What did it *say*?'

'It's all right,' said Mrs Downes, producing it from a drawer in a sideboard. 'In fact, it's good.'

'Good. How *could* it be good?'

'It *is*, though,' said Mrs Downes. 'You read it.'

Esther took the postcard, and rapidly ran her eyes over it. It read:

YOU HAVE DONE well and wisely You will receive NO MORE LETTERS FROM ME and BE No. longer BOthERED from ONE You have reas on to thank and WHO Thanks you

'Well, that's better, isn't it?' said Esther's mother. 'In fact, you're out of the wood now – aren't you?'

'Yes. I suppose I am,' said Esther, still dazed.

'Aren't you glad now that you did what I advised you?'

'Yes. I am,' said Esther.

There was no sense in telling her mother that she had not done what her mother had advised – that she had done exactly the opposite, and met Ryan.

'Well – now you're *right* out of the wood,' said Mrs Downes, and kissed her daughter congratulatorily. 'Mother always knows best about everything, you know.'

Here Mrs Downes was inaccurate. Mother usually knows best about everything, but not always. In this instance, as Esther perceived, she knew a great deal less than Esther.

After she had been kissed, Esther said: 'Yes. I know. And just think of it. I *am* out of the wood, aren't I?'

'Of course you are.'

And now Esther, who had come out of her daze, began to feel surges of inexpressible relief and joy.

'Well, what shall we do with the letter? Tear it up or keep it?' said Esther's mother.

'Oh no. I think I'd like to keep it,' said Esther impulsively. She was so joyous she wanted to hug it and look at it again and again.

There is only one type of anonymous letter capable of bringing joy – that which, after previous anonymous menaces, promises there shall be no more. But it seems that all anonymous letters have to be hoarded.

'Very well,' said her mother. 'It doesn't matter either way, now.'

'Yes. I'd like to keep it,' said Esther. 'And as a matter of fact I'd like to show it to someone I'm meeting tonight.'

'Is that the other one? The Metropole one?'

'Yes,' said Esther. 'You don't mind me meeting *him*, do you?'

'No. Of course I don't.'

'As a matter of fact,' said Esther, 'it's been him who's all the time been giving me exactly the same advice as you – almost word for word.'

'Did he?' said Mrs Downes. 'He sounds a good and honest boy to me.'

'Yes. He *is* good and honest. And he's got his head screwed on the right way, too,' said Esther. 'Well, I must be rushing upstairs to dress.'

She kissed her mother again and ran upstairs.

As Esther dressed her joy and relief grew greater, and, as she was walking on her way to meet Gorse at the Metropole, they grew greater and greater still.

It was the wording of the letter in her bag which particularly pleased her. She already knew them by heart. '*You will receive no more letters from me and be no longer bothered.*' The words carried complete conviction. Then '*From one you have reason to thank and who thanks you.*'

She liked the way he thanked her. And perhaps she *did* have reason to thank this unknown. Perhaps he was a very good character who had been absolutely forced, for some reason, to use underhand methods.

She inclined strongly to this view. After all, why should the man, whoever he was, go to the trouble, unless he was good, of writing her a third letter to reassure her and thank her?

It may be said that all this time the thought of Ryan had hardly entered Esther's head.

Anger atrophies fear: a really angry man will strike another man much larger than himself. So does great relief atrophy other emotions. Esther was impervious to regretful or romantic thoughts.

2   When Esther arrived at the Metropole (noticing the red dream-car outside) Gorse had risen from their usual table to greet her. Esther was radiant, and radiantly beautiful, with joy. Only a satanic creature, such as Gorse was, could, surely, pursue, as he did, his dark plans with so lovely a being.

'Hullo,' she said, sitting down. 'I've got something to tell you. I've got some good news.'

Gorse had seen her mood as soon as she had entered. It gave him pleasure and satisfaction. It was exactly the mood he had intended to induce in her when he had sent her the final letter.

Tonight was an important night for Gorse: the success of his plans hung upon what happened between Esther and himself in the next hour or two: and so he wanted Esther to be in a good mood.

'Have you?' he said. 'Well, I've got a bit of news too. But what's yours?'

'No,' said Esther rapturously. 'Let's wait till our drinks come. That's what you make *me* do.'

'Well, that won't be long,' said Gorse. 'I've taken the liberty of ordering them.'

'And what's *your* news? Good or bad?'

'Well, it could have been bad. But I think it'll be all right. In fact, I know it will. Though actually I want a bit of *your* help this time.'

'Well, you shall certainly have it,' said Esther, in her own happiness not taking Gorse's trouble in any way seriously. 'You help me, and I help you. That's only fair – isn't it?'

The drinks came.

'These glasses are larger,' said Esther.

'They're larger drinks,' said Gorse. 'I wanted a bit of bucking up, and I thought we might make a change. Well, go on. What's your news?'

'Here you are,' said Esther, producing the anonymous letter. 'Read that. I'm out of the wood now all right. And it's all due to you, really. I'm pretty grateful, you know.'

Gorse pretended to read the letter. Then he said:

'Oh yes. This is wonderful. You're out of the wood all right – there's no mistaking that. Well, let's drink to it. Congratulations. Well done.'

They drank.

'Shall I tear this up?' Gorse said.

'No,' said Esther. 'Give it back, will you? I want to keep it. I want to go on looking at it.' She took it back from him. 'And now. Tell me. What's *your* trouble? And how can I help *you* or advise *you*, this time?'

'Well – it's not really so much advice I want as help.'

'Go on, then. Tell me.'

Gorse paused, and took another sip at his drink.

'Well,' he said. 'It's this. That money – the money from my aunt – hasn't come through.'

'What about it? It hasn't *fallen* through, has it?'

'Oh – good heavens no. Nothing like that. It's just been delayed again. It'll be here on Monday for certain.'

'But what does it matter, then?'

'It wouldn't, normally, but just at this moment it matters more than anything else on earth. It means that I lose that car outside.'

'Lose the car?'

'Yes. Unless I get some help.'

Esther saw roughly what was coming, and her soul was emptied of joy.

'What sort of help?'

'Well – what do you think? Monetary help.'

'A lot?'

'Yes. A great lot.'

Esther's soul was now not only emptied of joy. Grave anxiety was pouring into it.

'But *why* do you lose the car?'

'Because the deposit of fifteen pounds I gave Gosling only lasts till twelve noon tomorrow. And if I don't fork up by then I not only lose the fifteen pounds, but the car as well. But don't look so worried. You can help me, and it's going to be all right.'

'Help you how much?'

'Well – in a pretty big way. I'm sorry, but there's nothing else to do. Thank heavens I've got you to come to.'

'But *how* big a way?'

'Well, I'll give you the details. The car's going – for a song – at eighty-five pounds. I've paid fifteen as deposit. That means seventy more to come.'

'Well?'

'Well, I went to Bell this morning, and he lent me five. He hadn't got it himself, but his aunt had. She happens to like me, fortunately. So that leaves sixty-five pounds to be found.'

'Well?'

'Well – don't you see? It all fits in. With your sixty-eight you can just do it for me. You get it back on Monday, and now I'm determined to give you a real share, and every sort of security as well. You and I are going to make a lot of money – between us.'

'But I *can't*!' said Esther. '*I can't*! Not all that money.'

'Oh, don't be silly,' said Gorse, utterly coolly and casually. 'It's as simple as pie – simpler. All you've got to do is to dig out the money tomorrow morning – early – and it'll have to be early, and then –'

'But I *can't*!' said Esther. 'It's all the money my mother gave me.'

'What's that got to do with it? You're going to get it back on Monday. And a lot more, too. I don't see where the trouble is.'

Gorse was still beautifully casual.

'But it's all I've *got*!' said Esther, and spoke incorrectly in her excitement. 'I ain't rich like you.'

'Not "ain't". I'm *not*,' said Gorse. 'You told me to tell you these little things.'

'Well, then, *not*. I'm not rich like you – and I just can't do such things.'

'I don't know what you're getting so excited about,' said Gorse. 'It's just a plain business transaction. If you go on like this I'll think

you're mean or something. Or that you don't trust me. And that'd
be worse. You *do* trust me – don't you?'

'Of course I do. You know that. But there must be some other
way round.'

'I wish you could tell me what,' said Gorse.

'Well – this man who's selling the car – what's his name?'

'Gosling.'

'Well – if you give him a little more money – say another fifteen
pounds – won't he wait?'

'Don't you think I've tried that? I've been haggling with him all
this afternoon. The man's as hard as nails. And he's got everything
in writing. I'm going to show you all the documents later. I don't
like the man, but I don't blame him for being a bit hard. He knows
I'm getting a bargain of a lifetime, and he knows, now it's too late,
that there're dozens of people after the car – people who'd be only
too glad to pay double the price, if not more. He's only praying in
his soul that I don't stump up.'

'But your money from your aunt might come through tomorrow
morning.'

'Not a hope. I've got a letter from my solicitor – I'm going to show
it to you in a moment – and beyond any suspicion of doubt it'll
definitely be here on Monday morning – but not a moment before.'

'But *still* there must be a way round. What about Bell's aunt?
Wouldn't she help?'

'No. I tried that one. That's no good. Not a penny more than five
pounds from *her*. Though she's got the money. It's funny how the
richer people in life are so mean, and the poorer ones so generous.'

'Then what about your uncle – the one in Preston?'

'If you can get water out of a stone you might get threepence out
of my Uncle Ralph. But I don't think you can get water out of a
stone – can you?'

'Then what about your people – your stepmother?'

'Yes. She'd probably give it to me in the long run. In fact, I'm
sure she would. And my solicitors would advance the money on
Aunt Lucy's legacy. But it's a question of *time* – don't you see?
There's no way of getting the money by *twelve o'clock tomorrow
morning.*'

'Then what about a money-lender?'

'Well – first of all, I don't know a money-lender in Brighton. And
then I don't like dealing with money-lenders. I never have and never
will. They're dangerous people. And, then, even if I found a money-

lender in Brighton, I'd never get the money in time. They put you through thousands of formalities, because they want security – quite naturally. Now you're *not* a money-lender, but I *am* going to give you security.'

'What does security mean – exactly?'

'Well – something which makes it absolutely sure that you get the money back.'

'What security are you going to give me, then?'

'You sound very stern and businesslike.'

'I'm sorry. But tell me. I can't help being anxious.'

'Well – I'm coming to that in a moment. But first of all I want to show you all the documents. You're quite right, really. In business one's got to be businesslike.'

'I don't really want to see them. I probably wouldn't understand them, anyway.'

'Oh yes. They're quite simple,' said Gorse, feeling for papers in his pocket. 'Now. Here we are. Exhibit one.'

Gorse now produced three documents – all typed.

The first purported to be a copy of an agreement with Gosling. In this agreement Gorse had promised to forfeit his deposit of fifteen pounds if he had not produced the remainder of the money for the car by twelve noon, Saturday.

The second purported to be an agreement, signed over a stamp, by Gosling, in which the latter acknowledged the receipt of the fifteen pounds' deposit, and declared that he would sell the car to Gorse for £85, provided the remainder of the money was given to him by Gorse by twelve noon Saturday.

The third document seemed to be a letter from a firm of solicitors. It had imposing-headed notepaper from a perfectly genuine firm of first-class solicitors. Gorse had acquired the useful habit of stealing notepaper from any hotel, club, firm of solicitors, or other owners of imposing-headed notepaper.

The letter from this firm of solicitors was half formal, half informal. It was apparently signed by one of the directors of the firm, whose name appeared upon the headed notepaper. The letter apologized for the unexpected and annoying delay in the sending of the cheque, and assured Gorse that it would reach him by Monday without fail. The name of this firm of solicitors was 'Rose and Loughborough'.

'That's Sir Charles Loughborough, Bart.,' said Gorse. 'It's pronounced Luffborough. I used to pronounce it wrong when I used to meet the old boy as a kid. I expect you've heard of him. He was pretty well known in his day.'

Esther had not heard of Sir Charles Loughborough, but she was awed by the name, and believed in the letter.

'No. I haven't,' she said. 'Are you related to him, then?'

'No,' said Gorse. 'No connection at all. Nothing so grand. You'll see the letter's signed Rose – Ronald Rose. That's the connection. The Roses are sort of distant cousins of mine. Ronnie's a jolly good sport – and a friend of mine, as you can see by the letter – but the rest of the firm's all very pompous and stuffy.'

Although Esther entirely believed in all these documents, and in Gorse, she still did not want to part with sixty-five pounds.

'You know, I *still* don't want to do it,' she said.

'Well – you haven't got to,' said Gorse. 'It's your choice. I've just got to lose fifteen pounds, and let's see – what's the exact double of eighty-five pounds? Yes – that's a hundred and seventy pounds to be precise. Well – I've got to lose that, if you won't help me.'

Esther did not perceive the flaw in his mathematics.

'But you haven't got to,' Gorse went on. 'In a way it's just fifteen pounds down the drain, that's all. But I lose the *car*! That's what's so important to me! However, there we are, if you feel that way. I'd have thought those letters would have been sufficient security for you. Actually –'

'Yes. I know *they're* all right. It's just I don't like the whole idea – that's all.'

'Now that's not speaking like the Esther I know – the Esther who does things in the right way. You know you've got to take risks if you're going to get anywhere. You've got to do things in style. Not that there's the tiniest risk on earth in this case. The whole thing's as safe as houses.'

'Yes. But I'm so *poor*. My *family's* so poor. Don't you see that –'

'No. Let me go on. You interrupted me just now. I was going to say that actually I've got much more security than I've shown you.'

'Have you?' said Esther miserably. 'What?'

'Well – first of all, I can give you an IOU for the money. You know what an IOU is – I take it?'

'Yes. I've heard of them, anyway.'

'Well – if it's signed over a stamp it's absolutely valid in law, and I could write it here and now. Then, if anything went wrong, you could sue me. Unless you think I'm going to vanish into thin air? Do you?'

'Don't be silly. Go on.'

'Well – even if I did vanish – I mean if I was run down by a bus – you could claim on the estate – the Gorse estate.'

'Could I?'

'Yes. But that's not all. You can ring up my solicitors – Rose and Loughborough – and simply get them to tell you that the money's there, and reaching me by Monday. You can't do it tonight – but you can early tomorrow morning. Of course, it's Saturday morning, and they may not all be there. But there's bound to be somebody in charge to tell you. Ronnie Rose himself'll almost certainly be there – though, as a matter of fact, I know that he likes, when he's given the chance, to sneak off and get a game of golf on a Saturday morning. He's a crack golfer, and he likes to play the whole of Saturday when he possibly can.'

All this wealth of inventive detail was convincing Esther more and more. Nobody, she thought, could possibly *invent* detail like this.

And, in fact, Gorse, had he not been what he was, might have been a highly successful novelist.

'But even *that's* not all,' said Gorse. 'There's more.'

'Is there?' said Esther, slightly less miserably. 'What more?'

'Well – it's half sentimental and half businesslike.'

'Sentimental?'

'Yes. It concerns a ring.'

'What sort of ring?'

'Well – not an engagement ring, or a wedding ring, actually. But this ring – the one I'm wearing. It's a signet ring. Would you like to have a look at it?'

'Yes. I've noticed your ring,' said Esther. 'And I've wondered what it was. I like it. It suits you, somehow.'

'Well, I should imagine it'd suit anybody,' said Gorse, taking it off and handing it to Esther. 'I'm very proud of it. Just take a look at it.'

Just as Gorse had adopted an old school tie which he had no right to wear, so he had adopted, falsely, a family relationship – a relationship with the peerage.

The ring he wore was of gold, with a cornelian stone, upon which was engraved the image of a horse's head – a head like that of a chess knight. A person related to Lord Belhaven and Stenton might have worn such a ring.

Gorse, whose real social snobbery was deep and bitter, had also thought it might be useful to exploit social snobbery for commercial purposes.

About a year ago, while he was lazily yet greedily turning the pages of *Debrett* in a Public Library, this crest had caught his attention, and appealed to his imagination as being a suitable one to adopt. The family to whom it belonged, it seemed to him, was of the correct type. It would be flying neither too high nor too low. It will be remembered that Gorse had been clever enough, when choosing a tie, not to have gone to Eton or Harrow.

He had had the ring made at Spinks', and it had cost him as much as ten pounds.

'Well – what do you think of it?' he said.

'It's lovely. What is it – exactly?'

'Well – it's been handed down in my family – that very thing you're holding now – from generation to generation. The crest's Belhaven and Stenton – Lord Belhaven and Stenton.'

'Good lord,' said Esther. 'Are you connected with a lord?'

'You got rather a lot of lords into that sentence,' said Gorse jocularly. 'Yes. I am. But it's all extremely distant and only on my mother's side. She had another name – the Belhaven family name. You can look it up in *Debrett's* if you like.'

'What's *Debrett's*?'

'Oh – just a reference book about all these things. You'll find one in any Public Library. There's probably one in this hotel, if we ask. However, it's a lovely ring – isn't it?'

'It certainly is.'

'And do you know how much it's worth?'

'No. Not the faintest idea.'

'You don't know about antiques at all?'

'Not a thing.'

'Well – it's worth about fifty pounds. It might be a little more or a little less. You see, it's got historical value. I couldn't tell you the exact date – but it's well over a hundred years old. And that sort of thing fetches money.'

'Yes. I suppose it does,' said Esther, quite believing all this piffle, and she tried to hand the ring back to him.

'No,' said Gorse, waving it away and looking at her earnestly as he leaned forward. 'I don't want it back. That's just the point. I want to give it to you – or at any rate lend it to you. That's half as security for you, and half sentimental.'

'How sentimental?'

'Well – don't you see what I mean? Quite apart from any question of security, I'm giving you something of great sentimental value, for great sentimental reasons. You must know what I mean.'

'No . . . I don't . . .'

'Listen, Esther. You know I've told you I'm going to ask you something soon – to ask you if you'll marry me. Well – I am. And I'd ask you tonight if I could, but your mind's on other things. So's mine, if it comes to that. But I want you to take that ring as something more than security. I'd like you to say that it means that there's a bond between us. Heaven knows I wouldn't give it into the keeping of anyone else – apart from its money value, its sentimental value's too great. And so I want you to say that it means there's a sentimental bond between us. Will you?'

'Well – there's certainly a bond between us, after what I've been through, and the way you've taken me out and helped me. I can certainly say that, though we've only known each other such a short time.'

'You know, it seems to me that I've known you for about five years. Funny, but there it is.'

'Yes. I feel I've known you a long time too.'

'And will you take the ring? Please say that you will.'

'All right. I'll take it. If you want me to.'

'And, although it's not an engagement ring – couldn't we look upon it as a sort of *half* engagement ring? Couldn't you say that we're sort of *half* engaged? It doesn't commit you to anything.'

'All right. I'll say it.'

'Thank you. I don't think you know how happy you've made me. Now don't let's say another word about it at the moment. You might say something to spoil everything. Now, you put that ring in your bag – it's too big for any of your little fingers – and let's get back to business.'

Esther, dazed and by no means unhappy at this firm proposal of marriage – her first from what she called a 'gentleman' – had almost forgotten about the horrible business on hand. But, somehow, it was much less horrible now. The large drink, too, was going to her head.

'Yes,' she said. 'I'd forgotten business.'

'Well. Just let me run through the details, and I'm sure you'll agree there's nothing in it – one's only making a mountain out of an absurd little molehill. Now, remember what your securities are. One, there's those letters I've shown you. Two, there's my I O U, absolutely valid in law. Ask a lawyer. Three, you can ring up my solicitors. Their telephone number's on their notepaper and I can give it to you now. Fourthly and lastly, but by no means least, there's that ring, which I wouldn't part with for anyone else on earth. Now, say you'll just help me out for ever such a little while. Will you?'

Esther hesitated. Then suddenly, and believing in Gorse's valuation of the ring, and not without the aid of the larger drink which Gorse had purposely bought for her, Esther was utterly convinced by Gorse's story, and was sure that she was secure.

'All right,' she said. 'I will. I suppose I'll have to.'

'Thank you for saying that. I can promise you you won't lose by it. In fact, you're going to gain a great deal. Because I'm now going to *insist* that you have a share in the car, and that means a share in the profit when it's sold. And now let's change the subject and be gay. It's worth celebrating. We're going to have good times ahead in that little bus. Come on. Drink up.'

They drank, and the subject was changed.

But soon Gorse saw that Esther's mind was unable to fix itself upon other subjects.

He had won a technical victory, probably a real one – but Esther still had a night and morning in which to change her mind.

Gorse had anticipated this situation and had up his sleeve what he believed was an unbeatable card.

The reader may be interested to learn, at this point, that Gorse was, in fact, the owner of the car.

The youthful but highly experienced speculator in cars had paid for it in cash only that morning.

It may also interest the reader to learn that all of Gorse's recent persuasion of Esther was merely an exercise in his own powers of persuasion. He had an unbeatable card, but he had wanted to prove to himself that he could win the game without it. He was deliciously satisfied with his success.

But now, as he saw that Esther's mind was wandering back to the car and to her promise, he decided to play his unbeatable card.

He interrupted the conversation suddenly, and said:

'Oh, good heavens! What a fool I am!'

'What? How?' said Esther.

'About the car. It's just come to me this moment.'

'What?'

'Well – I needn't have gone into all that palaver at all. I've got a *much* better security for you than *all* those I've mentioned.'

'What?'

'One that'll cut out all the IOUs and the telephoning, and all that. Although you can still have all that. It's so simple! And I didn't see it!'

'But what *is* it?'

'Why – the car *itself*.'

'How?'

'Listen. Tomorrow morning I can go to Gosling early, and I know he'll let me have it for the morning. If he didn't trust me he wouldn't let me have it now, and anyway, he's charging me three bob an hour for the loan of it – the old Shylock . . .'

'Well?'

'Well – all I've got to do is to call for you in the car early tomorrow morning. At the end of Over Street if you don't want the house. Then you give me the money. Then we pay Gosling – you can come with me while I do it. And then you need never let the car out of your sight. You can put it into any garage, of your *own* choosing, and tell the garage people it's *yours*, and that no one else – including me – can take it out. Either that, or leave it outside your house all day and night. In fact, you can *sleep* in it, if you want to. And it'll jolly well be *yours* until you get your money back on Monday. You see how simple it all is?'

'Why, yes. That does sound simpler than IOUs, and all that. But you mustn't think I don't trust you.'

'I know you trust me. But this way's so much simpler. It's *I* who've been so "simple", as they say. In fact, I'm afraid, if you *should* accept an offer I'm going to make so very soon, you'll be engaged to a complete idiot.'

He saw a glow of relief on Esther's face. Another of his reasons for telling her the long circumstantial story had been to put this glow of relief into Esther's soul. Gorse, all his life, was an expert exploiter of the emotion of relief in women.

'Well, it does seem simpler – though I'd hate you to think I don't trust you,' said Esther joyfully. 'In fact, the only trouble I can see is I'll be late for work tomorrow.'

'Well – you can get round *that*, can't you, for an occasion like this? Can't you pretend you're ill?'

'Yes. I could. Or I could get my little brother to go round and say I'll be late. They're very good to me round there.'

'There we are, then. By the way, there's only one other little thing. You might think the car might not be worth the money. But you can get the garage people, the people *you* choose, to assess that, and, believe me, they'll agree with me. There. Now let's have another drink and go for a little spin again. But only a small one this time. No driving under the influence.'

Gorse and Esther had another drink, Esther taking all of her own. Then, in a state of great exhilaration, Esther went for a ride in the car with Gorse.

He finally left her at the end of Over Street, arranging to be there, with the car, at nine o'clock tomorrow morning.

As Esther walked to her humble home she believed that she had fully decided to accept Gorse's offer of marriage or an engagement, when he made it.

Though she had pointed out that it was now unnecessary, Gorse had insisted upon her keeping the signet ring. Among other things, Esther did not totally dislike the notion of marrying one who was related, however distantly, to a 'lord'.

She looked many times at the ring in the dim gaslight of her bedroom, and she put it on to several of her fingers.

She was a good sleeper, and she slept beautifully.

II

The car and Gorse were at the end of Over Street next morning, five minutes before the appointed time, as Esther saw from her bedroom window.

Of course Esther had not told her mother about the car and the temporary surrender of her savings. Her mother would not approve: she would argue. This would cause delay and Gorse had only until twelve. Also, her mother might want to meet Gorse, and this would embarrass him. It would embarrass herself, too, for Esther was ashamed of the mother she loved. She was not so much ashamed of her as she was of her father, but all the same she was ashamed – afraid.

She therefore bribed her little brother with twopence and asked him to take a note to the sweet-shop. The note said that she would be late, and that she would explain why when she arrived. She would think of an excuse later: it would depend on how late she was. She made her little brother swear to keep the matter secret from her mother. He readily agreed.

Having met Gorse, Esther got into the red dream-car, and gave him (apart from three pounds fifteen shillings) her entire savings.

She had taken these from the old tin safe, hidden amongst clothes in her old tin trunk, the night before.

'And now to our friend Gosling in his royal residence in Portslade,' said Gorse when the car was moving.

'But I thought you said he was in the London Road,' said Esther.

'Yes. That's where his garage is. But it's Saturday morning, and he's over at his private house.'

'Oh lord,' said Esther. 'That's going to take some time, isn't it?'

'Oh no – not long,' said Gorse. 'With any luck we'll get the whole thing signed and sealed under an hour.'

They had not been driving long before Esther, who was very worried about being late for her work, and who utterly trusted Gorse, said that she would rather not accompany him to Portslade. She asked him if he would drop her near the sweet-shop at which she worked.

Gorse had rather fancied that she would do this. The matter had not bothered him, however, for he had many tricks to play had she not done so.

2   Gorse, on leaving Esther near the sweet-shop, said that, after he had paid Gosling and was the owner of the car, he would call in the car at the sweet-shop and buy some sweets.

He did this at eleven-thirty. She saw the car outside. He bought some sweets and spoke to Esther. He said that the car was now his – and hers. He asked her when they were to go to whatever garage she had chosen.

His future plans were such that he did not even care in the least if she insisted on a garage, or watching or sleeping in the car.

She said that she had chosen no garage: she trusted him. And she had his ring, she said jokingly.

He said that he could not meet her that evening because he had to go again to his uncle in Preston. What, then, he asked, was to be done with the car?

Esther said that she thought it advisable to take the car and drive over in it to his uncle in Preston.

'The old boy'll be a bit taken aback,' said Gorse. 'But the point is, when do I meet you again? What about Sunday afternoon and a real spin in the country?'

'Well,' said Esther. 'I'm supposed to give that up to seeing Father.'

'Oh – can't you make an exception?' said Gorse. 'This is a pretty big occasion, after all, isn't it?'

'All right, then. I'll manage it somehow,' said Esther. 'Where and when on Sunday?'

'Well – what about two-thirty – outside the Metropole? I'll be waiting there in the car.'

'All right,' said Esther. 'That sounds fine.'

'All right. Two-thirty – outside the Metropole – tomorrow. And in the meanwhile will you work out what sort of answer you're going to give to that question I'm going to ask *you*? I'm going to ask you it tomorrow afternoon.'

'Yes. I'll try and work it out.'

At this Esther had to serve a customer, and Gorse left her.

Gorse, having no uncle there, was, of course, not going to Preston. He had made the excuse simply because he preferred to spend the evening alone.

The girl and her company bored him.

It would have been possible, now, for Gorse to have fulfilled his plans at once – in which case Esther would not have seen him again.

But Gorse intended to meet Esther tomorrow. He wanted to recover his ring.

III

Esther, finding herself unexpectedly without a friend on a Saturday evening, became lonely as the evening wore on, and was even assailed by remote doubts and fears in regard to Gorse. These she shook off easily, but her loneliness remained.

For this reason she took the unusual step of calling upon Gertrude, who lived in another little street near Over Street, with the object of asking her to take a walk with her.

Gertrude was at home, but she was not free. She had arranged to go to the cinema with another girl friend, who was paying for the seats.

Esther knew perfectly well that she had no reason to be offended by Gertrude's having made an arrangement to go elsewhere with another patroness: all the same, she was slightly displeased. The slightly 'spoiled' girl had come to look upon her slave-companion, the ugly Gertrude, as one who would be ready to come out with her whenever called upon to do so.

But this is characteristic of slave-companions. They are finally compelled to lead some sort of life of their own, and, nearly always, at the very moment when they are most wanted by their owner-companions, are engaged elsewhere.

The matter was made worse because Gertrude (as she had to explain to Esther) could not very well invite Esther to join herself and her friend at the cinema. Her friend (who was unknown to Esther) was most generously paying for the seats, and it would look rude.

Also, Esther did not relish the idea of Gertrude having another patroness at all. However, she showed nothing of these somewhat base feelings, left Gertrude with a pretence of cheerfulness, and decided to go for a walk by herself along the front.

2   Ever since the receipt of the final anonymous letter, and the excitement caused by the car, a thought of Ryan had hardly entered Esther's head.

But Ryan, needless to say, had been thinking of practically nothing else besides Esther.

He had been forbidden to write to her or see her. But could he not possibly manage to meet her accidentally?

After his early-morning meeting with Gorse, he haunted the front and the West Pier – morning and night. He also tried the Palace Pier.

Then he thought that, although he had been forbidden to call at her house, he had not been forbidden to look at it, or at any rate haunt its vicinity. He made inquiries about the whereabouts of Over Street, and found it. He did not dare walk down it, but he loitered at one end of it, in the same place that Gorse had loitered and met Esther in the car.

He did this more than once, had cups of tea at Brighton Station, and was in the neighbourhood a great deal.

It was because of this that he ran into Esther on that Saturday evening after Esther had left Gertrude and was making for the Brighton Front.

He met her at the bottom of Queen's Road, very near the Clock Tower. There were many people passing on the pavement. The encounter was brief and most unpleasant.

3   'Hullo!' said Ryan, completely surprising her, for he had come up from behind her. 'Well – fancy running into you.'

'Oh – hullo,' said Esther, who did not smile and went white in the face.

Esther's emotions were of a mixed and peculiar nature. Ryan had not been in her mind for two days, and he belonged to, was the central figure of, a horrible episode in the past. In this past she had been tortured, and then she had been relieved of this torture.

Now a feature of torture, physical or otherwise, is this. The victim will endure much: some victims, indeed, will endure an incredible amount of it, without flinching. But, once having been relieved of torture, there are few, if any, victims who can tolerate the thought of having to submit to it once more. In the case of physical torture to extract a secret, it is usually at this point that the victim gives in.

Ryan symbolized Esther's recent torture, and the sight of him filled her with horror. She could not go back to it again.

In fact, her affection for Ryan had turned into a complete revulsion.

'How are you?' said Ryan.

'I'm all right . . .' said Esther, still white.

'It's very nice to see you again,' said Ryan. 'And funny meeting you here, of all places.'

'Yes, it is,' said Esther. 'And I told you I didn't want to meet you again. You know that.'

'I'm sorry. It was quite an accident. I was just in this part of the world.'

'Yes. And why were you in this part of the world – so near to where I live?'

'Oh – I don't know . . .' said Ryan, his whole manner and tone suggesting that he had been hanging about in the neighbourhood.

'Have you been hanging about and following me?'

'No – of course I haven't been following you,' said Ryan, and added foolishly, 'I'll admit I've been hanging about a bit.'

'Yes. I thought so,' said Esther. 'And I don't like it. You got my letter – didn't you? So will you leave me now?'

'But why?' said Ryan. 'I don't understand. Why can't we *meet*, even if there *is* someone else?'

'We can't. That's all,' said Esther.

'But *why*?' said Ryan. 'Anyway, couldn't I just have one more little talk with you? Couldn't we go into a coffee-shop or something *now*, and just have a little talk?'

'No, I'm afraid we couldn't.'

'But just tell me *why*,' said Ryan, unwisely raising his voice. 'It all seems so utterly *absurd*!'

Esther saw that his raised voice had attracted the attention of a passer-by. She anticipated some dreadful scene in public. This threw her into a panic. At the same time she realized that the unknown letter writer might still be watching her – might be watching them both at this moment. Her panic increased.

'I've told you why in my letter,' she said, also raising her voice. 'Now will you please *go* and leave me *alone*!'

Her anger was real. It was also, in a way, simulated and made to look greater than it was. This was for the benefit of the possible watcher.

'I can't see why you're so angry!' said Ryan, almost shouting. 'At any rate, there's nothing to be *angry* about!'

Now it seemed to Esther that people were definitely standing and watching them. She was in a public brawl. She was filled with even greater fear and rage.

'Look here, will you leave me this *moment*?' she said. 'Or am I to call a *policeman* and make *him* make you leave me?'

This, quite naturally, put Ryan himself into a violent temper.

'All right, I'll leave you,' he said. 'But I think you're a silly little fool – that's all – a damned silly little fool. Good-bye!'

He left her, walking in the direction of Brighton Station. Esther walked on towards the front.

4   As arranged, Ryan called upon Gorse early on Sunday morning. The ginger-haired young man was again found in bed with his breakfast.

After greeting Gorse, Ryan came straight to the point.

'Well,' he said. 'I ran into that girl again last night.'

'Really?' said Gorse, who was disturbed by this news. Those two, then, might still have compared notes about their anonymous letters. What Ryan said next, however, relieved Gorse.

'And it looks as if it's all over, as you said.'

'Why? What happened exactly?'

'Oh, we met in the street, and she wouldn't even speak to me. She ended up by threatening to call a policeman.'

'A policeman!' exclaimed Gorse.

'Yes. A policeman,' said Ryan. '*Me*! A *policeman*!'

'Yes. That does sound a bit stiff, I must say.'

'However,' said Ryan. 'I thought I might just call and ask if you found anything out. Did you?'

'Yes. I did my best for you. I sang your praises, and I pumped her as much as I could.'

'And what was the result?'

'It was just what I thought. There *is* somebody else, beyond any doubt, and that's just that. She was absolutely firm about it. I'm afraid you'll have to call it a day. I'm sorry, but there it is.'

'What sort of person is it? Did you find that out?'

. 'Not exactly. She was a bit reticent. But I gathered, pretty well for certain, that it was someone in her own class. They make strange choices, these girls.'

'Yes. I suppose they do. However, as you say, that's that, and there's nothing more to do about it. I'm pretty well fed up, anyway. Particularly after that threat about a policeman.'

'Yes,' said Gorse. 'That was rather low. But then, you see, they *are* low, these people, and that's why you're so well out of it. It's an awful thing to say, I know, but breeding does tell in the end. If they come from that class it always comes out somehow, though sometimes you have to wait for it.'

'Yes. I suppose you're right. But I thought her different, somehow.'

'Yes. She was a little unusual.'

'Yes. She was. She got under *my* skin, I must say. But now the whole thing's made me feel so fed up that I've decided to cut my holiday short and get away from Brighton. I'm packing up and going home this afternoon.'

'Well – funnily enough – I'm feeling just the same. I'll probably be going myself, tomorrow or the day after.'

They talked about other things for a little, and then Ryan prepared to go.

'Well,' he said. 'It's been a funny holiday. Nice in some ways – nasty in others – for me, at any rate. Anyway, it's been nice seeing you and Bell again. I hope we'll all be meeting again sometime.'

'Yes. I certainly hope so. By the way, have you got my address – my home address?'

Gorse had a minor reason in asking this.

'No. I did know it – I think – but I'm afraid I've lost your letters, and it's gone from me.'

'Well, it doesn't matter,' said Gorse. 'Because we're moving in about two weeks. And I'm going to be on the move for a bit. However, I've got yours and I'll write.'

'Good. Do. And now I think I'd better be buzzing off. Well. Good-bye and good luck.'

'Same to you.'

They shook hands.

'Oh, I'm sorry,' said Ryan, at the door. 'I completely forgot to thank you for trying to help me. It was really good of you, and thank you very much. Well. Good-bye.'

'Not at all. I was only too happy, and you're more than welcome. Good-bye,' said the nasal-voiced, imperturbable doer of good deeds.

PART TWELVE

JOURNEY

I

Esther found Gorse waiting for her in the car outside the Metropole at two-thirty on Sunday afternoon. He wore a motoring cap, and she was pleased by his appearance.

He drove her out into the country.

After about half an hour Esther, as they drove along, said:

'Oh – by the way, hadn't I better give you back that ring?'

Thus Esther had volunteered to give it back to him. If she had not, he had plenty of tricks with which to extract it from her: but he was glad that she had brought the subject up herself, and glad, too, that she had it with her. Otherwise he would have had to go to the trouble of using further tricks to make her go back to her house and get it.

'No,' he said. 'That's just what I don't want you to do. I love you keeping it – apart from all that security nonsense. And talking of rings, I've got another ring. I bought it yesterday.'

'What ring?'

'It's very cheap. It cost me exactly two bob, in fact. But it's an engagement ring. It's only a temporary one. Tomorrow, when my money comes through, I'll get another one – a proper one. That is, if you're going to give a favourable reply to a question I'm going to ask you this evening.'

Here Esther very nearly said, 'Why not ask it now?' For she had decided to become engaged to Gorse. She was not absolutely certain that she would marry him (though she thought she would), but what harm could there be in an engagement? What, after all, were engagements for? To enter, surely, into an arrangement which was not entirely binding.

'Oh – it's to be this evening, is it?' she said.

'Yes. Over our drinks, at the Met. I want you to be in a good mood, you see,' said Gorse. 'But I'll tell you what.'

'What?'

'If you've got it on you, I might as well wear it just while I'm with you. I feel sort of naked without it.'

She produced the ring from her bag and gave it to him. He stopped the car and put the ring on his finger.

'I was terrified of losing it, anyway,' said Esther.

At about a quarter to five they were in the vicinity of Shoreham.

'Now we're near Shoreham,' said Gorse. 'And I've got a bit of a bore to go through. I've got to go to my uncle.'

'What? *Another* uncle? Here?'

'Oh no. Not that sort of uncle,' said Gorse, giving a little giggle. 'Haven't you heard the expression "my uncle" – meaning a pawn-broker? I'm short of ready cash, and I've got to pay for tea soon, and drinks at the Metropole tonight. You see, Monday morning's an important day for all of us.'

'But isn't a pawnbroker a money-lender? And I thought you disapproved of money-lenders. And anyway, will he be open on a Sunday?'

'No – pawnbrokers aren't anything like money-lenders. And my friend Mr Fenton is a very high-class pawnbroker. And I'm calling at his private house. I arranged it yesterday over the phone.'

'You don't half arrange things – don't you?'

'Not "don't half". You told me to tell you.'

'Sorry. You *do*. And thank you for telling me.'

'Not at all. Well – I've got my typewriter in the back there, and Mr Fenton has promised to lend me a fiver on it.'

Gorse spoke the truth when he said that he had his typewriter at the back of the car. All his belongings were there too.

'But it's got to be delivered in an hour's time, or he might be out,' said Gorse. 'And that means we've got to go miles beyond Shore-ham. And I want my tea – don't you?'

'Yes. I must say I do.'

'But needs must when the devil drives. You haven't got any money to see me through, have you?'

Gorse had seen pound notes in Esther's bag when she had given him back the ring.

'Yes. I've got a bit.'

'How much?'

'I've got three pounds and a few coppers. It's what's left over from what I took out.'

'Oh well. That's fine. If you'll just loan it to me we can have tea at once.'

'What? The whole three?'

'No. Two'll be enough. More than enough, really. I can give you any change at the end of the evening. Well – shall it be that, or shall we wend our weary way to Mr Fenton?'

'No,' said Esther. 'Let me lend it to you.'

'Well – that's very good of you.'

'And have the whole three,' said the generous girl, taking the notes from her bag.

'All right,' said Gorse. 'It's all the same. I can give you the change in the evening. I certainly hope we're not going to spend three pounds. But there *may* be an occasion to celebrate in a big way – mayn't there?'

'There might,' said Esther. And she gave him, as he drove, three pounds. These, removing one hand from the steering wheel, Gorse put into a pocket of his coat.

Much as we may dislike the character of Gorse, it must be conceded that he did things thoroughly.

2   Gorse knew a large inn, a mile or so to the north of Shoreham, at which teas were provided, in the summer, in the garden at the back.

It was called 'Ye Olde Wheatsheafe', and it was of partially genuine, partially vilely restored Elizabethan architecture.

Gorse drove towards this. Then, at a walking distance of about two minutes away from it, he stopped the car in a quiet lane.

'We're just there,' he said. 'But we'd better leave the car here. It's one of those swanky places, and if you drive up in a car like this they stick up the price. I'm sorry to be so mean, but I know the place.'

They walked to Ye Olde Wheatsheafe, outside which there were one or two cars. Esther was deeply delighted by the foolish architecture. She was deeply happy in every way.

3   Gorse took Esther through Ye Olde Wheatsheafe (whose name enchanted her) to the garden at the back.

Here there were a few people having tea – few because it was late for tea.

Tea was brought to them by a pleasant waitress.

They had bread-and-butter, strawberry jam, and cakes.

After tea Gorse smoked a cigarette (Esther, although invited, would not do so in public) and then said that he would like to wash his hands before they returned to the Metropole. He asked her if she would like to do this. She said that she would.

'Well – who'll go first?' Gorse asked.

'I don't mind.'

'You go first, then,' said Gorse.

Esther left him, and returned to him in about four minutes' time. Gorse was smoking another cigarette.

He rose politely.

'Well,' he said. 'Now I'll just go and do the same. Will you excuse me? My hands are absolutely filthy after all that driving. Not at all the way to appear at the Metropole. I won't be a sec. And talking of the Metropole, I may tell you I'm pretty worried about what's going to happen there tonight.'

'You needn't be,' said Esther. 'At least not *too* much.'

It seemed that Gorse had the power to extract the last ounce of everything from this girl, who, really, was by no means more credulous or stupid than other girls of her age. He had not only taken her savings: he had recovered his ring; and had deprived her even of the three pounds left over from her savings. Now, in having made her tell him that he need not worry too much about what would happen at the Metropole, he had most ironically extracted from her what was as good as an admission that she would engage herself to him, or marry him. It is difficult not to believe that, had he desired them, he could have taken from her the clothes in which she stood.

In much later years it was rumoured that Gorse had Hypnotic Eyes with women. Indeed, pictures of these alleged Hypnotic Eyes, isolated from his face, were published in the newspapers. But all this was mere Press folly and sensationalism. Gorse had no hypnotic quality: all he did was to use common sense and take the greatest pains in a particular field of activity in which he was naturally gifted.

4   Left alone, Esther looked around at the pretty garden. There were now only two other couples left, and their tea was finished.

Esther watched one of these couples paying the bill and leaving the garden. Then she listened to the song of the birds, and watched the waitress clearing away the table which the couple had just left.

Amidst the song of the birds it would have been just possible for her to distinguish another noise – that of the engine of a car moving away at a high speed. This was the red dream-car, and Gorse was driving it. But Esther did not consciously hear this noise.

Gorse had had not the slightest difficulty in reaching the red car. He had walked straight and boldly through the hotel, and out to the front. Then, in the same calm way, he had turned to the right and reached the quiet lane in which he had left the car.

Then, because he believed (correctly) that he was unobserved by anyone, he had begun to run towards it.

In less than a minute after this Gorse had started the car and was on his way to London. He wanted to reach London before it was dark.

Although, for other reasons, he would have rather preferred darkness.

5   After about another minute the last couple in the garden paid their bill and left.

Although Gorse had been gone more than four minutes, not the faintest suspicion of his treachery had crossed Esther's mind.

After about six minutes she began to wonder why he was so late.

When about eight minutes had passed, the waitress asked Esther if their tea was finished, and, if so, whether she might clear the table. Esther said that they had finished and that she might.

The waitress was a blonde, rather pretty, big, amiable girl of about twenty-eight.

'Your friend seems a long time,' she said cheerfully to Esther.

'Yes, he does,' said Esther, who was still not in any way alarmed.

'And they always say', said the amiable waitress, 'that it's the girls that keep men waiting. *I* always say it's the other way about.'

Esther politely and smilingly agreed with her.

The table was cleared.

'Well, I expect he'll be along soon,' said the waitress, and, having put a bill on the table, she went into the inn.

Now all the tables were cleared, and Esther was alone in the garden.

6   When five more minutes had passed Esther became anxious – but not gravely so.

She had three theories with which she explained Gorse's absence.

The one she favoured most, for some reason, was that he had gone to the car to fetch something. Perhaps, telepathically, or by some subconscious means, she had sensed that he had walked in the direction of the car. She might even subconsciously have heard him do so.

Her other theory was that he had been taken ill while washing his hands. Her final theory was that he was, rather inconsequently and rudely, doing something the nature of which she could not guess but which he would tell her about when he returned.

The real solution to the mystery did not even cross her mind.

After five more minutes, still not suspecting the truth, she was alarmed, and, picking up the bill, walked towards the inn. At the door she met the amiable waitress, who saw that she was looking alarmed.

'What – ain't he come back *yet*?' she asked.

'No,' said Esther.

'What on earth could have happened to him?'

'I don't know. Perhaps he's gone to the car. That's what I expect he's done. I think I'll go and see, shall I?'

'Yes. Let's go and see,' said the waitress.

The waitress accompanied Esther from the back of the inn to the front for two reasons. In the first place, she knew that the bill had not been paid and dimly suspected that all this might be a swindle – a walkout. She had had experience of such things in her profession. In the second place, she was curious, and eager to help the clearly anxious Esther.

On reaching the front of the house the waitress said:

'Well – there's no car here.'

'No,' said Esther. 'He left it in a lane just near. Shall I go and see? It's very near.'

'Why did he do that?'

'Well, as a matter of fact, he said that if you drive up to a hotel with a swell car, they stuck on the price.'

'Well – *that's* nonsense, anyway,' said the waitress. 'At this place, at any rate.'

'Well – shall I go and see? It's only a minute's walk.'

'Yes. I'll come with you, shall I?' said the waitress, inspired by the same motives which had induced her to escort Esther from the back of the inn to the front.

On reaching the lane Esther at once saw that the car was not there.

'It's not there,' she said. 'It's gone.'

She was merely baffled by the mystery: she still did not suspect Gorse's treachery.

'Oh lord,' said the waitress. 'I hope he hasn't gone and hopped it.'

Now, and only because it had been suggested to her by another, a faint suspicion of Gorse's treachery came across Esther's mind. But she dismissed it from her mind.

'Oh no,' she said. 'There must be some explanation. He must have *moved* the car for some reason. He's probably back in the hotel. He said he was going to wash his hands. It struck me that he might have been taken ill or something in the bathroom. Shall we go and see?'

'Yes. Let's.'

'I'm sure there's some quite simple explanation,' said Esther.

'Do you know him well?' asked the waitress as they walked back to the inn.

'Well,' said Esther. 'Fairly well.'

'How long?'

'Oh – about three weeks, I suppose.'

'Well, that's not *very* long – is it? I don't want to put the wind up you – but it's not too long – is it?'

'No. I suppose it's not.'

'Where did you meet him – if it's not a rude question?'

'Oh – on the West Pier, Brighton.'

'You mean he picked you up?'

'Yes. You *could* put it that way.'

'Well – that's not as good as a proper introduction, is it?'

'No. I suppose it's not.'

By the time they had reached the inn Esther had had time to reflect upon the truth of the waitress's observation, and she was white in the face. The waitress saw this, and pitied her.

'Now – don't you worry,' she said. 'Even if he has gone, it's not the first time a man's walked out on a girl and left her to pay the bill.'

'Oh – I'd forgotten about the bill,' said Esther. 'And there's a lot more to it than that.'

'Is there? What?'

'Well – it's a long story.'

'Well,' said the waitress. 'Don't tell me now. I'll go and see if he's up in the bathroom, or anywhere else in the hotel. You come in here and sit down.'

She took Esther to a long, low, beamed room in which two residents were sitting.

These two residents were a married couple of the Anglo–Indian type.

'Now, you sit down here,' said the waitress, 'and then I'll come back to you. I don't expect there's anything to worry about.'

The Anglo–Indian couple had heard the waitress's reassurance, and, during the six or seven minutes in which Esther was alone with them in the room, they stared at her. They did this at times openly and rudely, and at times furtively, at times while pretending to talk to each other, and at times in silence.

The man, elderly and moustached, was particularly vulgar and cruel in this matter.

The waitress returned.

'No,' she said quietly. 'He's not in the hotel. Will you come with me? We'd better go to the manageress. I've told her about it.'

7   Esther followed the waitress into a small office. It had only a small window and was electric-lit, now and all the year round.

The manageress was a fat, dark, middle-aged disagreeable woman, who took an instant dislike to Esther's good looks.

'Well, young lady,' she said. 'You seem to have got yourself into trouble – don't you?'

'Yes,' said the ashen Esther. 'I'm afraid I have.'

The ashen face did not impress the disagreeable manageress.

'This is what comes from gadding about in motorcars at your age,' she said. 'How old *are* you – may I ask?'

'Just eighteen,' said Esther.

'Yes – so I thought. That's just seventeen, too, isn't it?' said the manageress. 'Well – young lady – I'm afraid you've got landed with having to pay the bill, haven't you?'

'But I haven't even the *money* to pay the bill,' said Esther. 'And there's more to it than that. You don't understand.'

Here the waitress cut in.

'Yes,' she said. 'You said there was something more. *What's* more?'

'Well,' said Esther. 'If he's really left me, he hasn't just left me to pay the bill. He's run off with all my money.'

'And is that a lot?' asked the manageress.

'Yes. A great lot,' said Esther.

'How much?' said the manageress. 'If it's not too rude to ask.'

'Oh, it's a terrible lot,' said Esther.

Even in her black predicament Esther retained a certain amount of pride. She simply could not name the real sum: it would make her look such a fool in front of this harsh woman.

'But *how* much?' asked the manageress. 'Of course you haven't *got* to tell me.'

'Well, it's all my *savings*, anyway,' said Esther, holding her own. 'Every *penny* of them. And they were a *lot*. My *mother* gave them to me, too.'

'Well, I wonder what *she's* going to say,' said the beastly woman.

'Yes,' said Esther. 'So do I.'

The manageress was now slightly appeased by the thought of Esther having lost all her savings, and adopted a slightly kindlier tone.

'Well, I'm very sorry for you, I'm sure,' she said. 'But what are we going to do about this bill? How much is it? Can I see?'

Esther was holding it in her hand, and the manageress took it from her.

'It's three and two,' said Esther.

'Well, three and two's three and two, isn't it? How much *have* you got on you?'

'Nothing!' said Esther. 'Not even a copper! Look at my bag.'

The manageress took the bag from her.

'A very nice bag,' she said. 'Who gave you that?'

'*He* did.'

'Well – there's certainly nothing here. So what are we going to do?'

'I don't *know*!'

'Who are your parents? Where do they live?'

'In Brighton.'

'Where?'

'In Over Street. Near Brighton Station.'

'I don't know it. But are they on the phone?'

'No. Of course not! It's only half a slum.'

'Then there's no way of getting into touch with them?'

'No!'

'Well – I don't know *what* to say – I must say. It's all very difficult, isn't it?'

'And I haven't even got the money to pay my fare back by train!' said Esther. 'We're right out at Shoreham, aren't we?'

'Yes. We're very cut off here, I'm afraid.'

Here the agreeable waitress, who now deeply pitied Esther, again cut in.

'Excuse me, madam,' she said to the manageress. 'But I've got an idea.'

'Yes?'

'Well, madam. That bag of hers. It's worth quite a lot. If she'll leave it here – leave it with me – *I'll* find the money – the money for the bill, and the money to pay her fare back. Then, if her parents'll give her the money later, she can come back and pay me back, and I'll give her back the bag.'

'Well,' said the manageress. 'That seems fair enough.'

'Very well, madam. Shall I go and get the money now? It's in my room.'

'Very well,' said the manageress, and the waitress left the electric-lit room.'

Esther had only to spend a minute alone with the manageress, who did not talk to her, but sat down and looked at letters on her desk.

The waitress returned, with a ten-shilling note in her hand, and addressed the manageress.

'Excuse me, madam.'

'Yes.'

'It's a long way to the station – ain't it? I was wondering if I might get Larry to drive her there. If we ought to charge her for it, it can all come out of the bag.'

'Yes. That seems all right. And I don't want to charge her. She's in trouble enough. Very well. You do that. And you'd better do it as soon as possible.'

They were clearly being dismissed.

'Thank you, madam,' said the waitress, and Esther, the erstwhile user of waiters at the Hotel Metropole, echoed the waitress and said, 'Thank you, madam.'

8   In the passage outside Esther said:

'Now I must give you the bag – mustn't I? And I can't thank you enough.'

'Well, I suppose you must,' said the waitress. 'And don't thank me. I'm only too glad to help. And then, later, when you've got the money, you can come back and get it – can't you?'

The waitress took the bag, and gave Esther the ten-shilling note. She also gave Esther a few small things from the bag.

'And I don't want the bag back,' said Esther. 'It hasn't got happy memories for me, but it may be luckier for you. You've been very kind to me, and I'd like you to have it as a present.'

The waitress protested, but Esther meant what she said, and never came back to claim the bag.

Thus Gorse had, indirectly, even deprived her of his one present to her, the bag.

9   When Esther and the waitress were outside, the waitress
told her to wait while she found Larry, who was the man-of-all-work
of the inn.

'He's very silly,' she said. 'But he'll drive you back to the station.
And mind you don't give him a *penny* – even if he has the sauce to
ask for it. I know old Larry. Promise?'

'Yes. Thank you.'

The waitress found Larry in a surly mood and, to make him
hurry and behave himself, told him something of Esther's pitiful
story.

In due course Larry appeared in front of the inn, and in due
course Esther stepped into an old and cheap car – what Gorse would
have called a 'tin Lizzie'.

Esther again thanked the waitress, said good-bye to her, and was
soon being driven on the road to Shoreham Station, which was
about three and a half miles away.

10   'Silly Sussex' is an old and well-known expression. Larry
was about fifty-five, and indeed silly – so silly as to be quite evil.

The waitress had told him about Esther's misfortune, and he
talked about it, with great relish, to Esther.

'Yes, you were *dished*, all right,' he kept on saying, and 'Yes – *you*
were ditched.'

Esther, hardly listening to him, yet felt the evil of the man.

Larry, along with his incessant 'Yes, you were ditched, all right'
or 'Yes – you were dished', related some of his own experiences.

He told her that, as a child, he had had an experience roughly
similar to hers.

For this, he said, he was given a 'good hiding' by his parents. He
used this filthy expression several times – even temporarily drop-
ping, for its sake, his 'ditched' and 'dished'.

He had noticed that Esther was a very pretty, very frightened girl,
and he was being lascivious sexually.

As they approached Shoreham Station he asked Esther whether
she was likely to get a 'good hiding' from her own parents. Esther
did not answer him. She did not even properly hear him.

This angered Larry, and, on leaving her at Shoreham Station, he
said:

'Well – what about a tip for the driver, miss?'

She said truthfully that she had only a ten-shilling note, and he
left her rudely and in silence.

She had to wait over three quarters of an hour on the station for a train back to Brighton.

It was now getting dark. The carriage, in which she sat alone, was lit by incandescent gas. The train stopped at many stations, but no one came into her carriage.

During this journey home she was too stunned and numbed to suffer very much.

II

That night the scene which took place between Esther and Mrs Downes was, perhaps, as painful a one as had ever taken place in a house in Over Street – and the houses of Over Street had had very many very painful scenes indeed enacted inside them.

Coming home in the train, Esther had decided that she could have tolerated having lost her entire fortune.

It was having to *tell her mother* which was so terrible!

She decided to do so as soon as possible, and did.

The scene began quietly, for Esther was still too stunned and numbed for tears or an emotional outburst. Her mother was at first quiet, too, for she was also stunned and numbed.

But at last the tears, the reproaches from the mother, the wretched explanations from the daughter, the recriminations from the mother, the anguished and passionate sobbing of the daughter, the anguished and passionate sobbing of the mother – all these began.

It was the sort of commotion which attracts the attention of children lying in bed, filling them, they do not quite know why, with hideous disquiet and fear.

The Downes children, Esther's little brother and sister, heard the commotion, and finally they were so alarmed that they came downstairs, the little brother opening the door of the sitting room.

At this particular moment Mrs Downes and Esther were sobbing and crying inconsolably at the same time. Needless to say, this was the cue for the two children to start sobbing and crying, equally inconsolably: and the general din and hysteria were appalling. The children did more than cry. They yelled.

The children were at last got to bed, still crying. Then Esther and her mother went downstairs for some further sorrow, anger, explanations, and tears. At times, actually, it was Esther who became angry and reduced her mother to tears.

This scene might have gone on all night and into the morning.

But Mr Downes was due to return some time after eleven, and in spite of all the hysteria, it had been decided that he must not be told.

When Mr Downes came in, therefore, Esther was in bed, by a magnificent effort controlling her tears lest she made the children cry again.

Mrs Downes put up an equally magnificent performance with her husband. But neither Mrs Downes nor her daughter had more than the barest semblance of sleep that night.

2   Esther, it need hardly be said, never recovered her fortune.

If she had been better advised, and had had better luck, there might have been a dim chance of her doing this.

If, for instance, at Ye Olde Wheatsheafe the manageress had been agreeable and sensible, or if the waitress had been sensible, the police might have been telephoned at once, and Gorse, conceivably, might have been intercepted before dark on his way to London. The car, after all, was conspicuous in colour and shape. But such a thing would not have been at all likely.

Then, if Esther had had better advice at home, it could have been just possible that Gorse might have at last been traced. But this again would have been most unlikely, for Gorse had not been so foolish as to neglect to cover up his tracks in every possible way.

The advice that Esther was given at home was as poor as it well could be.

The very poor, alas, do not usually behave at all wisely when they meet disasters of this sort.

Either they become angry, or even vindictive, and insist too much upon their rights, thus displeasing those who are trying to help them; or they sink into a state of hopelessness, and consequent apathy. The very poor, they believe, are the very poor, and it is useless to contend with the rich, their betters.

Mrs Downes was of the apathetic type. Mr Downes, though he was never told anything, would have been equally so. Esther herself was apathetic.

It must be remembered that in the veins of Esther and her father ran the blood of the runner, the consumptive follower of cabs. Inheritors of such blood are unlikely to fight boldly against a cheat or oppressor.

3   What Mrs Downes did was to consult her old friend – the ex-policeman, Mr Stringer. She could not have done worse.

Mr Stringer was elderly, and, in matters of law especially, pompous and a know-all. He really knew practically nothing about the law, and his little knowledge was in this case a fatal thing.

With her mother Esther had a long interview with Mr Stringer, who questioned her, thoroughly but foolishly.

Mr Stringer, like the manageress at the inn, did not like or approve of Esther's great beauty. He never had. He was not so bitter as the manageress, but it told against her.

Esther was to experience this disadvantage all her life, and always more than ever when she was in difficulties.

There is an absurd theory that juries take a favourable view of pretty women. Nothing could be further from the case. Juries, on the whole, take a suspicious and adverse view of pretty women.

Some of Mr Stringer's questions were to the point. Did Esther know the number of the car? Esther did not. This folly on Esther's part made Mr Stringer inwardly despise her more than ever.

Did Esther know the *make* of the car? Esther did not – but she described its colour and shape.

Did Esther know where the car was *bought*? Esther mentioned the man Gosling. This slightly encouraged Mr Stringer: but as there was no man Gosling, the clue was ultimately quite useless.

Did Esther know anything *about* Gorse? Esther did not. She did not even know his address in Hove. (This actually would have been of no use in tracing Gorse, for he had left a false address with his landlady.) Mr Stringer was made more irritable still.

Did Esther not know at least *something* about Gorse? Did she not know anything about his parents and upbringing? Esther thought. Then she said that she thought he lived in London, that his people were Army people, and that he had been to school at Westminster.

Her knowledge of his school again encouraged Mr Stringer a little, and he asked Esther if she knew any of his friends. She mentioned Ryan and Bell. And she knew Ryan's address.

This yet again encouraged Mr Stringer, but was finally of no value. (Inquiries were made at Ryan's lodging in Tisbury Road – but Ryan, in the flurry and misery of his departure from Hove, had left no address with his landlady.) And while he was staying with the landlady he had never given it to her. She trusted and adored him (as all landladies did) and the matter had been put off and off. Furthermore, Ryan did not know Gorse's address, as we have seen.

Oddly enough, the one who might have been of the greatest

assistance was Bell. He had kept Gorse's letters, and knew Gorse's stepmother's address.

But Esther did not know Bell's address. Bell, who might have 'counted' now, had not 'counted' enough in the past.

Probably the best thing Mr Stringer could have advised would have been to tell Esther to seek an enterprising journalist on a local newspaper. There was, really, a 'story' – which might conceivably have found its way into the London newspapers. But such a thing never occurred to Mr Stringer.

And, even if it had, there would have been little chance of tracing Gorse. Gorse was 'lying low', as he put it, and had already told plausible lies to his stepmother, to whom he had given a false address, and with whom he did not intend to communicate, until the thing had 'blown over'. He watched the newspapers carefully for a matter of months. The thorough Gorse also dyed his hair black, and took off his moustache, and wore new clothes.

4   A feeble approach was made to the police, but this was done by the apathetic Mrs Downes, for Mr Stringer had by this time developed an agonizing attack of lumbago. The police were infected by Mrs Downes' apathy.

The towel was thrown in at a later interview between Mrs Downes, Esther, and Mr Stringer, who was in bed. At this interview Mr Stringer happened to ask Esther whether she had given the money to Gorse *voluntarily* (a word he liked). Esther replied, in a dazed way, that she had.

In that case, said the pompous know-all (who was still in considerable pain), there was really no sense in pursuing the matter. Even if Gorse was found, there was no redress in law.

Esther was at last forgiven by her mother. But on the night when the dreadful news had been broken, Mrs Downes, in her anguish and anger, had told Esther that she would never forgive her until her dying day – and that Esther had practically killed her mother.

These words stuck, and when Esther's mother died, which she in fact did a few years later, Esther always had a feeling that she had helped to kill her, and that she had never been forgiven. This notion haunted her all her life.

5   And so (apart from Esther and Gertrude) none of those five ever met again in Hove, or went on the West Pier.

On that Sunday evening – so terrible for Esther, so fruitful for

Gorse – the West Pier, which had brought them all together, wore its own peculiar air of indifference about their departure.

This battleship – this sex-battleship – was on this Sunday evening more crowded than usual. Sunday evening was one of its best, and the season was at its peak. Many new curious acquaintanceships were made upon its resounding planks, and, as it grew dark, its secluded benches were used by many would-be lovers.

And, as it grew dark, Gorse, far away, was employing great speed in the use of his recently acquired car.

He had had the misfortune of having a breakdown on his way to London. This, before he had located the trouble in the engine, had delayed him nearly three quarters of an hour. He therefore had need of speed. He was late in his plans. He knew where he was going to leave the car in London for the night, and he did not want the place to be closed. At this place, he hoped, he was going to dispose of it at a great profit.

The car fancier's hopes were fulfilled. He sold the car, as he had promised Esther he would, at nearly double the price he had paid for it.

Gorse, as he drove, was deeply delighted by the superbly easy success of this – his first serious enterprise in his main profession in life – that of defrauding women.

But he was tired, and had to extract all the speed from the car that he could. Also, the breakdown had told upon his nerves.

There was, therefore, a set, ugly, hard, more than ever satanic expression upon the face of Ernest Ralph Gorse as he sped ahead – sped ahead to London, and to his very curious destination in life.

ENGLISH AND AMERICAN LITERATURE IN PENGUINS

☐ *Emma* **Jane Austen** £1.25

'I am going to take a heroine whom no one but myself will much like,' declared Jane Austen of Emma, her most spirited and controversial heroine in a comedy of self-deceit and self-discovery.

☐ *Tender is the Night* **F. Scott Fitzgerald** £2.95

Fitzgerald worked on seventeen different versions of this novel, and its obsessions – idealism, beauty, dissipation, alcohol and insanity – were those that consumed his own marriage and his life.

☐ *The Life of Johnson* **James Boswell** £2.95

Full of gusto, imagination, conversation and wit, Boswell's immortal portrait of Johnson is as near a novel as a true biography can be, and still regarded by many as the finest 'life' ever written. This shortened version is based on the 1799 edition.

☐ *A House and its Head* **Ivy Compton-Burnett** £4.95

In a novel 'as trim and tidy as a hand-grenade' (as Pamela Hansford Johnson put it), Ivy Compton-Burnett penetrates the facade of a conventional, upper-class Victorian family to uncover a chasm of violent emotions – jealousy, pain, frustration and sexual passion.

☐ *The Trumpet Major* **Thomas Hardy** £1.50

Although a vein of unhappy unrequited love runs through this novel, Hardy also draws on his warmest sense of humour to portray Wessex village life at the time of the Napoleonic wars.

☐ *The Complete Poems of Hugh MacDiarmid*

☐ Volume One £8.95
☐ Volume Two £8.95

The definitive edition of work by the greatest Scottish poet since Robert Burns, edited by his son Michael Grieve, and W. R. Aitken.

ENGLISH AND AMERICAN
LITERATURE IN PENGUINS

☐ *Main Street* **Sinclair Lewis** £4.95

The novel that added an immortal chapter to the literature of America's Mid-West, *Main Street* contains the comic essence of Main Streets everywhere.

☐ *The Compleat Angler* **Izaak Walton** £2.50

A celebration of the countryside, and the superiority of those in 1653, as now, who love *quietnesse, vertue* and, above all, *Angling*. 'No fish, however coarse, could wish for a doughtier champion than Izaak Walton' – Lord Home

☐ *The Portrait of a Lady* **Henry James** £2.50

'One of the two most brilliant novels in the language', according to F. R. Leavis, James's masterpiece tells the story of a young American heiress, prey to fortune-hunters but not without a will of her own.

☐ *Hangover Square* **Patrick Hamilton** £3.95

Part love story, part thriller, and set in the publands of London's Earls Court, this novel caught the conversational tone of a whole generation in the uneasy months before the Second World War.

☐ *The Rainbow* **D. H. Lawrence** £2.50

Written between *Sons and Lovers* and *Women in Love, The Rainbow* covers three generations of Brangwens, a yeoman family living on the borders of Nottinghamshire.

☐ *Vindication of the Rights of Woman*
  Mary Wollstonecraft £2.95

Although Walpole once called her 'a hyena in petticoats', Mary Wollstonecraft's vision was such that modern feminists continue to go back and debate the arguments so powerfully set down here.

ENGLISH AND AMERICAN
LITERATURE IN PENGUINS

☐ *Nostromo* **Joseph Conrad** £1.95

In his most ambitious and successful novel Conrad created an entire imaginary republic in South America. As he said, 'you shall find there according to your deserts: encouragement, consolation, fear, charm – all you demand – and, perhaps, also that glimpse of truth for which you forgot to ask.'

☐ *A Passage to India* **E. M. Forster** £2.50

Centred on the unsolved mystery at the Marabar Caves, Forster's masterpiece conveys, as no other novel has done, the troubled spirit of India during the Raj.

These books should be available at all good bookshops or news-agents, but if you live in the UK or the Republic of Ireland and have difficulty in getting to a bookshop, they can be ordered by post. Please indicate the titles required and fill in the form below.

NAME _____ BLOCK CAPITALS

ADDRESS _____

_____

_____

Enclose a cheque or postal order payable to The Penguin Bookshop to cover the total price of books ordered, plus 50p for postage. Readers in the Republic of Ireland should send £1R equivalent to the sterling prices, plus 67p for postage. Send to: The Penguin Book-shop, 54/56 Bridlesmith Gate, Nottingham, NG1 2GP.

You can also order by phoning (0602) 599295, and quoting your Barclaycard or Access number.

Every effort is made to ensure the accuracy of the price and availability of books at the time of going to press, but it is sometimes necessary to increase prices and in these circumstances retail prices may be shown on the covers of books which may differ from the prices shown in this list or elsewhere. This list is not an offer to supply any book.

This order service is only available to residents in the UK and the Republic of Ireland.